ABOUT THE AUTHOR

Louise Beech is a prize-winning author, whose debut novel *How To Be Brave* was a *Guardian* Readers' Choice for 2015. The follow-up, *The Mountain in My Shoe*, was shortlisted for Not the Booker Prize. Her next books, *Maria in the Moon* and *The Lion Tamer Who Lost*, were widely reviewed, critically acclaimed and number-one bestsellers on Kindle. *The Lion Tamer Who Lost* was shortlisted for the RNA Most Popular Romantic Novel Award and the Polari Prize in 2019.

Her novel *Call Me Star Girl* won *Best* magazine Book of the Year, and was followed by *I Am Dust* and *This Is How We Are Human*. Her short fiction has won the Glass Woman Prize, the Eric Hoffer Award for Prose, and the Aesthetica Creative Works competition, as well as shortlisting for the Bridport Prize twice. Louise lives with her husband on the outskirts of Hull.

Follow Louise on Twitter @LouiseWriter and visit her website: louisebeech.co.uk.

Also by Louise Beech
How To Be Brave
The Mountain in My Shoe
Maria in the Moon
The Lion Tamer Who Lost
Call Me Star Girl
I Am Dust
This Is How We Are Human

Nothing Else

Louise Beech

ORENDA BOOKS

Orenda Books
16 Carson Road
West Dulwich
London SE21 8HU
www.orendabooks.co.uk

First published in the United Kingdom by Orenda Books, 2022
Copyright © Louise Beech, 2022

A catalogue record for this book is available from the British Library.

ISBN 978-1-914585-16-6
eISBN 978-1-914585-17-3

Typeset in Garamond by typesetter.org.uk

Printed and bound by CPI Group (UK) Ltd, Croydon CR0 4YY

For sales and distribution, please contact info@orendabooks.co.uk

For my sisters, Claire and Grace.
Now you can both be Richard Clayderman.

And Patricia, or MrsLovesToRead, as I know you.
For your husband, and his music.

'Don't only practise your art but force your way into its secrets; art deserves that, for it and knowledge can raise man to the divine.'
—Ludwig van Beethoven

'Music was my refuge. I could crawl into the space between the notes and curl my back to loneliness.'
—Maya Angelou

'Music can name the unnameable and communicate the unknowable.'
—Leonard Bernstein

PLAYLIST

'Nocturne No 2' – *Chopin*
'Annie's Song' – *John Denver*
'I'll Remember April' – *Miles Davis*
'Clair de Lune' – *Debussy*
'Serenade No. 13' – *Mozart*
'Vincent' – *Don McLean*
'Lady Bird' – *Tadd Dameron*
'Moonlight Sonata' – *Beethoven*
'Bridge over Troubled Water' – *Simon & Garfunkel*
'Take on Me' – *A-ha*
'Für Elise' – *Beethoven*
'The Four Seasons: Spring' – *Vivaldi*
'Careless Whisper' – *George Michael*
'Toccata and Fugue in D Minor' – *Bach*
'The Thrill Is Gone' – *Roy Hawkins*
'Interstellar' – *Hans Zimmer*
'1812 Overture' – *Tchaikovsky*
'Dances with Wolves' – *John Barry*
'Sonata in C Major' – *Mozart*
'Now is the Time' – *Jimmy James*
'Yesterday' – *Lennon-McCartney*
'Une Barque Sur L'Océan' – *Ravel*

To listen to these pieces please visit
Nothing Else – **The Playlist** on Spotify.

HEATHER
(PRIMO)

1

Sometimes violence is neat. It happens quickly. A table is overturned and then righted. Food is spilt and cleaned up. Glasses are
smashed, the pieces swept up by dawn and sparkling new ones in
the cupboard by evening. Physically, it is fast, then over.
Emotionally, it lingers, then settles. There's a bloody, visceral beauty
to it, a sweet agony that leaves you breathless if you look at it.

But we didn't look.

We closed our eyes and played our song. The notes were an accompaniment to the crashes and the thumps and the muffled cries
in the next room. Our fingers flew over the keys; flashes of black
and ivory, ivory and black, back and forth, neither of us leading or
following. I recall that melody now in my dreams. I should hear
violence as the background percussion. But I don't. I only hear us.
Our song. 'Nothing Else'. Us, cocooned by the safety of our music.

And I wish I could play it again with her.

But she's gone.

Gone.

2

I arrived early at the town house; it was one of those tall new builds designed to blend in with the older architecture surrounding it, close to the river, and off a cobbled street. I always arrived promptly for a first lesson. I liked to chat to the new student, gauge what level they were at, how passionate they were, and ascertain whether music was something they wanted to pursue or something their parents had insisted they do. It was more often the latter, so I was always overjoyed when it turned out to be the former.

A willowy woman opened the door, tall like a new tree, but tired-looking, and I was sure she sported a bruise on her cheek that she tried to hide by repeatedly pulling her hair forward. Something in me stirred; an anxiety, a recognition, an urge to turn and walk away.

But I stayed.

'Come in, Heather,' she said cheerfully. 'I'm Ellen, Rebecca's mother. Thank you for agreeing to teach her. You came highly recommended.'

'Thank you,' I said.

I rarely agreed to teach very young students, particularly those younger than about eight. I mostly taught the bored teenage offspring of rich parents, who I knew would far rather be putting their long fingers to use on the skin of other equally bored teenagers. Dan, my ex-husband, had often asked why I preferred older, probably more stroppy kids, and I was always defensive, saying it was my choice, I didn't need a reason.

So why was I here, having agreed to teach eight-year-old Rebecca, who her mother had described on the phone as a natural; who, she had told me, always played her friend's piano, and then begged them to buy her one; who – when they did – ran to it as soon as she got home from school? Something about her mother's gentle voice and simple request had compelled me. I recognised it, that maternal warmth, from long, long ago, and my heart had given in.

Now I could not take my eyes off the fading bruise. When I looked at it, I saw a lace collar below, though hers was plain; I saw soft yellow hair, though hers was mousy; I saw tiny pearl earrings, though her lobes were bare.

'I chose you because...' Ellen looked around the bland, modern hallway, as though checking who might be listening '...Brandon's mother said you were very sensitive.'

So she was the one who had recommended me. I had wondered.

'Oh. I guess.' I didn't know what to say. 'Thank you.'

'It's just, I wanted someone ... *understanding*. Rebecca ... we adopted her, you see. When she was three. And it's been hard, at times, not knowing her full background. She's always loved music though. It's the one thing that calms her.'

I smiled. Oh, how I knew this. 'Of course,' I said.

Ellen gave a heavy sigh. 'Before you meet her, I need to tell you a couple of things that we now know about her background ... You see, she can go into black moods and not speak for days.'

I felt a little uncomfortable that she was being so open, sharing so much so quickly, but I just nodded along. Perhaps she needed to get it off her chest. And perhaps it would help me.

'We couldn't understand it at first, it was so difficult to deal with. Anyway, I decided I needed to know more about what had happened to her before she came to us. So, I got her care records from the social-services team.'

Ellen paused then, emotional. I told her she didn't have to tell me if she didn't want to.

'I must tell you,' she insisted. 'It's important, for you, if you're to teach her.' She steeled herself. 'It was a very sad read. Both of her biological parents were drug addicts. They left her alone for long periods, but they always put music on for her, classical, because ... well, they *did* love her, and they wanted her to feel comforted while they did what they had to.'

I nodded.

'Now she wants to play her own music,' said Ellen, softly.

'Well, I'd love to help her,' I said.

'Wonderful. Oh, I'm so glad you've come and that you still want to teach her, even after all I've told you.' I thought for a moment Ellen might hug me, but instead she wrapped her arms around her own body, eyes watery. 'Rebecca's in here. Come through, please.'

Ellen led me to a door and opened it onto a large, sparse room, the floors gleaming wood and the walls beige. In the corner, by a tall window, was a baby-grand piano, perfect and polished, making my heart sing; and sitting there was a little girl in a sunflower-yellow dress with auburn hair cascading down her back. She was the brightest thing in that room. And yet I stepped back involuntarily, not sure at my sudden reluctance. My throat tightened; my heart sped up.

What was *wrong* with me?

'I'll leave you to it,' said Ellen, closing the door.

I approached the little girl. She turned and I felt my knees give a little.

'Hi,' said Rebecca, shy, cheeks as pink as new roses.

I couldn't form the word.

'Are you OK, miss?' She looked concerned.

I wasn't. I thought I might be sick. And then I knew. It wasn't just the bruise on her mother's face. It wasn't just this child's background, the need for music as comfort. It wasn't just the hair spilling down her back. She reminded me of ... *her*.

I turned and ran.

'I'm sorry,' I called out, not sure where in the house Ellen was. 'I don't feel well. I'm sorry, so sorry.'

And I ran and ran and ran.

StarWind Entertainment Group are seeking a pianist to work onboard the Queen of the Seas *cruise ship. The successful candidate will be fluent in English and play a variety of styles. Vocals are a bonus but not essential. You will play easy-listening music at cocktail time as well as pop, party style after dinner. You should also be able to play acoustic solo piano at lunchtime during the day. You will be able to read the room and cater to a crowd.*

I didn't for one moment think I'd get the job.

I'd never played piano on a ship. I taught music and occasionally took month-long gigs in quiet city bars where no one really listened, and they rarely tipped. That had been my career since I left university twenty-six years ago.

But mostly, I played at home on my baby-grand piano. Its polished ebony was a dark mirror that created a second set of hands; and together we danced a ghostly duet. I bought the piano with money Margaret had left me when she passed two years earlier – the good woman who was my mother during the latter part of my childhood. Hours of practice – a habit instilled in me long ago by my beloved tutor, Mr Hibbert – were a joy on this beautiful instrument. The old upright piano Margaret bought when I was eleven was like a beloved friend, but this sleek baby grand, with its larger soundboard and longer strings, gave my music a louder, richer, fuller resonance.

My friend Tamsin told me about the job.

She regularly did six months at a time on the ships. 'You'd *love* it,' she'd tell me during the brief in-betweens when she was home, and we caught up over mojitos and her lurid tales of exotic men and foreign lands. 'It's all playing jazz at night and then playing whatever I fancy afterwards, if you know what I mean. It's not difficult to catch the eye of some velvet-skinned dream man when you're the one in the spotlight. What's not to love about that?'

I'd never felt much inclination to travel, beyond country get-aways or weekends in Dublin. But Tamsin showed me the job advertisement just two weeks after I'd run away from that sparse room with the little girl sitting at the piano in the corner.

Still, I resisted even considering it at first, which was ridiculous because I had no ties. It was just me. I'd recently downsized to a two-bedroom flat on Hull Marina, with a metal balcony overlooking the bleached boats and wind-swept walkers who dropped chip paper, with a mustard-yellow kitchen I kept meaning to paint, and with my piano in the corner of the cold-floored living room, sitting on a large grey rug to absorb excess reflected sound. It had taken two movers an hour to get my instrument up three flights of stairs on a hot August afternoon last year.

I was now divorced. I'd never really felt married, not the way I think you're supposed to. What did I know though, with the example my father had set long ago? I'd always chosen gentle men, kind men, quiet men. Just a hint of aggression and I was gone. Dan and I split amicably. How else do you separate when neither has done anything wrong? When you still love each other, but your love isn't quite enough for him, and his is more than you think you deserve?

'I'd have applied for the job myself,' said Tamsin, over at my flat one evening, with a bottle of Prosecco on the balcony and the cruise ship job description on her phone. 'But I'll be in Brazil by then. The *Queen of the Seas* is a magnificent ship. Made for me, really.'

She laughed. Her confidence was what I loved most. No one bigged up Tamsin more than she did, and I adored her for it. I wished I could be more that way. We met years ago, when she played the sax in a band at a pub where I'd played too. I was shadow to her sun; she was an extrovert, craving the spotlight, while I was quieter, loving my music but far too shy to shout about it.

'I think I've done four or five trips on the *Queen of the Seas*,' she said. 'You should go for it. You'd *love* life at sea, Heather. I'll never understand why you've never considered it.'

'I like my feet firmly on the ground,' I said, unsure about new things as always.

'They will be. These are big ships. There's hardly any motion. You don't even know you're at sea.'

Tamsin clicked her phone screen and showed me more of the job details. I skim-read them while she regaled me with the tale of Marco, who she met in Rio and 'almost married' on the beach.

> *Sailing area – Southampton to New York, two nights in the city, fourteen nights Eastern Caribbean cruise, return to New York for two nights, repeat fourteen nights Eastern Caribbean cruise, two more nights in the city, return to Southampton. Total of 42 nights (6 weeks).*
>
> *Contract length – from Friday 2nd August 2019 to Friday 13th September 2019.*
>
> *Working hours – up to four sets of 45–120 minutes a day.*
>
> *Accommodation – Cabin shared with a roommate or single.*
>
> *Included – Full board meals with the crew, laundry, and free Wi-Fi.*
>
> *Salary – ranges from £3,400 to £3,600 depending on musician's ability and experience.*
>
> **Additional duties besides a regular performance (helping in other departments) are tipped an extra £300–700 per month.*

'It does sound nice,' I admitted.

'Nice? *Nice*? It's a bloody marvellous life, woman. What's stopping you? You get to do the thing you love, around the clock, you get paid well for it, you have an actual attentive audience, *and* you're at sea.' Tamsin studied me; her skin was still tawny from the last trip. 'What are you doing now, eh? Playing melancholy shit all on your own here, for an audience of you and a nosy neighbour.'

'Thanks.' I shook my head at her.

'Heather, you're forty-eight an—'

'Seven,' I corrected.

'You're forty-seven and you're one of the most beautiful pianists I've ever heard play. You know that, don't you? You know I envy you, and trust me, that's a hard thing for me to admit. And you're teaching scales and C-major arpeggios to bloody thirteen-year-olds who don't care. You're wasted.'

'I like teaching,' I said.

I did. But I hadn't told Tamsin about the other day. About coming home from Ellen and Rebecca's tall townhouse, sure I couldn't do it anymore.

'You could be in New York, for God's sake. *New York. And* the Caribbean.'

'Maybe. Six weeks is a long time to be away though.' Could I do with that time though? To think about what I really wanted from life?

Tamsin swigged Prosecco, laughed. 'You big baby, it's nothing. I do months at a time. It will be a taster for you. And who knows, if you like it, you'll want to try longer.'

'Maybe.'

'Let's fill the application in now,' she cried.

I shook my head, still hesitant. 'Let me think about it. I promise I'll decide by tomorrow.'

'Are you OK?' she asked, studying me.

'Yes,' I lied. Then, '*Yes*,' more firmly.

'Don't wait,' she cried. 'People are killing one another for these jobs.'

I did think about it. When she had gone, I sat alone in the dark on my balcony. The harbour lights bounced off the water, mini flashes in a watery theatre. Tinny dance music drifted up from one of the nearby bars. But that wasn't what I heard. I heard a recital as the sailboat masts moved in the evening breeze. I heard a symphony of the sea in their chimes. Because I heard music in everything. A monotonous hum from the washing machine or from a food blender and I'd harmonise with it, moving my fingers across an imaginary keyboard, working out what chord progression worked best.

I tried to concentrate on less melodic matters and looked up cruise ships on my phone. Tamsin had told me plenty about them over the years, shown me all her travel snaps; they were her passion. I clicked on pictures of sleek white liners cutting through azure waters, of promenades with as many shops and bars as a high street, of art auctions and surf parties. Then I read blogs by people who worked aboard – some happy, describing wild crew parties, breathtaking cities, and friendships that lasted a lifetime, others listing the cons: no days off, tiny, shared cabins, and long shifts.

Could that life be for me?

I lived in a port. I should have been drawn to the ocean; Hull is a sea city without being right on it. The Humber Estuary took ferries daily from our port, across the North Sea, linking Yorkshire to Europe. It was a city I'd never left. They call it the end of line. Once you're here there is nowhere else to go but the water. And yet I'd never sailed. I was within touching distance of the waves; I witnessed currents and storms from the safety of my balcony. I played melodies with the double doors wide open, the stench of brine on the air. Could I play out there, at sea, for an audience of travellers?

Why was I so reluctant?

I wasn't sure. It was only six weeks. I'd be coming home again. No children held me here. Margaret and Harold – I'd never been able to call them Mum and Dad, though I loved them deeply – had passed away. I knew my ex-husband Dan would encourage me to go if I told him about Tamsin's idea. 'Be adventurous,' he'd say. 'See the world.'

And then there had been Rebecca two weeks ago.

I hadn't been able to put her of my mind; I kept seeing her turn around to look at me. I'd hardly been able to concentrate on teaching after I ran away from the house. I'd taken the last few days off, cancelling all my lessons, apologising and blaming a family emergency.

Family emergency.

Those two words were perhaps more truthful than I'd at first thought.

4

The morning after she had shown me the advert for the cruise job, I called Tamsin. 'I know you're busy, getting ready to go away again bu—'

'Have you applied for it?' she interrupted, excited.

'Tamsin ... I ... I know I said I *was* when you asked yesterday ... but I'm not OK.'

'I didn't think so,' she said. 'What's wrong, babe?'

'I ... I haven't been working these last few days,' I admitted. 'I just haven't felt like ... well, like I can.'

'Why? That isn't like you, Heather.'

'I know.' I went onto the balcony and looked out at the boats. 'There was this ... student...'

'Yes?'

'She reminded me of...'

'Lady Gaga? Miley Cyrus?'

I laughed. 'No.' I said her name then, one I rarely said aloud, one I only thought of when I was alone, and the past grabbed at me with greedy hands: 'Harriet.'

'Oh,' said Tamsin softly.

'Rebecca, my supposed new student,' I explained. 'She was this little girl, and her vulnerability, it just, it floored me. And I ran away. She broke my heart. I couldn't do it. I couldn't stay and teach her. I had to lie and tell her mother that I was ill. I feel terrible now.' I bent down low, as low as I felt, and put my forehead to the chill balcony railing. 'I've never liked teaching the little ones. And I think it's because...'

'Because they'll remind you of her.' Tamsin paused. 'I think perhaps it's because you've buried such a lot and you never talk about it.'

'It's hard to,' I breathed.

'Haven't you ever wanted to look for her, after she disappeared like that?'

'I've been ... afraid, I guess. I mean, yes, I've looked on Facebook and I've googled her name – or at least what *was* her name – but nothing more. I can't explain why I haven't taken it further. I can't explain why I'm ... *scared*. It's like, if I search for her, I'm going to have to face so many other memories.' I shook my head as though to free my fears. 'Anyway, I did something quite epic. I applied for my care records last week.'

'You mean, from your childhood?'

'Yes. Rebecca's mother told me she'd got hers, you know, to find answers about her past. They adopted her when she was three, you see, and she had some behavioural problems, so they wanted the full story. I couldn't stop thinking about it. What might such a document disclose? What might I find inside mine?' I came back inside and stood by my piano. 'So, I got in touch with the council after I googled how you obtain them, and I've requested them. They said they could take up to thirty days to arrive, because they have to redact other people's names and details first, by law, though it's often much quicker.'

'Oh God, this is so *Long Lost Family*,' gushed Tamsin.

'I don't think so,' I said.

'Are you hoping they'll give some clues as to where Harriet is? Do you think you'll actually look for her?'

'I'm not sure. It was an impulse. I might not even dare read them.'

'*I* will,' cried Tamsin.

'Anyway,' I said, 'I can't go on like this – not teaching. I need to earn a living. So, I've decided; I'll apply today for the job on the ship. It'll give me time to think about what I really want to do in my career. To decide if I want to ... finally face my past. And when I get home, my care records might be waiting for me.'

'I'm so happy.' Tamsin paused. I waited. 'I really am. You're supposed to be playing, not teaching. I've always said it.'

'I wouldn't be able to play if I hadn't had such a brilliant teacher,' I said quietly.

'Oh, you would. It's in your blood.'

Was it? Yes. And she was right. Maybe it was time to play.

5

The audition for the cruise job was the most intense thing I'd ever done.

An American lady – Pamela-Anne Garcia – called three days after I'd submitted my application to say that she loved my résumé and would I audition. I might have embellished how often I'd played for an audience and made the bars I'd gigged in sound more upmarket, but it was true that I was classically trained, and that I had studied music at Durham University.

'Oh.' I panicked, walked onto the balcony with my phone. 'An *audition*?'

My gigs in bars had been via word of mouth. I hadn't auditioned for anything since university. Not for the first time, I felt foolish that I'd even thought I could play anywhere beyond a local venue. I suddenly saw myself, twenty-one, reading the list of things I could do with my degree: composer, choral director, conductor, sound design, music therapist. But I'd realised that really music was *my* therapy. I hadn't studied with a career in mind, but for love. Now, I wondered if I had wasted my years.

'Do I come to you?' I asked Pamela-Anne.

'Oh, no,' she said. 'We come to *you*.' She laughed lyrically. 'Well, at least via the magic of video. The audition will be conducted via Zoom or Teams. We just want to see what you can do.'

What could I do? I could read sheet music and perform on the spot, but I preferred to listen to the music in my head and play that. I'd wake in the night with a melody in the room and hum it into my phone, so I didn't forget it. Then I'd play it by ear in the morning. But no one wanted to hear those songs. They wanted the oldies, the classics, the recognisable.

'We need to *see* you as much as hear you,' explained Pamela-Anne. 'For a cruise job, it's about the whole package. Make sure the device you use captures good-quality video and that your room is well-lit, and then set the device up so that we can see you *and* your instrument. The audition will last approximately two hours. The first half is a sight-reading test, and in the second half you'll play in a variety of styles, some jazz, some blues, some poppy tunes, and some classical pieces. Do you have all these styles in your repertoire?'

I nodded, then quickly said, 'Yes.'

I was growing more nervous with every word. Should I dress up? Yes. I tried to visualise my wardrobe, the simple trouser suits I wore to play in bars. Was that enough, or did they mean a cocktail dress? Ball gown? I was embarrassed to ask in case it seemed I was wrong for the job.

'We'll send you a PDF of some sheet music twenty minutes prior to the audition,' said Pamela-Anne. 'That gives you time to look it over but it's a brief enough period for us to know your sight-reading skills are top notch. A cruise-ship gig is more challenging than most people think, and we need to make sure you can do it.' She paused. 'Are you still interested?'

'Yes.' I sounded more confident than I felt.

And so, four days later, I auditioned.

I wore a simple black trouser suit with a gold blouse beneath, in case they wanted glitz, and a dash of red lipstick. I put a large cream lamp behind my phone – which was taped to the bookshelf – so I was in a sort of improvised spotlight. I'd quickly sight-read the pieces they had emailed twenty minutes earlier. I could look at printed music and hear it at once in my head, without having to whistle it aloud. It was a language I understood better than any other.

'Are you ready?' asked Pamela-Anne, when I was seated at the piano. She was one of three – the other two were men – all waiting to judge my performance.

Was I ready? I had prepared as much as I could; my nails were short, I'd warmed up for forty-five minutes that morning, I'd practised a little in the preceding days (but not too much because over-practice can result in muscle fatigue), and I'd done a test re-cording with my phone to check the quality.

'I'm ready,' I said.

'Then play for us,' said Pamela-Anne.

Play.

And I did. It was what I'd always done, since I was six. For me, it was a private thing, even when I was in a bar. I'd often close my eyes if I knew the music intimately, but now, for this, I had to con-centrate. I had to follow the set pieces.

What did they *really* want from me? I had asked myself this often during the last four days. To know I was capable, for sure. But maybe to know that I was creative too, and that I didn't play like everyone else did. Or maybe that didn't matter on a ship. Maybe blending in rather than standing out was the key. I'd asked Tamsin for advice, and she insisted, 'Don't play the pieces to make them happy, play them how *you* like to and how you want to play.'

Really, I couldn't do it any other way.

I composed myself for a moment; my fingers floated above the keys, pale and patient. I took a deep breath, and then another. Then I began.

Sometimes she was with me in these moments. Harriet. My ghostly partner. A girl, smaller than me, with long auburn hair that fell in waves down her back, curls that, no matter whether you dam-pened them or brushed them hard, sprang up like determined peonies after a cold snap. She didn't join in or look at me, she simply sat at my side, and that was enough.

Now, I felt her. I knew she was smiling.

I played 'I'll Remember April', 'Lady Bird', 'Now's the Time', and 'The Thrill Is Gone'. I played pop tunes from the seventies and eighties, ballads from the big musicals, and Chopin. There was no camera, there was no Pamela-Anne, no panel. I played for myself, and I played for the girl at my side.

Afterwards, there was a moment to ask questions. I had already asked Tamsin plenty so I could hardly think of anything new.

Eventually, I said, 'I presume you provide the piano,' knowing how stupid it sounded, but needing to make sure.

'Oh yes,' said one of the men. 'There's one in every lounge and bar that you'll play in.'

'Um, thank you.' That question freed some others. 'How should I dress when I play?'

'Classy. Simple. Elegant.' This was Pamela-Anne.

'Do I have to share a cabin?' I would if I had to but hoped I'd have my privacy, so I could read, escape, relax.

'Most musicians share with other members of the band, but the piano-bar entertainer always has a single cabin.' The man again.

Now I really wanted the job.

'We'll let you know,' they said.

They did. I hadn't had to worry for long about how well I'd done. Just forty-eight hours of responding to Tamsin's constant messages (*Any news yet?*) before she jetted off to Brazil. Forty-eight hours of checking my emails every few minutes. Then, 'We want you,' Pamela-Anne said when she called. *We want you.* 'You'll receive your itinerary, a letter of employment and other information to-morrow. You'll also need to sign a few forms, which I'll send you a link to. And we need a good, high-quality photograph for the bro-chure. Something elegant. There's no time to get it in the one for the first cruise, to New York, but it will go in the one for the Caribbean leg of the trip.' She paused and then added, 'You played beautifully. I was mesmerised.'

I beamed, despite myself, proud and happy.

But because it was a brief, six-week contract she gave me just two days' notice before I had to be in Southampton, ready to board the ship the morning after.

Those two days were a whirlwind of deciding what I might need, panicking that my passport wasn't in date (it was), and realising I hadn't asked what currencies I'd need for the trip. I went shopping for dresses, upset but accepting when the assistant in the posher section of the department store said, 'There's nothing in the sale here.' I bought quality products for my hair (Tamsin's tip), and new make-up, and some strappy black heels. I made sure my credit card bill was paid, my accounts were up-to-date, and that there was nothing urgent that needed dealing with over the next six weeks.

I had to let my music students' parents know that my recent absence was going to be lengthier, though I was sure their umbrage would not be shared by the teens, who were free of my instruction for a longer while. I told my neighbour I'd be away until the middle of September, gave her my number and asked her to make sure my post was pushed through the door properly. I got her to take a photo of me with my Nikon camera, dressed in black, sitting next to my piano, for the cruise brochure.

'I'll miss your music,' she said, and I wasn't sure if it was a dig or genuine.

Then I said goodbye to the people who cared.

Tamsin had left the country so that meant Dan.

Dan and I had coffee in the café opposite my building the night before my train left Paragon Station. He looked tired, but I didn't say so. Sometimes it felt more like he was my brother, which was lovely now, the affection and easiness, but it had been a problem when we were married.

'I can't believe I won't be there tomorrow.' I spooned froth off my cappuccino and then motioned to my flat.

He glanced at my darkened balcony and then at me. 'I'm glad,' he said.

'Thanks. Nice send-off.'

'No,' Dan said gently, his green eyes the same soft shade as when he'd first looked my way fifteen years ago. I saw us for a moment; him too tall and handsome-faced to be serious about buying *me* a drink; me clumsy, stammering, finally agreeing. He had said many times over the years that he would never get over how a woman could trip up steps and crash into people in the supermarket and yet play music as gracefully as I did. 'I think you need this trip, Heather. I think … it will anchor you.'

I snapped to the present. 'Oh, God. Sea metaphors. Please stop.'

'No, I mean … Look, don't take this the wrong way … but you drift.'

'I guess that's just me.' I was defensive.

'It's not a criticism. It *is* you. You sort of drift along, waiting for things to happen *to* you rather than making them happen. And now this. It's huge. I'm proud of you.'

I shrugged off his praise. 'It's only six weeks.'

'But who knows what will happen in that time? This could change your life.'

'Maybe.'

I knew he had met someone else; I'd seen him with the same woman twice, their hands entwined, oblivious to my presence. How had I felt? Not entirely jealous, because we would always be friends, but sad. I'd never been able to let my guard down, never really let Dan in, and these things affected a marriage. I had learned long ago to hide pain, expressing it only in the music I played. I was afraid that the ugliness I had experienced long ago might be seen as an ugliness in *me*. That if I trusted Dan, one hundred percent, and gave him every bit of my heart, he would turn into my father.

Better to be safe. Better not to love fully.

'Make sure you take condoms,' Dan said.

'Stop it,' I cried.

'I'm serious. Who knows what you might get up to out there? It's different when you're away from home. I've seen how women can be on holiday.'

'It's not a holiday,' I insisted.

'Yeah, yeah.' He grinned, and I knew he was teasing me.

'Be happy,' I told him, meaning it.

'Jesus, you sound like you're not coming back.'

'Of course, I am,' I said. 'Why wouldn't I?'

'Why now?' he asked. He knew me of old.

'What do you mean?' I knew full well.

'This is so sudden.'

I finished my cappuccino. 'I think it's time for a change,' I said. I thought of telling him about my overreaction to Rebecca, but I feared I might cry. I didn't want to ruin our last evening. 'Also, I applied for my childhood care records.'

'Really? Wow. I didn't know it's something you could do.' Dan paused. 'Why?'

'Maybe it's time to look at my past.'

'You've never wanted to talk about it.' Dan's voice was gentle. 'And I never wanted to push. But I know you saw some horrible things. You'd dream sometimes and cry out, "Where is she, where is she?", and it upset me so much. I always wished you'd tell me, but I understood it was difficult.' He looked at me. I tried not to look away, as I so often did. 'And what about her?'

'Don't,' I said, not sure what I meant.

I often did this. Got angry where anger wasn't required. Dan had suggested I have counselling over the years, but I couldn't face it. He often said that it wasn't normal that I hated eating meals at a table at home, preferring to eat food on my knee, or that I needed it quiet at night – no loud TV or radio – or that I hated slammed doors so much that I'd tremble.

'Don't you want to know what happened to her?' he asked.

'Yes,' I cried. '*Yes*! Of course I want to know, but I'm afraid. Afraid ... of ... everything else I'll have to face. Afraid of things I can't remember now. I wonder all the time what happened to her. But it's the rest ... It's the rest...'

'I know,' he whispered, putting a warm hand around mine. '*I know*.'

And then we sat in silence, one formed of comfort and years and respect.

I was sad when I watched him walk away, along cobbles bathed in gingery light, the last night of July tropical, my neck damp and my arms around my body. It wasn't that I wanted him back. It wasn't that I thought our split was a mistake. It was that I *longed* to feel that way. Sometimes I felt music was the only thing that fired me. That the world was too real, too average, too mundane. My feet walked the path, but my head floated in a cloud of harmonies.

Back at the flat, I finished packing.

What did you take on a six-week trip? The things you'd miss. Yes. The things you would rescue in a house fire. The things that brought comfort. The things to make whatever small cabin you were allocated a home. Plus the things you needed. And the things for just in case, like seasickness pills.

I wrapped framed pictures of Margaret and Harold in socks and put them in my case with the more practical items – the underwear and toiletry bag and spare phone charger. I chose four paperbacks I'd not yet read from my bookshelf; I found a soft, pink leather notepad I'd never used, in case I wanted to record the details of my trip; I packed my Nikon camera so I could capture pictures worth keeping; I selected sheet music for the songs I didn't know by heart.

Then I zipped the case up.

I dreamt of fire, my last night in the flat.

Brazen flames flickered and devoured everything around me; they crackled and snapped and then roared. There was music in the sound. Tempo. The sky blackened with billowing smoke. The air was thick with it. I couldn't breathe and yet I couldn't turn away.

Then I heard it. Music. Just behind me.

I turned. It was there, our cherry-coloured upright piano, sitting on the grass, grey ash raining down on the keyboard like tiny flying notes. She was there too. Harriet. Seated. Waiting for me. I joined her. We sat side by side, in the places we always took, me on the right and her on the left.

And we played.

Our song.

There was nothing else. The music swirled around us as wild as the flames, a physical force, a wave of love, a place of safety.

Then I woke, alone, my balcony doors wide open and the sounds of the harbour a cold reminder of where I really existed. I went to my piano in the dark and tried to evoke the full melody from my dream, but on my own the song was incomplete, a haunting tune without its ghostly accompaniment.

8

In the morning, a large brown envelope arrived in the early post. It was stamped with the local council logo. I knew what it must be – my care records – but there was no time to look now. I didn't even know if I wanted to. Just holding the delivery my heart pulsed like a quaver followed by a quaver rest. It had arrived more quickly than I'd anticipated. Should I take it with me? Would reading what was inside it ruin my trip? Should I leave it here for when I returned?

I couldn't decide, but I shoved it in my hand luggage anyway, and then left for the station.

I sat on a packed train for almost eight hours, stretching my legs and buying coffee when we changed at Sheffield and Birmingham New Street. Usually, I studied the other passengers when I travelled. I people-watched all the time, often creating their soundtrack in my head. An old man shuffling along might be a slow melody; a woman marching in crisp heels a faster beat; a running child joyful, her notes more random, jazzlike. But I couldn't concentrate.

I kept thinking about the documents in my bag.

In the end, just after Birmingham, I took out the envelope and opened it. Inside was a black plastic folder; different pages were clipped together inside the cover – some handwritten, some typed, some official-looking, some yellowing. Everything was digital now, but back then, there were paper records. I slammed it shut, hands trembling.

Yes, I wanted to know what had happened to Harriet.

But that meant opening a door I had locked long ago.

9

I was in Southampton.

I had really come. I'd left my routine behind (practise piano all morning, teach mid-afternoon, play occasionally in the evening), my fridge cleaned and empty, and the plants in a row on the balcony in the hope that it might rain occasionally and water them.

By the time I'd found the hotel in Southampton and checked in, it was past seven and I was exhausted. I wanted to collapse on the bed. But then I went onto my small balcony, and I could see the harbour – its sea bluer than the sandbank-muddied water I saw every day – and in the far distance two cruise ships docked, side by side, twin beauties. One could be mine. I can't deny that excitement livened me then. I put both my hands over my mouth like I was five years old, and I wanted to cry. It was just me and my future. 'Just me,' I murmured.

Just me.

For a moment it was as if there was an echo. Like someone else said 'Just me' at the same time. How curious. Perhaps I was tired. I stepped back and tripped over the bed, clumsy like always, laughing at my sudden joy.

I sat on the bed, wondering what this trip might really mean for me. Who might see me play? I didn't usually dream of acclaim or fame, but we're all human, and I enjoyed praise as much as anyone else. Once, a few years before, I'd played one of my own compositions at the end of a set in a small bar. It didn't even have a name; it was just a melody that had come to me on a walk by the water. Someone recorded me playing it on their phone and shared it on Twitter. Just for a few hours, it went viral. I only went on social media occasionally and I had barely a few hundred followers anywhere – mostly those who had seen me play and liked my music – but briefly I was in the spotlight. Tamsin was delighted. She put her entire life on Instagram, so she urged me to 'share the hell out of it and grab your moment'. She got everyone to share it with a hashtag she created: #GirlOnAPiano. Others added theirs: #RandomGirlInABar and #UnnamedSong.

I shared it twice, and of course, that 'moment' passed.

Unless you work on it daily, and share and promote your music hard, recognition doesn't come knocking on your door. Tamsin was a social-media natural, but I never really knew how to do it. What to say. Which pieces to share. Which hashtags worked best. Or if I preferred to play for the simple joy of it; for myself.

I looked around the small hotel room, designed for comfort and economy. I didn't unpack, other than my toothbrush and toiletries, and the next day's clothes, which I hung up. What was the point? I wasn't staying here. I found a menu and ordered chicken and salad from room service.

While I ate, I read through my cruise itinerary again. I had to board early, at eight, long before the guests, in order to be playing in the main lounge at lunchtime. I would be shown around the ship, meet other members of staff, and I'd get settled in my cabin. There would be a safety training drill where I'd be assigned my personal ship number. I'd also be given a special card to pay for anything I purchased while aboard, and this would be linked to my credit card.

It all sounded surreal, like I was reading about someone else's new life and not my own.

The sun finally died, its rays setting the room alight. I wanted to cherish my last moment in England, so I got my camera and snapped the very first picture of my trip; the harbour lights that weren't that different to mine back home, the now inky-black water, and the holidaymakers strolling back to wherever they were staying.

Then I went to bed.

I didn't sleep well. The mattress was comfortable, but I hated unfamiliar sounds at night. I'd become accustomed to the safety of my flat. The lift along the corridor pinged intermittently, and people chatted freely as they passed my door well into the midnight hours. I grew fretful that I'd not sleep on the ship either, and that only added to my insomnia.

I kept thinking about the black folder in my hand luggage. About what words might be written there. I kept seeing myself walking towards young Rebecca, my would-be student, then turning and running away. In my imagination she called after me, telling me to *Find her, find Harriet*.

In the end, I found a favourite Chopin piece on my phone and put my headphones in, hoping to get lost in his tranquil nightscape. Still, I heard laughter and doors banging, the crude sounds louder than 'Nocturne No 2 in E-flat Major'. I grew evermore restless. How could Chopin's piece not soothe me? Usually, no other music calmed me like his.

I knew my anxiety at these unknown and sudden nocturnal noises was to do with my childhood. Back then unexplained sounds were rarely good. The years until I was eleven and moved in with Margaret and Harold were turbulent. The nights were unpredictable. The mornings could never come soon enough. Time had not lessened my need to drown out ugliness with the beauty of music.

In the end, I got up.

I considered dressing and going for a walk on the waterfront, but it was almost 2am. I wondered then for a moment about going home. Not boarding the ship. No. That was silly.

Instead, I got my purse. I took it back to the bed, turned on the lamp, and clicked it open. I went to the place where I knew it was; the slot protected by a plastic window. A faded Polaroid, its hues mostly the colour of that era: dull tans and olives. Two girls. One tall and gangly, her flowered dress with puff sleeves clearly too big, her hair the brightest thing, as yellow as the sun she squints in. The other one much smaller, chubby-faced, red-cheeked, with auburn hair in two thick plaits. Arms around one another, cheeks touching, smiles shy. Two girls, parents recently killed in a car accident, now with no one but each other.

Not shadow and sun like Tamsin and I, but gold and auburn.

I put the photo on the pillow next to me and lay down. I wouldn't go back home. No; I'd go to sea. I'd play music at night, and during the day, if I dared, I'd read the documents in that folder. I didn't plan on finding a man, like Tamsin always did, or partying hard. I had no interest in that.

I finally slept, thinking of her.

The girl with auburn hair, who I hadn't seen for thirty-seven years.

Harriet.

My sister.

My phone alarm dragged me cruelly awake at six-thirty. I'd had barely three hours sleep, and I felt it as I tried to slug away the fatigue by making coffee with the sachets on the dresser; I then devoured the stronger one that arrived with my pre-ordered breakfast. Nerves and excitement churned my stomach, but I forced myself to eat a hearty amount of croissant, fruit, and cereal, knowing I likely had a long, eventful day ahead.

I'd booked a taxi for seven-thirty, though I could have walked to the ship in twenty minutes. I gave the room a final glance and spotted the photo of Harriet and me sitting on the pillow like a tooth fairy's note. I gasped. I had almost left it behind. I'd never have forgiven myself. I put it back in my purse, heart staccato for minutes after.

The car dropped me at the end of a grey pier. I stood alone for a moment, looking back at the departing vehicle, and then at the vast carpark, not yet busy, at the gentle, sun-sprinkled morning water, at the ships waiting for passengers. I walked along the cement pier, passing the occasional person who looked like staff too – one was clearly on his first trip, looking as anxious as I felt, and another two were marching with the confidence of the well-travelled.

I stopped in front of my ship.

The *Queen of the Seas* was white and graceful, putting me in mind, curiously, of a large swan. The trim along her decks was navy blue, and the only thing that broke the expanse of white was her name on the side, also in navy. I knew from my itinerary pack that she was classed as a mid-sized vessel, that she had thirteen decks – eight were public, those lower were for staff – and that she catered exclusively for adults. She had enjoyed a refit last year, and now a stunning atrium formed the heart of the ship, spanning four decks and dominated by a marble-and-gold mermaid sculpture.

In the 'sensual' pool you could apparently enjoy a 'chic environment whatever the weather thanks to the clear glass Skydome overhead'. The best views were said to be from the cocktail bar at the back of the ship, where you could relax during the day and watch the scenery float by, and by night enjoy a drink and the classical pianist.

That would be me.

I'd be giving them that music.

I found my Nikon in my hand luggage, fired it up and framed a picture of the ship, blue sky her backdrop, only two wisps of cloud on the horizon. Then I took the picture.

I headed for the terminal. It was much like one at an airport. I found departures – a huge, glass-fronted building with rows of empty chairs baking in the early-August heat and three escalators, one of which took me up to the check-in lounge and port security. Only two desks were open. I imagined they'd all be open later, and this place would bustle with excited holidaymakers. I approached one of the desks.

'Good morning,' beamed a white-uniformed man. 'You're very keen. We don't admit passengers for another—'

'I'm staff,' I said, shy. Perhaps I didn't look like they usually did.

'Crew,' he corrected with a smile. 'On a ship, you're *crew*.' He took my passport and the letter of employment that I'd been told to also show. 'Is this your first cruise job?'

I nodded, sick with nerves now.

Perhaps sensing this, he said, 'You'll enjoy every moment, I promise you. And there will be others who are new too. You're going to have a grand adventure.' He handed back my passport and my papers. 'You're good to go, ma'am. Just take the escalator on the right, follow the gangway to the end, and you'll be aboard. Have fun!'

'Thank you,' I smiled.

It had said in my itinerary that I'd be met at the bottom of the gangway with other new joiners, so I approached the end of the long tunnel with much apprehension. There was more security to go through, and then I was in a navy-carpeted lobby with gold handrails and ornate mirrors, where a group of people gathered, some chatting in pairs, others looking nervous, all surrounded by a mishmash of luggage. They represented every walk of life; every gender, colour, age and type, like they had been selected to show that it was a thoroughly inclusive ship. I was among the oldest, aside from a greying man with designer luggage – I guessed a musician, too – and a couple of carefully made-up women who were likely here in some beauty capacity. I stood quietly by a plant in a gilt pot, nodding politely at anyone who looked my way, fiddling with the strap of my bag.

After perhaps ten minutes a man marched purposefully towards us down a corridor. He smiled warmly, showing teeth almost too white to be real, his blue suit crisply ironed, his shoes polished, and his general demeanour one of efficiency and readiness.

'Good morning, newbies,' he said, accent slightly American, voice loud. I smiled to myself: I heard him as Tchaikovsky's '1812' overture, a bombastic work that uses artillery in the percussion section for effect. 'Welcome aboard the *Queen of the Seas*. I'll let you into a little secret – she's one of my favourites. I'm Aiden Miller, your crew manager. How are we all feeling?'

A couple of whoops from those feeling confident, and then ripples of laughter from the rest of us.

'Great stuff,' cried Aiden. 'Right, I want you to grab your luggage – sorry but you'll be responsible for that until we get you to your cabins, which will hopefully be mid-morning – and follow me to the crew office.'

We did as he requested, heaving our suitcases along a corridor behind him, crashing into one another and laughing and apologising.

'You're going to see what happens on a turnaround day,' he called from the front as we passed open doorways leading to the pier and saw multiple forklift trucks noisily loading vast crates aboard. 'Today is the busiest day, with the ship at the start of her journey.'

We descended a level, through a door that said *CREW ONLY*,

clattering down metal stairs. The corridors were different here, not rich blue and gilt-edged but stark white, paint chipped, wider and with plain, wood-laminate floors.

'Welcome to *your* world,' said Aiden. 'Down here, below deck five, it's crew only. Unless you are part of the entertainment team, mixing with passengers is a big no-no, so here, belowdecks, we have our own ecosystem, where we sleep, eat, work out, relax, and socialise.' He paused to open a door onto what looked like a very small internet cafe. 'As you can see, this is where you can log on for a little escapism or to catch up with those at home. You have Wi-Fi in your quarters but the signal in here is better.'

We moved along, our footfall inharmonious still, a gang of people not yet familiar enough to march to the same beat.

'We have our own gym down here,' continued Aiden, opening doors on a variety of rooms. 'And also, our own café, pool, hairdressing salon, dining room, laundry room, outdoor lounge, and bar – just between us, the drinks are a lot cheaper than abovedeck. Don't tell the guests...'

Eventually we reached a large room with *CREW OFFICE* on the door. It was wood panelled with plain-blue carpets, with numerous uninviting seating booths, and a main desk with a computer on. There were no windows, which was understandable as we must have been well below sea level.

'Find somewhere to perch,' cried Aiden, 'and we'll run through a few essentials.'

After brief introductions – where we had to say our name and describe why we were there; I lied and said, 'for a change of scenery' – Aiden gave us a rundown of what we should expect for the rest of the morning, including a safety and orientation induction, where we would be assigned an emergency duty. He handed out a map of the ship, including the crew area, and a personal itinerary, outlining where we needed to be and when. He also gave us the cards we would use to pay for anything we purchased onboard, and that would get us into our cabins and on and off the ship, plus an individual cruise number that we should remember.

We handed over our passports too. The crew office would keep them for the entirety of our contract. Letting mine go felt like a huge moment. Like I was giving up my identity. Like I was no longer Heather Harris, middle-aged divorced woman, nondescript, playing in half-empty bars. No, now I was *Heather Harris* – announced here by an imaginary compere – adventurous, traveller, playing the classics at sea to a rapt audience.

A young woman with multi-coloured plaits and lashings of indigo eyeshadow – probably musical theatre, I thought – glanced at me as she handed over her passport, perhaps feeling the same.

'I know it's a crazy hour or two,' said Aiden, 'but with passengers boarding from noon, many of you will be on duty soon. Make sure you grab something to eat whenever you can, and most of all enjoy it. You really are going to have the time of your lives.'

More whoops from some of the braver newbies.

Gentle laughter from the rest of us.

I left the crew office with my luggage, my map of the ship, and my cabin number, knowing I had safety training on deck seven in one hour, and then had to meet the entertainment manager and team in a green room – which was backstage to the theatre – at eleven-thirty, ready to perform for the lunchtime crowd in the main salon, the Sky Lounge, from 1pm.

I felt dizzy for a moment; it wasn't the ship's motion, because she was still docked. It must have been exhaustion. Even though we were still in England, she felt a million miles away. I paused. I prepared as I might for playing, with some deep breathing, taking air in through my nose, imagining my stomach filling up, holding it, then letting it out by pursing my lips and making an F sound. It calmed me as it always did.

I headed towards where the map said cabin 313 was.

Was I ready for this?

To play piano, here?

Yes. I was always ready for that.

11

I found my cabin and opened the door with my new card.

Though it was compact, windowless, plain, with dull hues of beige wall, tan wardrobe and desk, and worn white bedding, I smiled at my new transitory home. The only place for my case was on the bed, so once I'd unpacked – my clothes in the narrow wardrobe, electrical items, books, chargers and framed pictures on the desk, toiletries in the tiny bathroom – I stowed it perilously on top of the wardrobe, imagining it falling on me during a storm. A fat orange life jacket sat on the shelf. I'd need it for the induction shortly, and obviously if the ship got into difficulty. I tried to imagine having to grab it in an emergency, perhaps in the middle of the night, and rushing to the upper decks, the panic, the fear.

I sat on the bed.

Tried to take it all in.

One item I had placed on my pillow. The folder with the black plastic cover. Just in case I decided to start reading. For now, though, what to wear? I had to go for my safety training – God only knew what that entailed – and then on to the green room in readiness for performing, so I needed to be dressed for my audience, made-up, hair styled. Afraid there would only be time to dash back to the cabin to return my life jacket, I had no choice but to wear my black tailored jacket and trousers, powder my face, paint my lips, sweep my hair up into a classy chignon, and risk looking ridiculously overdressed for the induction.

I selected some sheet music and put it in my black leather folder; I knew hundreds of songs by heart, but I didn't want to risk not being able to play a request or something that was required as part of the set.

Before I left the cabin, I sent messages to Tamsin – I had no idea where she was in the world at that exact moment – and to Dan, letting them know I was safely aboard. I suddenly missed them desperately; it was silly, I'd only seen them days ago, and with the internet we were permanently connected to those we loved.

The training took place on a sunny deck; we learned what various emergency signals meant, what to do if we heard them, the direct number to the bridge to call if we needed to raise the alarm, where the fire extinguishers were, how to wear our life jackets properly, and what to do if someone jumped overboard. There was so much to remember. We were encouraged to ask questions if we were unsure, but I didn't have anything specific to query; my head was just buzzing with the tumult of new information in such a short space of time.

Afterwards, I returned the life jacket to my cabin and, using my map, headed for the green room. I knew it was at the Queen's Theatre, the main showroom, which was on deck seven, but I realised I had twenty-five minutes to kill. I desperately wanted to see the rest of the ship first, especially without the guests onboard, so I could explore undisturbed. I wandered through neon bars advertising unique ship-themed cocktails, through tastefully decorated lounges clearly geared for tranquillity, along a promenade – the Queen's Parade – where designer boutiques, beauty salons and jewellery stores circled a lavish fountain. It was an entirely different world to the one hidden below: a heaven, not above a hell, but certainly above a darker, dingier place.

I was glad I wore my suit and heels. Anything less would have felt underdressed, like going for a job interview in my dressing gown. Staff members – no, sorry *crew* – bustled about, readying everything, stocking shelves, cleaning floors, polishing bars. Some smiled as I passed, and I felt like a minor celebrity. They must have known I was part of entertainment; why else would I be wandering the place all dressed up?

I wanted to see the three places I'd be playing during the upcoming weeks: the Sky Lounge at lunchtime, the Piano Bar early evening, and the Sunset Bar later on. I found the first on deck nine. The Sky Lounge was all muted ash and silver, with marble columns and grey padded bar stools around a circular central bar, and with tables that looked out to sea. Right now, the view was of the bustling port, of cars arriving that no doubt contained excited holidaymakers.

In the corner, on a raised area, sat a piano. Not just any piano but a white Steinway grand like the one Lennon famously played in the 'Imagine' video. A piano I knew to be the gold standard of musical instruments. I approached. This would be *mine* for the duration of the trip, and I'd have panoramic views of the ocean and sky. I sat on the white stool. I longed to play; I placed my fingers just above the keys as though I might. I hadn't played for three days, which was rare – I usually practised for at least three hours every day. Then I looked around, unsure if I should even be in the lounge yet.

I could wait.

Soon. Just a few hours.

I found the Piano Bar on deck seven to be more intimate, with dim ambient lighting, ebony décor and a black baby grand in the centre, partly encircled by bar seating decorated to look like a piano keyboard. Higher up, on deck eleven, right at the back of the ship, was the Sunset Bar cocktail lounge, a more colourful venue with huge windows that would no doubt offer incredible views once we set sail. The piano here was white and set against the glass so that my backdrop would be water and sky. I had never played anywhere so perfect. I was sure it would influence my mood, as beauty often did.

I suddenly remembered when we won a piano.

The random childhood memory had me stumble as I stepped down from the raised piano area. I picked myself up, embarrassed.

I had been small then.

There had been a raffle ticket. Green. The number eleven. I could see the ticket, held with slender fingers – my mother's? Had seeing this most beautiful of pianos now triggered the reverie?

I realised that it was twenty-five past, that I had no time to think further about that raffle ticket now, and I headed for the lift, con-

sulting my map with eyes that couldn't quite concentrate. I needed
to be on deck seven. I found the Queen's Theatre, a russet-carpeted
auditorium on two levels, with rows of traditional red-velvet seats
and a large stage currently shrouded in gold curtains. But where
the heck was the green room? I asked a staff member – *crew*, I reminded myself again – who was vacuuming. He said I should go
onstage and through the door on the left.

The shabby room I found was already full. A hush settled over
the place at my arrival. When they realised that I wasn't anyone
important, they resumed their conversations. Dancers in casual
gear hung out together on two threadbare sofas near a table of
nibbles and hot drinks. Musicians dressed as smartly as I was gathered in the opposite corner on what looked like chairs that had
been rejected by one of the ship's bars. I guessed that the rest were
actors or singers or DJs. As earlier in the lobby, it was a cross section
of the world, of nationalities, judging by the pastiche of accents, of
age groups, of personalities. If the group was a composition, it
would be one that had used every single note on the keyboard.

I realised how hungry I was and grabbed two bananas and a
coffee from the table.

'I'm Astrid,' said a young blonde woman with what I thought
might be a Swedish accent. 'I'm part of the theatre orchestra.
Clarinet.'

'Oh, hi.' I had a mouthful of banana. 'Um, Heather. Pianist.
Solo.'

'Is this your first contract?'

'Yes.' I swallowed. 'You?'

'No, my ... actually, I don't know.' She laughed. 'Long time. I love
it.'

'What's the show?' I asked motioning to the stage.

'*Broadway at Sea* tonight. We alternate between that and
Mamma Mia.'

'I wish I could see it, but, well, I'll be playing too then.'

'I guess it could be lonely for you,' she said, nibbling on some
crackers. 'Do you mind that? Not being part of a band.'

I shook my head. I really didn't. 'I'm not really alone,' I said, but I didn't mention the girl who was often at my side.

'I'm in cabin 207,' she said. 'If you ever need company.'

'I'll try and remember,' I smiled. 'I'm in 313.'

'And we often hang between shifts in the crew café on dec—'

The door opened then, and a woman bustled into the room, perhaps in her late fifties, wearing pink lipstick and a blue suit like the one Aiden Miller had worn but finished with a striped scarf and with a skirt instead of trousers.

'Welcome everyone,' she said with ebullience as the din died down. 'I'm Sarah Briggs, your entertainment manager, and for those who are new among you, I take care of all daytime activities and evening recreation. Sorry I'm a little late – a few technical hiccoughs with stage lighting. How are you all?'

Lusty whoops: this was the showbiz team after all.

'Great,' she said. 'OK, I know quite a few of you already' – more whoops from the dancers – 'but we do have a couple of new team members, so I'll have a quick chat with you guys individually first, and make sure you know what you're doing for the rest of the day and where you have to be.' She looked at her clipboard. 'OK, that's Frederica Becker, Heather Harris and Barry Lung.'

I approached Sarah, along with a ruddy-faced, squat man, whose eyes disappeared when he smiled, which he did, lasciviously at the other new crew member, a young woman with rich auburn hair cascading down her back. I did a doubletake, breath trapped in my chest. Harriet. Her hair. I almost reached out to touch it. But it wasn't possible. This woman looked to be no older than thirty and Harriet would be forty-five now.

'Right, Barry, you're our guest comedian,' said Sarah.

'For my sins,' he bellowed with a hearty chuckle.

Despite the jolly demeanour, I had a bad feeling about him. It was like the smell of slightly off meat, subtle but foul. It happened to me occasionally – a sense of darkness; that's what I called it. Certain people I met triggered my 'never be alone with them' radar. It wasn't only men. I once taught the son of a woman who incited such a repellent reaction in me that I feared for the child. And yet I'd had nothing but a dark instinct to go on, one I was sure came from childhood. From knowing that kind of person.

'And Frederica, you're doing the daytime writing workshops,' said Sarah, bringing me back into the room. 'I *love* your books. I think I've read them all.'

'Thank you.' She seemed shy, how I imagined writers to be; how I was.

'And Heather, our pianist,' smiled Sarah.

That was me.

Barry Lung told his stories through comedy. Frederica told them via actual words.

I told mine with a melody.

12

Barry Lung wasn't performing until much later, and Frederica's workshops weren't until the next day, so Sarah spent twenty minutes with me, explaining what the lunchtime audience in the Sky Lounge would be like.

'This set is just an hour,' she said. 'Today's audience are newly aboard and therefore quite excited, so you're just background music. Generally, guests are least likely to engage with you at lunchtime – they just want the light snacks we offer in there, a few drinks, and are busy planning the afternoon ahead.'

I nodded, thinking of what kind of music to play; perhaps some John Denver and Don McLean, with 'Annie's Song' and 'Vincent' being two of my favourites.

'Sea days are busier because guests can't go anywhere else. On port days lunchtime numbers will be small, but you'll likely have that day off to go ashore. Treat the room the same though, whether your audience is ten or two hundred.'

'Oh, yes,' I said. 'I always do.'

'Shall we head to the lounge now and I'll introduce you to our manager, Phillippe?'

'OK, great.'

Phillippe was from Barbados, had apparently won awards for his cocktails, and had a smile was as bright as the large Sky Lounge windows. He wore a soft grey waistcoat the same tone as the decor, a dickie bow tie, and the customary name badge. He brought life to the still-empty lounge. If I had a strong sense of darkness, it was balanced by my sense for lightness, you might call it. Good people shone to me, and he glowed.

'We're gonna have some fun here,' he said. 'I fill them with drinks, and you fill them with music – and we're all full of joy.'

'I'll leave you with Phillippe.' Sarah seemed happy that I could get on with the job. 'You've got half an hour until the lounge opens at one. Phillippe has plenty of sheet music behind the bar, I believe? Yes. Great.' She looked at her watch. 'OK, I'd better get on. Passengers have been boarding since noon, so lots to do. I'll try and pop back before you're done, but if not, you're in the Piano Bar at five-thirty for a two-hour set. Michaela is manager there, lovely girl. Then the Sunset Bar at nine for two more hours, and manager Harvey will take care of you. We set sail at four so since you're between sets, you might like to go outside and enjoy that. OK. Good luck.'

I tried to digest all this information.

Phillippe busied himself behind the bar with a variety of young staff. I walked up the three steps and sat on the piano stool. Found my centre. Did the customary deep breathing exercises to decrease my heart rate. Stretched my body and wriggled my fingers. Tried to relax. Prepare. It was only a practice, but I treated it with the same respect as the actual performance. The only difference was that I tried not to play a piece the way I was going to perform it for real. I changed the key; I upped the tempo; I made subtle, purposeful mistakes so I could find my way back to the song.

Phillippe brought me some water with ice in it. 'We open in five,' he smiled.

'Thank you.'

I sipped from the glass. My stomach danced somersaults just as it always did before a performance. I knew I should begin, that the music should already be playing when patrons entered the room. I repeated my exercises. There was always a danger of beginning too fast, so I visualised the start of the first song and audiated it at the right tempo.

Then I played.

I opened with 'Bridge over Troubled Water'.

I went wrong about halfway through, and my heart beat so fast I followed its tempo over the song's, but I managed to find my way back to the chorus, not daring to look up in case I saw rows of dis-approving faces. A million thoughts exploded in my head; *I'm not good enough. I shouldn't have come. Go home*. I suddenly saw the little girl, the would-be new student whose house I ran from: Rebecca. I felt guilty now for being here and abandoning her – my responsibilities – so suddenly.

I had to pause before the next song.

But the notes did as they should, and my heart slowed again. I often forgot time when I performed. The beats did not mark passing seconds, but immeasurable moments. Between songs I looked around, remembering to smile at my audience, but they were wrapped up in one another. I rarely hoped for applause, and I didn't receive any this time.

When I finished the set, though, there was a light spattering of claps.

I nodded, polite, appreciative.

I went to the bar, wanting to thank Phillippe, but they were busy, so I headed back to my cabin. The ship was packed now. I passed through the central atrium, where a gold-and-glass lift joined four floors, and a floating staircase curled beneath a stained-glass dome the colours of the ocean. Guests milled about, casually dressed, faces alight. I wanted to be on deck when the ship departed, which gave me less than two hours, so I hurried through the throng, getting lost and having to retrace my steps a few times.

Finally, I reached cabin 313.

I sat on the bed and realised how exhausted I was. I should pace myself. I had two more two-hour sets still to do. I slipped out of my clothes and set the alarm on my phone, planning to have a one-hour nap, wake at three-thirty and freshen up before heading outside for the ship's departure, and then on to the Piano Bar. I saw the black folder on my pillow. I was too tired for reading, and I knew it might not be wise to enter my dreams with whatever words lay between these pages, but before I knew it, my hands were opening the cover.

Despite myself, I read the words there.

PRIVATE AND CONFIDENTIAL
Dear Ms Harris,
Re: Care Records Access Request

Please find enclosed copies of historical records held by the
East Riding of Yorkshire Council as requested under your
subject access request. Please be aware that redactions
have taken place, which is due to third-party information
being recorded where consent to share said information has
not been sought or given. If you have any queries, please
contact me and I will be happy to assist you.
Yours sincerely,
Lesley Smith
Senior Customer Relations Officer

It was an innocent enough page, but I closed the folder anyway,
my heart pounding. I could recall some scenes from my childhood
– the first part of it, the years with Harriet; moments that were
vivid, painful, joyful, too real. It was after that, when she had gone,
that was the great mystery. Answers about her disappearance were
what I wanted, but I feared that digging up our past in order to
find them would cause such pain, I might never recover.

I closed my eyes and finally fell asleep with her image whirling
about my brain, a lively auburn-haired girl cartwheeling through
flowers.

13

I dreamed we played our song.

She joined me on the white piano seat in the Sky Lounge, Harriet, against a backdrop of a raging ocean, of angry clouds that fought to win the heavens. As always, I was the primo on the right and she was the secondo on the left, and we looked at each other and whispered in unison, "'Nothing Else'." And there wasn't. Only us. Only our ballad. Our fingers in perfect harmony. And when we finished, applause came in the form of a clear, cloudless sky, and a sea we had calmed with our music.

When I woke, homesickness enveloped me – heavy, heartful. But I did not long for my flat on the marina, or for the people in my life now. The house of my childhood was opening its door, regardless of whether I wanted it to. Now I was far from anywhere, untethered by home or everyday life, it felt like the past was inching closer. It seemed as though reading even just that first page of my care documents had triggered something. She was creeping in. She had tiptoed again into my dream.

Harriet.

I moved my fingers in the air on an imaginary keyboard and played my part of our song. I could only play those chords. I'd even written them up once, years ago. I'd brought that sheet of music with me on the ship, the paper more yellowed than the others, standing out like a cheap paperback in the bargain bin. I'd always had to imagine Harriet's part. I'd tried playing it a couple of times, but I just couldn't. It was always slightly off, like when I was purposefully playing a song wrong in order to practise, except I was trying to play it *right*. I could hear it, but I couldn't repeat it.

Four-hand music – where two people play – is seldom heard in concerts. Musicians must have a certain chemistry, an innate under-

14·07

Hobbs, K

Reserved Item

Branch: Whitstable Library
Date: 30/06/2023   Time: 11:36 AM
Name: Hobbs, Katrina P
ID: ...5241

Item: Nothing else
         C334768456

Expires:14 Jul 2023

Instruction: Please process item

standing of one another, to do justice to a duet. It's about more than speaking exactly the same language. It's about being one.

And, back then, Harriet and I were.

Until suddenly we weren't.

14

I quickly showered, and dressed again in my tailored black suit, but added gold drop earrings and let my hair fall around my shoulders for the evening crowd. I ate some of the cereal bars I'd packed for emergencies, knowing I must eat properly later, and grabbed my folder of sheet music and my Nikon, and headed to the upper decks.

I had no idea where would be best for watching us leave land. I wanted to enjoy it somewhere tranquil, not as part of one of the boisterous, and infamous, Sail Away parties Tamsin had described. I went up to deck twelve and discovered one there: a DJ was playing dance hits for an audience of young and old who, if they weren't already in the large neon-lit pool, looked likely to end up in there before the day ended.

I went down to deck seven and headed outside. A path wrapped around the length of the ship. It would be a great place to walk and get fresh air when I needed to. I remembered Aiden's warning that mixing with guests was a big no-no, but it was deserted, and hadn't he said it was different for the entertainment team?

I walked along the wooden deck towards the back of the ship – the stern as I now knew it to be called – my heels clacking a jarring rhythm, blue-and-white lifeboats blocking any view to the left, wooden doors and windows looking into a packed restaurant on the right. At the end was pleasant area where white railings curved around a polished floor and a few guests sat with drinks in the randomly scattered cream wicker chairs. I stood where the railings reached a gentle point, where on one side I could see the port, the hustle and bustle there, the city of Southampton beyond, and on the other the sea shining like someone had sprinkled diamonds on the waves. I took a photograph of each side, two opposing images.

Just after four a gentle shuddering began, so subtle that I didn't realise anything was happening at first. Then we began to move. It seemed the port was leaving us rather than the other way around. I looked down into the sea, frothing and wild. This was it. We were going to New York. There was no going back. I was on this ship, like it or not, for seven days, until we arrived in the US. How did I feel? Not trapped, that was certain. Bound? No, not that either. The word that came to me was 'inevitable', and I had no idea why.

I took another picture.

A woman came over from one of the wicker chairs and asked if I wanted one with myself in the shot. I didn't particularly, but not wanting to sound ungracious I nodded eagerly and gave her the camera. Later I would study the picture; I looked uncomfortable, the way a five-year-old looks in her first school picture, and also, with the vast expanse of ocean behind me, like I was the only person in the world.

I wanted to stay longer, watching the sea churning, and the land disappearing, but I had to play in the Piano Bar soon.

As I headed for one of the wooden doors that would take me back inside, a voice stopped me. 'Excuse me, I think you dropped something.'

I turned. An elderly man with wild wisps of white hair and a camera similar to mine around his neck held out a small piece of paper. Green. I reached for it. A raffle ticket. The numbers 282 on it. Not eleven as my mind had pictured.

'It's not mine,' I smiled without taking it.

'Oh, how curious. It looked like it fell behind you.' He studied it. 'They were having a raffle in the lobby earlier to win some art at the auction tomorrow. I hope it's not a winning ticket or someone somewhere will be very disappointed.' He returned to a wicker chair, still studying the small scrap.

It could seem a strange coincidence, yet it felt perfectly commonplace to me. Jazz improvisation relies on such luck. On the synchronicity of the musicians gelling together, as if joined by a higher force, their music more than just notes that they play.

It was not my raffle ticket.

But it felt fated.

15

I was six when we won a piano.

It was the talk of the street. Who wins a piano? What an unusual prize, most people said when we told them. How lucky you are, they cried. My mother was a member of the local Women's Institute; a member had died after a long battle with cancer and asked her husband to make sure the beloved instrument was used to raise money for the hospice where she passed. The piano had 'brought her many years of joy' apparently, and she had played until morphine rendered her unable.

A green raffle ticket and the number eleven brought it to us.

'We don't want a bloody piano.' That was my father, at the dinner table. Six words that could have changed the entire course of my life if we had obeyed – words spat out with force and a mouthful of stew.

But my usually quiet, obedient mother was firm. 'I won it,' she said softly.

'Give it to the runner-up,' my father snapped, shovelling more food into his mouth.

'I think Mary would have been delighted that it was coming here,' she tried again, still gentle. 'I really do feel like it was supposed to.'

'If that was the case, she'd have left the bugger to you.'

'No, I meant … Oh, it doesn't matter.'

Let me tell you about my mum as I remember her. She was a timid woman who didn't know her own beauty, whose English-rose skin was wasted on a woman who often hid her face with her hands, both prepared for attack and as a nervous tic; whose soft gold hair was mostly pulled back as though there was shame in its glory; whose clothes were plain and chosen to hide bruises rather than show her delicate frame. I adored her. Of course I did – all children love their mothers. But there was a role reversal with us. I felt I had to protect her. She never asked me to and would have felt terrible if she'd thought I was burdened with it, but I worried that a strong wind might blow her away, and I had to be the paper-weight that secured her to us.

'Who the hell's gonna play a piano?' demanded my father. He was thickset, not tall, but powerful, raucous in everything he did, from his words to his footfall to how he closed doors. The house knew not to get in his way; I often felt that the windows and the walls held their breath when he came home. 'None of us know how to.'

'My mum did,' said my mother, her eyes sad.

'Yes, but *you* never have.' He shook his head and tutted.

'I will,' cried Harriet. 'I'll play it.'

She was just four then and spirited, far more than I was. I was my mother's quiet shadow, the same golden hair about my shoulders, but Harriet dared to come out of that shade into the sun. She bounced in her seat.

'You will, eh?' My father sounded amused rather than annoyed, which he often was with my little sister, who I knew he favoured. I didn't even mind, because I did too. She made me the happiest.

'I can, I can,' she insisted, wriggling her hands in the air. 'Mrs Cooper at nursery said I have piano-playing fingers. Look. They will play it very goodly.'

My father ruffled her hair and put some bread on his plate to mop up his gravy. 'If I did permit you to have it, where the hell would we put it?'

'I suppose it might go in here,' suggested my mother, well versed in making it clear with her tone that he would ultimately decide.

'Here?' He looked around. We were sitting at the dining table in the back room that overlooked a long garden. The only other things in the space were a cupboard full of our toys, a doll's house with a red roof, and a small tiled fireplace. 'I suppose. Where then?' He put the question to Harriet as he so often did, belittling my mother by placing more value in the opinion of a four-year-old.

'Oh, *there*,' cried Harriet, innocent to his game. She pointed at the toy cupboard. 'I will play on it there. Will you play with me, Heather?'

'Yes, if you want me to,' I said. 'We'll have to learn, won't we?'

'Oh, Mr Hibbert at number fifteen teaches piano in th—' started my mother, more excited than I'd ever heard her.

'I'm not paying some bloody nancy boy to come into my home,' said my father, dropping his knife and fork noisily onto the now empty plate. 'No, if I do let you have the bloody thing, the girls will have to learn themselves. Nobody ever taught me nowt, and I'm OK. That's that.'

My mother collected the plates, as she did every day, and my father lit a cigarette. As far as meals went, it had been a peaceful one. The food had stayed on the table, and the words had been amiable. Harriet and I waited until he dismissed us and then scurried away to read in the hallway, where we liked how the sun broke through the front door's multicoloured glass and speckled the floor, and where I told Harriet stories about houses that were full of light all the time, and she shone.

The 1968 Kohler and Campbell upright piano was ten years old but immaculate when it arrived with us on a hot June afternoon. I've since googled pianos and found it, but back then I didn't know the details of its origin – I only saw an instrument that was a beautiful polished cherry, with ornate legs, brass fittings and a long matching stool padded with black leather. Two men got it into the house while Harriet and I sat on the stairs, hardly able to keep still at the sight of this new and wondrous thing.

'How does it make the music?' Harriet asked me. 'Do you wind it up?'

'Haven't you seen one before?' I asked. 'Don't they have one at your nursery?' She shook her head, though I wondered if she might be playing with me. 'You lift the lid and there are these keys underneath.'

'Like those?' She pointed to the ones in the door.

'No,' I laughed, sure now that she being silly. 'They're black and white. And you press them, and they make a nice sound.'

'How do you know so much, Heather?' She studied me, her hazel eyes intense. 'Will I know all the things you do when *I'm* six?'

'I don't know much,' I said. 'But remember when we watched that man on telly with nice hair playing one? He was dead good, wasn't he?'

'I didn't see that.'

'You were probably in bed.'

'It's not fair that you stay up longer than me.' She crossed her arms.

'You don't miss much,' I said, thinking of when I'd gone to get some water the night before and seen our mother cowering on the kitchen floor while my father rained blows down on her. I wasn't shocked; I had seen this many times. But I didn't want Harriet to witness it too. It was enough that she saw food flying across the room at mealtimes. That she had heard muffled arguments while I frenziedly read her stories near the toy cupboard. That I lied away the sounds we heard in the night, the thumps and thuds and thrashes. Last night, seeing my mother cowering, I'd buried my thirst and retreated to the living room, to *Wonder Woman* on the TV, to the quiet place in my head that I found when I sat and stared at the screen with my hands over my ears; *Come to me, Diana Prince*, I thought; *come and rescue us all*.

She never came.

But the piano did.

As agreed, it was placed in the back room, between the doll's house with the red roof and the toy cupboard. When the two men had gone, my father came into the room, cigarette dangling from his mouth, and studied it, lifting the lid and patting the seat. I willed him not to touch any of the keys. Not to be the first to play them. I willed it so hard my head hurt. *Don't play a song, don't play a song*. But it worked and he put the lid back down again, more gently than was his usual way.

'I suppose it's quite a grand thing,' he said.

'A grand thing,' repeated Harriet with a giggle.

'You'd better bloody look after it,' he said to us, and went into the garden.

'Better bloody look after it,' repeated Harriet.

I giggled. She always made me laugh.

We sat on the stool, her on the left, me on the right, and we grinned at one another. I remember it as vividly as though it was yesterday. I can close my eyes and hear my mother washing dishes in the kitchen, hear my father cursing at something in the shed. I can smell the cake baking in the oven and the just-cut grass outside. I can see Harriet, her auburn hair plaited that day, her pink-checked dress that bit too tight.

Did we know what this piano was going to mean to us? Did we sense the music we would eventually play? I don't know. Perhaps it's only now, looking back, that I place such importance on the moment, as we all do when the things afterward have put it into context.

'You go first,' said Harriet.

I lifted the lid. I realised the bigger keys were not really white, more a creamy colour, and that there were more of them than the darker, much smaller keys that seemed randomly placed, in twos and threes. I know now that this particular piano had eighty-eight notes and that it had been well looked after.

'Do the music then,' said Harriet.

I had no idea which key to press or what any of them were called. I went for a central creamy key, middle C. It sounded like an announcement. I pressed it again, and then again. Announce, announce, announce. Harriet then pressed three at her end, over and over, A B C, A B C, A B C. Our mother came into the room, a tea towel on her shoulder, as it often was, her face red from baking.

'My mother started playing at about your age,' she smiled.

'Did she?' I asked, fascinated. 'Was she good?'

'A natural. I used to sit at her feet and just get lost in the music. I could tell her mood from what she played.' Mum paused as though she was about to divulge the greatest secret. 'Music is in your blood, girls.'

'Is it in yours?' asked Harriet.

'I suppose it must be.'

'So why don't you play?' I asked.

'I don't know. I've always preferred to listen to music than try and create it. And these things often miss a generation.' She kissed my forehead and then Harriet's. 'Music is the only language that every single person understands. Imagine a world without it? It would be lovely to have some in this house.'

I've often wondered why we never really did until then, apart from pop songs on the radio – never loud, and usually when our father was out. Did he not like it?

As my mother continued, I was sure she was speaking to herself: 'It would make me so happy if you learned to play.'

And, oh, I wanted to make her happy.

16

I arrived in the Piano Bar at four-forty. It was already busy. The seating, decorated to look like a piano keyboard, was hidden now under the many patrons. This unnerved me; there would be no chance to rehearse alone, to compose myself. Fortunately, I was invisible. No one knew I was the pianist. It might have seemed odd that I performed for an audience when I was shy, but many artists are – musical ability can strike the most introverted person, lumbering them with a need to do something that goes against what feels comfortable. Once I started playing though, I didn't so much transform as step through a mirror and become the right reflection of myself.

I approached the bar and found its manager, Michaela, a beautiful black woman with Beyoncé-esque hair and an American accent, the customary blue uniform somehow more of a statement on her statuesque frame.

'I'm Heather,' I said. 'The pianist.'

'Oh, hi, honey,' she said. 'You want a drink?'

I realised I did. 'A glass of Pinot Grigio if you have it.'

She brought me one, and I handed over my new card to pay. 'Oh, no,' she said. 'On the house this first time.'

'What do they usually like in here?' I sipped the wine, my heart racing now, going from moderato to allegro each time I surveyed the room.

'It varies, honey,' said Michaela. 'My last trip they had a guy who did a lot of Bob Dylan, and sang too, but the woman before that just played a mix of stuff from the seventies and eighties. You can't go wrong with that. They'll join in more if you sing, but I think as long as you chat to them, they're happy.'

When I'd worked in bars, audience engagement varied, but I'd never had to sing. I watched Michaela and her staff bustle about, making cocktails and greeting guests with much more enthusiasm than bar staff did back home. I guessed training was more specialised on a cruise ship, or perhaps they just loved what they did.

At five-twenty I couldn't wait any longer. I made my way to the black piano in the centre of the room – an unusual position, and closely surrounded on all sides. I stumbled on the two steps that led up to it, and righted myself, heart racing. It occurred to me, as I sat down and composed myself, that my father had been clumsy too, and I wondered if doors and walls ever quaked in my wake.

I saw Frederica – the girl whose auburn hair had reminded me of Harriet. The writer who would be doing workshops tomorrow. She smiled, and it comforted me to have a sort of familiar face in the audience.

'Good evening, everyone,' I said brightly, hoping I sounded more confident than I felt. I dreaded making a mistake like I had in the Sky Lounge. 'I don't know what you're in the mood for tonight, but I don't think you can ever go wrong with this one...'

And I played A-ha's eighties classic, 'Take on Me'.

I played perfectly, and it got a good reaction, some light cheers and a scattering of applause as gentle as spring rainfall. I decided to stick with that era, and gave them Elton John, Stevie Wonder, Chris De Burgh and George Michael. They lapped these hits up, clapping and swaying along, some even singing, which broke the ice and made it easier to chat in between. Now I didn't mind their close proximity; there was a warmth in it, and I could feel their joy. Frederica requested 'The Power of Love' by Jennifer Rush, and I played that. I knew these songs by heart; popular music is easier to master than classical.

Time flew by.

A two-hour set is generally around twenty-five songs, and always passes quickly. I graciously accepted the generous applause at the end – a heavier rainfall this time – and then made my way to the bar and ordered another glass of Pinot Grigio, figuring I had an hour until I played in the Sunset Bar, my final gig of the day. Frederica sat on the stool next to me.

'You were so good,' she gushed.

'Thank you. You're English,' I said, surprised. I'd presumed from the unusual name that she was German or Swedish maybe; she'd not spoken much at our meeting with Sarah Briggs, so I'd been unable to ascertain which.

'Yes,' she laughed. 'What else did you expect?'

'Frederica is an unusual name. Beautiful though. And your surname...'

'My father's German,' she said. 'It's helpful having a unique name, you know, when you're a writer. Are you hungry?'

I realised I was. All I'd had since breakfast was a couple of bananas and some cereal bars. 'Why, do you want to get some food?' I looked at my phone. 'I only have forty minutes though. I wonder where's best. Should we go back belowdecks? Not sure I have time.'

'One of the dancers told me there's a self-service café on deck eight for guests who don't want to dress up for the main Oceana restaurant. We could probably grab something fast there.'

'We're not supposed to, are we?' I said.

'Who'd know? We look like guests. And we're entertainment.'

'True. Shall we, then?'

I thanked Michaela for making me feel welcome, and Frederica and I went up a deck and found a bustling canteen-style café with a diverse mix of buffet food, from various pasta dishes to salads and vegetables, from every meat possible to pizzas and other fast food. I chose lasagne, Frederica the same, and we took our plates to a window table. I had almost forgotten we were at sea; Tamsin had been right about the motion of the ship being minimal.

Thinking of her, I smiled. Frederica, though very different, put me at ease in the same way. She was one of the 'light people' as I called them when I sensed this.

'It's so beautiful.' I couldn't take my eyes off the water. It was eight o'clock and though not yet setting, the sun was fast approaching the horizon. In its orange glow the undulating waves looked like melted chocolate.

'I know.' Frederica followed my gaze. 'The kind of lovely I could only dream of putting down on the page.'

'What kind of books do you write?' I cut my lasagne up.

'Psychological thrillers.'

'That's so exciting. Do you have any with you?'

'Yes, I'll be selling them at my workshops. You should come along.'

'What time are they?' The lasagne was surprisingly nice considering it had likely been sitting a while, and I devoured it.

'Eleven, in the theatre,' said Frederica.

My gig in the Sky Lounge was at one so if I went dressed ready for performance, I could go to her workshop first.

'I'll try and come before my set,' I said. 'Are you nervous?' I'd first assumed her to be shy, like I was, but she chatted quite freely. Or perhaps I just put her at ease the way she did me.

She nodded vigorously, mouth full. Swallowing, she said, 'God, yes. Most of my life is spent in isolation, writing. I've done loads of festivals and stuff, but this is different. It's like teaching a class in a way, and I'm no teacher. How about you? Do you get nervous?'

I nodded too. 'It's a strange thing. I can't not play, and yet I hate the limelight. When I'm up there – I know it's a cliché – but I do get lost in my music. It makes me feel ... safe. It always has.'

'I would never have known this was your first gig on a cruise,' she said.

'Thank you. I mostly teach. I do play in bars, but people there aren't always listening.'

'I was listening,' said Frederica, seriously. 'There's something hypnotic about you.'

I blushed. Didn't know what to say. So I kept quiet. Put my knife and fork neatly on my empty plate.

'What made you decide to do this?' I asked. 'Come on a cruise, I mean. I didn't know it was something writers did.'

'I was invited. Apparently, they often have guest speakers – not just writers, but artists, chefs, minor celebrities.' Frederica looked thoughtful. 'It came at the right time.' She paused again. 'I needed to get away. I was in … well, an…' She looked unsure but then finished her sentence. 'An abusive relationship.'

'I'm sorry to hear that,' I said.

She shrugged, not dismissively, more as though she were shaking herself free of the sadness. 'We're here, and that's all that matters, isn't it?' She changed tack, as fluid as when I crossed one hand over the other on the keyboard. 'How about you then? It's your first time too. Why now?'

Though I felt sure I could have shared anything with her in that quiet moment, I wanted to keep our conversation light. I had to leave for the Sunset Bar in ten minutes and needed my mood to be up. 'Like you, I do have my reasons, but let's leave that for another time. Are you writing a book at the moment?'

'Yes.' Her face lit up like the nearby sunset. 'I brought my laptop because I thought these six weeks would be a great opportunity to start something new. My workshops are only two hours long, once a day, so the rest of the time is mine.' She finished her food. 'And I fancied a change. So last night, in my hotel room, I started writing about the actual process of writing. I kept notes with each novel, you see. I just thought it might help other writers – after all, that's what I'm doing here on this ship.'

'That sounds incredible,' I said, meaning it.

'Quite a change from killing people.'

'Sorry?'

She laughed. 'In my fiction.'

I laughed too. 'Of course.'

'Your gift I really envy though,' she said.

'Oh, stop it. Writing an actual book. *That's* something.'

'Do you write your own music?' she asked.

'I have done,' I admitted.

'Do you play it, you know, in public?'

'Not really. Unless you're famous, people don't want to hear original pieces.'

'I'd like to,' she said.

'Would you?'

'Yes. Why do you sound so surprised?'

'I don't know.' I didn't. No one except Tamsin and Dan was ever interested in my own songs.

Harriet was, whispered a voice at the back of my head.

'You should play something. In one of your sets.'

I realised I should go. 'I have to get to the Sunset Bar on deck eleven,' I said.

'I'll come in a bit,' she said. 'I might go and put something a bit glitzier on and then come and have a drink and a listen.'

'You don't have to,' I said.

'I want to.'

'OK. See you later.'

As I walked through the café and out onto the Queen's Parade shopping mall, where guests milled about with designer carrier bags, I wondered why I was so surprised that anyone would like the music I had written. Was it that it was personal, created from a deep and private place within, and I dreaded judgement? Was it that I feared any criticism would feel like disapproval of my ability, of my life, of me? Or was it that I simply dared not share my full self in that way?

For now, let them hear me play the songs that others had created and that I interpreted as best I could.

17

Sarah Briggs, the entertainment manager, was waiting for me in the Sunset Bar. Though the place was flamboyant, the colours were tasteful rather than neon: dusky pinks, soft blush lighting, a circular bar as shiny as a new wedding band. The room was full. I didn't know if it was the hour, the number of drinks consumed or that people felt at home by now, but the atmosphere was convivial, and I felt less nervous about this gig than I had for my others. Perhaps I too had acclimatised already.

I approached Sarah.

'Ah, Heather, how are you doing?' She squeezed my arm. 'I can't stop for long, but I wanted to see how you'd got on. I dropped into the Piano Bar, and Michaela said you were fab.'

'Oh, that's good.' I was flooded with relief.

'I know it's quite lively in here,' said Sarah, 'but I'd go for some classical background music. This is where people want to relax and chat. There's dance music up in the top bar and in the nightclub. Is that OK?'

I nodded, happy. Classical was my favourite.

'Great,' she said. 'That's Harvey over there. He's the manager.' She pointed out a slight man with thinning black hair and aquiline features. 'How about we meet tomorrow morning for a proper chat, at nine-thirty, in the crew office?'

'I'll be there,' I said.

When Sarah had gone, I tried to catch Harvey's eye, but he was too busy to speak, and just put a glass of wine on the bar for me, flourishing it with a wink and a little bow. I sipped it, the calm of a moment ago leaving me, my heart a metronome switched suddenly to a faster beat. At eight-fifty I weaved through the crowd towards the white piano, which sat against the backdrop of fading sky and emerging moon and stars, my knees soft with anxiety, hoping I wouldn't stumble. I sat down. A few people looked my way and a brief hush settled before conversation was resumed.

Then I saw her.

Not Frederica. Not the auburn hair that reminded me. But *her*. Harriet. My little sister. In the crowd. Darting between guests. Peering out at me from behind legs. Laughing – I could hear it over the din – and then scurrying behind someone else, a teasing hide-and-seek, catch me if you can. It couldn't be. I blinked. And she was gone.

But not really; I always felt her when I played.

It was time. I stretched and breathed, in, out, in, out, slow, slower, slow.

Then I began.

I started with my favourite, Beethoven's 'Moonlight Sonata', and the room quietened.

My audience was receptive. Polite but sincere applause came after the final note of my first piece. I gave them some Chopin, some Bach, some Debussy, and then moved on to contemporary classics by Hans Zimmer, John Barry and John Williams. Some I needed my sheet music for, others I knew by heart. Each was received with similar warmth. I relaxed. Enjoyed it. In between, I glanced out of the huge window behind me, but complete darkness meant that all I could see was myself, the piano and the audience beyond.

As I neared the end of the two-hour set, I saw Frederica standing by a gold column, now wearing a shimmering black dress, drink in hand. She gave a little wave. I smiled. I thought of what she'd said – that she would like to hear one of my pieces. My favourite I didn't think I could play. I'd need Harriet for that.

But there was my other, the one that, thanks to Tamsin, enjoyed brief notoriety on social media with the hashtags #GirlOnAPiano and #UnnamedSong. I'd composed it after a solitary river walk, thinking about my childhood, my lovely mother, and how everyone from that era had gone.

I had come back to my flat and sat at the piano with this simple harmony in my head. That's usually how it started. Just three or four chords. The rest would scatter away from that, as I liked to describe it. I found the remaining melody by putting my fingers on the keys and playing the notes, this action freeing the rest of the piece. The song freely flowed in two parts that then joined, one of them light – allegretto – the other angry and dark – prestissimo – and eventually they alternated, like an argument, first gentle, surrendering, then wild again. I thought about how the people from my past had been both light and dark, and of my innate gift for seeing this in people I met.

Now I placed my fingers on the keys that opened this song, closed my eyes for a second, and played it. If the room enjoyed it any more than the previous music, I didn't know. I wasn't with them. I was in my own world. A world with a garden full of flowers and a car engulfed in flames and my mother crying and trying to hide it from me. It was only when I finished and there was a momentary hush, followed by applause, that I realised they had been listening at all.

I smiled and nodded until the clapping stopped. Then I found Frederica.

'I'm exhausted now,' I admitted, deflating after the long day, the many new experiences, and three sets.

'I'm not surprised,' she said.

It was eleven o'clock. My day had begun so long ago.

'That last song was beautiful,' she said. 'I didn't recognise it.'

'It's one of mine.' I felt shy.

'Wow. What's it called?'

Maybe it was time to decide. After all, Harriet and I had given our childhood melody a name. 'Oh … it's…' I realised what it should be. 'It's called "A Sense of…"' I paused, not sure which way to go; light or dark. 'It's called "A Sense of Light",' I finished.

'The perfect title,' she said. 'That's what it is. A lot of people stopped talking when you played it.'

'Did they?'

'Yes.'

I was overwhelmed. 'Thanks for coming. Look, I'm going to go back to my cabin now, if you don't mind?'

'Of course not. You've had a busy day. I've been able to relax. My turn tomorrow. So, you'll come to my workshop?'

'I will. See you then.'

I walked back through the ship, past couples who leaned into one another, looking like this was a first shared holiday, and past those who had definitely travelled together many times and were more interested in their surroundings, in the examples of artwork propped up along the passages to promote tomorrow's auction, in the table of designer luggage in a sale, in the other men and women who passed them, scantily clad, more appealing.

In my cabin, I collapsed on the bunk, not wanting to move. It took every bit of effort to peel off my clothes, wash my face, clean my teeth and return to the narrow bed. The day flashed before me – so many faces: Sarah, Aiden, Frederica. How could I have been on land only sixteen hours ago? It felt now like a place I'd imagined. This curious world at sea was all that truly existed. I wondered briefly if my usual dislike of strange noises at night would keep me awake – I could hear footsteps occasionally going past my door, voices somewhere down the corridor, curious chugging sounds I couldn't identify – but my eyes were so heavy with fatigue that I felt sure sleep would not be a problem. The extraordinary day had drained me. I could feel the subtle, gentle motion of the ship more now I was reclining, and it was soothing, as though a mother rocked me in a nursery.

Before I switched the lamp off, I checked the messages I'd not had time to read earlier. Dan wished me a *Bon Voyage!* and Tamsin told me get myself to the first crew party and bag myself a hot waiter. When I turned my phone on silent for the night, I saw the black folder still sitting on the bedside ledge.

I felt it was calling to me.

Read some more, it whispered. *You know you want to*.

But I didn't know that.

And yet I opened it.

Divisional Director of Social Services
16ᵗʰ July 1982
Placement of children in Birchwood Orphanage

Family:
Mother   Annie Johnson
Father   Robert Johnson
Children   Heather Johnson (10/03/72)
            Harriet Johnson (03/05/74)

Due to the recent sudden death of both parents, Heather and Harriet Johnson are currently staying with their paternal grandmother, ███████████, but this situation is temporary due to ███████████ ill health. There are no other family members able to care for them. Maternal grandparents are dead, there are no suitable aunts or uncles; there are only one of each and they either live overseas or have no contact.

I am therefore writing to ask if it would be possible for places to be financed for them at Birchwood Orphanage, subject to there being vacancies. Placement at Birchwood would have inestimable advantages in that both children could continue in their present schools, they can remain together, and it would provide some areas of continuity in their lives.

The hope is that foster care/adoption will then be looked into.

Simon Bishop

Memorandum from Divisional Director of Social Services
To: Area 4
Subject: Johnson Family

Thank you for your memorandum dated 16ᵗʰ July. Approval is given for the Johnson children to be admitted to Birchwood, as and when necessary.

I couldn't read any more. It jarred me to see us described so factually, no emotion about the fact that two young parents were dead, and their children orphaned. But that was the key word: fact. These were documents recorded only as reports to be shared among those dealing with our case. Because that's what we were once the social services team took us on – a case.

What could I recall about the days after we were told our mother and father had gone? Who told us? It's all a blur, a shrill symphony of strange notes. I do know that Harriet and I clung to one another; that at night we shared a narrow bed at the orphanage despite there being two; that we held hands underneath the long breakfast table; that because we could not speak our grief, and because we were without our beloved piano, we played our song in the air and hummed the tune.

And then Harriet disappeared.

One day. From the orphanage.

Thinking of it now, I wanted to cry like a five-year-old.

I sometimes asked Margaret (my 'mother' after I was eventually adopted at eleven) about Harriet, though not often, fearing I'd upset her with my questions; I always felt I had to keep the peace, not cause problems. Margaret said that Harriet had been long gone by the time they adopted me. I think that maybe she said the social-services team hadn't even known where she went, but I can't be sure after all this time.

But what if Margaret lied about it all? Not to be unkind, but to keep me from knowing something that might hurt.

I realised now, in my tiny cabin, floating on a vast sea, that I wanted to try and find Harriet. Properly. Through some sort of agency or DNA testing place. When I got home. I wondered then, was my sister even still alive? If so, what would she recall of me after all this time? Had I implanted myself in her mind as firmly as she had been implanted in mine? Did I ever enter her thoughts? Did she want to find me?

As I drifted into oblivion, I heard our song once again.

I dreamt hard, part replays of the day, part past memories – new songs and old ones. Frederica was there, in a beautiful silver gown that fell away from her like frothing seawater; she was reading from a huge book, her words not appearing as sounds, but written in bubbles that flew out of her mouth and drifted away and popped. Harriet was there too; she sat at the white piano in the Sky Lounge and played her half of our song. But when I tried to get to her, a gigantic tsunami rose outside and water smashed through the windows, washing her away. I struggled to breathe, to float, to swim, to get to her, but the flood's current dragged me away, down, deeper, and I choked and drowned.

I woke with a gasp.

I was exhausted enough to quickly succumb to sleep again.

But I took with me a sudden, vivid memory of the time our mother played us her favourite song.

Throughout the summer of 1978 Harriet and I played on our new piano. We abandoned the street games with the kids we usually played alongside; our bikes lay forlornly on the parched grass in the back garden, and we declined invites to our neighbours' gardens for paddling-pool play and picnics, just so we could sit side by side and find our way around the cream-and-black keys.

We always waited until our father had left for work.

'What a bloody racket,' he'd yelled the first day we excitedly plonked the keys, each trying to outdo the other with our speed, and with trying to press as many at the same time as possible. Our father marched into the back room, grunting and muttering, and I retracted my fingers from the keyboard in a flash while Harriet, always more mischievous, continued her messy song.

'Stop, Harriet,' he cried. 'It's bloody awful, girl.'

'Bloody awful, girl,' she mimicked.

If I'd have dared answer back, I'd have got a slap around the head, like I did when I once made the mistake of responding to something he hadn't required a reaction to. Harriet didn't seem to anger him the way my mother and I did. Mum only had to move in the wrong way or give him the wrong portion size at a meal and he punched her in the arm or dragged the cloth from the table, spilling food and smashing plates. In these moments, even my bright, rascally Harriet looked afraid, and I held her tightly to me, wordlessly willing her not to make one of her cheeky comments and further anger our temperamental father.

Ignoring her now, he said firmly, 'Until you two can make some sort of proper tune, you'll only play when I'm out or else I'll chop the bloody thing up and use it for firewood. Understood?'

Harriet didn't play but she kept her fingers on the keys in defiance. I loved her for her ebullience, but I feared that one day our father would tire of it and turn on her like he had on our mother and me. I often wondered if his obvious favouritism was because she was so like him in her candour, while I was more like my mother.

When he had gone, we settled into a gentler game. We mimicked one another; two delayed mirror images. I played six or seven keys in quick succession, and Harriet tried to copy this basic pattern at her end of the keyboard. We did it at the same time, and then with a few seconds gap, excited about the different effect. We learnt quickly that repeated patterns played up and down the keys made a basic song; that if we then did it backwards that created another; and if we changed the speed, another.

I know now, as a teacher, that a gauge for when a child is ready to learn the piano is that they have the dexterity to tie their own laces. I don't know if Harriet could tie hers that summer, but we were ripe for learning. I also know that an interest is essential, or the child's attention will wander, and they won't practise; we had that passion from the off. Only a tiny handful of the children I've taught are what you would call naturals, meaning they play with flair, have an innate understanding of the piano in a physical sense, and can improvise rhapsodies of their own.

We were naturals.

After a week or two of this instrument being part of our life, our mother watched us from the doorway, a smile dancing about her lips. 'You really love it, don't you?' she said, thoughtfully.

'Oh, we do,' we cried in unison.

'You're not going to take it away, are you?' I asked, always fearing the worst.

'Oh no,' she said, coming over to us. 'I'd never ever do that ... but...'

'But what?' asked Harriet. 'What is your but, Mummy?'

'Well, your dad...'

'What has he said?' I asked, dreading the answer.

She shook her head. 'He thinks that you should be able to learn to play yourselves, and fast. But I know it would be impossible to play like Chopin in a matter of—'

'Who's Chopin?' asked Harriet.

'My favourite,' said our mother, wistfully. 'Wait, I'll find the record...'

She disappeared.

'Who is Chopin?' Harriet asked me. 'Does he live on our street?'

I shrugged, and she looked disappointed. She always expected me to have the answers. I was more concerned about our father and his expectations, and what they meant for us and the piano. Our mother returned from the other room with the record player and an LP. On the front was a statue of a man with old-fashioned hair and the words *Chopin by Starlight – The Hollywood Bowl Symphony Orchestra*. She plugged the record player in and took the vinyl from its sleeve and then placed it on the turntable.

'This is "Nocturne No 2",' she said, as though she was announcing a royal visit, and she moved the needle to the second track.

I'm sure Harriet and I held our breath with anticipation.

Then the most delicate, lyrical, hypnotic tune filled the room. I felt like my heart opened up. Like my pores drank it in. Like the hairs on my neck stood not to attention but in awe. It was as though I heard it with more than merely my ears. I heard it in my veins and in my bones. Harriet's hand slipped into mine, and I saw from her face that at the tender age of four, she felt it too. I knew nothing bad could happen to the three of us while it played. That the safe hands of such beauty would not let any harm come to us. It's a moment I've never forgotten. The moment I knew that music was indeed in my blood; in my DNA; as much a part of my soul as anything ever could be.

'I want to play like that,' I said when it had finished.

Mum laughed. 'That's a big dream, Heather,' she said. 'But, yes, I want you to as well. I know your father expects so much from you, and that he can be critical of anything less than perfect, so he thinks that it will only take a few weeks and you'll be two mini Chopins but—'

'Mini Chopins,' giggled Harriet.

'But we won't achieve that unless someone *teaches* you. Natural ability is a start, and I can't show you how to read the sheet music or what the notes are.' She knelt down so she was at eye level with us and tenderly put a hand on each of our cheeks. 'Mr Hibbert at number fifteen teaches piano at the university.'

'But Dad said h—' tried Harriet.

'I know. So, it would have to be our secret.'

'What would?' I asked, although I was beginning to realise as I said it.

'I'm going to ask him to teach you twice a week when your father isn't here.'

Though I was excited at the idea, I felt sick at the thought of us being discovered, of him coming home unexpectedly. Perhaps my mother saw this in my face, because she said, 'Don't worry, Heather, you'll go to his house. And then if your dad does come home, for whatever reason, I'll tell him you're playing at Emma's house.'

'Yes,' cried Harriet. 'Emma's house. I like Emma.'

Mum laughed. 'I'll speak to Mr Hibbert, and I'm sure we can come up with some sort of arrangement. I just wanted to make sure you were serious about learning to play properly. Is that what you want?'

'Oh, yes!' we cried.

'I think your dad will enjoy it when you can. I think it will make us all happy.' If that was what she thought, I wondered why she looked so sad. 'But not a word, OK? Harriet, I'm very serious about this. I know I've taught you that you should never lie or keep secrets but, well, this one ... I suppose you can think of it as a surprise. That you're learning the piano so you can surprise your dad, yes?'

'Yes, we will surprise Daddy,' cried Harriet.

'So, you have to *shhhhh*.' Mum put her finger over Harriet's lips.

'Shhhhh,' repeated my little sister, not even silenced by this.

'I'll go and see Mr Hibbert this afternoon,' said our mother before returning to the kitchen.

She kept her promise. We were itching to ask what had happened, what Mr Hibbert had said, but by then Father was home, and we assumed our usual positions at the table and ate fish in parsley sauce while listening to him talking about an upcoming strike at the factory. Harriet had this big, stupid grin on her face, and I feared she was going to tell him about the plan.

'What on earth is that face?' asked our father, mouth full as always.

'I'm happy, Daddy,' she cried.

'I can see that,' he snapped. 'Does it have to ruin my meal? What are you so happy about?'

I gulped down my peas, willing her not to give us away.

'It has been very sunny today,' she said.

He shook his head and shovelled more food in. 'I'm glad the weather makes you so happy. I might find such joy if your mother knew how to cook fish properly.' He pushed the rest of his meal away, half of the cod still there.

Our mother didn't look up. She never did. If his criticism hurt, she never showed it. She probably never dared. I often found it hard to eat when my father's mood switched so abruptly from belligerent to cruel, and this inability only fuelled his anger, so I forced the peas and fish down my throat.

'It tastes like shit,' he said.

I dreaded Harriet repeating his words, as she often did, but even she must have known this was not a moment for silliness.

Still, my mother kept her eyes on her food and said nothing.

'Are you even listening to me?' he demanded.

She couldn't win. If she responded I knew he would argue more fiercely. When she kept silent that fired him too. It was choosing what seemed best in that moment.

'Fuck's sake.' He stood, shoving the table.

I braced myself. It was like when my bike wobbled in the street and I knew I would come off it; I'd try in a split second to foresee how I'd land, and how best I could cushion the impact. With my father, it was trickier. He might storm out of the room, not to be seen again for the rest of the evening, snooker loud on the TV in the front room. He might rip the cloth away from the table. But worst of all, he might ask our mother to go and 'talk with him' in the kitchen. Then I'd know to take Harriet upstairs and read to her, so we didn't hear the violence below.

That night he looked at our mother and said, 'Annie, let's go to the kitchen.' Then to us he said, 'Go and play upstairs.'

I wondered how he had chosen the worst thing when only hours earlier the beauty of that Chopin music had made me feel like we were eternally safe. I felt cheated. I wanted to play it now. To see if it calmed my father the way it had soothed me.

'Dad,' I said, feeling brave. 'Can we play a record?'

'No, we bloody can't,' he said, and they disappeared, slamming the kitchen door.

I took Harriet upstairs and read her favourite story, *Snow White and Rose Red*. She loved that they were like us, that fair-haired Snow White was me, shy and preferring to spend time indoors, while darker-haired Rose Red was Harriet, more outspoken and cheerful, and preferring to be outside. I was a good reader for my age, understanding the written word as easily and naturally as I would later understand musical notes. But that evening, even this story didn't distract Harriet from what was happening downstairs, from the occasional thick thud, followed by our father's raised voice and then the unnerving silence, before it all began again.

'Why is Daddy so mean to Mummy?' asked Harriet.

I was only six. I didn't know the answer. I don't even know it now, long after. Had *his* father been cruel to him? I didn't know because he had died years before and I'd never got to know him. Was it because his mum, our Grandma Dolly, was so cold with him? Was he angry at the world, at his life, at himself? *Why*?

'I don't know,' I admitted.

Harriet looked sad. 'But Mummy is so nice.'

'I know,' I said. 'We'll make her happy, won't we?'

'Yes. We will. We will make music!'

I hugged her and eventually we both fell asleep on the floor with our book and the sound of our parents being unhappy downstairs.

The following morning, our father was in an amiable mood, as though none of the violence of the night before had happened.

When he left for work, our mother told us that Mr Hibbert had said he couldn't teach us until October, but then we could go twice a week for an hour. She said things might be a bit 'tight' because, though it was a very small fee – one she was sure he had set because he liked us girls – we would have to sacrifice the odd day out and extravagant birthday gifts. Harriet and I danced around the room with excitement. Mum laughed and watched us. I noticed bruises she had tried to hide with a high-collared blouse, and my joy wavered for a moment before she hugged us both.

When the summer holidays were over, and I went back to school and Harriet moved up to primary, we only had an hour to play on our piano before our father came home from work. On Saturdays he sometimes went out and we grabbed these hours too. We asked our mother to put the Chopin record on and we moved our hands over the keys as though we were playing his music. Our father had said we could only play while he was home when we knew how, and we were determined to know how.

And soon we would.

Soon it was October.

When I woke, I was disorientated. Not only because I'd forgotten where I was and expected to see my bright-yellow bedroom walls and saw instead dull beige hues, but because the absence of a window meant no daylight to give a clue to the time. Then I remembered. I was at sea. And I had slept better than in a long time, despite the dream. It must have suited me. I looked at my phone; it was just past eight.

I was starving. I dressed casually for now and found the crew café that we'd been shown yesterday by Aiden. I expected it to be quiet, that people would still be sleeping at eight-fifteen, but it was busy. Not everyone would be working later, I realised. Many, like waiters and shop staff, began early. The air was rich with the smell of bacon and coffee. I grabbed a tray and a bit of everything from the buffet, and looked around the room for an empty table or a familiar face.

Frederica waved from a table in the corner. Relieved, I joined her. She was with the comedian, Barry Lung, and a woman whose face I vaguely recognised, perhaps one of the dancers. I greeted everyone with a 'good morning' and sat in the remaining space.

'I couldn't sleep,' said Frederica, devouring a sausage sandwich. 'Nervous.'

'Your workshop? You'll be amazing. I can't wait.'

'You're going?' asked the girl.

'Yes, definitely.'

'Wish I could,' she said, nibbling on toast. 'But I've got rehearsals all morning. Last night was a nightmare – everything that could go wrong did. The lights failed. One of the dancers was sick halfway through and it went everywhere. We've got to kill it tonight ... or maybe I shouldn't say kill ... yikes!'

We all laughed.

'I *did* kill it,' said Barry. 'Bloody great set. I had to wait ages until they stopped laughing to move on to my next joke. Then they hounded me in the bar afterwards.'

No one seemed to know how to respond. His jolly demeanour still didn't fool me; my sense of darkness flashed strong. It was like he was trying too hard. He was a comedian, but it felt like you wouldn't want to be around when the laughter stopped.

'You guys should come watch me tonight,' he continued. 'We can get drinks after.'

'I'll be performing,' said the girl.

'Me too,' I added quickly.

Frederica made her mouthful last longer and then added a diplomatic, 'Yeah, I'll see.'

After more small talk, Frederica said she should prepare. I stood when she did, said I had a meeting with Sarah Briggs, which I did but not for another half-hour. Outside the café Frederica said, 'He probably means well, but Barry's so pushy. I saw him in the crew bar last night after I'd seen you play, and he was leering at the young dancers.'

I thought about how yesterday she had said she was in an abusive relationship, and I wondered if Barry therefore made her more uncomfortable than most. Was my history why I found him repellent? Did he just remind me of my father, and I'd misjudged the poor man? I hated to think badly of someone innocent.

'I guess you're more tuned in to men like that,' I said kindly.

'Sorry?' Frederica looked confused.

'You said, you know, you'd escaped an abusive relationship.'

'Oh, yes. My ex-girlfriend. Daisy.' She shrugged. 'Such a sweet name. You'd never know.'

I nodded. How presumptive I'd been. I knew that not all men were cruel, just as I knew not all women were the angels my mother had been, but still I'd seen the darkness in the wrong place with Frederica.

'Right,' she said. 'I'm gonna go get ready. See you at eleven in the theatre?'

'I'll be there,' I said.

I returned to my cabin. I wanted to go outside and see the sea now I knew we were out on the North Atlantic, but I had to plan my second busy day. There would be time for that later. Just before nine-thirty I headed for the crew office and found Sarah waiting for me with folders and two coffees, one of which she pushed across the table to me.

'I bet you need it,' she smiled. 'Did you sleep OK?'

'I really did.' I was still surprised and pleased about it.

'Oh, it sounds like the sea agrees with you then. It's not for everyone. I just wanted a quick catch-up, one on one. Our solo acts are often left to fend for themselves, so to speak, whereas theatre performers and members of the band have their team.'

'I don't mind that,' I said. 'I'm quite a solitary soul.'

'Still, make sure you come along to the crew party nights and other social occasions, won't you?'

I nodded but I wasn't sure I would. I gave so much to my music that I doubted I'd have anything left to give a crowd of boisterous youngsters at the end of the day.

'Now, there are just a couple of forms and questionnaires to fill in,' said Sarah. 'And of course, if you have any questions while you have me...'

My questions were mainly practical: where I could get my laundry done, where I could purchase general items, like toiletries, snacks, paracetamol, and was it OK that I walked around the main ship as long as I didn't bother guests, which it was.

By the time I'd finished talking to Sarah it was past ten and I knew I should change so I could go to Frederica's workshop, and then play in the Sky Lounge at one. I saw my care records on the bedside table and recalled my reaction to those few pages last night. Despite my reluctance to read them, and the abrupt nature of the way they had been written, they had triggered my decision to try and find Harriet, properly.

I showered, put my hair up and chose a cream suit. I grabbed my sheet music, my Nikon, and, after a thought, my care records too.

Outside, on deck seven, the rows of deck chairs had checked

blankets on top, and I knew why. Though it was August now, and the sky went on, forever blue, the wind was wild today. I went to the railings and raised my face to its lashing. There was nothing but sea, a sonata that followed its own rhythm, oblivious to me. I took a picture, knowing it wouldn't capture what my eyes saw.

I had to tear myself away to go to the theatre for eleven. The atmosphere there was subdued without the big lights I imagined shone in the evening. About eighty people gathered in the seats near the stage, some with notepads, mostly women. Onstage, at the front, was a chair and a table with a pile of books set out in an attractive manner. How terrified must Frederica feel looking at it. Playing music meant I didn't have to say much – but she would have to talk for two hours. I found a seat in the third row just as Frederica came out, looking lovely in a green dress, which contrasted with her gorgeous auburn hair.

'Good morning,' she said cheerfully. If she was nervous, she hid it well, though I noted that she kept her hands firmly together, perhaps to stop them trembling. 'Wow, thank you for coming. I was afraid I'd step out into an empty theatre.' Gentle laughter. 'Well, I'm Frederica Becker, as you perhaps know, unless you accidentally wandered in here, hoping to see *Mamma Mia*.' She was a natural. 'I know from the brochure that you've been promised some lively discussion, some top writing tips, some helpful writing prompts, and a chance to ask questions, so hopefully we'll manage all of this. Before we get to that, I thought I'd kick off with a bit about how I managed to get published. Is that OK with you guys?'

An encouraging stream of yeses made her smile. She talked about her long journey to publication, about the three books that were rejected over and over and over, and about a lucky meeting with an agent in a lift and the eleven words that changed her life: 'I've written a book about ice skating and sequins and murder.'

After answering a few questions, Frederica suggested a writing prompt. 'One of the main themes in my new book, *Never Forget*, is memory. My main character has forgotten an incident from her childhood and her counsellor needs her to remember it, because there's a killer who hasn't been caught.' A couple of audience members had this book in their laps and nodded along. 'So, I thought we could write something inspired by that. I'm going to give you a phrase, and I want you to write solidly for ten minutes and see what it evokes. Then if you're happy to, you can share some with us all, and we can discuss. Yes?'

No one argued, though some looked unsure.

'OK, the prompt is: "If only I could remember." Ready?'

Clearly most of the attendees had known to bring notepads and pens. I only had my sheet music and care records. I borrowed a pen from an elderly woman with teeth too big for her mouth and took out my Mozart 'Sonata in C Major' song sheet. I chewed the pen; everyone else scribbled away. I caught Frederica's eye and she winked encouragingly.

If only I could remember...

What? There was lots I did recall about the days before my parents died and Harriet disappeared. It was mostly the end that was hazy. The time after Harriet left the children's home. Was it because I *couldn't* look at it? I did try. I saw us at the long meal table, taking baths in a huge, cold room with a window that looked out onto playing fields, pretending a cardboard box in an empty corridor was a piano and 'playing' it. Then nothing. Then just me. Unable to eat. Unable to sleep. Not speaking to anyone.

I only managed to write a paragraph:

What if someone took Harriet all those years ago? If I look away from the memory of our last time together, I can see it out of the corner of my eye. If I think of it as though it happened to someone else, I can almost watch it unfold. It was morning. Yes. We woke in the same narrow bed, the other empty, like we had saved it for our mother, should she arise from the grave and come and rescue us. After breakfast – soggy cereal and cold toast – someone, a gruff woman who worked at the children's home, came and said she needed a word with Harriet. And off she went, my sister, half ready for bed in her pyjama bottoms, and half ready for the day in a pink top. And she never came back.

I was embarrassed to realise that tears had fallen down my cheeks.

Trying not to draw attention to myself, I squeezed past the others on my row, and sneaked up the aisle. In the area outside the theatre were some toilets, which I slipped into. There, I tried to compose myself. Dabbed my eyes. Took some deep breaths. Looked at the time. I was playing soon, so I made my way to the muted ash and silver of the Sky Lounge.

Cheerful Phillippe greeted me and lifted my mood again; he was a disco tune after a sad love song. 'Ah, Harriet, you bring the music again,' he cried.

'I'll try,' I laughed.

'Drink?'

'No, not this time, thank you.' I feared getting into the habit of drinking before every performance. Yesterday had been an exception.

The room was already full of lunchtime drinkers. I guessed this place opened at noon, not one, now we were at sea. The white piano awaited me in the corner, the sea blue and inviting beyond. I mounted the three steps, self-conscious as always, still emotional from my writing session, anticipating a fall but avoiding it. I was sure a slight hush fell as I took my seat; that meant the audience had some sort of expectation and this always unnerved me.

I began with 'Bridge over Troubled Water' as I had the day before, not sure yet if this audience enjoyed routine.

Contrary to how it seems, playing is not effortless. It sounds like it is because we hear it that way; that beauty, that gentleness, that calm. So much work goes into producing a piece that sounds like there is no effort. Though it's relatively easy to learn how, and most can pick up a melody or two, having finesse, being able to coordinate both hands simultaneously, and, if you're a true artist, using the physical, the mental and the emotional all at once, that takes great stamina. Yes, for me, this now came naturally, but if I was feeling vulnerable or tired or hadn't rehearsed enough, I could lose my way.

That lunchtime, I felt every movement. My finger joints ached. My back hurt. My arms felt heavy. I didn't speak between songs, afraid I wasn't up to it. I just gave the audience what they were there for.

After my hour was up the applause wasn't polite, like it had been yesterday, but more enthusiastic. I was surprised. Somehow, despite my mood, I must have performed well. I thanked them. It had only been sixty minutes, but I was exhausted.

'You are melancholy today,' said Phillippe as I left.

I needed to snap out of it before my next set. That was three hours away, thank goodness. I decided to eat. That would revive me. I went to the main buffet-style café, grabbed some pizza and a napkin and took it out onto deck seven. I found a deckchair in a quiet spot where I could watch the sea gushing by between the railings. I ate and my energy levels were restored.

Perhaps it was foolish when I wanted to keep my mood up, but I thought about the care records in my folder. Curiosity was stronger than my fears now. This felt like a safe spot, with the ocean a soothing song beside me. So I opened them, skimmed through the few pages I'd already read, and I resumed.

21

East Yorkshire Council Social Services Department
MEDICAL CERTIFICATE PRIOR TO BOARDING OUT
DATE: 18/07/1982

FULL NAME OF CHILD: Heather Johnson
SEX: F
DATE OF BIRTH: 10/03/1972
PRESENT WEIGHT: 4st 12lb

I examined this child on 18th July 1982, and I found no marks of injury, no evidence of an infectious illness and he/<u>she</u> appeared physically healthy.

ADMISSION FORM
Date: 18/07/1982
CLASS OF CASE
Section 2 Child Care Act 1980

PARENTS
MOTHER   **FATHER**
ALL REDACTED   **ALL REDACTED**

OTHER CHILDREN IN FAMILY
Sister ▮▮▮▮▮▮▮▮▮▮.

INTERESTED RELATIVES OR FRIENDS AND OTHER AGENCIES
None at present.

RELEVANT FAMILY MEDICAL HISTORY
None.

CIRCUMSTANCES RENDERING ADMISSION INTO CARE NECESSARY
No one to care for Heather and her sibling ██████ following the death of both parents. Paternal grandmother had the children for nine days in total, but ill health means she cannot continue. There are no other family members able to care for them.

INITIAL ASSESSMENT AND TREATMENT PLAN
Heather Johnson appears in good physical health. She is very close to her sister ██████. This bond appears to be a comfort in her grief. When spoken to separately, the children say very little. I worry that a separation would cause further trauma for both children and I've advised the social-services team that they must be fostered/adopted together if possible.

Signed
Alan Flemming

22

I stopped reading when my tears made it impossible. Looked around. Remembered where I was. Far from home. Even further from my past, and yet here it was, catching up with me. Reading the pages was like reading a story about another child, one I didn't know, Snow White separated from Rose Red. I was heartbroken. Seeing our situation coldly assessed, reported, only made its tragedy greater.

I concentrated on the horizon, remembering how Tamsin told me it eased seasickness, and hoping it would stem my tears. Still, they fell.

I knew it was around this time that the Polaroid picture of Harriet and I had been taken, in the grounds of the home, our smiles shy because the photographer was an older child who had a new camera and was testing it out. He had given the picture to me, and I'd never let it go.

I was already beginning to realise that because so many pages were photocopies and because so many were entirely blacked out (they probably contained information about my parents and the details of their deaths) I might not get what I needed from these records after all. But they were triggering odd memories, just as Frederica's prompt had.

When I read the line about Alan Flemming worrying that a separation would cause further trauma for us, I saw again the scene I'd written in Frederica's workshop. How was the moment I last saw Harriet clearer today, when all these years the memory had evaded me?

Now I wondered where Harriet had gone. Who took her? Someone must have. She can't have just walked out of the children's home alone, aged eight, never to be seen again. And why didn't that person take me? Had I been too quiet, too dull, not the kind of child that prospective adoptive parents viewed and wanted immediately? I could understand anyone falling in love with Harriet's vivacious nature, obvious at once in every joyful action and word. Yes, Margaret and Harold had adopted me, but I knew I'd been in the children's home alone for a while before that happened. I recalled lonely nights, shivering without my bed mate, trips to school alone in the yellow bus, unable to hear our song in my head without her.

I decided to read more, see if the pages included the date each of us left the home, but a shadow fell over me and a voice interrupted.

'You OK, Heather?' It was Frederica.

'Oh, yes.' I was embarrassed, knowing my make-up must be smudged, my eyes red. 'I just … I felt a little seasick…'

'Not homesick?' she asked kindly.

'Not exactly. Is there a word for when you long for a time gone by?'

'Nostalgic?'

'Of course,' I said. 'But not that either.'

'There is a word…'

'Yes?'

'*Saudade*,' said Frederica. I repeated it, softly. 'I came across it when writing my second book,' she said. 'It's Portuguese, and apparently there isn't an English equivalent. It's what refugees often use to describe what they have left behind: an intense, wordless, longing for everything that encompassed home, and is gone.'

'That's beautiful.'

'Do you want company?' Frederica shrugged. 'I can go to the crew café if you just want to relax here.'

'Oh, no, stay,' I said. 'Or we can eat? I'm still hungry. I only had a small slice of pizza. Up to you?'

'Well, I'm lucky to be free now, but you still have to play twice, yes?'

'I do, but I still have' – I looked at my phone – 'two and a half hours.'

We headed to the buffet-style café; I got a hearty lunch this time:

rice, chicken curry and some salad, and Frederica chose fried chicken. We sat in a window seat. I still couldn't get enough of being surrounded by ocean; it seemed to move in a different way each time I studied it, choppy this time, like an excited puppy.

'What did you write?' asked Frederica.

'Sorry?' I wondered if she was referring to my music.

'In my workshop. You don't have to tell me, if it's private. Just curious.'

'Oh. Yes.' I swallowed my curry. I didn't mind telling Frederica. It might be good to share it. 'I wrote about the last time I saw my sister.'

She nodded. 'And when was that?'

'Thirty-seven years ago.'

'*Really*? You must have been tiny.'

'Ten,' I admitted. 'She was eight.'

'What happened?'

'I don't really know. Sounds like something in a novel, eh?'

Frederica laughed. 'Be careful. I'm always looking for inspiration.'

'Our parents died,' I said quietly. I glanced at the sea; now it appeared calm. 'We both went into a care home. And then...' I had never spoken it aloud like this. I'd told Dan, just loosely, and with Tamsin I'd shared bits, after drinks, but with neither of them had I opened up enough to cause me grief. Now I was in a place that felt like everywhere and nowhere, and it freed me somehow. 'She left.'

'Your sister? What do you mean? Where did she go?'

'I have no idea.'

'In all this time?' Frederica sounded shocked.

I nodded.

'Have you tried looking for her – as an adult I mean?'

'Not properly,' I said, feeling embarrassed that it might seem like I hadn't cared enough to. 'I mean I tried Facebook and Google. But I was ... afraid. Because it meant ... well, looking back on things I've tried not to.'

Frederica nodded; no judgement apparent.

'I can't ask anyone because there's no one to ask. I was adopted, and my new parents told me that even the social-services team hadn't known where she went.' I paused. 'That might not be true. My adoptive parents could have been protecting me. That was my instinct.'

'Protecting you from what?' asked Frederica. I could tell she would research all her books thoroughly.

'I don't know,' I said.

'What about paying someone to find her?'

'I think I'm going to do that once I get home.'

'What do *you* think happened to her?' asked Frederica.

'I told you, I don't know.'

'No, I mean in your head. When we don't know something, we fill in the gaps, don't we? We imagine it. How do you see it? If you created a fiction, what would it be? The prompt I gave you all earlier was about memory. But what if it had been to write what you think happened, if you really, *really* had to create that.'

'I ... I...' I returned my gaze to the sea, hoping its cadence would inspire something. 'I think the person who took Harriet ... well, they must have ended up being someone good and this makes me happy.'

'Why do you say that?'

'She must have had a nice life or else she would have come looking for me.'

'But you haven't looked for her,' said Frederica, kindly.

'I suppose.' Suddenly I remembered something; it almost had me gasp. 'She would have had...'

'What?'

'She would've been wearing it.'

I closed my eyes. Saw us in our shadowy and foreboding room at the children's home, Harriet upset and unable to sleep. Saw myself freeing the chain from my neck and fastening it about hers. Saw the necklace with the quaver pendant dangling from it, gold against Harriet's creamy skin. Our mother had given us one each when we passed an important piano exam.

Why was this only coming to me now? Had Frederica's probing forced the memory out of its previously locked box?

'Wearing what?' asked Frederica.

'My necklace,' I said. 'We both had one, but she lost hers while riding her bike and then cried for days. There was a night in the children's home she was crying for our mum. I knew how much she adored this necklace, so I gave her mine, and she settled. And then ... she was gone.' I paused, to compose myself. 'Oh God, what if she *hasn't* had a good life? What if the person who took her was someone evil?'

'That only tends to happen in bad fiction,' said Frederica, not flippant but trying to console me.

'I guess. And what if she has ... you know ... *passed*?'

Frederica finished her salad, looked thoughtful. 'Then you'll grieve.'

'Yes.' I was choked.

'I definitely agree that you should try and find her.'

'I applied for my care records recently. But, having read a few pages, I don't know if they'll tell me the full story.'

'Is that what you were reading earlier?'

'Yes.'

'Do you want to continue now? I can leave you be.'

'I'm actually tired.' I was. It was all catching up with me – the travel, the change, the new schedule. 'I might have a nap and then go to the Piano Bar.'

'I might go for a swim,' said Frederica.

'Oh, that sounds good. I might do that tomorrow.'

We headed belowdecks together. Already, I seemed to have found my way around the many stairs and decks and corridors. Humans are so adaptable. Put us in a new environment and we quickly find its rhythm. I got to my cabin and sat on the bed. I looked at my care records but knew I'd fall asleep after one paragraph. So, I laid down and let oblivion take me.

They waited for us to play. I could sense them, an infinite, ethereal audience in the dark, but I couldn't see them. The spotlight made it impossible; I was blinded by its white radiance. I could only see Harriet, on my left. She was an adult. I knew I was dreaming. My unconscious told me it had to be a dream if Harriet was forty-five. Her childish face had morphed into one still impish, still bright with mischief, but now lined with life, marked by the experiences she must have had, the difficulties she must have faced. She smiled; I melted. If it was a dream, I didn't care, I had her in this moment.

"'Nothing Else'", she whispered.

And we played our song; I began, and she joined me, not following, not mimicking, but perfectly in sync.

Afterwards, applause echoed around us. When it quietened, she put something cold in my hand, closed my fist around it, and said, 'I came to give you it back.' Then she was gone, and I sat alone at the glossy black piano in an empty auditorium, my reflection in the sheen sad. I opened my fist. The necklace. The quaver pendant glinting in the theatre lights.

But when I woke my hand was empty.

One day in October, when autumn's gold covered the path, and the leaves scurried away in the wind as though they were escaping an invisible brush, two small girls went to number fifteen, dressed in matching gingham frocks, and knocked so quietly on the door that no one came, and they had to knock again.

Mr Hibbert was an older man who always called a cheery hello to us when he was trimming his rose bushes, and who always had a silk scarf tied around his neck and a pastel handkerchief in his top pocket. I know now what my father had meant when he insulted the dear man by calling him a nancy boy, and what neighbours really meant when, with raised eyebrows, they described him as eccentric. Those were different times, cruel times for men like Mr Hibbert. Children are without such judgement, however, and we thought he was Mr Pink-Whistle come to life from the pages of the book, and that he was going to turn us into the mini Chopins we longed to be.

'As I live and breathe,' he said when he opened the door, and as he would every time we arrived. 'If it isn't Heather and Harriet from number three who are quite the talk of the street with their new piano.'

We giggled, and he told us to come in. His house smelled of polish and some sort of sweet flower, and everything was dark wood, and the surfaces were cluttered with interesting trinkets and photographs of Mr Hibbert at the piano. He offered us a glass of lemon barley water which was tart, but we drank it anyway because we'd been taught to have manners, and then he suggested we wash our hands before we sat at his piano.

It wasn't like ours. It was flat not tall, a baby grand, and it was a creamy colour, and the bench was longer.

'That's not like ours,' Harriet whispered to me.

'It will do the same music,' I whispered back.

'Take a seat,' said Mr Hibbert, with a slight bow and a sweep of his arm.

So, we did, me on the right as we always sat at home, and Harriet on the left.

'You think you're the primo then,' he chuckled, looking at me.

'I don't know,' I stammered.

'In a duet, the primo sits on the right and plays the high notes.' He looked at Harriet. 'And the secondo sits on the left and plays the low notes.' We listened, rapt. 'That's how you play when there are what we call four hands. Now, I've never taught two students at the same time, so this is quite unusual for me, but we'll find our way together, won't we?'

We nodded enthusiastically.

'OK, show me what you can do,' said Mr Hibbert.

Since becoming a teacher myself, this was how I would always start when I was teaching a beginner, particularly a young child. It's how I assessed their imagination and ability. It was about getting to know *them*. I usually suggested my student improvise a short piece, using descriptive words and imagery to inspire them, for example an ocean that is angry or a storm that is just beginning.

'But...' I felt shy, nervous. 'Mr Hibbert, sir, we don't know anything.'

'You must have played around on your piano at home?' When we didn't respond, he said, kindly, 'It isn't a test. I just want to hear you. There is no right or wrong. You can't fail here. Just play.'

So, we did. We mimicked one another like we had at home, me playing keys in quick succession and Harriet copying, and then swapping over. We showed Mr Hibbert repeated patterns we had played up and down the keyboard, changing the speed, then how delicately or hard we pressed the keys. When we stopped the silence was huge.

'Very good,' said Mr Hibbert, and he did sound happy.

Harriet clapped her hands, and he chuckled.

'Yes, you deserve that applause young Harriet,' he said. 'You both have an affinity for music, that is clear. You have what we call "an ear". I'm delighted that I'm going to help you learn more. Tell me, why do you want to learn? Harriet?'

'To make Mummy happy,' she said cheerfully.

'And what about *you*?' he asked her.

'To make me happy too. And to surprise Daddy!'

'How so?'

'This is a big secret so we can surprise Daddy and play him a song.'

Mr Hibbert looked thoughtful. Then he chuckled. 'Heather?'

I thought carefully. I remember trying to find the words for why I had felt so drawn to our instrument the moment it arrived. 'I think ... I think I just *have* to,' was all I could come up with.

'A very good reason,' he agreed. 'I think that was my reason too.'

'Play us a song,' cried Harriet.

'Very well. I was going to suggest that to begin with.'

We leapt up, and Mr Hibbert took the seat. We watched him sit up straight and wriggle his fingers and pause for what felt like a long time. Then he played. We held hands. To us, he sounded like Chopin. It wasn't the same piece, but it affected me the same way, and I know it did Harriet too, from how tightly she was gripping me, and from how I could tell she was trying hard not to bounce on the spot.

We clapped and jumped when he was done.

'Now,' he said, after a moment, 'take your seats again, and we're going to find middle C and then all the other Cs, and we're going to create a little piece together using them. Look, here it is – middle C.' He pressed it and the announcement – as we had first heard it on ours – rang out. 'You will know a piece by the end of today.'

'A piece by the end of today,' repeated Harriet.

'Yes, a very simple one, that we'll put together.'

'What about those pages that have music things on?' I asked, pointing to a pile of sheet music on the nearby cabinet.

'Sheet music. Oh, one day we shall get to that. For now, I'd like to simply play. For the first few lessons we're going to look at the music alphabet, how it goes from A to G, and how to curve your hands correctly, like you're holding an orange, and the importance of practising daily.'

And that was what we did. Twice a week – I think Tuesday and Thursday, it's so long ago it's hard to be sure – we went there for an hour after school. Looking back, Mum really took a risk letting us go and keeping it from our father. Anyone on the street could've seen us going into Mr Hibbert's house and told him. Our mother kissed us each time we left and reminded us that we had 'been playing at Emma's house', and Harriet repeated it in her usual sing-song way. Still, there was a tension associated with going there that shaded it grey for me. A fear of being discovered.

Being in trouble.

Until we made music. Then, like when we practised at home, nothing else mattered. Until we did physical exercises to strengthen our fingers, which was a bit like when we made spiderwebs with string in the garden. Until we played the escalator game where we went from C up to G and then G down to C. Until we learned the notes by having each one of them marked as an animal on the keyboard, C being cat, D being dog, and so on. We were hungry to learn, and we devoured everything Mr Hibbert fed us.

But still, I was always anxious on the walk there.

'Are you OK, Harriet?' Mr Hibbert often asked when we arrived and accepted his lemon barley water.

I nodded but found it hard to swallow my drink.

'Do you enjoy coming here?' he asked once, and I feared him sending me away.

'Oh yes,' I gushed. 'My best days are when we're here!'

I wonder now how much he knew; if my mother had told him her situation and how these lessons had to be hush-hush. He was very gentle with us, very patient, so my instinct is that he did.

'That makes me happy,' he said.

'That makes me happy,' cried Harriet, and we all laughed.

Once we had been going for a while we began to play alone, not as a twosome, because the majority of pieces are performed solo.

This felt odd at first, and I had to sit on my hands while Harriet attempted 'Twinkle, Twinkle, Little Star' for the first time. I was proud though. My little sister, four years old, her fingers tiny, and yet they moved over the keys like spider legs scuttling back and forth. When it was my turn, she could not help but mimic me, playing on her leg as though it was a piano.

'Lovely,' said Mr Hibbert. He was always encouraging, even if we made mistakes, which of course we frequently did. 'There is no wrong,' he insisted. 'Just the song we played in order to find the right one.'

When he played for us at the end of the lesson, which he did every time, we shivered at the beauty, and I floated home, only coming back down to earth when our father's feet tramped a clumsy, discordant beat through the house, and the doors quaked and the music died.

One day our mother said she thought we were more than good enough to play a piece for our father. 'I think he'd really enjoy "Twinkle, Twinkle" by you, Harriet,' she said, 'and I think "Clair de Lune" by you, Heather.'

We had been practising while he was out. Mr Hibbert had recommended at least an hour a day, but on a Saturday, in our father's absence, we played all afternoon.

'Tonight, after tea, let's see if he wants to listen?' Mum suggested.

I should have been excited, but I feared his harsh words. I feared we wouldn't play well enough and that our father would banish the piano.

'Don't look so worried, Heather,' said Mum gently. 'I don't think you know how beautifully you both play. You've come on so much since you started your lessons. I never imagined you'd pick it up so quickly, and so well. I think you'll make your dad fall in love with music too.'

I could hardly eat. Our father, however, devoured his stew as messily and hungrily as usual, even though he grumbled that it was disgusting slop. Harriet bounced in her seat between mouthfuls.

'Got ants in your pants?' he demanded.

She giggled.

'The girls have been practising the piano a lot,' said our mother gently. 'They're really good now, Robert. They want to play for you.'

'The snooker's on.' He mopped up the remains of his gravy with his habitual slice of bread.

I saw my mother think hard, probably afraid to push it. Harriet saved the day.

'We are better than snooker,' she said.

He laughed heartily. Only Harriet could make him laugh that way. 'Are you now? Well, I suppose if you're quick I can decide whether that's true. Go on then. Play something for me.'

Harriet didn't need asking twice. She climbed onto the piano stool, lifted the lid, and, just as Mr Hibbert had taught us, she wriggled her fingers and paused for a second. I was overcome with love for this little girl, the brightest thing in my life. Our father lit a cigarette, the smoke curling as though spellbound by the music when she began to play 'Für Elise'. We had only learned the first, easier part of the melody, but she did it beautifully, with a light and deft touch.

'Well, well,' said our father at the end. 'You really have been practising, haven't you? Didn't I tell you that if you want to learn owt in life, you have to do it yourself?'

I saw in Harriet's face that she wanted to argue with that and willed her to remember our secret. Fortunately, she did. 'Does this mean we can play when you're at home, Daddy?' she asked. 'And you won't chop the piano up for firewood?'

'I suppose,' he conceded. 'Yes, play the bloody thing when I'm here if you must.'

'Now Heather is going to pl––' started my mother.

'Snooker's on,' he said, and disappeared into the front room.

The food in my stomach felt like heavy books. But I saw how heartbroken my mother looked and couldn't bear it, so I buried my own sadness at my father's indifference and said, 'I don't mind, Mum. He heard Harriet, and now we can play whenever we want.'

Mum nodded, quiet, sad still, so I went and hugged her. I still remember the smell of her hair – lemony – and the coolness of her skin and the tickle of the creamy lace chosen to hide the bruises on her neck

♪

'Now,' Mr Hibbert said one day. 'I want you to meet my metronome.'

'Meet my metronome,' repeated Harriet.

On the piano was a triangular wooden device with dashes and digits marking some sort of measurement along it, and what looked like the pendulum in the large clock in our hallway, but the other way up.

'What does it do?' I asked.

'It keeps the beat,' said Mr Hibbert. 'It makes a clicking sound and you set it to the tempo you want – a rhythmic command. Listen.'

'Listen,' whispered Harriet.

He wound it up, set it to one of the markings and the pendulum swung back and forth, back and forth, back and forth. Harriet and I swayed to its beat. Mr Hibbert smiled.

'See, it sets the pace for you,' he said. 'Timing is one of the hardest things to master as a pianist. According to Aristotle: "We are what we repeatedly do. Excellence is not an act, but a habit." So, girls, we must now begin practising with the metronome at a very slow rate. If we begin at forty beats per minute, we're teaching your internal clock to sync to a super low speed, and that trains you to play in time.'

I have since taught my own students the very same thing.

By this time, we had perhaps been going to Mr Hibbert for three seasons, not quite a full year. It's hard to know exactly. It might have been the following summer, the year Harriet turned five and I turned seven, when we were as brown as toffee from the sun, our noses covered in freckles, and so thirsty we almost enjoyed the lemon barley water. By then we could play basic one-octave scales, had a good grasp of sheet music and could play 'Yesterday', 'Hallelujah', and 'Happy Birthday' by heart.

My favourite part was when we improvised.

We did this at home too. Mostly when things got stormy. Now, instead of me reading stories to Harriet, we played music to drown out the arguments and thudding and plates crashing to the kitchen floor. Playing solo – the pieces we'd learned with Mr Hibbert – wasn't enough, because one of us had to sit still and listen, and this meant the background discord got louder for that person. It needed to be both of us engaged, transported, soothed. At first, we didn't name our creations, because we rarely repeated the same tune. But there was a song we produced on a particularly difficult Sunday afternoon.

Father had been in a foul mood all day. Our Granny Dolly had visited for an hour, and this always set him off. She was not your typical grandmother, not warm and chubby, not affectionate and loving. She barked and ordered, and she was the only person in the world who made my father cower. Something had also happened in the shed – perhaps something had broken – and our father cursed and stomped and slammed doors. Our mum knew to keep herself out of the way. She baked furiously, cake after cake. Even now, the smell of baking evokes that day. When she dropped something with a clatter, Harriet and I ran to see what. Two Victoria sponges were splattered across the floor.

Our father came to see what the commotion was. When he saw the destroyed cakes, something snapped. I'd seen him angry, but now he was incandescent. He lashed out at our mother, hitting her in the head. We rarely saw the violence. He always hid what must have actually shamed him behind closed doors.

'Mummy!' Harriet ran to protect her.

Our father had never hurt Harriet. Now he yelled at me to 'get her the hell out of here', which I did, dragging her by the arm when she shouted that her daddy was wicked, knowing that even his favourite girl wasn't safe. I got her into the living room, hot, sweaty, still shouting. I held her to me, whispered in her ear, 'Harriet, hush up. If you keep shouting, he'll hurt Mummy more.'

That did it.

'But we have to help Mummy.' She sobbed more softly.

'We can.' I squeezed her. 'I know how. We play. She loves music. She loves us. If she can hear us playing, she'll be OK.'

Harriet wiped her nose on her sleeve and climbed onto the piano seat. I joined her. We lifted the lid. Looked at one another. I was never nervous that we wouldn't know what to play.

But something happened when we began. Something that even now I can't define, a unity, an understanding, a synchronicity. I played a tune that I'd had in my head, that evoked the way I heard the wind in the trees at night, the way I heard Mum's musical jewellery box when she was searching for pearls to hide bruises, the way I heard my father's footsteps, a mix of lyrical and dissonant, light and dark. Harriet mirrored me, her version at the other end of the keyboard, the same but different, complementary and yet its own truth.

When we stopped, it had gone quiet.

'Nothing else,' I said.

'Nothing else,' whispered Harriet.

25

I woke from my afternoon nap with the dream about Harriet giving me the quaver pendant necklace back flashing before my eyes, and I looked again at my now-empty hand. I'd slept hard, yet again the motion of the ship agreeing with me. I reached into my purse and found the photograph of Harriet and me, needing to see it, our gold and auburn, side by side.

'Where *are* you?' I whispered, stroking her face.

I realised it was almost half past four and I should get ready for the Piano Bar. I showered and dressed, grabbed my now customary things – Nikon, sheet music and care records – and headed up the metal stairs to deck seven, passing crew members whose faces I vaguely recognised and exchanging pleasantries. I needed a quick glance of the ocean first. I let the wind and brine whip up my hair, inhaled the air and absorbed the salty energy. Then I went to the Piano Bar.

Despite it only being five-fifteen, the place was full, the dark, windowless place thick with tipsy people and laughter. I had yet to experience days when we docked and the ship was apparently deserted. I supposed guests had nowhere else to go but to the bars or the pools once they had shopped to their heart's content.

Michaela greeted me cheerfully and gave me some iced water when I declined an alcoholic drink. I spotted Frederica at a corner table and realised she was with Barry Lung and a red-haired woman I was unfamiliar with.

'I've only ten minutes,' I said, joining them.

Frederica glanced at Barry and raised her eyebrows at me as though to say, *What can you do?* 'This is Jen,' she said, introducing the young woman. 'Jen, Heather.'

She smiled; her freckled nose made me smile, putting me in mind of Harriet in the summer. 'I'm the singer in the band. Got an hour off.'

'Aren't I the lucky one,' grinned Barry, pint in front of him, cheeks red as though it wasn't his first. 'Lovely ladies all day, just two short gigs in the evening, and party all night.'

'I think your schedule is pretty exhausting, isn't it?' Frederica said to me.

'I don't mind.' It was true. The time was flying; two days had gone in two seconds.

'Mine too,' said Jen. 'We rehearse more than we perform. But I bloody love it. It's only my second cruise contract, but I know I'll be doing it again. How about you? Frederica said it's your first.'

I nodded but wasn't sure how to answer. This was like nothing I'd ever experienced, but I wondered if I'd want to leave it as a one-off, in order to retain that unrepeatable, never-before feeling. 'Ask me at the end,' I said.

'I'll be back,' said Barry. 'This beats empty backstreet comedy clubs.'

It was time for me to play. I felt the mood of the room was fun, so I should be upbeat too. I approached the ebony piano.

'Good evening,' I said. The room responded warmly, particularly Frederica's table. 'How are we all this early evening?' More positive reaction. 'I think we'll start off with this...'

And I played 'Gloria' by Laura Branigan, which had them singing along heartily. The requests came thick and fast this time, mostly for songs where they knew the words, Culture Club, Nik Kershaw, Whitney Houston and Kenny Loggins; some I played from memory, others via my sheet music or the ones Michaela had behind the bar. The atmosphere was joyful, and I was sure the ship moved in time with my appreciative audience.

I was deflated when the two hours were up. I could have played for another two. The applause went on for a few minutes. Then I tore myself away and rejoined Frederica and the gang.

'Not bad,' said Barry, cheeks even redder now.

'So good,' gushed Jen.

'Thank you.'

'You're a bit magic,' smiled Frederica. 'But her own song is even better,' she told the others. 'She played it yesterday. "A Sense of Light". I tell you; the room went quiet.'

'Oh, stop it.' I was uncomfortable with the attention. 'You're kind, really, but let's talk about you guys now. Barry...' I couldn't think of a question, but luckily, he was happy to take the spotlight.

'My audience likes it best when it's about me as well,' he said. 'They like jokes about my lunatic ex-wife and mother-in-law. They go crazy for them, belly laughing and cheering.'

'Keeping with the eighties theme then,' smiled Frederica, but the subtle criticism was lost on him. 'What are you going to do now?' she asked me.

I looked at my phone. It was almost eight. 'I've only an hour until I'm in the Sunset Bar. I think I'm going to grab a snack and then take a quiet moment on deck.'

'Yeah, I gotta head to the comedy lounge,' slurred Barry, standing up. I wondered how he would get through his routine, but perhaps alcohol and comedy went well together.

'I might come and watch you,' said Frederica.

'Oh, great.' Barry leered over her.

'No, I mean Heather.'

I saw Jen suppress a smile.

We all went our separate ways. I got a sandwich from the buffet, then headed out onto deck seven and found a deckchair in a quiet corner near a lifebuoy. The sun was beginning its descent, slowly swallowed by the water. Clouds dark against the orange turned the sky into a bright-striped tiger. As I ate, I sent messages to Dan and Tamsin, describing how much I was enjoying the trip, and including a quick snap of the sunset. Dan replied immediately, saying how glad he was. I wondered what time it was there. Were they now an hour behind? Two? My phone had probably updated itself to whatever time it was here on the ocean, and my body must be naturally adapting to the slow change. In a way, I was going back in time, which I found profound.

I was drawn again to my care records.

I read the next few pages.

EAST RIDING COUNTY COUNCIL SOCIAL SERVICES DEPARTMENT
SOCIAL WORKER'S REPORT

NAME OF CHILD: Heather Johnson
DATE OF BIRTH: 10/03/1972
DATE OF VISIT: 25/07/1982
RESIDENCE: Birchwood Children's Home

Condition of Child (appearance, general health)
Heather's physical health appears normal. She doesn't have a large appetite but appears to sleep well, often in the same bed as her sibling. In terms of her mental health, she often ignores questions she is asked. It is hard to say whether this is intentional or if she is simply unable to respond at times. In terms of her emotions, there is concern that she hasn't mentioned her mother or father at all during the week in the home. It would be natural that a child might cry for at least her mother. Concerns have been raised with the school and they are monitoring both of the children too.

Progress and Conduct of Child
Heather is well-behaved and quiet. She only engages when she is with her sister███████████████. The two are insep-arable and while this is a lovely thing, I'm concerned that they are too dependent on one another. Encouragement to mix with other children is important. It might be worth sug-gesting the sisters share a bedroom still, but otherwise sit at separate dining tables and take part in activities separ-ately too.

Signed
Alan Flemming

MINUTES OF CASE CONFERENCE HELD AT EAST YORKSHIRE SOCIAL SERVICES DEPARTMENT – 27th July 1982

Subjects – Heather and ▇▇▇▇ Johnson.
Received into Care, Section 2, Child Care Act 1980 on 18th July 1982.

Family
REDACTED

Those present: Marjory Cummins, Health Visitor.
Alan Flemming, Social Worker
Gina Smith, Principal
Social Services Officer
John Blackwood, Head Teacher

Reason for Case Conference:
The case conference was held at the request of Gina Smith to formulate a plan to effect the Johnson children being either temporarily fostered or adopted.
Alan Flemming proposed that adoption would be the best plan since the parents are deceased and there is no chance of the children returning home. Fostering, however, could be a temporary measure if finding adoptive parents who want both girls takes time, but he suggested that keeping them together at Birchwood until a permanent home is found might be the best option for maintaining some stability.

Gina Smith suggested that fostering until adoptive parents are found is a more suitable plan, since it can take up to two years for an adoption to happen, and the security of an actual foster family during this time might be more beneficial than the children's home. She added that the sisters would benefit from a more 'normal' and 'natural' family life with a foster family at this difficult time.

John Blackwood added that it is imperative these sisters remain together, even if that means a long wait for adoptive parents who will take both of them.

Marjorie Cummings agreed with John, saying that in her opinion, the wellbeing of these sisters must be the priority, and since they have lost both parents, it is vital that they remain together.

Recommendations made:
Adoption social worker Carol McGee to be contacted to begin looking into options.

I had to close the folder after just those few pages, emotional again, the words blurring. I understood that Harriet's reports weren't included, due to confidentiality, but I wondered what they might say that mine didn't. Had she been described differently? Had she still been my livelier shadow, or had she been as quiet as I seemed to be in the home? I found it curious that we were described individually in some cases, and as a set in others. And I was sad at the thought of these discussions going on while our hearts quietly broke.

They had clearly wanted to keep us together.

What on earth had happened that prevented that?

Where the hell had Harriet gone without me?

My bright mood from playing earlier faltered, fell into the ocean with the orange fireball sun and was eaten by darkness.

There was no time to read anymore, so I headed inside, stopping in one of the public toilets to powder my nose and reapply lipstick. The ship was alive with guests; coins clunked in the gaudy casino and winners cheered; a DJ in some bar encouraged her crowd to light up the night; the corridors were busy with people moving from one enticing place to another, tanned, happy, free.

In the Sunset Bar there wasn't a table empty. Harvey was as busy as he had been yesterday, but made time to wish me a good evening, and, with a flourish of the arm and a small bow, left me a glass of water on the bar where men in suits and women in cocktail dresses gathered.

I made my way through the crowd to the white piano.

In music, we're drawn to repetition; we find safety in its recurrent beat. So, I played the same set I had the night before, beginning with the 'Moonlight Sonata'. But as the two hours drew to a close and I saw Frederica by a gold column with a glass of wine, I changed my mind about sticking to a routine. I coughed quietly into the small microphone, and when most of the room looked my way I said, 'Thank you. It's been wonderful playing for you all this evening.'

Gentle applause then.

'Last night I ended with a song of my own.' I wished I could steady my voice. 'And if you don't mind ... I'd like to do that again tonight.'

More applause, slightly louder, which I took as encouragement.

I realised then what I was going to do.

I hadn't known until that moment.

Or maybe I had. Maybe everything had been leading to it: my decision to take the job, to leave land, to sail away, to play at sea.

'I've never played this for anyone.' I finally found my voice and was able to speak more evenly. The room was silent. Frederica sipped wine. 'When I was small...' I faltered, took a breath '...I used to play music with my sister. And we ... we created our own song. I've tried to play it alone since then and never succeeded. I don't know how it will sound without her part. I don't even know if I'll manage, but I'd like to try.' I paused. 'This is ... "Nothing Else."'

Gentle applause. Then quiet.

I closed my eyes. Imagined Harriet with me. I remembered how I'd first created the song, inspired by the whistle of the wind in the trees at night, by the tune from my mother's jewellery box when she was searching for pearls to hide bruises, by the thud of my father's heavy footsteps; a mix of lyrical and dissonant, light and dark.

And I played.

In my head, I heard Harriet's part, the lightning to my storm. And we were together again.

When I finished, I waited for the last note to fade. I didn't dare look up. I imagined my father in the corner of the bar, indifferent, disapproving, judgemental. I began to shake, from my feet up to my hands. I wondered suddenly if Harriet ever played her part, wherever she was.

Then it started. Low clapping that slowly built into enthusiastic approval. I still couldn't look up. Finally I did, and saw Frederica, shaking her head, not with condemnation like my father, but with a smile and damp eyes. I accepted the ovation, hand on heart. The shaking stopped.

I left my small stage, and people returned to their conversations.

Frederica pulled me into a hug. 'That was beautiful. You should release it or something.'

'Oh no.' I shook my head. 'It's too personal. And there's no market for that kind of thing. Plus, it's only half a song.' I wondered if other people heard it that way. Perhaps not. After all, they didn't know the full thing.

'A few were recording you on their phones,' she said. 'That really says something. Don't you have a website for your music? I bet it would be super popular.'

I shook my head. 'I mostly play other people's pieces, remember.'

'You should write more of your own.'

'Maybe.'

'You *should*,' she insisted. 'Stop being so coy.'

I laughed. 'OK. I'll think about it.'

'Don't think, do it.'

I realised how tired I was. It often happened after an intense gig.

'Do you mind if I retire for the night?' I said. 'Sorry to be boring.'

'No, of course, you've been working. Don't worry about me. I might go and catch Barry Lung's second gig – I'll report back.'

When I arrived in my cabin I sat on the narrow bed with my face in my hands for a while, letting the emotions and experiences of the second day at sea wash over me. How had I gone from hardly knowing how to play our song right to performing it for an audience? What was changing in me? Was it the freedom felt by being away from home? Were these crowds somehow more encouraging than those in small backstreet bars? Were the pages of my care records giving me more than just words?

Whatever it was, I felt I was exactly where I was supposed to be in that moment.

26

Days three and four on the ship passed as quickly as the first two had, a blur of sunrises and sunsets, of songs and sea. I barely had time to get to know the rest of the entertainment team the way Frederica did, but I didn't mind. I began to recognise the odd guest, mainly in the Sky Lounge at lunchtime, where it was an older audience, but occasionally at my last gig in the Sunset Bar. There I played 'A Sense of Light' as my final piece each evening, even though a woman in a creamy frock with a huge corsage at the shoulder approached me before I began on the fourth night and asked for 'Nothing Else'.

'Oh, my word,' she said, touching her arms. 'It gave me goosebumps.'

I'd already decided I didn't want to play it every evening; that I would only do so if the urge absolutely overwhelmed me. I wanted to say that it was only half of a song, but I smiled and said, 'Thank you,' feeling as though I was famous. 'I might play it again, but not this evening.'

'I wish you would. This is my first cruise with my fiancé, Charles.' She looked around the bar for him. 'I've no idea where he is. But it could be our song, you know, to remind us of this trip. Do you have a CD we can buy?'

'No, sorry.' It was something I'd occasionally thought of, but there was such a small market for that kind of thing, and I'd have to pay to produce it.

'That's such a shame,' she said.

'Maybe I'll play it on the last night.' I wasn't sure I would. 'But, thank you, you're very kind.'

A similar thing happened when I was having a late lunch with Frederica in the buffet café. We were eating lasagne and laughing about the fact that Barry Lung had been too drunk to perform the night before, and how Sarah Briggs was apparently furious, when an elderly couple in matching burgundy gilets approached our table, clearly nervous about interrupting us.

'She's eating,' the woman said to her husband, accent American.

'Honey, she won't mind,' he insisted.

I didn't. They melted my heart.

'Excuse us for being rude' – he gripped his wife's hand – 'but we couldn't not say something when we saw you. You see, this is our anniversary trip – fifty years married.'

'That's wonderful,' I said. 'Congratulations.'

'Thanks, honey.' She took over now, as though he had laid the groundwork and she was OK to take the lead. 'We saved for years – we just spent a week in London, didn't we, honey?' Here she looked at her husband with great affection. 'And now we're doing this cruise and right after it, the one to the Caribbean.' Frederica and I smiled at one another. 'Sorry, I haven't even introduced us – I'm Ruth and this is Gerry.'

'Ruthie, get to the point,' he said. 'The poor woman wants to eat her lunch.'

'Yes, I am.' She raised her eyes heavenward. 'We wanted to say how much we loved your song. Last night in the … what's it called? We had a little nap in the afternoon so we could stay right until the end.'

'The Sunset Bar?' I suggested.

'Yes, there. Oh, we had us a blast, even a little slow dance, didn't we, honey? And that last song. What was it called?'

It had been 'A Sense of Light' and I told her.

'Ah, yes. Oh, we fell in love with it. And that's it really. We just had to tell you, and we hope you'll play it tonight for us?'

'I will. Thank you for being so generous with your comments.'

'Let's leave the girl to her lunch now,' said Gerry.

'That's incredible,' gushed Frederica once they'd left. 'How do you feel?'

'Thrilled, for sure,' I admitted. 'It's a bit surreal. No one has ever really told me what they actually thought of my playing – you know, aside from friends.'

I'd been to all three of Frederica's workshops. My routine tended to include waking early – sometimes as early as six to catch the sunrise from the ship's stern (I was becoming an expert now in cruise language) – followed by breakfast, reading a few more pages of my care records on deck (mostly repeats or rewrites of previous pages), attending the first half of Frederica's workshop, playing the Sky Lounge, having a late lunch and nap, and then playing the Piano Bar followed by the Sunset Bar.

At her second workshop Frederica gave us another writing prompt; she asked us to choose a song that had meant a lot to us and write how it made us feel. Her third novel, she explained, had involved a character who had amnesia, who had forgotten every-thing that ever happened to them, but yet still knew – word perfect – the lyrics to all the songs they had ever heard.

'I explore memory a lot in my books, don't I?' she laughed, and the audience joined her. I found it quite serendipitous; her prompts were proving helpful in jogging my own childhood recollections. 'Scientists are still trying to understand how amnesiacs lose all memory of their past life and yet remember music. They think that musical memories are stored in a separate part of the brain.' She glanced at me. 'In a very special part, I reckon.'

I've always thought it astonishing that there are only twelve musical notes, far fewer than there are letters in the alphabet, and yet we create millions of different melodies, telling millions of dif-ferent stories. For Frederica's prompt I chose Chopin's 'Nocturne No 2', the song our mother had first played that day long ago.

But I wrote of a different memory – the time I first tried to play it myself, perhaps a year and a half after we'd begun learning the piano. I closed my eyes in the theatre and I was in our childhood back room again.

I was alone that day at the piano. It was a Saturday, I think, because we were all in the house. Luckily, by then, we were allowed to play at home when our father was there, not that he ever said what he thought of my music. Occasionally he praised Harriet, calling her his 'clever piano girl' but not me. I never resented her. I agreed with him. But inside I longed for his praise too. That day I was alone because poor Harriet was ill in bed. I had listened to Chopin over and over, just low, so as not to annoy my father, who was busy in the shed as usual. I didn't have the sheet music for this song, so I had to play by ear. At first, I played along with the record, Chopin and me, across time. Then I went it alone. It was strange without Harriet there. I heard a sound and turned. My father stood in the doorway, but he didn't say a word, and went upstairs. A moment later my mother came in and hugged me tightly. 'You have a gift,' she whispered in my ear. But I desperately wanted my father to say it.

I didn't share my piece with the room. I left shortly after, while Frederica was reading from her new book. I played Neil Diamond in the Piano Bar. Later, in the Sunset Bar, I performed 'A Sense of Light' as my final number and dedicated it to Ruth and Gerry, who then danced, slowly, cheek to cheek, him tall and thin, her delicate in his hold, the rose lighting a kiss upon them, and the crowd moving back to give them room and smiling at the romantic scene.

Frederica was waiting as usual, glass of wine in hand.

'How cute was that?' she said. 'You're making people's memories right there.'

'I guess.' I didn't know what to say. It did feel special though.

'How's the reading going?'

'Reading?' I was confused.

'The care records.'

'Oh. Yes. Not particularly productive. There's a lot of repetition, lots of reports on 'how we are' in the children's home; apparently we were quiet, didn't say much, were inseparable.' I glanced at the bar; I needed a drink. 'But I get a sense of time. According to the dates, we've now been in the home for five months. I don't know whether that's longer or shorter than I recall it to have been. But it is forcing me to explore my own memories.' I paused. 'Weird that two of your books are about memory.'

'I know.' She sipped wine. 'Three actually. But yes. Fascinating topic to me. Daisy, my ex, she buried some things from her child-hood, and I think that's why she had a lot of issues.'

'Still, it's no excuse ... you know, to be abusive.'

'No, it isn't, but I suppose it's a reason.' Frederica finished her wine. 'In the end, I couldn't take it anymore. She was possessive, insecure. She burned my hand under a grill once because she thought I'd been chatting too long to another woman at a party.'

'Oh Frederica, that's terrible,' I said.

'I'm gonna go to the crew party.' She obviously wanted to change the subject. 'There's been one every night apparently. Come! Go on, don't shake your head like that. It's just one night, and I know you're tired, but sleep in tomorrow.'

It was hard to argue with her bright face. 'OK, OK,' I conceded. 'Just for an hour though.'

I followed her belowdecks, along the shabby corridor to a room that certainly wasn't as tastefully appointed as those above, with a scratched bar, faded leather stools, and *Crew Bar* in pink neon on the wood-panelled wall. What it lacked in sophisticated décor it more than made up for in atmosphere and capacity. It was mid-night now and the music was loud, and we had to squeeze through the bodies to get to the bar. I recognised Aiden Miller, the crew manager who, since that first day, I'd only seen in passing, and Sarah Briggs, and a few other faces.

'No Barry Lung,' said Frederica as we reached the bar, eyebrows arched. I could only just hear her.

'Do you think they'll let him perform again?' I shouted.

'Doubt they'll have a choice unless there's someone to stand in. Wine?'

'Yes. Maybe they'll just cancel his show and abandon him in New York.'

Frederica laughed and handed me my drink. There was nowhere to sit so we stood in a corner near a faded poster of a 1920s cruise ship.

'Nah, he'll be back,' said Frederica. 'I bet most of the crew, es-pecially the entertainment team, have done worse than be too drunk to work. Doubt it's a dismissible offence.' She paused. 'How about you?'

'How about me what?'

She held my gaze. 'Did you leave a partner behind in the UK?'

She was fishing and I was flattered. 'That was quite a change of topic.'

'You're blushing,' she said.

'There's just an ex-husband. Dan. Ended amicably.'

'A girl can try,' said Frederica with a wink.

'You could have any woman in here.' I surveyed the room, the dancers, the beauticians, the other musicians.

She didn't say anything. Then, after a long moment, she said, 'I think I'm happier single, though of course I'd never say no to a fling at sea.'

I laughed. The wine warmed me, made me sleepy, sentimental. I suddenly missed Tamsin, wondered what she was doing. Even Dan, not in a longing way of wanting him, but the familiarity, the comfortable way I felt around him. Home, I supposed. That was what I missed.

'Let's dance,' said Frederica.

'No, you go, I'm happy here.' When she looked at me with pleading eyes, I insisted, 'No, you go, find a hot girl and have a fling.'

I laughed at Frederica as she sashayed through the throng and joined some girls on the makeshift dance floor in the corner. I watched her for a while, and when I was happy that she had forgotten me, I made my way to cabin 313.

The end of day four. Day *four*. How did it feel more like four weeks already? I had a shower and crawled into bed. I reached for my care records – a postcard of the ship that I'd picked up in the gift shop marked where I was up to. I opened the folder and read the entry there.

East Yorkshire Social Services Department

NAME OF CHILD: Heather Johnson
DATE OF BIRTH: 10/03/1972
DATE OF VISIT: 21/12/1982
RESIDENCE: Birchwood Children's Home

Condition of Child (appearance/health)

I spoke with Heather today and she was more vocal than she usually is. She told me that she and her sister do not want to stay here for Christmas. She admitted that she knows Father Christmas doesn't exist but that her sister still believes in him and is afraid he won't come and see her here at Birchwood. She also said they miss their piano and would like it to be brought to Birchwood for them to play. I believe said instrument was given away, but I said I would look into it. Heather then said she wanted to go to her friend Emma's house for Christmas Day and to take ▓▓▓▓ with her. I will contact her headmaster and see if this might be possible. I used this opportunity of her being talkative and asked how she was feeling about us possibly finding new parents for her and ▓▓▓▓ to live with, and she didn't answer. I told her that her ▓▓▓▓▓▓▓▓ had said she might visit them if we could find them a home in the local area, though she hasn't so far visited the home. I think that once the two children are settled in a new, more permanent home, Heather should be offered some form of counselling.

Signed:
Alan Flemming

I was crying by the time I read Alan's name. I had little memory of this conversation, and certainly couldn't recall if we remained in the children's home that festive season, or if we did indeed go to Emma's house. Had I blocked it out because it was too painful?

The next page was a repeat, then a couple that were entirely blacked out, followed by a report from January, so I'd never know where we spent that first Christmas Day without our parents.

I closed the pages, too upset to go on. Closed my eyes. Let the sea's motion and the emotional exhaustion take me into complete darkness.

I dreamt of fire.

It was a car; no, not a car, a fireball spitting angry flames that crackled and snapped and roared. To me, as always, there was music in its thunder. The sky filled with evil smoke. I could hardly breathe, and yet I couldn't turn away from the hypnotic spectacle.

Finally, I escaped from it.

I ran home, choking, desperate to find my childhood house.

It emerged from a mist, and I ran into the back garden. It was there, our cherry-wood upright, sitting on the grass, a whirlwind of grey ash engulfing it. The flames had followed me. Harriet was there too. Seated. Waiting for me, impatient, and somehow in this hot dream, oblivious to any fire. I joined her. We sat side by side, in the places we always took.

And we played.

Our song.

There was nothing else.

When I woke, alone, it was pitch-black and I panicked. Then I remembered where I was and tried to find sleep again.

But my mind raced with images of fire. My parents died in a car accident. Though I hadn't seen this happen, because Harriet and I were at home that day, I occasionally dreamt of a car aflame; perhaps my unconscious was processing what that must have looked like. And in these dreams our piano was often on the grass behind the house. When I awoke, I would be absolutely sure that it really had been there, in the garden, the day my parents died.

But if so, how had it ended up there?

And why?

There was a time – perhaps when we had been having piano lessons for a year and a half – that our mother went into the hospital. I remember it vividly, not only because Mum had never left us before, but because the day it happened Mr Hibbert told us he thought we were ready to take the grade one piano exam.

And because we played him our song.

Spring had scattered her colour everywhere as we walked up his drive: red tulips and lemony daffodils danced in the well-tended front garden, and pink blossom floated down from the small tree by the gate. In my head, I could hear Vivaldi's delightful 'Spring' from The Four Seasons, a tune we had recently been practising, and now I knew why Mr Hibbert had chosen it as our April piece. Originally written for the violin, it was a challenging piece to master, but we were eternally keen and did our best.

'Well, as I live and breathe,' said Mr Hibbert when he opened the door. 'It's Heather and Harriet Johnson, yet again.'

Harriet, at almost six, had stopped repeating everything anyone said by now, but still she giggled and said, 'As you live and breathe.'

He ushered us into the back room, today decorated with jars of pastel flowers, where we politely drank our lemon barley and began our scales. Our lessons consisted of these, followed by practising whatever piece had been set, some improvising, and having to perform one random number from sheet music and one from memory. We were comfortable at the piano by now; we had mastered the keys and had strong forearms, which strengthen after years of dedicated practice. Dexterity is a lifetime pursuit for pianists, but at almost six and eight we were already nimble and confident.

Harriet asked me once why we still had to keep the lessons secret when we had 'done the surprise' for our father now. I wasn't sure what to tell her. My head hurt from having to decide how to make everything OK and how to make a lie into something decent. In the end, I said that our father didn't like Mr Hibbert, but we did, so it was best for everyone that we said nothing, and Harriet just nodded, and she kept quiet.

As the lesson came to an end that day, Harriet whispered something in my ear. I didn't understand her properly and felt unkind sharing secrets in front of Mr Hibbert. 'Maybe just say it to both of us,' I said.

'Should we play our song?' she whispered.

I knew which one she meant. The one we played at home when our father took Mum away to the kitchen. The one we hoped she could hear. The one that meant we didn't hear the ominous sounds that even Harriet now knew meant our mother was in danger. The one we then hummed in the night when chaos reigned downstairs. Why didn't we tell anyone about this violence? Because we were afraid. Afraid of the trouble we might be in. Afraid no one would believe us. Afraid that it would only mean our father got even angrier with our mother. Afraid, afraid, afraid.

'Your song?' asked Mr Hibbert.

Harriet looked at me, clearly nervous, unsure. 'It's just ours. But...'

'It's OK,' I said. 'I think Mr Hibbert is one of us.'

A million things crossed his kind face, none of which I could fathom. 'I am one of you,' he said gently. 'Tell me, what's your song?'

'"Nothing Else",' we said at the same time.

Mr Hibbert repeated the two words, like an older Harriet.

'We play it at home,' said Harriet. 'When...'

'When?' he asked.

'When things ... aren't nice.'

He nodded. 'And how often are things *not nice*?'

I couldn't speak. My throat felt tight.

'Maybe ... most days ... but not *all* days,' said Harriet.

'Do the not-nice things happen to you?' he asked.

Harriet shook her head. I looked down. Perhaps Mr Hibbert knew not push it.

'Why don't you play me your song?' he said.

I didn't know if we'd be able to in the tranquillity of Mr Hibbert's presence; in that sunny back room with the tart scent of flowers in the air and the sun slicing the room in two, and two empty glasses on the cabinet dribbling lemon barley drops onto the wood. Crashing and thudding was our usual backing track.

But we played. It felt softer. Slower. We weren't hurrying to outdo horrible sounds. When we were done, we waited for a moment without moving, as Mr Hibbert had taught us, to let the song settle. Then we looked at him. His eyes were moist.

'As I live and breathe,' he said. 'That was beautiful.'

We beamed. Harriet clapped her hands.

'I think...' He paused. 'I think you girls have been my best students. Do you realise that you have taught me as much as I've taught you?'

'What have we taught you?' asked Harriet.

'You have taught me that some things can't be taught. Really, I knew this already. I've told you that some people simply *know* how to play, and that many use it as an escape, but I've never seen that in quite this way.' He paused. 'How do you feel when you play this song, and the not-nice things are happening in the house?'

'Like we're floating above it all,' I said.

'It's finally time,' said Mr Hibbert.

My heart sank. I anticipated him telling us we were done; that we had each taught one another enough now.

'I've thought for a long while that you're ready to sit your grade one piano exam, but your mum has had to save up the money. Now she tells me she has it.'

'An exam? Is it scary?' asked Harriet.

He laughed. 'For some, yes. I'll prepare you. But you girls won't have any trouble and you'll pass easily.'

'What would we have to do?' I asked. 'Will we know it all?'

'You know *more* than enough. I'd have you take your grade two, personally. You can sight-read, you can play at least two scales in two octaves, with separate hands, you can play both hands, and you can differentiate between the first three tones of each major scale. These are some of the things you'd have to do, as well as learning some new set pieces, which need lots of practice beforehand.'

I was still nervous, and I knew Harriet was too.

'Don't trouble yourselves. I just think we should consider doing exams because you both have a long future in music ahead of you.'

'When I grow up, I want to be Richard Clayderman but with long hair and a nice green dress,' said Harriet.

Mr Hibbert laughed heartily. The sound followed us down the path, past the dancing daffodils and twirling tulips, past the billowing blossom, where Harriet suddenly cartwheeled across the grass. The sound stopped at our gate. Our father's car was on the drive.

'We were at Emma's,' I reminded Harriet, firmly.

The mood in the house was dark. Mum had laid the table: knives and forks parallel, salt and pepper smartly side by side in the centre, napkins crisply folded, as though this symmetry would keep her safe. We knew to wash our hands and sit down, quiet, obedient. Father clomped into the room and dropped into the chair without a word. I often felt things had happened that we didn't know about. That were slowly changing our entire future. That I'll never know about, even now.

Mother brought in the white dish that held stew, and a canteen of mashed potato, and placed them on mats. I noticed that her hands were trembling. That her wedding ring caught the light, then didn't, caught the light, then didn't, an awful flashing song that said, *Help me, help me, help me.* But I didn't know how.

We could only eat when our father had begun; it was an unspoken thing we had learned as toddlers. He devoured his meal. Mine stuck in my throat like it always did. Still, he didn't speak. It was worse than when he criticised Mum's food. When he was done, he had his usual cigarette and then went into the front room.

We all breathed a united sigh of relief.

That night, as usual, I stayed up an hour later than Harriet, watching *Wonder Woman,* wishing I had her superhuman strength and could protect my mother. It was always my bedtime when the credits rolled, but before they had finished, I heard a *thud thud thud* and then a horrific scream, and the vase on the hallway table smashing on the wooden floor. Fear held me back for a moment; then instinct had me rushing into the hall. My mother was on the floor at an odd angle, all arms and legs, head bloody, eyes rolling back in her head. My father was at the top of the stairs, face shocked, pale.

And I knew.

She hadn't fallen.

I glanced back at him as I knelt down to her, and he held my gaze. I knew that look. Be quiet. You saw nothing. You know nothing. You *are* nothing.

An ambulance arrived. Mrs Charles from number eighteen came over, and our father went with Mum to the hospital. Mrs Charles let me have some cake before ushering me off to bed, where I couldn't sleep. Harriet snored on the bunk below me. Oblivious. In the morning, she cried when our father told her that Mummy had fallen and hurt her back and her head, and would be in the hospital for at least a few days. I watched from the doorway as he cradled her as tenderly as a man with a decent heart. I blinked away hot tears for the affection I'd never received, for the pieces I'd played that he had never acknowledged, for the mother I wanted back and yet was glad wouldn't sleep here tonight.

But I said nothing. I let Harriet think it had all been a terrible accident. I didn't want her to feel how I did.

Women from the street came with dishes of lasagne and chicken and stew, and they fussed over our father, and they patted our heads, saying, 'You poor things.' I heard him tell one of them that our 'poor mother' had been tired and doing too much, and must have collapsed, and that he was heartbroken. I was angry that he got their sympathy; I was angry that they were stupid and blind. I was angry, angry, angry.

Grandma Dolly came too, and she also seemed angry, and I

couldn't understand why. My father ate the meal she made, quietly, saying it was delicious – it wasn't, it was gristly and tasteless – and thanking her. Though I didn't like it when she came over, bossing us about and demanding to know what we knew (I never knew how to answer this), I did like how her presence affected my father. He didn't lose his temper. He walked more quietly. I only wished that my mother had that effect on him too.

We played the piano more quietly while our mother was gone, not sure what the rules were in her absence. Our music was mournful, the lament of lonely souls, the unspoken grief of feeling semi-orphaned. Because our father came home from work much earlier during this interlude, we were nervous about going to Mr Hibbert for our lessons.

'We *have* to go,' said Harriet, anxious. 'He'll wonder where we are.'

'Let's ask Daddy if we can play at Emma's,' I said.

Harriet nodded enthusiastically, and we found our father in the shed, where he was chopping something up, cigarette dangling from his mouth.

'Can we go to Emma's please?' I asked.

'Not today,' he said. 'You need to set the table. Mrs Charles is bringing a casserole over for us at four.'

'How is Mummy today?' asked Harriet, as she did every day.

'Much better. Not long until she comes home. Now run along and get that table set.'

We went back into the house, hearts heavy. What would Mr Hibbert think? We could not bear the thought of him being cross or upset with us. What if he came looking for us? He didn't. Did he know not to? Who can say? I imagine he heard, via street gossip, about our mother's hospital stay, and I'm sure he had his own concerns and didn't want to add to ours.

When she finally came home, our father told us to be very good and to not trouble our mother. She walked with difficulty at first, clumsily, knocking things over the way our father usually did. He, however, was kind, quieter than usual, lighter in his footfall, and less harsh with his words. They had swapped roles. She had finally affected him the way Grandma Dolly did.

But it didn't last.

29

On day five of the cruise, I slept in a little longer than usual. The late night in the Crew Bar with Frederica and the heated car-fire dreams meant I was exhausted. I'd missed one of my favourite parts of the day at sea – the sunrise, and the ocean turning from inky black to aqua in her light, the sky a palette of orange and gold that any painter would envy.

I realised also that the motion of the ship was different. My bed dipped slowly left and then slowly right. There was a pause, as though the ocean was waiting for a reaction to this new rhythm, and then again: left, right, pause, left, right, pause. I sat up. Did I feel queasy? No, I was just hungry, as I had been every morning.

In the crew café I grabbed a tray and got some eggs, sausage, and bacon, and a strong coffee and some orange juice, then tried not to spill any of it as the ship continued swaying, more violently now. I looked around for a familiar face. I realised the place was emptier than usual, but Frederica sat with a black coffee at a table by the door. She looked quite white.

'Hungover?' I smiled, sitting opposite her.

'How can you eat all that?' she sniffed.

I realised it was the motion of the ship that had her tentatively sipping coffee and wincing at my food. 'Oh, bless you, I didn't realise.' I tried not to devour my eggs with too much enjoyment. I guessed I must have what they call sea legs. 'My friend said you feel better if you sit where you can see the horizon. I'll eat this and we can go on deck for a bit if you like?'

Frederica nodded. 'Aiden was in earlier. He told us this storm is coming down from Greenland, and it probably won't pass until at least midnight tonight.'

I glanced at the TV screen, where a red dotted line showed the ship's progress across the vast North Atlantic Ocean. We were much closer now to America than we were the UK. Nearby, cups piled up on a plate clashed suddenly at a particularly sharp dip, and two fell to the ground and smashed. Frederica groaned.

'I brought seasickness pills,' I said.

'I've had a couple already, but thanks. Sorry, I think I need to lie down, try and get myself together for today's workshop.'

'Take care,' I called after her as she staggered to the door. 'See you there.'

I climbed the metal stairs and headed out onto deck seven. The wind wrenched the door out of my hands as I opened it, and then dragged me onto the walkway; it lashed my hair and whipped my skirt away from my legs. The ship dipped again and sent me hurtling towards the railings. For miles around, the slate grey waves were chaos; there was no pattern or symmetry in their anarchic rise and fall. I looked down into the torrent and tried to imagine what it would be like to fall into its frothing oblivion. I heard the explosive ambience of the last of Chopin's twenty-four preludes, my fingers readying themselves to play the stormy piece along the wood-topped railing. I tried to recall on what day of her journey the *Titanic* sank and was sure it was on the fourth or fifth, which made me smile morosely to myself; we too were on our fifth.

This was not a day to sit outside and read my care records. The loosely attached pages could easily be ripped out and blown away, my past forever consumed by the ocean.

I came inside when I was wet from the drizzle and my cheeks glowed. It was already past ten, so I returned to my cabin, had a shower, changed into my cream suit, applied some lipstick, and grabbed my sheet music, care records, Nikon, and my notepad for the workshop.

However, a makeshift poster had been stuck to the theatre doors: *Due to illness, Frederica Becker's eleven o'clock workshop is cancelled.* The poor girl. I wondered whether to go and make sure she was OK, and realised I didn't even know her cabin number.

I decided that perhaps it was time to buy a few gifts to take home. The boutiques on the Queen's Parade were quiet. Stormy days were perfect for browsing in peace, it seemed. The jewellery store caught my eye. I looked in the window, where polished gems and unique ship-themed pieces tempted. I did a double-take at a gold necklace; was that a quaver pendant dangling from the chain? No, just a delicate anchor. I bought two, one for myself and one for Tamsin.

Then I got a snack from the buffet café and found a corner sofa in the atrium, near the marble-and-gold mermaid sculpture, where I watched the glass lift ascending and descending, often empty, and then the ocean, still wild, through the three-floor-high windows. I loved the sight of it, even wild. After a while, I opened my care records and found my place: just after the Christmas I had wanted us to spend at Emma's house.

East Yorkshire Social Services Department

NAME OF CHILD: Heather Johnson
DATE OF BIRTH: 10/03/1972
DATE OF VISIT: 15/01/1983
RESIDENCE: Birchwood Children's Home

Condition of Child (appearance/health)
Heather appeared thin and pale. She has apparently just got over the 'flu, which both she and her sister had at the same time. There is concern over how little she eats, both in Birchwood and at school. I have suggested a star chart for when she finishes meals. There was also an incident yesterday where she and her sister got as far as a mile away from the home, with all of their clothes and a few toys in a bag. Heather said they were 'going home'. A passer-by thought they seemed young to be out alone and with luggage, and brought them back.

I had to smile at this. The idea of us packing what we had and attempting to run away. I couldn't remember it, despite reading it in black and white, but my imagination created us an escape song, marching, triumphant, soaring.

The following pages were photocopies of this one, and then ones mostly blacked out apart from the dates and my name.

I stopped smiling at the next entry that was visible.

East Yorkshire Social Services Department

NAME OF CHILD: Heather Johnson
DATE OF BIRTH: 10/03/1972
DATE OF VISIT: 10/02/1983
RESIDENCE: Birchwood Children's Home

Condition of Child (appearance/health)
Now that her sister has gone there is much concern that Heather's general health is rapidly deteriorating, both physically and emotionally. She hasn't spoken since that day and barely comes out of her room. It has been very hard to decide what we tell her. A meeting has been booked for next week. We are pushing to speed up the adoption process, which is always easier when there is only one child. ▨▨▨▨▨ has said that she might visit Heather, though she hasn't so far. Due to the circumstances, she isn't interested in seeing Harriet, and even suggested it better that they now live apart.

'Fancy seeing you here.'
I looked up at the booming voice: Barry Lung.
'Oh, hi.' I tried to compose myself.
Shit. Why now? I needed to process what I'd just read, that Harriet had gone, that the care home found it hard to decide what to tell me. Did that mean they *had* told Margaret and Harold when they adopted me? I needed to read on, to see if the care staff decided what to tell me. I figured out from the two redacted words and their length that Grandma Dolly had been mentioned and thought it better Harriet and I were apart. What circumstances

had she meant? God, she could have had the answers, but she never visited me once when I was adopted, and Margaret told me she died when I was thirteen.

'Guess you're like me,' he grinned.

'Sorry?' I couldn't concentrate on Barry.

'Not seasick.'

'Oh. No.'

'Fancy a drink?'

I felt unkind, being blunt, but wasn't in the mood. I looked at the time, still distracted. Luckily it was twelve-thirty so I could use the excuse of having to go and play in the Sky Lounge soon.

'Oh, I'll come with you,' he said. My heart sank.

'Great.' I forced myself to be friendly.

We headed up one deck, holding on to the railings as the ship continued rocking, him grumbling about how badly he'd been treated for missing 'just one bloody gig', me nodding and hmm-ing as animatedly as I could manage to, my head still in my care records.

The Sky Lounge was deserted. Phillippe and one other waitress polished the bar and restocked; even he wasn't his cheerful self and merely nodded a brief acknowledgement. It was hard to find energy for a performance when you had a handful of people, because there was nothing to lift you, but I was accustomed to this experience from the many deserted bars I'd played.

I just kept seeing the words, 'It has been very hard to decide what we tell her'.

Would the next page reveal what they did tell me?

I played some John Denver classics for the small audience, despite everything, still in awe of the beautiful white grand piano and the fact that I was here, in the middle of an ocean, providing music. Barry guzzled beer. Had he learned nothing? The sea was the liveliest part of my set, swirling and crashing behind me. Guests slowly left the room, one after another, looking green and holding on to chairs to steady themselves, so I finished ten minutes early to zero applause.

The rest of the day blurred into one.

Perhaps the eeriness of a half-empty ghost ship, where most were probably suffering in their cabins, made it feel surreal, like I was walking through a dream. Each set merged into the next. I wasn't in the mood for jolly eighties tunes in the Piano Bar, and I could tell from the sombre mood that the fifteen or so patrons weren't either. I gave them some of ABBA's more muted melodies.

Then, in the Sunset Bar, I brought Chopin to life, and it didn't matter that no one cared. The fiftieth-anniversary couple, Ruth and Gerry, must have been more stoic than most, because they came for the final hour and danced again when I played 'A Sense of Light', the only two on the floor, a delicate duo who could have been transported from a long-gone era, in chiffon dress and tuxedo, heads dipped close, lost in the music and each other.

With no Frederica waiting afterwards, I went straight to my cabin, glad of my bed. Just two sleeps and we'd be in New York. At the thought of it, of the skyscrapers and electric lights and yellow cabs, I couldn't help but feel excited, despite my morose mood all day.

I opened the care records to see what else they might reveal, but I must have fallen asleep before I could read more than a sentence or two, perhaps lulled by the deep rocking of the ship, because I woke the next morning with them stuck to my face.

30

It only took a few weeks of our mother being back home from the hospital for life to resume its cruel sameness; her back healed, and her head, though she always had a scar above her eyebrow after that, and she once again moved in her graceful, unobtrusive way; and our father – perhaps to oppose this – returned to his lumbering, look-at-me-I-exist manner. Harriet and I changed only in that we endeavoured never to annoy him, two mini Wonder Women with the superpower of invisibility, trying to keep their mum safe. We kept out of his way. We played the piano quietly when he was home. We played more exuberantly when he was out, and we loved the joy it evoked in our mother. And we continued to keep a most magnificent secret: Mr Hibbert.

He never asked about the lessons we had been missed while our mother was away. We were just relieved when we first knocked on his door again, terrified he would have forgotten us, and he let us in with a flamboyant sweep of his arm, saying, 'Well, as I live and breathe, how happy am I to see you both.'

The lemon barley water had never tasted so good, and we asked for more.

'I hope you've been practising,' he said.

'Of course,' we cried in unison.

'It isn't practice to me,' said Harriet. 'Practising is times tables. I hate them. Playing piano is like...' She looked thoughtful. 'Like dancing with my fingers.'

Mr Hibbert smiled. 'Very good. I like that. Beethoven said that we should not just practise our art but force our way into its secrets.'

'So, some secrets are good.' Harriet looked at me.

'Did Beethoven really go deaf?' I asked.

'Some say it wasn't fully,' said Mr Hibbert. 'He first noticed difficulties with his hearing when he was twenty-eight, and some say that by the time he was forty-four he was totally deaf. But others say that he had a tiny bit of hearing left in one ear. Whatever the case, I can't even imagine it. How about you girls?'

I have always thought it the cruellest trick of fate to do this to a genius who created symphonies to make the heart soar. 'It would be awful,' I said then.

Mr Hibbert paused and leaned closer as though he was going to now share *his* great secret. 'However, when it happened, he apparently said that now, with this affliction, he could hear what no one else could – music from heaven.'

'Music from heaven,' we both whispered.

'That's how I hear it,' I said.

He nodded. 'Right, scales, or there will be no music at all, and then show me what you've got.'

At the end of the lesson, he took our empty glasses away and returned with a box wrapped in purple tissue paper.

'It's not my birthday,' said Harriet.

'This is for both of you,' he said. 'You'll need it, to practise properly for your exam.'

'Exam?' I had forgotten his suggestion last time.

'We'll come to that on Thursday,' he said. 'Open your gift.'

It was a beautiful light-wood metronome with a gold pendulum and digits. We oohed over it and held it up like a holy grail.

'But where will we say we got it,' Harriet whispered in my ear.

'We'll think of something,' I hissed back, not wanting to upset Mr Hibbert and ruin his lovely gesture.

When we got home our father's car wasn't yet on the drive, so we hurried inside with our prize and found Mum in the kitchen, lost in the steam of boiling vegetables and bubbling gravy.

'Mr Hibbert gave us this,' I told her.

She touched the metronome. 'It's beautiful.'

'But where will we tell Daddy it came from?' asked Harriet.

Our mother's face clouded over and even at the tender age of eight I knew she felt guilty for teaching us to lie. 'Put it in the toy cupboard,' she said. 'He never goes in there. And only use it when he's out, OK?'

We heard his car then and scurried away with our metronome. I can see it now in a spot between my Tiny Tears doll with the missing arm and the xylophone that had long ago lost its mallets. Our father never found it and we only took it out when he was at work. A metronome's cyclic beat, even now, comforts me, because it evokes those perfect moments, when it was just Harriet and me, side by side, Mum in the doorway, drying dishes, smiling, briefly safe, and the music, always the music; nothing else.

That summer we sat our grade one piano exam. We had practised with Mr Hibbert for months. We had to go to Hull University's music department and take it alone in a dusty room, with a bespectacled invigilator sitting on a chair nearby. Mum told our father we were going to the coast for the afternoon and then, when they finally arrived, she hid our exam certificates beneath tea towels in the kitchen drawer, another spot our father would never look in.

We both achieved distinction, which brought tears to her eyes, and had Mr Hibbert patting out heads, and all three of us saying at the same time, 'Well, as I live and breathe,' and then laughing.

The following autumn we sat the grade two exam, and in winter, grade three, each visit to the university disguised as a trip to the park and to the cinema. Generally, the expectation is to advance one grade a year, so this was quite the accomplishment. But our celebration had to be muted, private, just a card from Mr Hibbert with poppies on the front, later hidden inside an English exercise book, and a kiss and a fevered hug from our mother. She gave us each our quaver-pendant necklaces around this time, telling our father they were selling them off at a closing-down jewellery store to appease his annoyance at the extravagance. I wonder now how she afforded our lessons and the exams. As a teacher, I know what they cost.

Did Mr Hibbert help? Take pity on us?

I'll always associate spring flowers with him. If I think of his garden, it's a splash of pastel pigments, and if I picture his house those blooms are displayed there too, effortlessly arranged in large vases, the scent sharp in the air. By the spring of 1981, when I was nine and Harriet was turning seven, we began preparing for our grade four piano exam.

At the end of that day's lesson, Mr Hibbert sat on the chair opposite our piano seat, the scarf at his neck that day as bright as the rows of pink peonies along his driveway. 'You need to be ready for a challenge, dear girls,' he said. 'We're really going to find out if you're true maestros.'

'True maestros,' whispered Harriet, in a, by then, rare repetition of his words.

'Grade four is slightly more challenging than grade three,' he explained. 'Most children who sit this exam have been playing piano for five years, and we all know it's just over two and a half years for you two. If we wait until autumn for you to sit it, it will be three years. But I'm confident, especially after the distinctions you achieved in the previous ones.'

'I'm still scared,' I admitted.

'That's understandable,' he said. 'Even when we're good at something, our desire to perfect it means we expect a lot from ourselves. And this is good. Always be scared, Heather. It keeps you sharp.'

'Do we get to learn new pieces?' asked Harriet.

'Oh, yes. This is where the music becomes more elaborate and interesting. You'll need to learn five pieces – two etudes and three repertoire pieces, including a couple from the Baroque era, some minuets, marches and musettes.' Mr Hibbert smiled at our rapt faces. 'We shall begin next time by learning more about Johann Sebastian Bach and mastering "Toccata and Fugue in D minor". OK, that's it for today, girls. Keep practising. Keep forcing those secrets.'

'You mean keep letting my fingers dance,' said Harriet.

'That's exactly what I mean.'

We never sat that exam.

We never found out if we were true maestros.

Instead, our father found out about Mr Hibbert.

I'm not sure how long after this it was, but, as with most of the dark drama of our lives then, it happened during a meal. Our father was in a surprisingly good mood. He had come home from work, cheerfully describing how a colleague had won 'two grand' on the horses. He'd even asked about our day at school, and praised the beef lasagne Mum had attempted for the first time.

Then there was a knock on the door.

It was unusual for anyone to call by, and perhaps it was this more than a premonition that had me feeling sick. We three remained quietly sitting at the table while our father went into the hallway. We heard voices; our father's was surprisingly amiable. Then he returned with two police officers, which had Mum's hand flutter to her chest and all colour drain from her face.

'What is it?' she asked, voice cracking. 'Who's...?'

'No, it's nothing like that,' said the taller officer, his glossy black hair as slick as the paint our father used on the metal gate. 'We had a phone call about an incident.'

'An incident?' She looked confused.

'Darling,' said our father, and I know Harriet was as shocked as I was to hear him use such an endearing term. 'Someone called the police station and told them that I'd hurt you.'

'We have to look into a complaint like that,' said the smaller officer. 'They didn't give a name, but they said that there were often noises coming from the house, and that Mrs Johnson often has bruises.'

Our father got lucky that day. Mum happened to be bruise-free, and looked healthy and content, her cheeks pink from cooking the meal, mouth upturned from his rare praise.

'This person said they heard something this evening.'

'As you can see, all is well.' Our father sounded like the dads in the TV shows we watched: calm, jolly, warm.

The officers looked at us children, and we automatically smiled as though our world was the technicolour of happy movies.

'Was it our piano?' asked Harriet suddenly.

'Sorry?' The taller officer.

She pointed to it, between the doll's house and the toy cupboard. 'We can be noisy sometimes.'

'I don't think that's the sound they heard,' he said.

'There are some gossipy people on this street,' said our father. 'Nothing better to do than report trivial things. Him over the road said my lawnmower was too loud the other day.'

The police officers must have been happy with what they saw and satisfied with what our father told them in the hallway, because they didn't stay long.

When they had gone, the mood changed; a black blanket fell on the house. Clearly trying to control his volume, our father ranted and raved about 'which fucker' had dared to interfere in his business.

'Who did you speak to?' he demanded of our mum.

'No one,' she whispered, eyes bright with fear.

We believed her. Our father must have too because he left her alone that night, perhaps afraid of who might hear.

Things settled a little after a week or two of him stomping around the house, tearing apart one neighbour after another. We hoped the storm had passed. If he hurt our mother, he did it more quietly then, and hid it well. Then, one Saturday, he saw the card with the poppies on the front that Mr Hibbert had given us for passing our exams. It fell from my English book while we were doing homework at the table. My heart dropped to the floor with it.

'What's that?' asked our father.

I knew if I lied, I'd be in more trouble, so I simply passed it to him.

'What piano exams?' he asked, reading it.

Harriet fidgeted in the seat next to me. I wanted to protect her, and our mother too, but what was best to do?

'It was for you,' I said.

'What do you mean?' he demanded.

'The lessons. We ... we only kept it from you so we could ... *surprise* you,' I stammered. 'With how well we played. We couldn't learn on our own.'

'You had lessons? With that nancy boy? When I specifically said not to?' He left us then, to find Mum. We cowered together when we heard him yelling at her. We didn't dare play 'Nothing Else' to escape the sound, not even quietly, fearing it would incite him more. 'I bet he rang the police too, didn't he?' our father shouted at her.

The next Monday, when we walked to school, every single flower in Mr Hibbert's beautiful garden had been destroyed; rows of headless green stems stood like sad stickmen. I don't think our father had the guts to deal with Mr Hibbert in person, he just took out his rage on that beloved sanctuary late at night. I realise now that my father, like many men who beat women, was not as brave with his own gender.

We never had another lesson with Mr Hibbert.

We saw him on the street after this, and I always wanted to run and hug him, but feared the consequences, both for him and for us. But he always caught my eye. He often smiled and mouthed something that it took me ages to work out. I eventually realised that it was, 'Keep letting your fingers dance.' For a while, I couldn't walk past his house without choking back tears at the barren front garden.

I've never forgotten Mr Hibbert and the gift he gave us – not the metronome, not the lukewarm lemon barley water, not the sweet card with poppies on the front, but his absolute faith in our ability, a need to practise and perfect, and an ear for music from heaven.

31

Day six and the storm had passed. I woke to calmer seas, to a sunrise like butter melting over liquid-gold waves, and to the thrill of knowing this was the last full day at sea before the ship sailed past the Statue of Liberty first thing the next morning. 'I always think of Annie Moore when I first approach Manhattan along the Hudson,' Tamsin had often said back home. 'She was the first immigrant processed at Ellis Island. Imagine how she felt seeing the green lady of liberty, tired but excited to start a new life in a city of dreams.'

I too felt that the land awaiting me, out there, ahead, held some unspoken, unknown, indefinable answer. It was a strange emotion; not quite a premonition, more like when you feel like you've been somewhere before and then you realise it's only because the place is so iconic that it feels familiar.

I was desperate to finish reading my care records, not only to find out if and what the care home had decided to tell me about Harriet's whereabouts, but so I could put them aside and enjoy my two nights in the city. I picked them up, tried to find where I'd got up to, but a knock on the door disturbed me.

It was Frederica, her colour and liveliness returned. 'Hey,' she said. 'Wanna get some breakfast?'

I looked back at the black folder. It would have to wait.

In the crew café we grabbed eggs and coffee, and found a table. 'I'm excited about New York,' said Frederica.

'Have you been before?'

'Yes, I've an ex there and I'm staying at her apartment. Have you been before? Where are you staying?'

'It's my first time,' I admitted. 'I'm in a hotel near Times Square.'

'We can hang out if you want.'

'That's generous, but honestly, I'm excited to explore.' I was. I preferred it, not having to follow someone else's schedule, being able to go where the mood took me, as it took me, for as little or long as I wanted to.

I went to Frederica's last workshop on this leg of the journey. I took my Nikon out and – without using the flash, in case I distracted her – I got a shot of her talking. It was a beauty; the light caught her face, lit up her eyes, added depth to the silky green fabric of her dress. I got her email from one of the workshop flyers and later sent her it from the internet café. She was delighted, said she would use it as a promotional picture.

I didn't stay for the writing prompt.

The Sky Lounge beckoned. The room was the busiest it had been so far. I was no longer clumsy. I sat on the stool, breathed slowly, composed myself, and began with 'Bridge over Troubled Water' as I had the first day, and my heart matched its pace, not competing, not disruptive, but perfectly in unison.

The applause was the best I'd had.

Afterwards I grabbed a snack and found a quiet spot on deck seven to finish reading my care records. This was it. There were only a few pages left. I might finally find out where Harriet went that day. I looked out to sea for a moment, feeling I must prepare. The sun was hazy today, shimmering behind thin layers of cloud.

Then I began reading. The first few pages were dull reports about my adoption process, and the usual photocopies and duplicates, but no mention of what the care staff had decided to tell me about Harriet. I scoured each page a few times, certain I must have missed something. Finally, there was something of interest.

East Yorkshire Social Services Department

NAME OF CHILD: Heather Johnson
DATE OF BIRTH: 10/03/1972
DATE OF VISIT: 10/04/1983
RESIDENCE: Birchwood Children's Home

Heather met with her prospective adoptive parents today.

████ and ███████████ came to the home and sat in the garden with Heather, at first supervised by Sue Wilkins, and then alone. Heather was quiet but not impolite. ███████ asked questions about what Heather liked, but it was only when she mentioned that she loved classical music that Heather came to life. She then asked if they had a piano and ███████ said they didn't, but that they could certainly look into getting one.

I couldn't remember this visit, but I did know that within a short time of moving to Margaret and Harold's white cottage in a village on the outskirts of Hull a scratched upright piano arrived. It wasn't quite the immaculate, polished cherry 1968 Kohler and Campbell with ornate legs that Harriet and I had fallen in love with, but I remember being touched by Margaret's kindness; how she wanted me to have it. I was eleven by then, and it had been two years since our last lesson with Mr Hibbert and a year since my parents had died, so a long time since I'd played at all. It wasn't the same without Harriet. I felt stiff. I couldn't play with both hands. I didn't know if the tinny sound was me being out of practice or the piano being out of tune. But I pushed on. I slowly relearned all the classics Mr Hibbert had taught us. My fingers remembered how to dance.

But my heart faltered.

Margaret was patient with me in those early days, I know that. I wasn't a difficult or unruly child, but I must have been a challenge when I hardly spoke and had trouble eating. Maybe it was a good thing that Margaret and Harold were an older couple who had waited a long time for a child. I could not voice my pain about having Harriet ripped out of my life. I never said her name aloud. But I cried every night for her. And when I had mastered the keys once again, I played in the hope that she would somehow hear, wherever she was, and return to me.

And then we would play 'Nothing Else' again.

Now, I composed myself.

The next and final page in my care records was the adoption certificate.

Certificate of Adoption   Application No: 6464839575-21

Date: 25th July 1983
Registration District: Hull, East Yorkshire
Name and surname of child: Heather Johnson
Sex of child: Female
Name and surname adoptive parents: Harold Winters
                                          Margaret Winters
Occupation of parents of adopted child: Engineer
                                              Housewife
Signature of officer to Registrar General to attest the entry:
Stanley Bowers

I closed the folder. I was done. I had read everything.

There had been no mention of what I'd been told about Harriet's disappearance, so I guessed it was nothing at all, and there was no mention of whether the care staff had informed Margaret and Harold. Perhaps those facts were on documents not sent to me. I had all the answers these pages were willing to give. I might never know where my sister had gone. I would definitely never know if Margaret and Harold had known and not told me.

How did I feel? I wasn't quite sure.

Numb. Sad.

But how could I be, sitting there in the sun on that beautiful ship? I felt ungrateful for the trip I was lucky enough to be on.

Memories hit me with the force of the waves that had smashed against the ship during the storm; I saw us at the piano in the back room, I saw Harriet cartwheeling through Mr Hibbert's dancing garden flowers, I saw our fingers fast, playing to drown out the daily discord.

I couldn't hold the tears back.

'Oh, Heather.' It was Frederica. She sat in the next deckchair and put a hand on my arm.

'I'm done,' I sobbed.

'That sounds so final.' She looked concerned.

I laughed, couldn't help it. 'No, I meant finished. I've read all there is to read.'

'No answers?' asked Frederica.

I shook my head. 'Yes, answers about dates and names, and little things I didn't know. But nothing about where Harriet went.'

'I'm sorry.'

'It is what it is.' I didn't know what else to say.

'There must be something else you can do.'

'Yes. There must be. When I get home, I'm going to pursue it properly. I am. I'm going to find her.'

'Amazing,' cried Frederica.

I shrugged. 'I think, for now, I should just enjoy the rest of this trip. I'm so lost in the past I could be missing what really matters. Now. Here. *This.*' I looked out at the ocean waves.

'I guess I just like answers,' said Frederica. 'Resolution. I'm a writer remember.'

'You write me my happy ending then.'

After enjoying the sun for a while, I left her and headed for the Piano Bar. As I walked into the dark room, I remembered my nerves that first afternoon at the audience's close proximity, being encircled by the piano keyboard seating. Now, like in the Sky Lounge, I felt comfortable here. I gave the packed room the eighties hits I'd given them all week and smiled as they sang along. I might have gone back in time with my music, but that was it, from now on it was all looking to the future.

I allowed myself a glass of wine before the performance in the Sunset Bar. Frederica joined me, the soft blush lighting flattering, the white piano in the corner awaiting me.

'Give me your camera,' she said.

'Sorry?'

'You took that great picture of me. Let me get some of you.'

'Oh, no, I'll be self-conscious.' I covered my face.

She took the Nikon anyway. 'I looked at your so-called social media,' she said, shaking her head. 'Heather, it's pathetic. Why don't you share your music? Pictures of yourself playing?'

'I ... I just...' I didn't have any excuses.

'I'm going to get some good pictures with this, and some footage, and you are going to share it. OK?'

I didn't respond.

'OK?" she repeated firmly.

'OK.'

I went up to play my last set of this cruise. I tried not to look at Frederica but could see her out of the corner of my eye, moving around the bar with my camera. I played the gentle classics as usual. Then 'A Sense of Light' for Ruth and Gerry, who came onto the floor and glided around. I then played a brief version of 'Nothing Else', trying to keep my emotions in check.

In my cabin, later, I looked through the pictures on my Nikon. I realised that though I'd taken quite a lot of photographs, I'd written nothing in the soft, pink leather notepad I'd brought along with me. I paused at the photo of me on that first day, looking un-comfortable against the sea. I clicked through multiple glorious sunrise and sunset shots, smiling at the one of Frederica in green, remembering the Southampton harbour lights and the first one of the ship, and finishing at the ones Frederica had taken of me earlier.

I was taken aback.

I liked them.

I *never* liked pictures of me. But Frederica had caught something I'd never seen in myself before. Perhaps it was because I'd never really seen myself perform. When that one-off video went viral, I'd barely been able to watch it. But these I thought I might share on social media; yes, I would do it if I had Wi-Fi in the hotel tomor-row. In the photos and footage of me playing 'Nothing Else', my face was serene, my back was straight – just how Mr Hibbert had taught us – and my eyes were aglow.

I looked like I belonged there.

On my small stage.

In the light.

32

In my dream that night, we were both in a glow. Harriet and me. Side by side, we shared it. First it came from flames that devoured a car; then from the sun rising over the ocean; finally, it came from a theatre spotlight, intense, blinding.

But really, we *were* the light.

33

There was a quick meeting in the crew office first thing on the seventh day, where Aiden Miller returned our passports to us and advised us on when to be back on the ship in two days. It was clear that everyone just wanted to rush outside and see New York.

Most guests gathered by the pools to catch that first glimpse of the city, so I found a quiet spot at the bow of deck seven and stood by the railings with my Nikon. Frederica and I had said goodbye last night. I wanted to do this alone. We travelled beneath a bridge – which one I wasn't sure – and then, far in the distance, thin spikes of skyscraper emerged from grey mist. It took forever to reach them. I was as excited as a child, taking picture after picture of the silver buildings – click, click, closer; click, click, closer – a rhythm that was musical to me. Then I saw her, emerald green, torch aloft: the Statue of Liberty. I almost clapped my hands in delight. While she greeted us port side, starboard, rows of mirrored buildings flashed their bright welcome.

I had to tear myself away when we docked.

Crew had to let guests disembark first, so I'd left my packing until now. It was odd to put away things I knew I'd be getting back out in this cabin again in two days, but still, it had to be done. I'd made sure all my laundry was clean yesterday and carefully folded these fresh clothes in my suitcase. I took my care records from the bedside table and touched the plastic cover. I was finished with them and should pack them at the bottom of my case now.

But something had me open the pages one final time.

Something had me flick through.

Something had me check inside the front flap, and then inside the one at the end.

And there – there was *something*.

Folded up, small, as though someone had placed it there when they shouldn't, perhaps hoping for it to be discovered, was a piece of paper. Had whoever put these records together *wanted* me to find it there? I opened it up.

It was a photocopy of a newspaper article. The date at the top was 12th August 1982. I knew what this was going to be: it was about the car crash. I'd never seen any newspaper articles, not as far as I could recall. I hadn't thought there would be any. So many people died in car accidents – they rarely made the news. There was a picture of a car being pulled from a river. I frowned, something uneasy stirring in my gut.

Hadn't it burned?

And then, a picture of my parents.

This had me sob. I had not seen them in so long. I stroked my mum's sweet face, ached for her. Often, over the years, I'd thought it better that I had no photos of her. That it meant I could move on, cope. Now, here she was, my beautiful long-gone mother, eyes sad and lowered, while my father glared at the camera. And I wanted her. Oh, how I wanted her.

Then I saw the headline:

'Fatal Crash in River Ruled Murder-Suicide.'

I sank to the floor. Murder-suicide. *Murder-suicide*?

It couldn't have been. It had been an accident. Someone would have told us such a thing. Wouldn't they? I felt sick, but I had to read on, the sheet trembling so much in my hand that I could hardly see the words.

'An inquest today ruled that a fatal car crash into the River Humber five weeks ago was a murder-suicide. The driver was named as Robert Johnson, thirty-eight, who died alongside his wife, Annie, thirty-six. The submerged vehicle, which was driven off King George Dock at 6.45pm on 9th July, sparked a major rescue operation. Witnesses described how beforehand Annie Johnson tried to get out of the car but was dragged back inside by her husband, before he drove into the water. The couple were declared dead at the scene.

Their two young daughters were discovered safe in the garden of their Hull home and were taken into the care of social services. Police had been previously called to the address. A spokesman for Humberside Police, Detective Sergeant Rice, said: 'We were sent to the Johnson house a year before the car crash to investigate an incident. Neighbours reported their concerns, but we found no evidence of a problem.'

Local resident, Paula Moran, forty-five, paid tribute to Mrs Johnson. 'Annie was a lovely woman,' she recalled. 'I cannot believe this has happened to her.'

I had to read the report twice more, to try and absorb what it said. It hadn't been an accident. After the third read, I dashed into my small bathroom, only just making it to the sink before I retched.

My father killed my mother.

Killed himself.

Killed.

No. It couldn't be. It was too horrible. *Why*? There had been violence and disruption, I knew that; we had tried to drown it out with music. But murder. Suicide. These words had no place in the story of my childhood. They happened to other people. They happened in the psychological thrillers Frederica wrote. How frightened must my mum have been? I saw her, suddenly, vividly, high-necked lace blouse hiding bruises, tea towel on one shoulder, baking, cheeks pink. She had tried to escape. I could not bear it.

I put my hands over my face to stop the horrible images. I didn't have time to deal with this – I was supposed to leave the ship. I was in New York, city of dreams, city that never sleeps, a city that I would now associate with this shock.

I put the paper back where it had been hidden.

Shaking, unsteady on my feet, afraid I might be sick again, I got my luggage and left the cabin. I must have gone to the correct deck, I must have found the gangway, I must have made it onto the dock and found a cab, but I can hardly recall it now. The next thing I remember is emerging into bright light, the centre of it all; August sunshine flashing off glass buildings towering on each side, cars honking and trying to push in, a rammed sidewalk, hotdogs sizzling on a vendor's stand. But all I could see was that car being pulled from the river. I was missing what should have been a great moment because of a terrible truth.

The cab driver was speaking to me. 'That's fifty-five dollars, ma'am.'

'Oh, yes.' I panicked, realised the dollars I'd bought on the ship were in my case. 'Do you take cards?'

'Sure.' He passed me the machine. 'Love your accent,' he said.

'Oh, thanks.' I forced a smile. 'Love yours too.'

I got out. It was madness, heaving, too hot after the car's air-con, a million odours bombarding me at once. I was in the middle of Times Square. It was as flashy as the images I'd seen. Electric billboards competed for attention, advertising Broadway shows, new TV pilots and junk food. The red steps on the pedestrianised square were packed with sweaty tourists taking selfies. If this place had a theme song, it would be jazz: improvised, unruly, different every time.

I felt sick again.

Needed to sit down.

My hotel was on the corner. Glass doors led to a bare hallway. I saw on a sign that the reception area was on the fifth floor and accessed by one of four lifts. An efficient woman at a desk checked me in – complete with a warm cookie – and told me I was on the forty-fourth floor. I expected the lift to take forever to reach such a height but, in a flash, I was stepping out onto a long corridor and found my room.

The view was spectacular, shimmering skyline against blue, forever.

But I felt wretched.

I sat on the bed, left my luggage by the door.

All I could see, everywhere I looked, inside, outside, was water; gushing, devouring, stealing the breath from my mother. And I sobbed.

That day came to me. I'd not so much forgotten it as been unable to look at it properly all this time. Now I did.

Now I did.

34

There was a meal. Always the meal. Earlier than usual, I think. Yes, earlier. I found it odd that our father was already home that day and that we were called to the table so soon after school. Harriet and I had been reading, each lounging in our bunks, me above, her below, feet bare that summer afternoon, dangling from the beds like forgotten leaves on a dying tree. I no longer had to read stories aloud to her; she was eight and devoured her own books now. Nor did we go near the piano when our father was home. In the year since lessons with Mr Hibbert had ended, it felt like an unspoken rule that we shouldn't. Only when our father was out did we sit side by side, frenziedly practising, forcing our way into the secrets Mr Hibbert told us were there.

'Teatime,' called our mother, her voice shrill and unusual.

I peered down into Harriet's bunk. 'Already? We've only been home ten minutes.'

'And why is Dad even here?' she said. 'He's doing my head in. He's in *such* a bad mood.' She was still the only one who dared be feisty with him.

We went downstairs. The table was set, neatly as always, our father already there. I had never seen such subdued menace in his face. It was as though he was trying to contain a fire inside his head. He didn't look at us, but held his knife and scratched the table, scrape, scrape, scrape. I couldn't take my eyes from the small, slow, deliberate action, from the scar he left. I dreaded Harriet asking what he was doing, but she just glanced at me and sat quietly in her seat.

Mum brought in the food. She was trembling so much that the casserole dish lid made a clattering sound against the rim, until she put it down and took her seat. Her skin was so pale I'd have believed she was a ghost if you'd told me; if you'd said that my true mother had died, and this creature was all that was left.

No one spoke. It was an agonising silence.

We ate in that quiet, our chewing and the cutlery scraping against the plates the only sound. At the end of the meal, our father lit a cigarette, the one thing that was customary and so had me grasping at straws, praying that it meant this horrible oddness was over. The police had not called since that one occasion a year ago. Now, I wanted them to come. I didn't feel safe. The whole room simmered with unnamed danger. In the corner, our piano begged to be played.

'Go in the front room, Annie,' said our father.

I could tell she was trying to hide her surprise. He always went in there while she washed the dishes.

'I want to talk to Heather,' he said.

To me? What had I done? I thought I'd be sick, vomit beef casserole all over the table.

I saw my mother struggle with leaving us there. What had happened? Why was he so angry, so different? Why was she so terrified? Mum stood, wringing her hands, looking at us and then him. She kissed each of our foreheads. I felt that kiss long after. I smelled her when she was close, a sweet, sticky warmth, familiarity, and security. She went into the front room.

It was the last time I saw her.

'Your mum and I are going away,' said our father, ash tremulous on the end of his cigarette.

'On holiday?' asked Harriet.

He ignored her, and only looked at and spoke to me. I was confused – they had always taken us on holiday with them.

'Yes, tonight,' he said. 'I don't want any fuss. Do you understand? You two are to behave. You are going to wait in the garden while we pack and leave. You are not to come back into the house until it's dark, no matter what happens.'

Why did we have to go in the garden? It made no sense. Who was going to look after us?

'But it's not dark until after we go to bed,' said Harriet.

Again, he ignored her, and I feared she too was a ghost, like our otherworldly mother. He had never ignored his golden girl. I'd longed for his attention at times, but now I had it, full force, I didn't want it. And I couldn't bear that Harriet was in the shadows.

'You can take something you enjoy. But you stay there until it's dark.'

'But where are you going?' I asked, voice small.

'That's our business.'

'When are you coming back?' asked Harriet, still bold. 'Who will look after us?'

He ignored her. 'What do you want to take outside?' he asked me.

'I want to stay inside,' I said quietly. 'With Mum.'

'Me too,' said Harriet.

'Right, out you go, right now.' He stood up, voice cold, stubbing the cigarette out on his plate.

'We'll take the piano,' cried Harriet.

'The piano,' I repeated softly, not daring to tell him I wanted to go to my mum, that I was terrified he was going to hurt her, more than usual.

'For fuck's sake,' he grunted. 'I can't get that outside.'

'I won't go out without it,' said Harriet.

He ignored her.

So, I repeated it, not as brazenly, but still. 'We won't go without it.'

'Right.' He kicked his chair over. Stormed out of the house.

Harriet and I looked at one another. We didn't dare move. Didn't even dare go into the other room to our mum. I had no idea what would happen next.

Our father returned with Graham from down the street, who he often went to the pub with. The two of them approached the piano. 'You take that end,' said our father, gruffly, 'and I'll take this. Bloody kids, eh?'

If Graham thought this odd, he didn't say. Thankfully the piano was on wheels and our rooms had those tiled wooden floors so popular in the late seventies, so they were able to wheel it, noisily and clumsily, with much exertion, scraping of walls, and causing an awful clanking inside, through into the kitchen. Harriet and I followed, fearing the damage, but afraid to say anything. After all, we had asked him to move it. They let it drop in two horrible clunks down the small step into the garden and then half pushed, half dragged it onto the grass. They stood panting next to it.

'Thanks, Gray,' our father said gruffly, and our neighbour left.

Then our father went and got the piano stool.

'Right,' he said, red-faced. 'You stay here, with your bloody piano.'

'But who's going to look after us if you're going away?' I asked.

'Grandma Dolly will come later,' he said. 'Listen to me.' We did; we heard nothing else. 'Sit there at your bloody piano and don't move.'

We sat, regretting our request for it to come outside. Was it ruined?

'Stay there, no matter what,' he continued. 'Do you hear me? If you leave this seat before it's dark, your mum and me, we'll never come back. We're all packed and we're leaving now.'

Harriet sobbed. I nodded.

'No. Matter. What. Stay here.'

He went inside, and we heard him lock the door.

We looked at one another. I had never seen my feisty Harriet look so afraid.

I had to be the stronger one. The big sister. 'It's fine,' I said. 'We can do this. We'll sit here and play, and soon Grandma Dolly will come, and we'll go inside to bed, and Mum and Dad will come back next week.'

'But Dad locked the door,' said Harriet.

'I think Grandma Dolly has a key.'

'I don't like her,' said Harriet. 'She's grumpy.'

I had to smile at that.

'Shall we play?' I said after a moment.

What else was there to do?

We played Chopin. It sounded different because we were

outside; dense, less crisp, like it was annoyed with us. We heard the car start up on the drive out front. They were going. Our parents were leaving us for a holiday. Without even announcing that we would, just instinctively, we played 'Nothing Else'. That too sounded strange in this outdoor position, but we played harder, tried to force the magic. We sat up straight, just as Mr Hibbert had taught us; we flexed our fingers, inhaled, and we played our song. It was the last time we performed together, though we had not known then that it would be. The last time our fingers danced. The last chance we had to find its secrets.

I don't know how long it was before we stopped. I don't know if we grew tired, or if it was when Grandma Dolly arrived at last, but the sun was low in the sky by then. I'm not sure if we found out that night or the next day that our parents had died. I can't recall my reaction, so deeply buried it must be. I do remember going to stay at Grandma Dolly's house for a while, where, despite that fact that we had been orphaned, she was as gruff and indifferent as she had always been.

Then we went to the children's home.

I thought our parents' deaths had been an accident. I understand that adults would not want to tell such young children the truth about that car crash. That they would let us think it had been a slightly less horrific end. An accident, not a murder and a suicide. And I suppose it would have been a hard thing to bring up once we were separated, me with my new family – Margaret and Harold – and Harriet wherever she had gone.

But if I had known, would it have helped?

Would I have slowly come to terms with it?

Instead, I now felt like my entire life had not been what I thought it had.

And I hated my father for what he had done.

35

I woke from a hot sleep on my New York hotel bed, hair stuck to my face and luggage still unpacked. I was alone in a place I'd never been, not just geographically, but mentally. The hidden newspaper article had answered a question never asked. I dragged my suitcase to the bed, opened it, found the cutting and read it again. My tears fell onto the sheet. Had a part of me known, deep down, that it had been a murder-suicide? Could trauma do that? Mess up memories? Was that why I'd always been so afraid of searching properly for Harriet? Had I known this truth and hidden it from myself?

Did Harriet know?

Wherever she had gone, whatever had happened to her, had she known?

I wanted to enjoy my time in the city, but it proved impossible. That afternoon I bought a ticket for a hop-on-hop-off bus and sat on the open top deck for hours, going round and round the same route, watching tourists get on and off, pointing out famous land-marks, getting excited at the Chrysler Building and Fifth Avenue and Bloomingdales. I took pictures with my Nikon. Later I would look through them, sad that my shocking past had darkened this special experience now, and that all I had to show for my day was photos of places I'd barely even seen.

I slept fitfully even though it was quiet so high up. I wished I was at home, and I could go to the piano and play away my anxieties.

I remembered that restless night in Southampton. Was it only eight days ago? If I had travelled far in physical distance – just over three and a half thousand miles from England to New York – then I had travelled even further in time. As we approached this land of dreams, I'd been getting closer to a nightmare truth. Now, I turned to Chopin in my hour of need. I found 'Nocturne No 2' on my phone, and I was in the back room with my mother and Harriet, listening to it for the first time – and with more than merely my ears; hearing it in my veins and in my bones. I had known nothing bad could happen to the three of us while it played. That the safe hands of such beauty would not let any harm come to us.

This was what broke me.

The music had lied.

We had played while my mother drowned, at my father's hand, and it had not saved her.

I turned my phone off.

The next day, I hoped to put this revelation about my parents to the back of my mind and enjoy New York. I walked as far as Central Park and bought an ice cream from a vendor and sat on a rock in the sun, wondering about the people who lived in the apartments beyond the trees. Did they enjoy the spectacular vista they had or were they complacent? I suddenly missed the view from my balcony. The murky-brown water of home. My simple life. My not-knowing-this-horrible-truth life.

I caught a showing of *Les Misérables* in the afternoon and then, later, sat with a glass of wine in a bar where the pianist performed Billy Joel. For the first time in my life, I didn't move my fingers in time. For the first time in my life, I didn't feel the urge to go to the piano and play during his break. For the first time in my life, I thought I might not want to make music ever again.

Early the next morning it was time to return to the ship.

As I boarded, knowing that at one o'clock I was to go and play in the Sky Lounge for the new guests, I felt weak. I didn't know if I could. I had never felt this way. It was like I'd lost the ability to walk – or to breathe or think. I attended the safety training and the meeting of new crew members in the green room, hardly taking anything in. Frederica was there, full of joy about her whirlwind New York visit.

'Are you OK?' she asked.

'Yes.' I forced a smile.

I knew she wasn't convinced, but luckily, we were supposed to be listening to Sarah Briggs introduce the new comedian. Absentmindedly, I wondered what had happened to Barry Lung, but didn't care enough to ask.

I changed into my cream suit and made my way to the Sky Lounge just before one. It felt like I was a character in a show. I sat at the piano and played. But I wasn't me. I wasn't there. I was acting. I was a fraud, pretending to love what I did, but my heart had died. No one applauded. I didn't care. I went back to my cabin. Slipped out of my clothes. Curled up on the narrow bed. No care records to read now. No hope of answers about Harriet. No point in being here.

After all this time, I wanted my mother.

I wanted my sister.

I had neither of them.

I dreamt that Harriet and I were trying to play our song, but no matter what we did, the music had gone. There was no sound. I could not hear her words; I could not hear the notes. We pressed the keys, again and again, but all we heard was our own fingers tapping, tapping, tapping.

Something woke me. A gentle tapping. Pause. Another gentle tapping. By the time I realised it was on my door and not fingers on a keyboard, they must have gone. I sat up. The ship was moving. We were away again, heading for the eastern Caribbean – there would be four days at sea and then we would arrive in Road Town in Tortola, the capital of the British Virgin Islands. How excited I should have been.

How lost I felt.

I stood and realised there was something on the floor. Someone had pushed a white envelope under the door. I frowned, picked it up. On the front was simply my name: *Heather Johnson*. Except it wasn't my name, not now. I'd been Heather Harris since marrying Dan. I'd briefly been Winters when I was with Margaret and Harold. But I hadn't been Johnson for years. Who on earth called me that? No one.

Not anymore.

I opened it.

Something shiny inside. I took it out. A delicate chain, tarnished with age, sliding through my fingers like liquid gold. On the end, dangling, quivering as though it had been played, a quaver pendant. How? Only one person could have…

I opened my door and ran into the corridor, looked up and down. Empty.

'Harriet?' I whispered. Then, '*Harriet*,' louder.

Empty.

'Harriet,' I cried.

Nothing.

I came back inside and fastened the chain around my neck, put my palm over the musical note high above my heart and felt Harriet's hand on top of mine. I had no idea how or why, but I knew that the music had not lied after all. It only ever spoke truth. It had not died either. I saw in my head the two diagonal slashes that indicate a break in the music; a caesura; a pause.

It had only paused.

HARRIET
(SECONDO)

36

I sat in the waiting room, flicking through one of the glossy real-estate brochures on the glass coffee table, hardly seeing the images of expensive, minimalist apartments. The man opposite wore a barely visible, flesh-coloured hearing aid in his left ear; I only noticed because I was looking for it. I told myself he was much older than me, that his hearing loss was age-related.

I crossed and uncrossed my legs every few minutes, unable to keep still, fearing I might get up and run at any moment.

A large photograph of an apartment on one page caught my eye; there was an Andy Warhol-esque print of Beethoven on the wall. I touched it. Thought of the tutor I'd had when I was small; 'Mr Hibbert from number fifteen' was how I recalled my mother describing him. He explained once how this great composer slowly lost his hearing. I knew now that by the time he'd got to my age, Beethoven was reputed to be totally deaf. The idea of a pianist being unable to hear his own music had haunted me ever since I was six.

I closed the brochure, choking back tears.

What if that happened to me?

I hadn't even realised for a long time that I might be slowly going deaf. It was ridiculous really. Me, a woman who had once volunteered for five years at the Sound Sensation Theatre, a group for children with hearing loss. Me, a woman who helped those kids confidently speak and perform on stage for a packed auditorium. Me, a woman who struggled to learn the basics of ASL (American Sign Language) but ended up as proudly fluent in it as I used to be with sheet music.

But I suppose the things we are so aware of in others we often disregard in ourselves. Especially if it's the most terrifying thing of all: a fear we've had since we were small.

The secretary, who sat at an impeccable desk, called a name, and the man opposite got up and went along the corridor to my left; it looked endless to me, though it wasn't overly long, and I dreaded being sent along there.

I put the brochure back on the coffee table. I couldn't recall exactly when I first noticed subtle changes in the world around me. I was always so busy, and living alone I had no one to point out the odd new habits I had at home, ones I just put down to laziness, to hitting forty-five, to middle age.

'Mrs Romano,' said the secretary crisply and loudly. 'Dr Resnick will see you now. Room three.' I wondered if she spoke with clarity because she worked in an audiologist's office.

I felt sick. I thought my legs might give way as I went along the corridor of doom. I barely took in room three when I entered, except for the ceiling-high window overlooking Times Square, and Dr Resnick, who was efficiency personified, as though not only his suit had been ironed an hour ago, but his hair, tie and forehead too. I told myself to grow up, that the hard-of-hearing children I'd volunteered with had come to places such as this, had dealt with this, had then joined the Sound Sensation Theatre and made their lives glorious.

'Take a seat,' said Dr Resnick warmly, speaking clearly and looking at me the whole time. 'How are you today?'

I couldn't speak.

'Tell me why you're here, Mrs Romano,' he tried.

So, I told him what my daughter Sera had said. That she was the reason I had booked the appointment.

37

Sera had arrived home on a Friday evening two weeks earlier – with her washing, as always, two bags of it

'What the heck do you do with it when you're not home?' I asked, dumping it in the laundry room. She was studying gender, sexuality and women's studies at Pennsylvania University, a BA that her father, Michael, said was 'pretentious' and not the kind of degree that would get her a 'proper' job.

'Mom, I do it,' she sighed, in her beautiful, weird accent. Even after all this time, I had miraculously retained a lot of my Yorkshire accent. I often thought that I'd clung to it as a way of keeping my true home close. Sera's dad was originally from Italy, so she spoke with a hint of three countries, her home, mine, and her dad's.

It was a weekend in the early summer when the pots on my balcony sprouted lilacs and lupins, and the trees on the street blossomed pink, and she was home from university. A weekend when I would realise I could no longer ignore the fact that everyone mumbling around me was not the result of some sudden, mass speech affliction, and that the softer sound of my footsteps on the polished marble corridors of the apartment building was not because my shoes had somehow lost their clickety-clack; and that the Manhattan streets had not quietened because the city residents had suddenly found patience and calmness amidst the splashes of new summer colour.

'Are you hungry?' I asked Sera. 'Shall I cook, or shall we get take-out?'

'Let's do Chinese food and watch old movies.' She paused. 'Why are you looking at me like that?'

'Like what?' I frowned at her.

'You're studying me.'

'Am I?' I wasn't aware that I had been.

'Yeah, it's weird, Mom.'

'Sorry. I'll try and stop being weird.'

She was as feisty as I had been at her age. I often regretted only having one child. I suppose we were busy, Michael as an investment banker, me as an editor and with all the voluntary work I loved. Sometimes I did wonder if I subconsciously feared having another girl, and then something happening to Michael and me that meant the two of them ended up separated. Being an only child ensured Sera never got deeply attached to a sibling who one day disappeared, leaving her sad and broken, and probably never being able to forgive her.

'I'll go and get the take-out now,' I said. 'What do you want?'

'Just call them,' she said, going into the bathroom. 'I'm gonna have a shower.'

'I like to go in person,' I said. 'It's only a block away.'

'Whatever, Mom. Weirdo. Can you get me that Wulong steamed pork with sticky rice? And get me some of their hand-pulled noodles too. And some ribs.'

'I guess you don't eat *or* do laundry at uni,' I said on my way out.

I walked to the takeaway on the corner, never tiring of my beautiful city. I'd moved here when I married Michael twenty-two years ago, and before that I'd lived in Jersey City. Each new season had me thinking *it* was my favourite; when the dying leaves turned Central Park's ground into a carpet of crisp cinnamon, I thought fall was the most beautiful; then winter's white made New York pure, followed by spring's birth of buds and blossoms, and I was sure those were my favourites. But now, early summer, the heat not yet stifling and the sky clear, this was truly perfect. The city suited my passion for the arts; there was always a new concert, a new hot book and all the ensuing events, a new gallery exhibition.

A bike almost knocked me over, wrenching me from my thoughts.

'Hey,' I cried, angry.

'I rang my bell,' she yelled over her shoulder, and sped away.

'Bloody didn't,' I muttered to myself.

I remembered a young boy – Martin, aged ten – from my time

six years ago when I was volunteering at the Sound Sensation Theatre, how he said that everything in life made him jump. He was moderately deaf so got by with lip reading, but when people called him from another room or tried to warn him about something approaching, he rarely heard and was caught unaware.

But *I'd* just been distracted. That was why *I* hadn't heard the bell.

When I got back, Sera was in the living room, lounging on the sofa, wearing my fluffy pink dressing gown, hair damp; her locks were the same colour as mine – deep auburn – with curls that sprang back no matter what she did. Each time she came home I realised how much I missed her. How much I feared that one day she might not come home. It was a ridiculous, irrational fear, but it had me sitting up in the night, dripping sweat.

I put the food on the kitchen worktop.

'Mom, did you hear me?' Sera was right next to me, and I jumped.

'What? No. When?'

'Just now. I said it twice.'

'Said what?'

She started to open the trays of food. 'I sort of met someone.'

'Oh, that's nice. At uni?'

'It's *college*, Mom. You're still so damned English at times.'

'I try to be,' I said, touching her cheek.

'What?' She shrugged me off, not unkind, but more with the affection that permits such rejection.

'Who is he then, this young man? Is he decent?'

'No, he's wild, has a criminal record and six wives.' Sera took her food into the living room.

I followed with mine, pausing for a moment at the entryway from the kitchen to the L-shaped living room, where floor-to-ceiling windows gave views over the East River and city, with hardwood floors, oversized sofas, and pieces I'd picked up on our travels over the years, and most cherished of all, the black baby grand in the far corner. Michael bought me it on our tenth wedding anniversary, a complete surprise that I cried over, replacing the out-of-tune upright I'd had since I was ten. Michael lived downtown now, near his offices. I'd kept this East 60th Street apartment; from here I could walk to the Penguin Random House offices, where I'd been a senior editor for fifteen years. Plus, Michael wasn't as attached to the three-bedroom place that I'd made a home; he hadn't decorated it, he hadn't given up work for a year and nursed Sera here, he hadn't felt that if he stayed in one place for as long as possible rather than moving around, he would be easier to find – if someone happened to be looking for him.

As I often did when I walked past the piano, I touched the lid. I didn't play as much as I should, perhaps a couple of times a week. I loved having it in the apartment, but I felt sad when I played alone. Sera had never shown much interest. I had encouraged her when she was little, but beyond a childish tinkle with her friends, she never took it up properly. Hadn't my mother once said that the gift of music missed a generation?

'How's your father?' I sat on the opposite sofa to Sera.

'My *father*?' she laughed. 'Can't you say "Dad" like normal people?'

Despite finding out afterwards that Michael had been seeing a much younger woman for the final six months of our marriage, it had actually ended quite amicably. Though he was fifteen years older than me, once I got to forty, I knew I was getting too old for him. He liked young women, and I knew eventually he would replace me with one, so I got out while I had my dignity, before he dumped me.

'Maybe I'm not normal people, you cheeky monster.' I filled my mouth with noodles.

'Dad's fine,' she said. 'I saw him last month ... with Scarlett.' She said the last two words gently, like she was trying to be sensitive about mentioning another woman, even though I'd told her many times that I still loved Michael, that I always would, and I wanted him to be happy.

'I know. He said. Did he go to the doctor about those heart palpitations?'

'I dunno. I don't talk to him about that kind of stuff.' Sera studied me. 'Mom?'

'Yes?'

'You're doing it again.'

'What?' I paused with a fork to my mouth.

'You keep staring at me.'

'Bloody hell, I'll look the other way if it bothers you so much.' I felt defensive about it and wasn't sure why. 'Let's find a movie to watch, and then no one has to look at anyone.' I found the TV remote and switched it on, and then flicked through the channels that showed older movies, stopping at a black-and-white film with Lauren Bacall in it. Then I moved onto the same sofa as Sera so I could see it properly.

She nudged me.

'Yes?' I was annoyed.

'I *said,* why have you got the subtitles on?' She sounded exasperated.

'It means I can have the volume low and still know what's going on,' I said. 'Shall I open some wine?'

'But the volume isn't low,' she said. 'It's loud.'

'Turn it down then.'

I went into the kitchen to get a bottle from the rack and two glasses. I put the cold glass to my forehead for a moment, suddenly wanting to cry and needing a moment to compose myself.

When I returned to the sofa, Sera put her head against my chest. How I loved her. I remembered suddenly how she repeated everything I said when she was tiny; how much it made me laugh. I'd say, 'Well, isn't this a lovely day,' and she'd squeak it back in a singsong voice. I had only ever loved girls this much – a mother, a sister, and now a daughter. This was why I gave everything I had to Sera, dropped everything at a moment's notice for her, answered every late-night message, and forgave every word she ever said in tantrum or anger. All the love I could not give to the first two females I'd loved burst out of me, entirely for Sera.

'So, this boy,' I said to her now. 'What's his name?'

I couldn't hear what she said with her face against my chest but didn't want to ask her to repeat it, so I just stroked her damp hair, sipped my wine, and read the subtitles like I had for months now. I'd never analysed why. I liked being able to read what people said. I was a fan of foreign films, and subtitles were essential then.

Eventually, Sera fell asleep, so I laid her carefully down with a cushion and covered her with a throw.

In the morning, the living room was empty. She must have gone to bed. I made coffee and sat at the piano. Lifting the lid, I looked at the keys. Shut my eyes. Suddenly saw us there, side by side, her on the right and me on the left. My older sister. The sister I hadn't seen since I was eight years old. I didn't have a single picture of her, though I had one of our mother. I struggled to conjure Heather clearly; she was part creation, part fantasy, part faded memory to me now – golden-haired I was sure, tall and lithe maybe, kind and softly spoken, definitely.

My shadow, my reflection, my missing half.

I was currently editing a book in which twins had been separated at birth – the mother was addicted to drugs and at that moment in time, no one wanted to adopt twins. When they found one another years later they had lived almost identical lives, both trained dancers and having dyed their hair exactly the same colour. In my job, I loved memoirs that explored missing family most. I was obsessed with reunions, particularly ones that happened by chance.

I started to play our song; Heather and I had played it when she was trying to protect me. I had a vague memory of our mother in the kitchen, cowering, blows raining down on her, and Heather pulling me away, taking me to our piano and playing a melody to make me feel better: 'Nothing Else'. I followed along, as I always did; she set the rhythm and I fell into it. I could still play my part. My fingers couldn't let go of the tune; they returned to it every time they were close to the keys. But I had to imagine Heather's notes, which, now that mine were softer when I played, seemed to swirl around me. I wondered if, wherever she now was, she still played it.

A hand on my shoulder then. Sera. I hadn't realised she was there and jumped violently.

'Your nerves are terrible, Mom,' she laughed. 'You should see someone about that.'

'Well, don't sneak up on people.'

'I said good morning twice.'

'Oh. OK. You want some breakfast?'

'Nah, I'll just get some coffee.' She returned from the kitchen with a steaming mug. 'I can tell you're melancholy,' she said.

'Why?'

'You always play that song when you are.' She sipped her coffee. 'It's beautiful. So ... melodic and mournful, but yet still weirdly uplifting.'

Though Sera knew about my other, long-ago life in England, I'd never told her the story behind 'Nothing Else'. I didn't want to burden her with the traumatic reasons why we had created it, and played it over and over. Sera knew nothing of the violence I'd witnessed, only that I once had a sister and we had been separated when our parents died.

Separated was the word I used. But, really, I had left her.

And I'd never forgiven myself.

'Does the piano sound right to you?' I asked Sera, turning to look at her.

She flopped on the sofa, flicked through some magazines. 'What do you mean?'

'Well, the notes ... I don't know... they're more muffled when I press the keys.'

She said something I couldn't make out.

'Sorry?'

'Sounds the same as always to me,' she said loudly.

I took my coffee to the sofa. 'What do you want to do today?'

'Don't mind.' She put the magazine down and looked at me. 'Mom?'

'Yes?'

'Don't get annoyed ... are you watching my mouth when you keep studying me?'

'Your mouth?' I laughed. 'Why would I be doing that?'

'There's a girl at college,' she said, 'she's deaf in one ear so she part lip-reads when we talk. You remind me of her, the way you look intently at me when I speak. Is everything OK?'

'Of course it is.' I sounded defensive and I knew it.

'Is that why you went to the take-out place instead of calling them? Because you find it harder to hear people on the phone?'

'No. I just like Charlie who works there. And I can never decide what I want on the phone.'

I could tell she didn't believe me. 'You text me instead of ringing.'

I didn't respond.

'Mom, when I've spoken to you, and you couldn't see me, you didn't hear me.'

I thought I might cry. A few people at work had said the same, and I'd made excuses. I knew the signs. I'd volunteered with kids who were deaf or hard of hearing. I knew how they needed to lip-read, while also using the information they had from the context of the conversation, knowledge about the language itself and its lip patterns, and any residual hearing they might have, with or without a hearing aid. Hadn't I been lip-reading as much as listening recently?

'It's probably my age,' I said. 'The start of menopause...'

'Mom, you're only forty-five, Jesus.'

Why did I try and explain it away? Because I was afraid. I knew what it might mean.

'You used to volunteer with those youngsters,' she said. 'You know the signs.'

I did. But I was in denial.

'You told Dad to get his heart palpitations checked out,' Sera continued. 'You should get your hearing checked out too.'

'OK, OK. For you. Though I don't think they'll find anything.' I forced a smile.

Sera kissed my cheek. I hated that she looked sad.

That afternoon we went to the new exhibition at the Guggenheim, ate at her favourite Italian restaurant on West 44th Street, and got last-minute tickets for *Madame Butterfly* in the evening, but I couldn't concentrate. In the theatre, in the dark, I felt lost. The music did not soar. When we cried at the suicide scene, Sera's tears were at Puccini's glorious music, while mine were for my memory of it. The world was growing quieter. And I was not ready for that silence.

Dr Resnick took notes, nodded, encouraging and non-judgemental, while I told him about my recent experiences. 'How long would you say it's been going on?' he asked.

'That's hard to answer.'

'How long, then, that you've noticed it? That it has impacted your life in some way.'

I didn't want to admit it. Not only because it meant facing up to the idea that I was losing my hearing in some way, but because it meant I'd avoided coming here when perhaps I should have.

'Six months,' I said hesitantly. Then, 'A year...'

Dr Resnick nodded. He asked about my medical history, which was very good: I rarely visited the doctor – only for routine smear tests – and I had a good constitution, seldom getting colds or the 'flu.

'Is it one ear particularly?' he asked. 'Or both?'

'Both,' I admitted, sadly.

'Do you work in a job that involves a lot of noise?'

I shook my head. 'I'm a book editor.'

'You mentioned that you play the piano. I know this isn't particularly loud, but do you listen to other music at a high volume, via say headphones? Go to lots of loud concerts?'

'No,' I said.

'And how about your parents, grandparents?' he asked. 'Is there any history of age-related hearing loss?'

As always, this was difficult to answer, so I simply said no. I wondered suddenly if in a room far away Heather was being asked the same question? How curious would it be if we were like the twins in the book I'd edited, and we were living the same life?

'OK,' said Dr Resnick. 'I'm going to do a series of routine tests.' I must have looked scared because he added, 'Nothing painful, I assure you. First, I'd like to have a look in your ear canal with my otoscope, which is just a small magnifying pen. OK? The first thing I'll be checking for is that it isn't simply a case of ear wax, something we can easily deal with.'

I nodded, hopeful that that was the problem. Once he had checked inside my ears, he said it didn't appear to be ear wax. My heart sank.

Then he took me into a small, black-walled soundproof room, where I had to sit at a table, don some headphones and press a button each time I heard a sound. This produced a graph – an audiogram, Dr Resnick explained – which showed the quietest level where I could just hear a sound. Even without understanding all the data on it, I could see that my range was below normal hearing ability.

We returned to Dr Resnick's office, and he explained that he was going to do two final tests. He stood across the room, about ten feet away from me, and spoke a series of words, in a normal voice, and then asked me to repeat them.

'Avoid,' he said.

'Avoid,' I repeated.

'Ditch,' he said.

'Ditch,' I repeated.

'Fraud,' he said.

'Fraud,' I repeated.

I wanted to laugh despite my nerves. After seventeen more words, all of which I felt sure I'd repeated correctly, Dr Resnick said I'd got eighteen out of twenty right. The relief was immense. I couldn't be doing that badly. Surely most people would mishear one or two?

Then he put a sheet of paper in front of his face. My heart sank. Another test. Behind the white, he said something. It sounded like shoelace.

'Shoelace,' I said, tentative.

Another word. Maybe shoelace again. Was it a trick?

'Can you repeat that please?' I asked.

He did. Maybe it was interface? But that was so random.

'Shoelace again,' I said.

This time, I scored just five out of twenty correct. I was embarrassed. I wanted to cry. I felt like a failure somehow. When I couldn't see Dr Resnick's lips moving, I had missed seventy-five percent of what he said. But hadn't I been doing this for months? Essentially lip-reading.

'Is this bad?' I asked him.

'No, nothing is bad. There are always ways to help you. I think we need to do further tests.'

'Oh.' I felt sick.

'I'll get an ear, nose and throat specialist to check you out. We also need to eliminate certain conditions, like diabetes, which involves a simple blood test, and do a neurological exam, just to rule out anything more serious. I'll book those now.' He looked at me. 'The audiogram suggested that you may be suffering with moderate to severe hearing loss – you're exactly between on the score. That may change at some point in your life, though of course it may not. I'm just surprised you've managed for so long like this. Please, sit down.'

I did and I began to cry. I couldn't help it. He passed me a tissue.

'What's caused this?' I asked. 'I'm healthy. I take care of myself.'

'It could be hereditary, but without knowing your history, it's hard to say where it might have come from. Let's get some further tests done first. But there is plenty we can do, I assure you.'

'Like what?' I dried my eyes.

But didn't I know? Hadn't I spoken in sign language to children who were profoundly deaf, even though I was rusty now because, as with any language where we don't speak it all the time, we lose the fluency? Hadn't I known to articulate as clearly as Dr Resnick did, to always look them directly in the eye? Hadn't I seen hearing aids in a variety of colours and styles? Those children had either been born deaf or become slowly harder of hearing, because of illness or injury or genetics, and they had got on with it, brave and hardy. And here I was, pathetic and weeping.

'You could try a hearing aid,' suggested Dr Resnick, writing something down.

I nodded. I wasn't keen. I didn't even know why. Resistance to admitting this was happening. Maybe. It was all brand new. I needed to digest everything, see what the other tests showed.

'It may be that you don't need one,' he said. 'Let's see what results the tests give us. You'll receive the appointment dates in the next few days. For now, I can give you some information, and you can go home and think about it. Talk to your family. I'll talk to you again soon. And don't worry.'

'Will I...?' I couldn't finish the question.

Dr Resnick, didn't speak, gave me space to find the words.

'Will I go completely deaf?'

'That, I can't answer,' he said. 'Until we know more.'

'OK' I said quietly. 'Thank you.'

I left his office and stood outside on the busy street. The noise – the traffic and some builders nearby and music from a restaurant somewhere – was not muffled because of my ears, but because of my heart. I did not *want* to hear a thing right then. Not that I needed further tests. Not promises that there were ways I could be helped. Not consoling words from a friend. Not even music.

Now I feared that I might never again hear 'Nothing Else' played by Heather and me, together once again. I'd occasionally wished that something, somehow, would reunite us, like the relatives in my favourite memoirs: a chance meeting, a coincidence, fate. Maybe I'd just been editing books too long, tweaking those happy and serendipitous moments. I'd looked for Heather a few times on social media, wanting to see what she looked like now, and then been sort of relieved when it failed. I could've done more, I knew, but I was *afraid*.

What if she had never forgiven me for leaving her?

Because, in essence, that was what I had done.

What if I found her and contacted her – and she rejected me?

I knew that living in another country (though, of course, she might also have left England) it was less likely that luck might have us cross paths; that we might one day sit in the same bar, listening to a pianist, and recognise one another while basking in the beauty of Chopin. I dreamed of that ... and yet feared it.

I wished she would find me instead.

Because that would mean she still loved me, after all.

39

Having taken the whole day off for my appointment, I wandered aimlessly around. The sights and smells were intense now I depended more upon those senses: the sun sharpened the reds and oranges of rows of umbrellas at outdoor tables; the heat of the day deepened the odour of diesel and fried food and tar. I loved my city but, in that moment, I longed to be anywhere else. A place where ... I just didn't know where.

I ended up back at the apartment. The day loomed ahead of me. I liked to be busy, even more so when I had things I didn't want to think about. The place was immaculate, and I hadn't brought anything home to read. I sent a quick message to Sera, telling her I probably had mild hearing loss and it needn't be a problem. She asked if I wanted to talk, and knowing how tricky that could be on the phone, I said we would do our usual FaceTime call at the weekend.

As I often did when I was troubled, I went into my bedroom, to the silver jewellery box that played 'Für Elise' when you opened it, just as my mother's had when I was small. I thought of her every time I lifted the lid. I could feel her slender hands on my head, smell her Yardley perfume (I'd ascertained this one day by sniffing every fragrance in Macy's, trying to 'find her'); see her kind, soft grey eyes looking at me with love. I hated what *he* had done to her. When I was looking to do voluntary work, I'd considered a women's shelter. But just reading about what the women who went there had been through was too much. Too close. Too real. I knew those bruises. I had seen such injuries. I had, at first, not understood what caused them until the day I saw *him* hitting her in the kitchen. The day Heather began our song. In the end, I chose to give my time to somewhere that wasn't so close to my old life: The Sound Sensation Theatre. Oh, the irony.

The silver jewellery box's music had been growing quieter recently, but I'd ignored that, and hummed it in my head. I found my favourite piece in the secret drawer at the bottom, which only opened if you knew to push it gently.

The gold quaver pendant.

It wasn't mine. Not really.

But I felt close to Heather when I held it, cool against my skin. I remembered the day her chilled hands put it around my neck. I had not taken it off for years after that. Only when I was a teenager and feared it would wear out did I remove it from my neck and keep it safely in a drawer. Since then, I'd always held it when I felt sad. When, much as I was glad to have it, I wished I had never taken it from her. When I wished I could give it back to her, and say sorry I took your beloved chain.

Sorry I left you and never came back.

Because I've never forgiven myself.

40

My feet were cold that night. I remember that. I could never get warm in the children's home. The ceilings were so high, and the radiators were often broken. Heather always let me in her bed even though it was so narrow we had to squeeze close just so we didn't tumble to the floor. That night was the same. It must have been winter by then, because there was ice on the tall windows, and we could see our breath in the room.

'I'm thinking about the car,' I whispered to Heather. We always spoke quietly. There was a woman who got cross if we stayed awake after lights out. 'Did it go on fire with them inside, do you think? I keep imagining it crackling and snapping. Don't you?'

'Put it out of your head,' Heather told me. 'It'll make you sad.'

'I'm already sad,' I said, 'But I'm thinking about fire to get warm.'

'Snuggle up, you'll be fine.'

I did.

'Your feet are like ice,' she hissed at me.

We switched position and slept top-to-tail so she could hold my feet and warm them. I don't know why, but this made me sob. It was the kindness. The way she mothered me when really, I just wanted my own mother back, not this small, slight girl who should-n't have to be my comforter and caregiver.

I was inconsolable. Though I must have cried when they told us our parents had died – I can't recall that moment, no matter how I try – this was the breakdown that has cemented itself in my memory. When Heather was my mini-mum. When she took care of my feet and my heart. Looking back, she must have been as heartbroken as I was, and who comforted her? Some of the people in the care home were lovely, but they had dozens of children to look after and they didn't *know* us. That was what I craved. A mother *knows* you. She senses what you need before you ask. She reads your thoughts before you know they're there. She feels every bit of *you*.

'I don't have anything,' I wept.

'You do,' said Heather. 'You have me.'

'No,' I said, all snotty and trembling. 'I mean I don't have anything of hers. I want to smell her again, Heather. I want to have something that she touched ... and I don't.' More sobbing.

'You don't need those things,' said Heather, kindly. 'She's with us in here.' Heather touched her chest. 'And in here.' She touched her head.

'But that'll fade,' I sniffed.

'She's with us when we play our song.' I know now that must have made Heather sad to say.

'But we can't even play it here.'

'One day, when we go somewhere ... somewhere better ... somewhere nice ... to a nice family ... then maybe they'll have a piano.' I realise now, with hindsight, that Heather was close to tears too, perhaps controlling herself for my sake. I wish I had left it there, been more sensitive, but I was only eight, and I was grieving.

'You have that,' I said to her.

'What?'

'The necklace Mum gave us.'

'Oh.' She put a hand over it.

I think we both got our gold chain and delicate quaver pendant for doing well in a piano exam – it's hard to be sure after all this time. I know I loved mine. When we first got them, I ran back and forth in the hallway, loving how it felt, swinging and alien against my chest. I felt like a grown-up. Special. I couldn't wait to show Mr Hibbert at our next piano lesson.

'Go careful with it, Harriet,' my mum called from the kitchen. 'That chain is very delicate. Why don't you just wear it for special occasions?'

'Heather wears hers all the time,' I cried, still skipping back and forth.

'Don't come crying to me if you snap it then,' Mum sighed.

I showed Mr Hibbert and he showed me a gold chain his mum had left him when she died, that he kept in a black velvet box. It had a heart-shaped pendant dangling from it, and he had a photo of her inside. She looked just like him except with masses of curly black hair and glittery eye shadow. 'Look after your precious gift,' he told me.

But then I wore it on my bike. I liked to race against the boy three doors along. We lived on a cul-de-sac, so it was a safe street to ride in. We tore back and forth, back and forth, competing, me winning. When I got home and undressed for my bath, I realised it had gone. I panicked. Put my clothes back on, sneaked out of the bathroom, and went into the street to look for it. I couldn't find it anywhere. Not on the road, not in the gutters, not on the path, not in the gardens. I came home bereft. My mum was kind but reminded me that she *had* warned me to be careful.

'Can't I get a new one?' I wept while she washed my hair.

'I think you have to learn something here, Harriet.' She gently massaged my scalp. 'Not everything is easily replaced.'

'But it is,' I cried. 'I know which shop you got it in. You could go back and get me another.'

'Maybe in a year or two when you've shown me you can look after things. If I just buy you new things because you're careless, you'll never cherish anything.'

I pleaded and begged. But she was firm. And when a year or two arrived, it was too late; my mum had died.

When I reminded Heather that she had the necklace in the home that night, I was upset. But I feel bad now because, even in my grief, I probably just wanted that necklace. I've felt guilty ever since that I let Heather give me hers. That I stopped crying and hugged her tightly when she unclipped it in the half-light of our bedroom and reattached it around my neck.

'You have it,' she whispered. 'There.'

'Oh, thank you, Heather,' I gushed. 'I'm warm now.'

I didn't stop to think how she must feel, only that I wanted something of my mother's, and that, after all, she had promised that in a year or two, I could have another one, if I learned my lesson. Children are selfish. I was. Now, I would never have taken it from her. Now, I wished I could tell her I was sorry and return it to her.

Because the next morning was our last.

The next morning, I left the home without Heather.

41

I returned to work the day after my appointment with the audiologist. I didn't know whether to tell a couple of my closer colleagues about it. It might help me if I admitted I was – how had Dr Resnick phrased it? – possibly suffering with moderate to severe hearing loss. Then they could allow for me needing to look at them when they spoke; understand when I missed so much in meetings and had to read the minutes afterwards.

But I simply wasn't ready to talk about it.

In my corner room, where the summer sun scattered the tiled floor with tiny brass buttons and where the double windows gave a view of more mirrored offices, I finished editing the book about the twins separated at birth. I loved the scene where they found one another after twenty-two years, spotting each other across a busy carpark before even going inside the restaurant, mirror images in all ways except that one of them wore jeans and the other wore a denim skirt. It had been thirty-seven years for Heather and me. Would I even recognise her if I ever saw her? Or she me?

Just as the music was an escape when I was small, getting lost in editing words took me to another place. If back then the songs had drowned out the discord in our home, now the prose counteracted the negative thoughts swirling around my head.

Before I knew, it was noon, and my assistant, Beth, put a hand on my shoulder and asked if I wanted her to pick me up a sandwich from my favourite bakery. I knew she had probably also asked this from across my office and then approached me when I hadn't heard, but she never said so, and neither did I. For the rest of the day, I quietly went about my work. At least any further deterioration in my hearing would never prevent me from working on my passion: the books.

That night, at home, I poured a glass of wine and made meatballs the way Michael had taught me to, baking rather than frying the meat, and adding extra Cabernet Sauvignon. I watched the sauce simmering and realised I couldn't hear it at all. I leaned in. Still nothing. Closer. The tiniest bubbling sound. What would I do if I went completely deaf? I could polish my sign language, but what else would it mean? The end of music. I glanced at the piano. Not that.

I remembered one of the children I'd volunteered with telling me, in sign, that most people assumed that the only way to enjoy music was by listening to it. In a world dominated by those who can hear fully, it's a prevalent theory. But he told me that he felt the vibrations – the humming from a bass string, the boom of drums – as long as the volume was high. And he had his memory of it.

'The memory of it,' I whispered to myself now.

Would that memory fade, though, like so much of Heather's face had, without a photograph to remind me? Really, it was the music that had kept her alive for me all this time. When I played, or when I listened to someone else playing, she was near again. Without it, would she disappear altogether?

I stirred the sauce and sipped more wine.

When I searched, now and again, for Heather online, on social media, just in case, it always left me bereft. Some women used their maiden names on Facebook so they could be found, but either she hadn't done that, or she wasn't on there. I wondered sometimes if she ever found fame, if she'd continued playing, but I never saw anything.

I turned the hob off and took my food into the living room.

I went back to England once, to Hull, to our childhood house. Sera was only eleven, and I wanted to show her where her mother had originally come from. She was enthralled by the Old Town and its cobbled streets, by the flat, 'weird' accents people had, by the rundown side streets, and by how 'quaint' it all was. We went to the street where Heather and I had grown up. It was all very different by then. I was trembling inside as we approached my childhood home. It looked nothing like I remembered. There were new windows. White paint over the brick. An extension above the garage. It was like the four of us had never existed at all and had just been a sad fairy tale in a book long lost.

I was tempted to knock on the door and ask if we could look around, but I knew it would likely look nothing like it once had. We passed the house where Mr Hibbert had lived, and that affected me far more. I stopped in my tracks, swallowed my pain. The flower-filled garden had been bricked over and was occupied by two large cars. I knew there was little chance he still lived there after thirty-seven years, but still I loitered by the wall with Sera, explaining who he had been, until a young woman came out, reversed one of the cars into the street, and confirmed what I'd thought.

He had gone.

Every corner Sera and I walked around, every avenue we strolled along, I was nervous that I would bump into Heather. I had given the universe a helping hand in a way, coming here; a grand opportunity, like those in the books I edited, to somehow send her my way in the brief two-week window of my trip. I didn't want to look for her, face that possible rejection, but as throughout my life, I was hoping that she would find me – to demonstrate that she wanted me.

Sera and I went to our old school; we visited the park we had loved; we went to shops and cinemas and cafes we had been to, once upon a time.

But we never saw her.

Was I sad? Yes. Was I also relieved? Yes.

Now, I ate meatballs and drank wine while watching old *Coronation Street* episodes on some random BBC channel, subtitles essential, of course. I remembered when I had to go to bed as soon as the credits rolled, while Heather could stay up that bit later. How I'd grumbled endlessly at that. Now, it brought tears my eyes. I could see the matching nightgowns we had with scratchy lace about the cuffs that made my wrists itch. I could smell the fading odours of our evening meal. I could later hear chairs overturning downstairs and the soft thudding that made me sob until Heather crawled into my bunk and held me.

I realised my phone was dancing on the coffee table. I hadn't heard it ring. I looked at the screen – Sera making, luckily, a FaceTime call.

'Are you OK?' I was always afraid she was ringing with bad news or that she was in trouble in some way. I knew it was a common worry for parents of students who were away, but my fears ran way deeper.

'Yes, Mom.' She shook her head. She had clearly just showered and was pink-faced, and looked so young that I wanted to scoop her up. 'Just seeing how *you* are.'

'I'm fine.' I sipped my wine as though that would prove it.

'I didn't like only messaging yesterday when you'd been to see a doctor, and I know you won't answer a normal phone call. How are you really?'

'Really, I'm fine.'

'But moderately deaf,' she said.

I remembered that was all I'd told her. 'Yes. Only possibly. It's not that major. Many people are and don't even know it.'

'But what if it...?'

'Gets worse? It won't.'

'Did the doctor actually say that?'

I didn't answer. 'If it doesn't bother me, it doesn't need to bother you,' I said instead.

'But I think it does though,' she insisted. 'Mom, I know you. You're protecting me like you always do. God, I wish Grandpa was here. Everything was better with him around. You said you could always talk to him. He wouldn't have accepted your "everything's fine".'

My throat tightened. He was the one person I'd avoided thinking of. It was too recent. Too painful still.

'I miss him,' said Sera.

I nodded but couldn't speak.

'Oh God, I have to go,' she said suddenly. 'Kerry's here and we're going out. Talk soon, Mom. Love ya!'

'Love you,' I said, but she had gone.

I reclined on the sofa and realised my glass was empty. *Coronation Street* had finished too. 'Bedtime, Harriet,' I whispered to myself. I saw him then. Suddenly. In the doorway, as though he had risen from the dead to treat me as he had our mother, cigarette in hand, gravy on his chin. How he had hurt the woman dearest to me. How he had degraded and insulted and criticised her. But I knew now that as well as her two children and hearing them play the piano, she had had one other joy – a glorious, occasional happiness in her life.

She'd briefly had my father.

My real father.

Sera's grandad.

Dad.

42

The morning after Heather gave me her necklace, following the usual breakfast of soggy cereal and cold toast, one of the women who worked at the children's home came and said she needed a word with me. I remember I still had my pyjama bottoms on, and my favourite T-shirt. I looked back at Heather as I walked away, my hand over the quaver pendant. She smiled, maybe sensing my nerves, maybe to comfort me, maybe to say, *Never ever forget me*. I was nervous, afraid I'd done something wrong. The last time I'd been spoken to alone was because I'd broken a swing in the field behind the children's home.

The woman – I can't recall her name – took me into an office I'd never gone in before. An ugly desk almost filled the room, and a man was sitting in a tan leather chair. He got up as I entered and put his hands on his face. Then he got down on one knee in front of me. I giggled. It was like when the prince proposed to Cinderella, glass slipper in hand, except this man wore a checked shirt and jeans, not finery, and held no shoe.

'You're little Harriet.' His accent was weird.

'I'm little Harriet,' I couldn't help but say.

I had no idea who he was, but I liked him all the same. His hair reminded me of conkers in the sun. A bit like mine. He smiled at my words and put a warm hand on my cheek.

'I'll leave you a little while to get acquainted,' said the woman. She gave the man a large bag, the kind you took on holiday, and she left the office.

'What does acquainted mean?' I asked.

'Getting to know one another,' he said in that weird accent like David Banner's off the TV. He studied me. 'I'm ... well, I was a very close friend of your mum's.'

'You knew Mum?' I whispered.

'Yes.' He looked sad. 'I ... She ... she was very special. You look so like her.'

'Do I?' That made me happy.

He nodded. 'I think she would have wanted me to meet you. And I've got permission, but only if you're happy to ... Harriet, would you like to come out with me for the day?'

'But I don't even know your name,' I said.

He looked thoughtful, like he had perhaps forgotten it. 'Call me Bill for now.'

'And where did you meet my mum?'

'At an event where I was doing a talk. The Women's Institute, where she used to go.'

'The lady who had our piano was there.' The pain at talking about our beloved instrument and our beloved mother in the same sentence was intense.

'It's OK, Harriet,' Bill said kindly.

I sniffed, determined to be tough. 'So, where would we go if I did come out with you?'

'Wherever you'd like to.'

'Oh, I want to see *ET* at the cinema,' I cried. All the kids at school had seen it. I was fascinated by the little alien, just wanting to go home. Like Heather and me.

'Sure, we can do that,' he said.

'What about Heather? Can she come?'

'Not this time,' he said, sadly. 'But if you enjoy it, maybe I'll come back again, and we can take her out too.'

I wasn't sure. I looked at the door. I had never left her out of anything. But I felt oddly like I knew this strange man very well. Like I had maybe seen him before, fleetingly, then forgotten, and was now remembering. His accent might have been different, but his voice felt familiar. I so wanted to go with him and see *ET*, but loyalty to my sister tugged at me.

'How about we get Heather a gift,' he said.

'Oh, yes. I'd love that. Can I get her anything I like, anything at all? Can we go to the big toy shop in town?'

He laughed and nodded.

'I'll just say bye to Heather,' I said.

'There isn't really time,' he said. 'And wouldn't you rather surprise her? Imagine how delighted she'll be when you come back with a gift.'

I paused. I remember now that there was a spiderweb in the corner of the window. I remember it looked like a wonky star in the sunlight. I remember feeling excited yet guilty. Did I sense that this would be a moment that changed my life? Maybe. Did I follow a path already carved in the ground, or did I tramp that trail myself?

'As long as we can bring Heather something back.'

'Yes,' he said.

We left the building via the back door, where Bill's car was parked. It smelled brand new inside but didn't look loved – there were no cushions or stickers of boxes of tissues in it. As he pulled away, I realised I still had my pyjama bottoms on.

'Oh, don't worry,' he laughed when I pointed it out. 'They look like jazzy trousers really.' I guess no one realised. 'And we can buy you some clothes. How about a whole wardrobe full, huh?'

We spent the morning looking around a department store. Perhaps it should have felt unusual in Bill's company, but it didn't. He let me choose some new trainers with Snoopy on, three pairs of jeans and an Adidas T-shirt like the one my friend Claire at school had. In the jewellery department I chose a delicate silver bracelet with various charms dangling from it for Heather. I was beginning to feel bad about taking her necklace. Buying the bracelet for her eased my guilt a little. A tiny ballerina and a tiny moon and a tiny star swung from it, and I knew she would love it.

I felt special with my bag of purchases. Children are fickle. Easily seduced by pretty things. I changed into a pair of my new jeans and my T-shirt in the toilets, and pulled on my new trainers. In the mirror, I was a different girl. A different person. Heather's quaver pendant flashed in the fluorescent light. She should be with me. At my side. Enjoying this. I felt sick.

'Can we go and get Heather now?' I asked Bill, who was waiting for me outside the toilets.

'We'll miss the film.' He looked at his watch.

'Oh.' I really didn't want to miss *ET*.

Bill bought me popcorn and fizzy orange, so we missed the adverts, but I didn't mind. I fell in love with ET. I wanted to be taken into the home of a lovely family like he was. But, even more, I wanted my real family, like he did. I cried when he finally flew home. Bill patted my arm; he was probably nervous about comforting me in any other way.

Afterwards, in the carpark, Bill and I sat in the car. 'I need to talk to you about something, Harriet. Can you be a big, grown-up girl, for me?'

'I'm eight,' I said. 'I *am* grown-up.'

'I agree. You are. You've been through so much. You've been a very brave girl.'

'A very brave girl,' I whispered.

'I'm not just Bill,' he said.

'You have another name?'

'Well, not another name, as such ... I'm another person.'

'What? Like a spy?' I was transfixed.

He laughed. 'No. Not a spy. Look, I don't want to ... well, to upset you. Or, I guess, shock you, but I also have to tell you something that... well, it probably *will* shock you.'

I didn't speak. I waited for his shocking thing.

'Harriet, I'm your real daddy.'

It wasn't shocking. It was more ... odd. Confusing. And yet, somehow, expected.

'But I *have* a real daddy,' I said. 'He died in a car crash.'

'I know.' Bill ran a hand through his conkers-in-the-sun hair. 'But he was only your daddy because he was married to your mum. I'm your biological daddy. Do you know what that means?'

'I think so.' I knew what sex was. Heather had been having lessons about how bodies work, and she had told me about it late one night in bed. 'You and my mum made me. Is that what you mean? But how? I've never seen you before. Did she love you? Why didn't she marry you?'

'It's complicated, Harriet. When you're a bit older, I'll tell you all of that. I promise. I've always known you existed – it's just now you know *I* do.'

'We have the same hair,' I said.

'We do.'

'Heather doesn't,' I said.

'Heather isn't my biological daughter,' said Bill.

'Oh.'

'Your other daddy is her real daddy.'

I remember feeling sad for Heather, still having our unkind, cruel dad as her father, while now this nice and unusual man was mine. Her daddy was dead, but mine was alive. It was exciting news blighted by that fact that it was only my news, not Heather's.

'Would you like to live with me?' Bill asked suddenly.

I didn't know what to say. I didn't know what to think; how to feel.

'I know it's overwhelming,' he said.

'Where do you live?'

'It's a long way from here. We'd have to fly there. But I have a lovely house with a large garden, and two dogs, and a lovely wife.'

'But won't she mind having us there if she isn't our mum?'

'She won't mind,' he said, but he didn't look entirely like he believed himself. 'She has accepted that you are my daughter, and that you don't have anyone to take care of you now.'

'I do. I have Heather.'

'Yes,' he said quietly. 'But she can't...'

'Heather can come too, can't she?'

He didn't speak for a moment. I remember then that a car backed into the one beside us and two men started yelling at each other. 'Not this time,' he said. 'I was only able to get permission to take you, because you're my family.'

'But she is too,' I said. 'She's *my* family.'

'Yes. She is.' Bill didn't look at me; he looked at his hands. 'And

I would take her too if I could, I really would. But listen, if you come and we show them what a great daddy I am, and what a great family we are, I know that after a while they'll send Heather.'

'They will?'

'Oh, yes. We can get a bed ready for her in your room. And you can write her when we're there. You can start a letter on the plane, and I'll send it as soon as we land if you like. You can explain to her that you had to leave suddenly, but we are coming soon for her too.'

'On the plane?' I had never been on one before.

'Yes. We need to go the airport now.'

'*Now*?' I wanted a wee and thinking of this distracted me. 'But can't I say goodbye to Heather? Give her the charm bracelet? You promised I could. I *must* tell her we'll be coming back for her soon or she'll be sad and worried.'

'We'll miss the flight if we do,' he said kindly. 'And I think she'll get upset saying goodbye. Don't you? She won't want to let you go. A letter would be better. If we go to my house, then we can get everything ready, and then I can talk to the care home, and we can have her flown over. Sadly, as I say, they'll only let me have you for now because you're my daughter, but I know we can persuade them once we get Heather's bed ready.'

I really needed a wee. I told Bill. We went back into the cinema, and he waited outside the toilets. I was surprised at my reflection. Reminded that I was a different girl, in different clothes. But I wanted Heather to be different with me. I cried. When I went into the lobby, I was still sniffing.

'I know you're sad.' Bill started the car up. 'I really do. Sometimes we have to think of what they call the bigger picture. This feels sad now, but think of how happy you'll be when you're finally with Heather again, and you give her your gift and show her your new bedroom.'

I couldn't speak. Eventually, 'I don't have my toothbrush,' I croaked, thinking of the worn, almost bristle-free thing in the home. 'And I don't have any pyjamas.' I'd left the bottoms I'd been wearing in the department store toilets.

Bill glanced at the holiday bag on the back seat, the one the lady in the care home had given him. 'We have a few of your things,' he said.

'But ... you ... did you...' It was all too much.

I cried and asked more questions as we drove over the Humber Bridge, coming up with things I thought might make him turn back and get Heather. It wasn't that I didn't want to go with him, to this new and exciting home, only that I wanted my sister to come too. I remembered a TV show Heather and I had watched in the care home lounge the night before, where a bad guy on the run had been unable to escape the country because he didn't have his passport.

'I don't have a passport,' I said to Bill.

'I do. I had one done for you,' he said.

'Oh.' I paused. 'And Heather isn't on it?'

'No, I wasn't allowed to. She isn't my daughter. But we will sort getting her one of her own.'

After that, I fell quiet.

That day is as clear to me still as if it were yesterday, perhaps because it stuck firmly in my young head, the way superglue sticks your fingers together if you spill it on your skin. I think of it often: us travelling across the bridge, away from the care home, away from where I'd grown up until that point, away from my darling Heather. Would I have fought harder to stay if I'd known what would come about? I'm sure I would have. But I was just eight. What power did I have?

And yet I still feel guilty that I just left her.

The flight is more of a blur. Perhaps I slept a lot. I know I wrote a letter to Heather. And I know now that my dad – Bill, the man who eventually became simply Dad – never sent it to her. Not to be unkind. But because he had known when he came forward to apply to care for me – a process that took some weeks before he left with me – that it could only ever be me. The staff at the home had known he would be taking me that day. They knew how it would affect Heather and me, and perhaps thought they were being kind in having me just leave, rather than putting us through the trauma of a painful goodbye, one we would likely both have fought against. They had apparently spoken to Grandma Dolly, asking what she thought should happen, and she had said that at *least* one of us didn't belong to her 'good for nothing' son, and had agreed that Bill should take me.

Things would likely have been very different today; the research I've done when editing books about children going through the care system has taught me that much. So many new laws have been passed since the early eighties insisting that the welfare of the child should be the court's main consideration, and that every child has the right to survive, grow, participate, and fulfil their potential. Before this, it was what was easier on an overburdened system, and one child was easier to find a home for than two siblings.

I can't help but feel angry when I think of Grandma Dolly's cool dismissal of me. I can't help but feel angry when I think of how maybe, just maybe, someone could have fought harder to let Heather come with us. I was angry at Bill too for a good while, back then, during my teen years, but now he is simply the dad I came to love.

So many decisions were made for us.

And yet – *still* – I feel terrible about leaving Heather that day.

43

I woke in front of the TV, wine glass in hand. I hadn't been a good girl; I hadn't gone straight to bed after *Coronation Street*. It was late. I would be tired tomorrow at work. I left the empty glass on the coffee table and went into my bedroom. I picked up the framed picture of Dad, as I'd called him since I was nine. It sat on the bureau with all the snaps of Sera growing up, some of them with Michael too, some where all three of us looked like happiness personified within jewelled frames – rows of photos telling the story of my life. The one I had of my mum sat in the middle of them all, at the heart. She was young, the way I remembered her, smiling shyly at the photographer, gold hair behind one ear, showing a tiny pearl earring, delicate and simple against her lovely neck.

But there was an absence that told the secret story of my long-ago loss.

Not a single picture of Heather.

I touched the glass on the picture in my hand. Dad. It had taken a whole year for me finally to see him that way. He was patient when I first arrived in America. He gave me space. He waited for that love. Although he had made an ill-judged decision regarding how he took over my care, forsaking my sister in doing so, he was not an unkind man. His house had indeed been lovely, with Labradors Sabre and Winston, whom I adored as soon as I arrived, a bedroom that I chose *ET* wallpaper and matching bedding for, and Gabrielle, who I never truly got close to, sensing resentment at my existence bubbling beneath the smiling surface.

♪

This is my real father's story:

He travelled the world back then, giving advice to failing companies and doing talks on how to succeed in business. He met my mother after doing one at her WI. He told me there had been an intensity neither of them could ignore. and that they shared brief moments when he was back in Hull once a year. They wrote letters in between – missives that she sent to his office and he sent to my mother's friend Sheena at the Women's Institute, so they would be kept secret. She had felt terribly guilty about their moments, but adored him, and couldn't not see him. He said her eyes shone when they were together, while my then-father was working. When she suddenly found out she was pregnant with me, she wrote and told Bill. She knew I wasn't Robert's baby. Their sex was apparently infrequent, and the dates didn't add up. Fortunately, Robert wasn't savvy about this and never questioned when I arrived a 'little early'.

She said to my real dad, 'Now I have a piece of you.'

I asked him once why she never left my cruel first father.

'It was one of those things that never happened,' he said. 'My wife, Gabrielle, kept thinking *she* was pregnant, so I stayed. Your mum was afraid to leave Robert, much as she wanted to. It just ... wasn't to be. And times were different then. There was no support for women, and still a lot of judgement about divorce.'

Dad found out from a newspaper that my mum had died in the car, at Robert's hand. He had been planning to visit her after his next talk but saw the article before he could go to their usual meeting spot in a café. He knew from a letter he received later – the overseas mail was painfully slow then – that Robert had found out about me not being his; and this was the reason for the murder-suicide. He said that being unable to grieve properly or go to the funeral was agony; and knowing he had, in part, caused her death would forever haunt him.

Back home, he confessed the nine-year affair to his wife, Gabrielle.

She eventually agreed to forgive him and take me in, since they had never been able to have children together. But not Heather, she said. This was her condition, her punishment, if you will, for his affair. And Dad had known this when he applied to care for me and then came for me that day. Understandably, my relationship with Gabrielle was strained at times.

When we first got to America, I wrote to Heather at the care home for months, but got no answer. I saw her over and over in her head, smiling as I walked away from her that last time. Bill, as he was then, said he was still trying to bring her over to us. Then, one day, after I'd been there months, he sat me down and said we were too late. Heather had gone to another family. He obviously knew as he said it that he had never intended to bring her over; now he had a real reason for me to give up the dream.

'Did she forget me?' I sobbed. 'She got sick of waiting; I know it.'

'No, not at all,' he insisted. 'These things are so complicated.'

'But why didn't she write back to me?' I cried.

'Maybe...' Bill looked thoughtful. 'Maybe they told her you were here, and how hard it was proving to send her over here too, and she simply wanted you to be happy. She let you go so that you could find happiness with us. That's how much she loves you.' I know he must have felt bad telling me these lies. He told me in later years that he had desperately wanted to bring us both, but it would have meant the end of his marriage.

I cried for weeks. Months.

And then I didn't.

Then, as children do, I adapted.

I don't know what the care home told Heather after I'd gone, after that final night of my cold feet and her warm gesture. I have no idea what happened to her. I have no clue whether she blames me; whether she even remembers me.

Dad bought me an out-of-tune upright piano when I was ten, but it was never the same without Heather to my right. It was like the notes had lost their clarity. Like my fingers no longer knew how to dance. Dad also gave up the job that meant he travelled so much; I never knew if it was at Gabrielle's insistence or to be home with me. Sadly, they divorced when I was fifteen. I always felt guilty that my presence caused the separation. This was ridiculous; he had the affair that began it all. But children often shoulder burdens that are not theirs to carry.

I was a rebellious teen, feisty and full of fight. Once Dad revealed to me that he'd known all along we wouldn't be bringing Heather to the US, I gave him hell. I played angry songs on the piano late at night and then climbed out of the window and ran off with local 'bad' boys, returning in the morning, tired and sweary, ranting at my dad for stealing my sister from me.

I settled down eventually. Grew up.

Forgave him.

Started playing my part of 'Nothing Else' again instead of the angry songs.

Dad died nine years ago – cancer of the pancreas. Sera was only eleven and was devastated at the loss of her beloved Grandpa, a man who – once he had retired – spent every free moment with her, collecting rock samples on walks and swimming in the ocean. I was glad Dad had come into my world. I was glad my mother found brief happiness with him during a terrible marriage that left her dead at a young age. And I knew my darling Sera would not exist if he hadn't brought me to America.

But I had to give Heather up for it all.

After Dad died, I found letters my mother had written him all those years ago, hidden in a shoebox. During my grief at his death, I found again the woman I'd lost so long ago. I read her passionate, flowing, curled words and could hear her voice for the first time in years. It was also there that I found the picture that was now framed on the bureau. I kept her notes in a box with the baseball cards Dad had collected and some of the rocks he'd found with Sera.

♪

Now, I paused, there in my bedroom, with no lights on, and put Dad's photograph down, wanting to read one of my mother's letters, to feel as close to her as they always made me feel. But it was late.

Instead, I went into my jewellery box and found the charm bracelet I'd bought that first day with the man called Bill, safe in the secret compartment alongside the quaver pendant. It was silver, the moon, star, and ballerina tarnished a little at the edges. I put it to my cheek, then returned it to its sacred spot and went to bed.

In the morning, the alarm, at its highest volume, eventually pulled me from a sleep that felt drugged. I'd taken ages to drop off, worrying about my hearing and what it would mean for my life. When I sat up, it was my sight that I questioned. The room was soft in the dawn light. But the scene was harsh.

My wardrobe doors were wide; drawers hung open like slumping, old hammocks; the bedroom door was ajar when I knew I'd closed it; and my jewellery box was on its side and empty. I gasped. Someone had come into my room. Who? When? *How?* Were they still here? I'd left my phone charging in the living room so I couldn't call anyone from my bed. I must have remained there for ten minutes, straining to hear if anyone was in my apartment, angry at the impediment that hindered me from knowing for sure.

Eventually, I got up, crept to the door, heart hammering. I thought I might be sick. So many people I knew had guns, but I was too English, even after all these years, and refused to possess such a thing. After an eternity, I tiptoed into the hallway and slowly approached the living room. There, the same carnage: coffee table overturned, expensive paintings gone, leaving faded squares on the wall; bureau ransacked, no sign of my laptop or my phone. But no one there. Not in the kitchen or the other rooms. I went to the front door, where the chain had been cut, and locked it, knowing I'd never feel safe again.

With no landline, I'd no way of calling anyone. I went to my neighbour Jill, stammered an explanation, and used her phone to ring the police, though I barely heard their responses to my garbled words. Jill wanted to come and sit with me, but I insisted not, that I was OK.

Two officers arrived, a too-young man and an older woman with a kind face; I wondered absentmindedly if she was always sent to lone women who'd been violated.

'I'm Officer Seabold,' she said gently. I had to study her hard to hear the words. 'Shall I get some coffee on the go for us?'

Her kindness broke the seal, and I started to cry, pointing to the kitchen so she could make the drinks.

'I'm Officer Jenson,' said the man. Fortunately, he had a loud, clear voice. 'Do you want to tell me what happened?'

But I couldn't stop crying. I rarely let go like that. The incident – being a crime, a violation, an invasion – made me picture my poor mother drowning at the hands of that monster. I had only known this horror since Dad got ill ten years ago and finally shared what he knew about her true end. That it had not been an accident.

Now, with so many of my belongings gone, I cried for it all: for my murdered mother, for my fading hearing, for my raided home. For my lost sister.

'Take your time,' said Officer Jensen. 'Can we call anyone to be with you?'

'I guess my daughter,' I sobbed, though I wanted to keep this from her, protect her. At the same time, I longed for her. 'But I don't have a ... I don't ... I can't...'

Officer Seabold brought three mugs of coffee and sat next to me.

'I can call her,' said Officer Jensen.

I gave him the number. He got hold of her, but I was too upset to speak, so he told her what had happened and then hung up. 'She's going to get on a train,' he said, 'so she should be with you by this evening.'

'Can you tell us what happened?' asked Officer Seabold, still so gently I turned to watch her mouth. 'What was taken?'

'I must have been asleep.' My voice broke.

How had I not even heard anything?

The question came despite the answer already being lodged deep in my chest.

'I woke and ... it was like this. It's the same in the bedroom. Oh,

God.' I stood, cold. Without explaining my fear to them, I ran to my room, to my overturned jewellery box. Hand trembling, I opened the secret compartment. Thank God. Still there. The quaver pendant and the silver charm bracelet.

Officer Seabold followed me into the room, looking around sadly at the mess.

'If you could leave things how they are, just for now,' she said, 'that would be helpful. Someone will come and brush for prints this morning and then you can tidy up.'

I nodded, still holding my precious items to my chest.

'Will your daughter be able to stay with you for a few days?'

'Yes, perhaps.' How would I feel when she was gone?

'Someone will change the locks today. We'll get them to fit some extra security for you too.' Officer Seabold paused. 'Didn't you set the alarm?'

'I always forget,' I admitted, wondering if I'd have even heard it. Surely I would, a sound so shrill. 'I felt so safe in this building. I won't now.'

'These things rarely happen,' she said. 'And we'll do all we can to find who did this.'

I didn't care. I didn't want my things back.

They wouldn't be the same now.

When they had gone, when I had listed everything I could see that was missing, and they had been more honest about how small the likelihood was of me seeing my items again, I closed the door and leaned on it until I felt strong enough.

Then I went to the piano. Thank God such an item would prove impossible to steal. I sat on the seat, on my side, as though Heather was with me again. I saw us in Mr Hibbert's house, the scent of freshly cut flowers sharp in the air. I saw us in the back room at the old house – mini Chopins. I *felt* her. So powerfully, I turned around. Nothing. No one. And yet I had never felt so strongly before that she was somehow closer. I put my fingers on the keys and played my part of our song; I would invoke her with the music. But I could barely hear it. I played harder. Then I heard the notes.

But they were not mine. They were hers. I heard them like I hadn't in so long. I saw the keys dipping and rising as though her fingers danced there.

It felt like that day when we played outside. That day when my then-father was suddenly cold and indifferent with me. When he acted like I didn't exist anymore. The day I now know that he had found out I wasn't his golden child after all. That I wasn't *his* child at all. It felt like that day, when we played our song in the garden.

Except now I was alone.

44

Sera got to my apartment just after five. She had clearly left university in a hurry; her hair was hastily clipped up, her face was bare of make-up, and she only had a rucksack and was starving hungry. She hugged me in the hallway, something she had never done. It was all I could do not to cry again at the sight of her.

'I didn't want you to come.' I was exhausted now.

'Thanks, Mom. Nice welcome.'

'No, I didn't mean it like that. I mean … just … this isn't your problem. You have enough on your plate with all your work an—'

'Jesus, Mom, of course I'm gonna come home when you've been burglarised.' She paused. I was reading her lips but tried to hide it. 'Does Dad know?'

'Not yet.' I went into the living room, and she followed me. 'I don't have a phone. I'll tell him when I get a new one.'

The fingerprint team had been, and I had tidied up after they left, though no amount of scrubbing and polishing would erase the feeling that this beautiful apartment was sullied now.

When Sera saw the gaps where my paintings had been, her eyes filled up. 'Oh, Mom,' she said, going to the empty wall. 'You loved them. This is so sad. The evil fucking fuckers. What else did they take?' I didn't hear the rest because she was looking at the square spaces.

'Sorry?'

She turned to me. 'I said I guess you can replace certain things with the insurance money, but not the paintings.'

'No. Or my jewellery. They took those diamond earrings your dad got me.'

'No. Oh, Mom. I'm so sorry.'

'It isn't your fault.'

'You didn't hear them, did you,' she said.

I couldn't answer.

'It's getting worse, isn't it,' she said. 'Your lack of hearing.'

'I don't want to talk about it right now,' I snapped. 'I've enough to deal with.' I didn't tell her that in the post a few hours ago I'd received two appointments for further tests: one with a neurologist in three days, and one at the diabetes clinic the day after that. 'I'll cook for us. Spag bol, OK?'

She followed me into the kitchen, where I rummaged in the fridge and began frying the minced beef and chopping onions. I knew she was talking to me, but I couldn't hear it all without turning to look at her. I let the tears fall. I could blame the onions. A hand landed on my shoulder. I finally turned and looked at my beautiful, willowy daughter.

'Maybe it's better I didn't hear those intruders,' I said. 'The blessing, really, is that I slept through it.' I laughed, but it was more of a bark. 'They must've wondered what the hell was wrong with me, not even stirring.'

'Oh, Mom, it's not funny,' said Sera. 'Can I have some wine?'

'Of course. Help yourself. I will too.'

She poured us both a large one. 'You're not just moderately deaf, are you?'

I could pretend I hadn't heard. But, ironically, I had. I shrugged and sipped my wine.

'What did the doctor really say?' she asked.

'That I'm moderately deaf.'

'For God's sake,' cried Sera, and I heard every word. 'Quit the bullshit. It's worse than that. Why are you in such denial? There's stuff they can do, surely. Hearing aids. You should know, you can sign, and you worked with those hard of hearing kids.'

'Because I'm scared,' I snapped. There it was. The truth.

Sera put her glass down and came and lay her head on my shoulder as I mixed the sauce in the frying pan. 'It'll be OK,' she said close to my ear, so her lovely, weird-accented voice was rich, warm and clear in my head. 'Some of those hearing aids are invisible, so no one need ever know you're old and decrepit.'

I laughed. 'It's not just about that.'

'I know, I know. I can't imagine. It must be scary.'

'I'm not ready for the world to go quiet,' I said.

'It never will be,' she said. 'I'm here. And I'll never shut up.'

I kissed her forehead and then served our food, and we took it into the living room, where we sat on the sofa with the TV on. Since I'd lived alone, I rarely ate at the table. And Sera was happy to be as slovenly as I was. I occasionally wondered if my aversion to family meals at a dining table came from my early childhood, when food often ended up on the floor, and we never knew what mood my then-father would be in.

Sera fell asleep, as she almost always did on my sofa, so I covered her with a blanket, but I couldn't leave her there. I was afraid that if I went to bed and someone broke in again, I wouldn't hear, and they would hurt my girl. I got my duvet and lay on the floor alongside the sofa. I kept imagining sounds – I *knew* I had to be imagining them – and got up to go and see that the door was still locked. I couldn't settle.

When I did, I dreamt of a car hurtling into water. I woke chilled to the bone. I knew the burglary had triggered it, the feelings of life not being in my control, of dark things happening that could change everything, of losing what I had. I lay in the half-light, thinking of my mother. The day before her death she wrote to my real dad and told him that my then-father knew I wasn't his. He had found some of their letters, ones she had risked hiding between the tea towels so she could swiftly and surreptitiously slip them out and read them when she desperately wanted to, to stay sane. Unfortunately, one of them was Dad's loving response to the news that he had made my mother pregnant.

Dad heard no more from my mother for weeks – he had never had a phone number to call her on, or her home address, because she was afraid. So he had to wait until he was next in England and he contacted her friend at the Women's Institute, and of course, then he saw the newspaper article. When he told me how my mother had really perished, what my then-father really was, I died a little too. I wondered if, wherever she was, Heather knew. Would it have been easier if we had found out together and could share the agony? We could have played 'Nothing Else' and balanced the black with white, the ugly with beauty, the pain with music.

I slept again, deeply then, fortunately. Until a hand woke me. I gasped, confused about where I was. Sera's face loomed above me. 'What the hell are you doing down there, you weirdo?' she hissed.

Protecting you, I thought. 'I didn't want to wake you,' I said.

We both went to bed; she slept in mine like when she was tiny and had a nightmare. I curled my body around hers and wished Heather could meet her. How she would love her, this young woman who was both of us in one human, feisty like me, willowy like Heather, and utterly perfect, like herself.

Sera stayed another night, and then I went back to work. It was better to be there and lost in books than at home. I got a new phone and laptop. But each time I entered the apartment in the evening, I was nervous. I thought about moving, but then why should I? Fate had pushed me around too many times when I was little. I would fight her all the way now.

45

Anxiety at my hearing loss and the shock of the burglary was how I ended up inside a small travel agency tucked away on a side street a week later, seduced by the last-minute deals on their board. I hadn't been thinking about getting away, but when I saw the pictures of blue skies and palm trees, I realised it had been years since I'd gone anywhere, and it was exactly what I needed right now. I had gone to my two appointments a few days ago. The results to both had come back fine: I passed the neurological exam, and I didn't have diabetes. But this only meant a return visit to the audiologist, which I hadn't booked, though I knew I should.

I deserved to get away instead.

Inside the small space filled with plants and exotic posters, I took a seat opposite a tanned woman who asked where I fancied going and when – thankfully with a booming voice.

'I don't mind where, but as soon as possible.' Aside from for my recent appointments and the few days around the burglary, I'd taken no time off that year so far.

She tapped away on her computer with blood-red nails. 'Just you?'

I thought about it. Sera wouldn't be able to get away at such short notice. I couldn't expect anyone else to come. Plus, the idea of a trip on my own sounded like heaven. 'Yes, just me.'

Just me. I heard the words again in my own head. Except I didn't say them. Someone else did. Who? I saw a woman on a balcony, sea and ships beyond. I shook my head, sure I must be losing my mind as well as my hearing.

'Anytime?' the travel agent was asking.

Still, I saw this woman. It looked like an English city. Not Hull, I thought. I couldn't see her face, but her hair was as light as the sun. 'Just me' she said.

'Anytime?' repeated the travel agent.

The vision died. But something remained. A sense. A sense of a woman embarking on a trip. A sense of ... *I must go too*.

'Yes, anytime, just soon,' I said with new urgency.

What had just happened?

'Cruises make a great trip for solo travellers,' she said, head tipped. 'They can sit you at a table with other solo travellers in the evening and—'

'Oh, that wouldn't be necessary,' I said, still distracted. 'I just want to read and relax and escape.'

'Ah, cruises are perfect for that. Shall I look at some options for you?'

Cruises. The woman in my vision had been looking out at ships. I'd never been on a cruise, despite so many sailings out of New York and enjoying many a walk past the harbour, but the idea of being at sea sounded like bliss.

'What have you got?'

'The soonest available is in ten days. August eleventh. Too soon?'

That's the one, I thought. 'No, perfect.' I would use recent events as an excuse, take compassionate leave.

'Can you do two weeks away?' asked the tanned travel agent.

I was sure I could. 'Yes,' I said.

'Do you want to know where it goes?' I wasn't bothered but she told me anyway. 'It sails from New York Harbour and visits Barbados, St Kitts, St Maarten and Tortola, with plenty of days at sea in between so you can do your reading and relaxing too. There's lots to do. While you're at sea there are art auctions, writing workshops, and dance lessons. And the shopping aboard is world class, with stores selling—'

'What the hell, just book it,' I said.

'My kind of customer,' she smiled. 'Impulsive.'

I smiled too.

'You'll have to pay in full with it being so close. Is that OK?'

'Sure, whatever.'

I left the agency with a detailed brochure. I had to sit down on a nearby bench. What on earth had happened in there? Was I hallucinating now? And yet it hadn't felt like that. It felt like I saw someone, far away. And it felt like ... Could it have been ... *Heather*? Was it because I'd been thinking of the past a lot recently? Yes. I decided that all the hearing appointments and the burglary had caused some sort of neurological reaction. That I was dreaming while awake, perhaps through exhaustion.

I went home.

It was the day before I set sail when I finally picked up the cruise brochure and flicked through the pages, excited now. My suitcase sat in the corner, matching hand luggage on top. I'd been buying new clothes and bikinis through the week, and some paperbacks I wanted to read, just to look at the competition. Sera had been impressed by my 'adventure', as she called it. 'Mom,' she said in a FaceTime chat. 'You go get yours, girl.' I didn't dare ask what she wanted me to go and get, but I was sure that whatever it was, I'd at least pretend to her that I'd found it.

I was excited to read about the daily art auction; in a colourful article it said it would include some genuine pieces by an artist I loved, so maybe I could get some new work for my walls. The restaurants looked good too, with one run by a New York chef I liked. I looked at the shows – *Mamma Mia* and *Broadway at Sea* – and who the DJ was, not that I would be going clubbing.

Then I turned a page.

And I saw ... *her*.

Saw the words: 'Heather Harris, our resident pianist.'

Saw the picture.

Heather.

I could not process the image. I shut the magazine, sat for ten minutes, more, with it in my shaking hand, heart choking me, throat taut. It couldn't be her. I was seeing things, like I had in the travel agency.

Then I opened the brochure again at that page.

It *was* her. My Heather. My sister. Unmistakable. Older, but the girl I remembered still there, hiding behind the new wrinkles on the face, wearing a black blouse that tied at the neck, not the dungarees we often played out in; lips painted red, not smeared with chocolate after we'd finished off our mother's cake mix; golden hair swept up, not wild from playing songs for hours at a time; sitting next to a polished, black baby-grand piano. Of course. Where else? I looked closer. Was there space on that piano seat for me? There was.

On the left.

I'd always hoped that a chance meeting, a coincidence, fate, would bring Heather to me.

I sobbed into my hands like a small child.

Then I laughed. Put the brochure to my chest. Studied the image again, unable to get enough of it, taking in every shadow, every tiny flaw, every laugh line, because she was real, real, *real*. She was alive. She still played music, obviously did it for a living. She would be doing so on the very cruise I had chosen. But no. I hadn't. It had chosen me. I remembered feeling I had given the universe a helping hand when I visited Hull; a grand opportunity like those in the books I edited to somehow send her my way in the brief two-week window of my trip.

Now it had sent her to New York. I realised, if the ship was sailing tomorrow, she must either be on it, or in the city having flown here to then board. I paced the room, unable to contain my excitement at the thought of her closeness. Was there a way to find her, now, before we set sail tomorrow? She was near, yet still so far. This was almost worse than when I'd had no idea where she was, because now she was real, she was in my city, and I couldn't do anything.

That day seemed like the longest I'd known. I couldn't concentrate on reading. On the TV; nothing held my attention. Even the piano didn't calm me: my fingers were clumsy, heavy dancers, except with two left thumbs.

In the middle of the night, awake, still I was anxious that Heather might not even *want* to see me. That she might not have forgiven me for leaving her. Perhaps there was something I could do to ensure she did?

I got up and found the quaver pendant and then an envelope. I thought of writing a letter but had no idea what I should say. So I simply placed the chain inside and wrote her name on the front. Then I got the framed picture of our mother, the letters she had written to my dad, and the charm bracelet, and packed them in my case.

I finally fell asleep.

♪

I got a taxi to the harbour at eleven, my stomach churning. The *Queen of the Seas* was white and sleek, and put me in mind, curiously, of a large swan. Her trim along the decks was navy blue and the only thing that broke the expanse of white was her name on the side, also in navy blue. I knew as I stood on the dock, the wind pushing me towards the check-in, as though it was a helping hand from the universe, that my sister was somewhere aboard this vessel.

Once I'd gone through check-in, up an elevator and along a gangway, room key in hand, I found myself in a beautiful reception area with a grand, curved staircase, glass elevators, and a rather ostentatious marble-and-gold mermaid sculpture that spouted water. I approached the main desk.

'Good afternoon, ma'am,' said the cheery receptionist. 'Welcome aboard the *Queen of the Seas*. How can I help you today?'

'Good morning ... I wondered ... well, is it possible...' I took the envelope from my hand luggage. 'I know someone on your staff, and I wondered if you might be able to have this delivered to their cabin?'

'I can see if we can get hold of them to come up here?' she suggested, pink lipstick smile perfect.

'Oh, no, that won't be necessary.' I wanted to give Heather a clue that I was here. To give her time to let it in. To give me time to continue letting it in. To let us find our way to one another. 'The name on the envelope is her old name, but she's Heather Harris on here.'

'Ah, yes, our pianist,' she smiled.

'Your pianist,' I said.

'I'll make sure someone takes it to her cabin. Is there a message?'

I shook my head. 'No, thank you.'

I didn't quite know what to do next. Where was Heather right now? What was she doing? What if I saw her on my way around the ship? In the end, I found my cabin on deck seven and unpacked in the pastel room with a small balcony, which for now overlooked the harbour. It would be my home for the next two weeks. A home I would share with my sister for the first time in thirty-seven years.

I recalled the time long ago, when we first played 'Nothing Else' for Mr Hibbert. He asked us: 'How do you feel when you play this song, and the not-nice things are happening in the house?'

'Like we're floating above it all,' I said.

We would float now on the sea; united.

HEATHER
(PRIMO)

46

Now, I wanted to play music again. Now, I felt like myself again.

I must have sat for half an hour, perched on the edge of my narrow cabin bed like a patient awaiting life-changing news from a doctor, bristling with renewed energy, my hand over the quaver pendant, as though to stop anyone taking it away again. I still couldn't believe it had appeared under my door. It *must* have been her, or at least someone on her behalf.

She must have kept it, all this time.

Harriet.

And she must be *here*. On this ship. Somewhere. Somehow. I couldn't take it in. I said it aloud: 'My sister is here.' And still it felt unreal.

Did she live in New York? If so, I could have walked past her on the street. Had she come from somewhere else to board the cruise? How had she known I was here? Was that why she had booked the trip? Was she alone or with a family? What did she look like now? The questions whirled in an endless cycle, no answers to stem them.

We were leaving New York, a city I'd barely taken in after the shock of learning the truth about our mother's death. For years, the fear of my past had prevented me from looking properly for Harriet. Now I knew it all, I was free to find her. But perhaps I didn't need to. She had found me.

More questions came, over and over.

Had my mother – somehow, from somewhere beyond this earth – put this into action. Had she witnessed my grief at learning of her violent death and stepped in from some other world to send my sister back to me?

Did I believe such things?

I realised it was almost four-thirty. I had to be in the Piano Bar in an hour. I must go about my sea life now. I must perform. But there were more questions: Would Harriet be there? Was that her plan? Had she gently let me know about her presence with the chain and would then turn up for my set?

With clumsy fingers, I dressed for the performance. I unbuttoned the top of my cream blouse so the pendant was visible, flashing in the fluorescent light like a gold wink. I put my hair up so nothing would detract from the charm.

Then I headed for deck seven, weaving along the shabby below-decks passages, greeting crew I knew, and striding down the lushly carpeted corridors above, expectation fire in my heels. New guests gazed over the polished rails, in awe of the atrium below, gushing at how luxurious the ship was, just as the previous holidaymakers had done over a week ago. It was all new to them. In a way it was to me too; I knew my full history now. And we were heading for a new destination, new waters – the Caribbean. And my sister could be a passenger.

I studied the guests as they passed me, face after face after face.

Were they her? Would I know?

Would I sense her?

Was she going to come and see me perform?

The Piano Bar was full. I'd missed the dim lighting, ebony décor, and my – it *was* mine – black baby grand in the centre. It felt like forever since I'd been here. Michaela and her staff bustled about, serving cocktails and warm smiles. She put a glass of water on the bar for me, said, 'Welcome back, honey. Here we go again!'

I spotted Frederica at a table with a young woman whose name my mind hunted for – Carla, one of the dancers, eventually came to me – and I joined them.

'We were just talking about Barry Lung's disappearance,' said Frederica. She looked healthy, golden brown, and was dressed in rich crimson.

'Of course. Sarah Briggs introduced a new comedian earlier, didn't she?' I sipped my wine. I hadn't been concentrating then. I barely could now. I scanned the faces in the room.

'He didn't come back to the ship,' said Carla. 'Completely disappeared.'

'What do you reckon happened?' I returned my attention to them.

'Who knows,' said Frederica. 'Killed by the mob, joined the circus, died laughing at one of his own jokes...'

I giggled. 'Imagine that.'

'What a lovely necklace.' Carla reached to touch it.

'Thank you.' I looked at Frederica. 'I think she's here,' I said.

'Who?' Frederica smiled, added, 'Beyoncé? Taylor Swift? Michelle Obama?'

'Harriet,' I said.

'What? You mean ... *your* Harriet? How do you know?'

'Who's Harriet?' asked Carla.

'Her sister,' said Frederica. 'They haven't seen each other for...?'

'Thirty-seven years.' The words choked me.

'What happened?' asked Frederica.

'I woke in my cabin earlier and someone had posted this under the door.' I touched the necklace again. 'It's the one I gave her the last night we were together.'

'It's like something I'd write,' cried Frederica. 'She *must* be here then. Do you think it's a coincidence? That she ... well, just turned up and saw your name around the ship somewhere?'

'I don't know.' I looked at the time. I had to play in five minutes.

'Was there a note with it?'

'No.'

'She could really be here.'

'I know.'

'How do you feel?'

'Just...' I couldn't find the words, sitting there, suspended between the last trip and this one, a woman out at sea, all the answers to everything I wanted to know right on the tip of my tongue. I thought suddenly about telling Dan and Tamsin, but it would wait. 'I feel ready ... but yet not.' When we were alone, I'd tell Frederica the truth about the car crash, but not now, just before I had to play. I hadn't digested it fully myself.

I stood. It was time.

I made my way to the piano, my knees as weak as the first time I'd played here. I glanced around the room at the happy, flushed people, looking for the auburn hair that fell in waves, that no matter if you dampened it or brushed it hard, it always sprang back as curls. Harriet wasn't here.

I sat. Heard the long-ago reminder from Mr Hibbert to sit up straight, to keep the neck in line with the spine, to relax the shoulders, to hold the elbows a comfortable distance from the body. Hearing his voice calmed me. I made sure there was space on the left for Harriet; I glanced at the spot and then at the room again. I waited. The bar fell quiet. She didn't come.

I played alone.

I gave them the eighties hits that the previous guests had enjoyed, took requests, and answered the questions from this lively crowd. After each song, I waited a few seconds. But she still didn't make herself known. It didn't make sense. Maybe she wasn't on the ship after all. Maybe she had asked someone to deliver the necklace on her behalf. Maybe she would make herself known once we returned to New York in two weeks.

How would I wait that long without knowing?

And what if she didn't?

The applause when I finished was rapturous. I joined Frederica, who now sat alone. 'You get better and better,' she said. 'I could listen to you forever.'

'Thank you.' I was touched, but still distracted, looking around.

'Surely if she's on the ship, she'll come.'

'But what if she isn't?'

Frederica didn't seem to know what to say. After a while, she said, 'Hey, did you share those gorgeous pictures I took on social media yet?' When I didn't answer she asked, 'Did you retweet the footage? Follow me, I shared it. I'm @franniewriter.'

I hadn't thought about that since I'd looked through the photos on my Nikon before leaving the ship, surprising myself with how much I'd liked them. I'd meant to upload them onto my platforms in the hotel, but completely forgotten. 'I ... I will...'

'Wanna get something to eat?' she asked.

It felt like a routine older than time. It anchored me. 'OK,' I said.

We headed for deck eight, through the Queen's Parade shopping mall; the designer bags in the guests' hands were gaudy, flashes of bold print and colour, as though they were trying to outdo one another. We grabbed some pizza and went outside to eat on the deckchairs. I inhaled the salty air. I'd missed it. The sun was heavy in the sky, though not low enough to kiss the horizon. It hovered, seductively close. The water waited for that full kiss.

'Did you enjoy New York?' I studied every woman who walked past.

'Yeah. We went out clubbing, did a show, and I spent way too much. How about you? I felt for you, being on your own.'

'It was probably best,' I said.

'Why?'

I composed myself. 'Before I left the ship, I found something in my care records.'

'Oh, yes?'

'A newspaper cutting. About the car accident.' I couldn't even remember if I'd told Frederica about it, so I explained how I'd thought my parents died in a car accident. That now I knew my father had driven it into the water on purpose, with my mother as his passenger. I put the remains of my pizza down, appetite gone.

'Heather, that's awful. I'm so sorry.' Frederica put her pizza down too. 'I can see why that was kept from you when you were small. But why didn't anyone tell you when you grew up?'

'My adoptive mother is gone now, so I'll never know whether she was oblivious or whether she was protecting me.'

'Poor you, wandering around New York, knowing this.' Frederica touched my arm.

'My father was horrible to Harriet the day it happened, and I've never known why.' I glanced at Frederica; she was listening intently, food forgotten. 'She was his favourite. I never minded because I loved her so much. But that day ... all of a sudden ... she wasn't.'

'I don't know what to say.'

I nodded. I didn't either.

'And she could be here now,' cried Frederica.

'I know.' The sun was lower, lip to lip with the horizon now. 'But if she is, why didn't she come and see me play?'

'She might come later, to the Sunset Bar.'

'I suppose.' I was deflated after the excitement earlier.

'It's going to happen. Why would she give you back your necklace and then not find you?'

'I can't sit here like this,' I said suddenly. 'I have to look for her.'

'Yes,' cried Frederica.

I stood. 'I can't just *wait*.' I looked at my phone. 'I've got half an hour until I play again. I'm going to search the ship...'

'Want me to come?'

'No, I'll be fine.'

I started on the top deck, where the pool was, looking out of place amidst the bikini-clad guests. Would Harriet be here though, having fun and not looking for me? No matter: I searched. One woman with auburn hair caught my eye. But she was too young. I came down to deck eleven to the casino, the flashing machines as fast as my heart, keeping beat with my feet. It was deserted. I hurried to the top of the atrium, mindful of the time, racing down the grand staircase. I knew my hair was frizzed, my brow damp, but with every step, it felt more urgent that I find her.

A woman on deck nine – cascading reddish hair down her back, face turned away to study a menu – caught my eye. It was *her*. I was sure of it.

'Harriet.' I grabbed her arm, spun her around.

Not her; I knew immediately.

'Do you mind?' she demanded.

'I'm so sorry, I thought...'

She shrugged me off and marched away.

I wanted to cry. I couldn't bear it. Where *was* she?

And it was time for me to perform again.

When I arrived in the Sunset Bar it was full. The first night, and guests were ready for life at sea. Elegant, they milled about the softly lit room with fizzing champagne glasses; some of the men clearly weren't accustomed to wearing tuxedos and fiddled with their bow ties. I spotted Ruth and Gerry, remembering they were on this cruise too. Frederica was sitting with one of the dancers she knew.

I felt detached from it all.

I went to my piano. I surveyed the fog of faces: all strangers, none the one person I longed to see. I realised the crowd was waiting for me to start playing; the room had fallen silent. I gave them Chopin. I gave them Bach. I gave them Beethoven. I gave them everything I had.

I feared the end of the set. Should I play my part of 'Nothing Else' in the hope of summoning Harriet – a white witch incanting a spell to find her soulmate. But I didn't think I could bear it if the invocation failed.

'I'm going to finish,' I said just before eleven, 'with a song of my own. Guests on my previous cruise seemed to enjoy it at the end of the evening. I hope you do too. Thank you for joining me.' I was about to play, then added quickly, 'Oh, it's called "A Sense of Light" and I dedicate it to my friend, Frederica.'

She was at the bar with the dancer whose name again evaded me and smiled and raised her glass. Then I gave them the last song.

I willed Harriet to emerge from the crowd, having held back until the very end. Ruth and Gerry took to the floor in the centre of the room and danced slowly, eyes only on one another. Cameras flashed, both at them and at me, silver capturing an eternal moment. No Harriet. I bowed for the applause and joined Frederica.

'No?' she said, and I knew what she was asking.

'No,' I said.

'I'm sorry.'

'I'm going to my room.'

'OK. You sure?'

'It's been a long day.'

'Coming to my workshop tomorrow?'

'Yes,' I said. 'See you there.'

I took the long way back to my cabin, looking in every bar and restaurant doorway, scanning the rooms. In my room, I peeled off my clothes and stood under the shower, hot water merging with tears. The joy I'd felt at first seeing the quaver pendant disappearing with the steam curling away from the bathroom door.

I couldn't sleep. My mind whirled. I wanted to close the lid on the insistent keyboard, but the erratic song wouldn't cease. In the end, I sat up and got my phone, hoping to distract myself. I found Frederica on Twitter and followed her back. I shared her pictures and video footage of me playing.

Maybe Harriet would see it too. The hashtags Frederica had used were #PianoGirl and #HeatherHarris and #ASenseOfLight. I'd looked for Harriet on here and on other platforms before, using both our childhood surname and words that might be key, like 'music' and 'piano' and 'Nothing Else'.

Now, she was so close.

Eventually, I feel asleep, phone still in hand. I slept erratically, the blue light and the re-shares and the comments perhaps somehow infiltrating my night rhythms.

I dreamt I was searching for Harriet along endless corridors that grew longer the faster I ran. I knew she'd be around the next bend, but each corner yielded a crowd of drunken guests who prevented me going on. They took out their phones and filmed my distress, moving closer to capture the tears on my cheek, clicking frenziedly as I begged them to let me past. I managed to escape outside, to a moonlit deck where flecks of white light were discarded ribbons on the waves. Harriet was there too, at the ship's stern, the railings curving around her in an embrace. But as I approached, she climbed up the metal rungs and leapt into the sea.

I woke with a gasp, my hand over the necklace.

Just a nightmare. Just my own anxieties manifested into dreadful dreams.

Just the darkness.

In the morning I went for breakfast in the crew café, hungry despite it all, my voracious sea appetite back. It was comforting to see familiar faces again, dancers and musicians and shop workers, the ones whose names I still didn't know but with whom I always shared a cheery hello, and those whose names I knew and had become briefly acquainted with in the five-minute moments we caught here and there. And of course, Frederica, who arrived ten minutes after me, looking tired but happy.

'Late night?' I asked when she sat opposite me with juice and eggs.

'Oh, God,' she groaned. 'There was a crew party until three.'

'Why did you get up so early then?' I laughed.

'I haven't planned my workshop yet.' She glugged her juice. 'What the hell should I do it about, eh, Heather?'

'Didn't you say that you're working on a book about writing? Maybe talk about that.'

I glanced at the TV screen that charted the ship's journey. It would be another two days until we reached Road Town, Tortola. Another two days of everyone on the ship being unable to go anywhere else. Another two days of wondering if today would be when I saw Harriet.

As though hearing my thoughts, Frederica said, 'Maybe today?'

'Maybe. I'm going to look around again after this.'

'Go knock on all the cabin doors.' Frederica was joking, but I was considering it.

'Thank God I have my music to distract me, eh?' I said.

'That's it,' said Frederica, squeezing my arm. 'My workshop. I'll talk about how my writing got me through some difficult times ... you know, the power of the arts to uplift and transport...'

Didn't I know this so well?

After breakfast I had a meeting with Sarah Briggs in the crew office. It was positive: both my account of my experience onboard so far, and her feedback from the bar staff and guests. I returned to my cabin and dressed up so I could attend Frederica's workshop before I entertained the lunchtime crowd in the Sky Lounge.

I moved through the ship, scrutinising every face that passed by, feeling taller than usual in my heels, buoyed by the guests who stopped me on my walk to say they had enjoyed my music, and asking if I had CDs to sell. At home I had business cards to give to those who wanted piano lessons, but I had nothing here, now.

'You remind me of my mom,' said one guest, American, a young woman with an older man – I presumed her partner rather than her father from how he looked at her. 'She played in concert halls. I used to go when I was a kid and look up at her like she was some kind of goddess – because she made magic. So did you last night.'

I didn't know what to say. How could I feel blue after a compliment like that? How could I not feel grateful for this extraordinary opportunity, for the chance to do what I loved in a place like this?

In the theatre, I took my seat for Frederica's workshop. It was packed. Perhaps this cruise had sold out. Perhaps the people aboard loved reading. Perhaps they just knew and loved Frederica. Whatever the reason, I was happy for her. When she came onto the stage, I could tell by her reaction that she was speechless at the crowd.

'Well, well, well,' she said. 'Thank you all for attending. This is, really, quite lovely. I hope you'll be glad you came, and that we'll have some fun this morning. I hope too that you all have your imagination heads on, because we're going to do some writing prompts. But first, if you're thinking who the heck is this weird English writer, let me tell you a little about myself...'

After a ten-minute introduction, Frederica read a passage from her newest novel. I studied the faces around me. Would Harriet come to something like this? Did she love to read, to write? Frederica announced the first writing prompt.

'Think about how important art is in our everyday lives,' she said. 'What do we do to relax? We read, listen to music, watch dramas, visit galleries, look at beautiful paintings. Music evokes emotion. Imagine your favourite film without the soundtrack. Imagine the love scene without soft piano or a war film without hammering drums? Strange, huh? Now, I want you to reflect on a particular piece of music that helped you through a difficult time in your life. What was it about the piece that touched you?'

I didn't need to think about this. I stared at the blank sheet on my lap, unable to write. I thought about the day my parents died. I thought about the time before; the moment leading to our garden song. Our father's indifference towards his beloved Harriet. I thought of something I hadn't recalled until then. Something earlier that morning.

I started writing.

I was up early, disturbed by something, I'm not sure what. An argument? Possibly, though they were so customary it would have been unlikely to lead me down the stairs alone, to the piano. Did I somehow know it would be our last day in the house? Did I know everything was about to unravel? Did I sit there, my small fingers ready, preparing to play alone, because I knew soon I would have to play alone all the time? No. I can't have. I'm only thinking that as I write now. I didn't play 'Nothing Else', not without my Harriet. I played Chopin. Quietly. Gently, as he would have intended, poetry in the form of music. My father came into the room, and I paused, anticipating his grumble that it was early, expecting his gruff coolness. But he hovered there. 'Don't stop,' he said. I finished the piece. 'I never really listened to you,' he said. 'I don't know much about music, Heather. But I think yours is ... something else. It's you.' Then the rarest of affection; a kiss, on my forehead. 'I'm sorry.'

Frederica's voice interrupted. 'OK, that's time,' she said.

I shivered.

My father had said *sorry*. How had I not remembered it until then? What had opened me up to it? Frederica's prompt? Had the things I'd learned recently gently chipped away at the wall built around the forgotten memories? What had he been sorry for? For what he was about to do? For what he had already done?

'Anyone want to share their piece?' asked Frederica.

As I sneaked out along the aisle, a man with a walking stick hobbled to the stage and started reading about the time he played Queen's 'I Want To Break Free' at his second wife's funeral.

I walked along the deck, needing a blast of sea air before my performance. The wind snatched the new memory from my hand, sending the sheet of paper and my words overboard. I gasped and watched it fly away, somersaulting and then skimming the waves, until finally they saturated and swallowed it, drowning that one rare, better moment with my father. But there was no overlooking his murderous behaviour. Why had he been so violent? There were always things that drove us. I would never forgive that he had taken our mother, but could it have been learned behaviour? A lack of love? His dad had died when he was young, and Grandma Dolly was a cold woman – after all, she didn't want to care for Harriet and me when our parents passed. Did this excuse his behaviour? No. Many people had tough formative years and still found the strength to shine their light.

But maybe it was a reason.

In the Sky Lounge, Phillippe seemed happy to see me. His light was bright, as always. I had never sensed one so strong before and wondered what his homelife was, who he loved, how he lived. The place was busy, mostly older couples. I sipped my iced water and, as was now my habit, checked the faces for *her*. At one o'clock I walked to the piano. The waves rolled in the window behind me. At times, when I played, it was all instinct. I didn't hear the pieces. Like exercise, it's a routine you know; you do it without thought. Muscle memory. That afternoon, it passed that way. Except for when I played Debussy's 'Clair de Lune' for the first time in a while. A memory of Mr Hibbert performing it in his back room almost had me forget the next note.

At the end, when I stood, a woman with hair the colour of long-burning flames approached. My heart caught. *Harriet.*

But her hair was the wrong hue.

'You're going to think me a bit crazy,' she said, accent like the cast of *Gone with the Wind*, 'but I swear, in my head, I knew you'd play Don McLean's "Vincent". Then when you did, well, I...' She dabbed her eyes. 'It was our song ... my husband and me. I ... he passed away just six months ago, and ... well, this is my first trip without him.'

'I'm sorry,' I said.

'It was like he was with me again when you played.'

Afterwards, I got some pizza from the buffet café and sat on the deck, letting the sun burn my face. Should I knock on every cabin door to see if Harriet was there, as Frederica had suggested? What if something had happened to her and that was why she hadn't turned up at one of my sets? Then I realised something. I finished my snack and headed to the guest reception desk, impatient when I had to queue behind holidaymakers who had lost key cards or who weren't satisfied with room service.

Eventually I got to the front and asked the cheerful receptionist, 'Is it possible for you to tell me what room a guest is in?'

'I'm not supposed to,' she said with a smile that didn't falter.

'I'm the resident pianist, not a guest.' I realised she might not know this, and it might mean she was more likely to help.

'Yes, Heather Harris. I really shouldn't ... but, do you have the name?'

'Harriet Jo-' I started and then realised. It probably wasn't even her name. But it was worth a try. 'Harriet Johnson,' I said.

She tapped away on her computer. 'No one of that name,' she said.

'Damn. Could you find all the Harriets on the ship?'

She shook her head, still smiling. 'That I really can't do.'

'*Please?*'

She shook her head, still smiling. 'Wait,' she said. 'Someone came.'

'What do you mean? Where?'

'A woman,' said the receptionist. 'She came here the first day. Wanted me to get something sent to your cabin.'

'What did she look like?' My heart beat molto allegro.

'Um, maybe early forties ... reddish hair, clipped up ... pretty...'

'What did she say?' I knew I was speaking too fast.

'Well, after she asked if she could send the envelope to your cabin, I asked if she had a message and she said no. That was it. She just left.'

'She was definitely a guest?' I asked.

'Yes, she had luggage, had checked in.'

'Thank you.' I moved away to let her serve the guests behind me.

Harriet *was* on the ship. That was a fact. Somewhere. Here. *Near*. She must have her reasons for returning the necklace but remaining shy. I had to respect that. She would find me when she wanted to. I could wait. I had already waited thirty-seven years.

But what if something had happened to her? That was silly, I knew it.

I browsed the shops, trying to distract myself. I had a latte in the speciality coffee bar, where I sent messages to Tamsin and Dan, telling them I'd learned lots about my past, and I'd share it when I got home. Tamsin responded: she was in Puerto Rico and delighted at my news, hoping I'd bagged a few hot men along the way. I missed her suddenly. I wondered if I'd seem a different person when I got back. I *was* altered; but would it show? Dan responded after an hour, sending love, telling me to stay safe.

I played for the crowd in the Piano Bar at five-thirty. Frederica was absent. I missed her but hoped she was having fun with the dancer. I looked for Harriet as I played George Michael's 'Careless Whisper'. I felt an odd motion, like the ship had maybe slowed down. I was sure some of the guests felt it too because they looked at one another, shrugged and then looked around. Perhaps we had changed direction or there was something in the water that we had to avoid.

Afterwards I enjoyed a glass of wine at the bar. Frederica turned up.

'Did you hear?' she asked, not even sitting down.

'Hear what?'

'The emergency broadcast. Maybe they didn't play it in here.'

'What's happened?' I asked. 'I felt like the ship stopped.'

'It did. It turned to go back. Someone fell overboard.'

'No?' I touched my chest. 'How *awful*.'

'I know. The broadcast went out, Code Oscar, man overboard, though it was a woman apparently. They don't think it was suicide though. One of the guests saw her trying to take a picture from the railings, and she apparently lost her balance and fell.'

'Good God, that's *terrible*. Poor woman.'

'This guest alerted the teller in the casino, and of course she let captain know.'

'They turned the ship around?'

'Yes. They're searching for her. Someone threw a ring in the water, and someone else continued pointing at where she was so they wouldn't lose sight of her. I think after a bit they did though. I mean, God, the sea is vast...'

'Will they find her, do you think?'

'I hope so. Gemma said they've more or less pinpointed the area.' Gemma must have been the dancer Frederica was often with. 'They've called on another ship to help, and they'll probably search now for hours.'

'We should go and see.'

We went onto the deck. Sunset was close. The water was aflame. Onlookers were watching some small boats in the distance, circling and searching. Some took pictures and filmed videos, which I felt wasn't the right thing to do at such a traumatic moment. But weren't we as bad, coming out to ogle? I moved away, unable to keep watching, sad for the lost soul. Frederica and Gemma remained, watching from a respectful distance.

I looked at the time; I had to play in half an hour.

'Will they cancel activities, do you think?' I asked Frederica when she and Gemma joined me in a quiet corner near a lifeboat.

'What do you mean?'

'The workshops, dance lessons, shows etc. It doesn't seem right to carry on, does it? Not when a poor woman might be...' I couldn't finish.

'Generally, they're supposed to continue,' said Gemma, who I knew had worked on many cruises. 'The crew will want to keep the atmosphere normal. Not many people might attend though. I reckon until they find her, guests are going to stay out here.'

'Until they find her,' I repeated softly. 'What if they...?' I suddenly had a terrible thought. 'What did she look like?' I asked Frederica.

'The woman who fell?'

'Yes.'

'I'm not sure. We didn't see her.'

'I *need* to know. Who saw her fall? Can you point them out?'

'Wait.' Frederica grabbed my arm. 'What's wrong?'

'What if it was *her*?'

I saw the realisation dawn on Frederica's face. 'You mean ... Harriet? No, it won't be, surely not. There are hundreds of guests on the ship. The chances of tha—'

'But what if it *was*? Which guest saw her fall?'

'I don't know.'

'Did you see, Gemma?'

'No, sorry, we were in the buffet café – we heard the announcement and came out here.'

'I need to find out.'

'Heather.' Frederica spoke kindly. 'She's probably not even on the ship.'

'She is,' I cried. 'I went to the reception desk, found out.'

'But it still doesn't mean...'

I was crying. All my recent emotions would not be contained now. 'I dreamt that she fell into the water,' I sobbed. 'And now this. You can't tell me not to worry. I have to find out.'

'OK, OK,' said Frederica. 'We will. Let's go and speak to Dennie who works in the casino. Gemma, I'll meet you later, OK?'

Frederica and I headed inside, to the gaudy, coin-clanking casino area, deserted now, machines flashing a pointless invitation. Dennie was an attractive older woman; she had the look of someone tired of this role but determined to smile and keep going.

'Did they find her?' she asked us.

'Not yet,' said Frederica. 'Did that guest say what she looked like?'

Dennie shook her head. 'Not that I recall. The poor man could hardly speak, he was so shocked. Just ran in here and said that a woman had fallen. Said they had thrown a ring, and his wife had stayed outside to try and keep an eye on where the current took her. I've only ever been on one other cruise where this happened.'

'Did they find them?' I asked.

Dennie didn't answer.

'What did the man look like?' I asked.

'Heather, we can't go harassing him,' said Frederica. 'He's probably still in shock.' She took me aside, to a quieter area by the exit. 'Look, do you want to cancel your set? I can go and find Sarah Briggs, speak to her.'

I realised I only had ten minutes to get to the Sunset Bar. 'I can't let them down,' I said. 'I might just tell Harvey I'll be a bit late. I need half an hour. That's all.'

'I can go now and tell him,' said Frederica. 'You take a few moments, and I'll see you there soon, yes?'

I nodded, grateful. I felt stupid now, being such a drama queen.

But I just couldn't shake the heavy feeling of doom.

My sense of darkness.

49

I found a secluded spot outside on deck. There weren't many. I wrapped a checked blanket from a deck chair around me but couldn't stop shivering, despite the balmy temperature. It seemed most of the ship's occupants had come out to ogle the spectacle of flashing lights from the small boats in the distance, many dressed in their finery for a night of music and dance but having exchanged that for this entertainment. It would be completely dark soon. The light was dying, embers from the thin slither of sun fading fast. I didn't want to imagine being in the water at night. How cold it might be. How disorientating. How lonely.

How hard to hang on to the hope that someone would come.

Surely Frederica had been right. The chance of that poor woman being Harriet was slim. There were almost two thousand guests aboard the ship. But our history – the shadows of our childhood – had me thinking anything was possible. Hadn't we lived out the tales we read so hungrily in bed, hidden under the covers with a torch? Hadn't we lost our parents, as so many princesses had done? Lost one another?

This could not be the end of our story. One of us lost at sea. It wouldn't be fair. To finally find ourselves together aboard the same ship, at the same time, and never meet. I refused to think of the original endings of the many happy-ever-after tales that had been Disneyfied. I refused to think of the Little Mermaid throwing herself into the sea and dissolving into foam because the prince married a different woman, as had happened in the Hans Christian Andersen version. I refused to think of the original story of Sleeping Beauty by Giambattista Basile, where she was raped by a passing king while she slept, awoke to find she had given birth to twins, but forgave the king his violence anyway.

Looking out to sea, I remembered, suddenly, the wind stealing my words earlier. The piece I'd written about my father in Frederica's workshop whipped away and devoured by the waves. No. Harriet could *not* be there too. I paced the deck, blanket pulled tight about my shoulders.

Two guests walked past, arm in arm, her diamond bracelet glinting in the half-light, her heels a jarring tune on the wood.

'How long do they search before they give up?' she asked her partner.

'No idea, honey,' he said. 'I guess they don't. They can't. It's a human life, after all.'

'But we're supposed to arrive in Tortola the day after tomorrow. Won't this upset the whole itinerary?'

'They'll probably just shuffle things around a little. They won't want to let the guests down. Let's go get a martini.'

'Such an inconvenience,' she hissed.

I wanted to trip her up.

I looked at the time. Nine-fifteen. I should go to the Sunset Bar now. I had to force myself. I waited a second longer, a minute, praying there would be news, so I could go and play with hope still in my heart that Harriet might turn up. But the boats stayed out on the water. The crowd continued peering out into the almost-darkness. And despite the blanket, I was as cold as the sea.

I headed inside, along quiet corridors, past half-full places, to the Sunset Bar. It was busier than I expected but not as full as usual. Perhaps guests were tiring now of watching a search that yielded nothing. The soft pink lighting gave everyone line-free faces, as though they hadn't a care in the world. Could I pretend too that all was well?

Frederica had a table with Gemma. They were sharing a bottle of wine. I nodded but headed straight for the small stage. Harvey caught me, willowy, concerned. 'Are you OK?' he asked. 'If you really can't play tonight, I think under the circumstances, everyone would understand.'

'The music didn't stop on the *Titanic*, did it?' I realised that was quite a dark analogy. 'These people need some joy, don't they?'

'We all do. Such a tragic thing to happen.'

'Will they announce it if they find her?' I suddenly thought of it.

'They'll definitely let the crew know, so if I find out, I'll try and let you know too, with a nod or some signal.'

'Thank you,' I gushed, grateful.

And I went to my piano. I unfurled, as I always did, like a swan first discovering her wings. The crowd was subdued, the atmosphere quietly tense. It was my job to lessen that. Didn't we all turn to music's beauty in our darkest moments, when we were heartbroken, lonely, grieving, lost? Didn't it say all the things we couldn't? It was time for me to speak the sadness of this room.

I began with Ravel's sea-inspired 'Une Barque sur L'Océan'. The motion of water is effortlessly portrayed in this piece by flowing arpeggios, and later tremolos and glissandi. Halfway, the ocean stirs from its opening serenity into a storm, leading to a huge, dissonant climax, one I had so loved playing in my flat, back home, by the river.

'Thank you,' I said when the applause afterwards surprised me with its ferocity.

They must have needed me. I had spoken a language they understood.

I caught Harvey's eye, but he shook his head.

'If you have any requests,' I said, 'please just let me know.'

I played some Bach, some Debussy, and my eternal favourite, Chopin. I recalled when I first learned to play all those years ago. Mr Hibbert told Harriet and me never to look at the piano as a machine for reproducing exactly what someone else had invented for it. He said, yes, follow instructions, learn to read sheet music, study the score, practise, practise, *practise*, but the piano was a tool for expression, for sharing emotions with the audience, whether it was our own song or one we were bringing to life for someone else. That's what we were doing – Chopin had created his composition, but he wanted us to see our own song within those notes.

My song, that night, was desperate.

As the evening came to its conclusion, I caught Harvey's eye again, and he shook his head once more. I looked at Frederica, and she too looked miserable. Everyone in the room was waiting for news of this poor, lost woman. I had been waiting for news of one my entire adult life. Sadness choked me with slender hands; they snaked around my neck with years-old knowledge of exactly how to hurt me.

I couldn't play anymore.

There was nothing left in me. No more dance in my fingers. No more fire to play against. No more heart to rescue this room as I had once tried to rescue my mother. I put my forehead on the piano's surface. The room fell quiet with me.

'I have a request,' said a voice.

Still, I couldn't look up. I wanted to tell her I wasn't doing them anymore. *Go play your own song*, I thought. *Let me be*.

'I think you'll know it,' she said.

She sat next to me, in the small gap on my left. In the place that had been cold for thirty-seven years. In the place I had been saving – like a friend sitting in the theatre waiting for a companion who's late.

I looked at her. Long auburn hair fell in waves down her back, the kind that no matter how often you dampened them or brushed them hard, they always sprang back into curls. Eyes now surrounded by delicate lines, but that still said mischief, still promised eternal loyalty, glinted at me, tears there. Fingers she had once wriggled in the air before we played music were now slender, older, perched above the keys, ready. Lips that once repeated all the words I spoke, were now smiling, shy.

Harriet.

My sister.

I grabbed her. Hugged her tightly. Never wanted to let go. She squeezed back. And there was only us. No crowd. No ship. No hurt.

'"Nothing Else",' she said eventually.

Could we? Would we know it?

"'Nothing Else'", I said.
Of course we could. Of course we would.
And we played our song.

HARRIET
(SECONDO)

50

I had been in my cabin since the ship left New York, plagued with horrific sickness that left me barely able to stand, groaning when I made it to the bathroom, hunching over the toilet, hoping for vomit that might relieve the nausea but never came.

I'd never known anything like it, not even when I was pregnant with Sera. I ordered room service but couldn't even manage a torn-off bread crust. I paid for and activated the Wi-Fi on my phone and googled seasickness, which this seemed to be, even though I could barely feel the ship's motion. It was recommended that I sit outside, that if I could see the horizon it would ease the symptoms. But even on my tiny balcony, with views of a rippling sunlit sea, I felt wretched. I happened upon an article suggesting that deaf people were less likely to experience motion sickness than those who weren't hard of hearing; something to do with a weakened vestibular system within the ear. The irony. The one – the *only* – benefit of losing my hearing might be never feeling car or seasick, and here I was, suffering so badly I could barely move.

I cried. Felt desperately sorry for myself. This was supposed to be my getaway from real life, from the burglary, from my health issues, and I couldn't even read the books I'd brought. It was supposed to be my fated moment, my chance moment, the one I was finally reunited with Heather.

I tried. I left my room late one night, hair matted with sweat, inching my way along the corridor, determined to see my sister play. Another guest found me collapsed and helped me back to my room. After that, I didn't leave my bed. Sera messaged to ask how it was going, so I lied, said I was sunning myself by the pool with a cocktail, not wanting her to worry or fuss. I hadn't even told her before I left that I'd seen Heather in the brochure. I wanted to wait and see what happened, in case it didn't turn out right; in case my sister rejected me.

And here I was, unable to even find her.

In the end, my kind room attendant, Edie, brought some sea-sickness pills to my cabin – the one thing I'd not even thought to pack – and eventually, after taking two regularly for twelve hours, the nausea eased. Enough that I was able to shower, make myself presentable, and finally leave my cabin. I took the silver charm bracelet from the drawer, held it in my fist for a minute, and then put it in my pocket.

I knew where I was going to go.

I had wanted to go there since I first unpacked in my cabin and the decision came to me that I would simply turn up that evening, at Heather's piano. I hadn't even been sure I would approach her. I just wanted to see her. Hear her play. Then the ship departed, and sickness consumed me. I read the entertainment itinerary over and over while ill, miserable at each of her performances that I missed, watching the time pass, counting the minutes, feeling sicker than ever when I knew her pieces were over, and I'd not heard them. I longed to see her in the Sky Lounge, the Piano Bar, the Sunset Bar, all of which sounded exquisite.

Now I was *finally* going to see my sister play.

I was surprised by how empty the ship seemed. I expected it to feel claustrophobic after my time in solitude, to feel overwhelmed by the crowds, but the atrium was quiet. It wasn't just my impaired hearing. Glass elevators rode up and down without passengers; a mermaid sculpture spilled water alone.

A young couple passed me, deep in conversation, pausing near me, surveying the place. I strained to listen, caught the odd word when I was able to look directly at them, and put the rest together in my head.

'It's so sad,' she said. 'I mean, they *said* she fell, but...'

'But what?' he asked.

'Well, who falls, really.' I missed a chunk here, then heard, 'Those railings are high.'

'You mean ... *no*. In front of people like that?'

'Maybe it was a cry for help,' she said.

'But ... what a cry. Risking your life like that.'

I missed another chunk and then heard her simply say, 'I know.'

They disappeared up the curved stairway.

A woman had fallen. Jumped? It sounded like this guest thought so. That must have been where everyone was. Outside. Watching the drama unfold. I took the nearest exit and found myself in a humid night, the sea inky black, small crowds gathered at the railings, their grey faces looking out at small boats zigzagging in the distance, the lights shivering eerily.

It hit me then, a gust of violent wind almost taking me off my feet. What if the woman was Heather? The sickness I'd fought for days returned. I approached an older man at the railings.

'Do you know what happened?' I asked him.

He answered without tearing his eyes from the boats. I only heard 'woman', and that was vague, but I didn't like to ask him to repeat his words.

'It was definitely a woman?'

'Yes.' Clear that time.

'Do you know what she looked like? When did it happen?'

He glanced at me, frowning, perhaps annoyed that I had disturbed his viewing, not that much was happening. 'No idea. I heard about it maybe two hours ago. It was still light then. That's all I know.'

There was one definitive way to find out if it had been Heather. I went back inside and took the glass lift to the eleventh deck. I felt the music before I entered the Sunset Bar, and I *knew*. I had to take a moment, leaning against a column, hand trembling against my neck. I could hear the music too, though it was faint. I wasn't only overcome that it meant Heather was safe, but that my hearing was still good enough to hear her play. I was about to see her for the first time in thirty-seven years.

I pushed the double doors open. Chopin. Delicate, reflective, performed with an air of quiet reservation, exactly how the song is played best. I was in the presence of a far greater pianist that I could ever be; even my poor, failing ears could hear that Heather had somehow forced her way into music's secrets and been raised to the divine.

Momentarily, I was back in our living room, 'Nocturne No 2' on our mother's record player, the scent of her perfume around us, Heather holding my hand, and both of us at that exact second falling in love, completely and absolutely, with music.

I entered the bar.

There were enough people that I could remain hidden near a column. I wanted to watch without being seen. To enjoy her privately. I had this unfair advantage, but I used it joyfully. She must have known I was on the ship, maybe hunted for me, maybe wondered when or if I'd approach her. And I still didn't know if I would. Still there was that fear of her turning away from me.

I spied between the rows of heads in front of me. The piano was white, a grand, on a slightly raised stage, against vast windows that now only reflected ... *her*.

There she was.

I put my hands over my face, like I often had when I was a child trying to contain my churning emotions, trying not to jump on the spot or fidget in my chair or say something I shouldn't. Heather made me six again. Then I removed my hands so I could see her. She sat, graceful, black suit simple, blonde hair swept up, face rapt. Time had been kind to her. It hadn't stolen her smooth skin, hadn't tugged down too hard on her cheeks; rather it had shaped them affectionately into a mature version; the defined edges of youth were slacker but lovely still. Even from afar, I could see she wore the quaver pendant. It caught the light; held it.

Did that mean she had forgiven me?

Was she wearing it to say she still loved me?

When she finished the song, and the warm applause died, she looked across the room at someone, responded with a sad nod, and then looked in my direction, but at someone else. Then she stopped. Sagged. Guests looked at one another. Heather put her head on the piano's surface. It was heart-breaking. I couldn't bear it. I *had* to comfort my big sister, no matter what. I pushed through the crowd, the room deathly quiet.

Had I suddenly gone fully deaf?

I stood in front of her, not sure what to say. Then I knew.

'I have a request,' I said. I wasn't fully deaf. Not yet.

I couldn't hear if Heather responded because she kept her head down.

'I think you'll know it,' I said regardless.

Still, she kept her head down. So, I took the seat. On my side. Where I belonged. I placed my fingers above where I knew they needed to be.

Finally, Heather looked up.

The only time I'd felt that much joy, staring into a face, was when Sera was born and they first gave her to me, bloody and squashed, but the most beautiful thing to behold. I had drunk in those new features. Now I drank in this familiar but slightly different face, one whose look of speechlessness and emotion I knew mirrored mine. Her mouth hung open.

We hugged like we would never let go.

'"Nothing Else"', I said.

I saw her gulp; I knew she was struggling to speak.

'"Nothing Else"', she repeated. I didn't know if she'd whispered it or if it was just me. But it didn't matter. Because I heard her.

And then we played our song.

Heather began, like she always had. I was afraid of how little I would hear, but as her fingers landed on each key, I heard the note as clearly as when we had been small; perhaps it was my knowledge of the tune, my joy at this moment, my desire for this to work that opened my ears once again.

Mr Hibbert once told us that when it came to music, muscle memory is actually *nerve* memory; that when you repetitively practise a movement, you're changing the way your brain reacts to it, and therefore even after years of not playing a certain piece, the physical action will bring it right to the front of your brain again.

'Nothing Else' was at the front of mine. It was all that existed. I knew exactly when to come in, I knew the tempo, each beat, each pause, and, as the secondo, I pedalled to sustain the chords. We had not lost the ability to anticipate one another, to listen and adapt, to quickly move a hand when the other needed to play that note straight after.

That was the physical.

But our song was more than that.

Our song had been created to lift us out of a traumatic childhood experience. Now the melody united us, allowed us to say hello, to speak for the time in thirty-seven years in a language we both knew fluently.

When it was done, there was roaring applause. We hugged. She smelled warm and familiar and right, and my head fit perfectly into the curve of her shoulder. I didn't know how I would ever leave her side again.

'That was a song called "Nothing Else",' Heather told the audience. 'I played my part of this duet last week on another cruise. But it wasn't complete. Now it is. Because this…' She paused, tears in her eyes. 'This is my sister, Harriet, who I haven't seen since I was *ten years old*. And we wrote it and we played it when we were small and…' She shook her head and couldn't finish.

Cameras flashed like stars had fallen from the sky to join us.

'Thank you.' She looked at me, shook her head again like she couldn't quite believe this was happening.

As we left the small stage, hand in hand, a willowy man came from behind the bar – possibly the manager judging by his name badge and smart jacket – and stood in the centre of the room and asked for everyone's attention. 'I'm very happy to report,' he announced, 'that the woman who fell overboard earlier has now been located and rescued, and she's back on the ship and recovering well.'

The entire crowd broke into gleeful whoops and more applause. The bar was warm with happiness. The lost woman had been rescued. Two lost sisters had been reunited.

We had finally found one another.

51

It could have felt like an anticlimax to walk out of that room, to leave behind the waves of warmth, but we were moving into the quiet waters of our new life together. This was real. I still couldn't get my head around it. Couldn't stop studying Heather, the way she walked, the fine greys hidden in her blonde, the quaver necklace about her neck, where it belonged. We paused in the foyer outside the bar, looked at one another, laughed, not knowing what to say, and laughed again.

'What do you want to do now?' Heather asked eventually.

'Right now... or forever?' I smiled.

'Shall we just start with right now?' She smiled too and then studied me, the way I had to watch people now to be sure what they were saying. I was glad, not only for a chance to see her fully, but because then I heard everything she said. 'I was afraid the woman in the water was you,' she said, serious. 'When I got this' – she touched the necklace – 'and knew you were on the ship, but then you didn't show up, God, I imagined all sorts. Then when they said someone had fallen overboard...'

'I thought the same,' I cried.

'Oh, thank God, you're here.'

'I am,' I said.

'You accent is so cute.'

'Is it?' I laughed.

'Yes, so American.'

'Really? Everyone I know thinks I sound so English.'

'Where *were* you?' she asked suddenly.

'In my cabin, I ha—'

'No, where did you go all those years ago?'

Did she sound angry about it? Was she just, understandably, wanting answers? We were in the way of people trying to get into the Sunset Bar for late-night drinks. 'Should we go somewhere, talk properly?' I suggested.

'Yes, sorry, of course.'

'No need to apologise,' I said. 'I have so many questions too. Are you hungry?'

'I guess, yes. Where do you want to eat?'

'I've no idea,' I admitted. 'This is my first time out of my room. I was seasick. That's why I took all this time to come and watch you play.'

'*No.* Oh, poor you.' Her obvious concern touched me. 'Are you OK now?'

'I think the seasickness pills are finally doing the trick. Either that or I'm accustomed to the ship's motion.'

'The buffet restaurant is always open,' Heather said. 'It's casual, nothing glitzy or anything, but the food is nice.'

I laughed, because her words were so normal, so unremarkable, and yet they made me happy.

'What?' she smiled.

'Just … us. Here. It's real.'

'I know.'

'Let's go to the buffet restaurant then,' I said.

I followed her down some stairs to deck eight, where she led me into a large lounge that offered food at different stands. It was busy, even considering the time: eleven-thirty. Cruising must be hungry work. I realised that after two days of barely eating I was ravenous, and glad it was eat all you wanted. We both laughed when we reached for the same chicken pasta, the same cold potatoes, the same feta cheese salad.

There was no point trying to locate a window seat; night-time made mirrors of the glass. We found a small table in a quieter corner near a large tiled mural of three identical ships, and I was glad we sat opposite one another because then I could read on her lips the words I missed.

'Where do we even begin?' Heather shook her head.

'I know. This isn't like we saw each other a year ago.' I started my salad, unable to take my eyes off her. 'Why don't you ask me whatever you want to know, and then I'll ask you? There might be things you remember that I don't, and vice versa. Plus, I want to know all about your family, your life, everything...'

'How did you know?' she asked.

'*Know*?'

'That I was on the ship. Did you know before you boarded?'

'I saw you in the brochure after I'd booked the trip. Can you even imagine how I felt, seeing you? I knew right away it was you.'

Heather studied me. 'Where did you go? That last day ... at the children's home...' Her voice broke and I reached across the table and wrapped my hand around hers, not letting go until she recovered. 'I was devastated when you disappeared. I know it wasn't your fault, you were just a child.'

I couldn't stop the tears at these words. She knew it hadn't been my fault. She didn't blame me. I paused, knowing the possible impact of what I was about to say. I had no idea if Heather knew we had different fathers. I'd had years to get accustomed to it.

'Heather, this may be a shock, so we can talk about it as much or as little as you want tonight.' I inhaled and then let it go. 'My real dad took me.'

She blinked. 'Your *real* dad? I don't...'

'Our mother ... our lovely mum...' We both teared up at mention of her. 'She had an affair. She was in love with someone else. I brought the letters she wrote him to give you, not now, another day, when everything has sunk in. Heather...' I gripped her hands again. 'It means she was briefly happy.'

She nodded, clearly overwhelmed.

'When my dad found out she'd died in the car accident...' I paused. 'You know about what really happened?'

'I do.' Heather's voice was almost inaudible, but I understood her perfectly. 'I found out, here.'

'What do you mean?'

'I've been reading my care records. There was a newspaper cutting. It said the crash wasn't an accident. Our father...' She faltered at the word father, and I knew she was fully comprehending that *her* father wasn't the same man as mine. 'My father drove them into the water.'

'I know. It's ... I *know*.'

'So, who is your real dad?'

'Are you OK?' I asked because she looked so sad.

'I am ... it's just...'

'Heather...'

'I...'

She stood. Shook her head. And left me. I jumped up, catching the table, spilling food, delayed by trying to rectify the mess. When I got into the corridor, I couldn't see her anywhere. I looked left, right. The shopping mall was quiet. She wasn't there. I went outside, onto the deck. I could not lose her again. I called her name. Nothing.

Then I saw her at the front of the ship, staring down into the darkened sea.

'Heather.' I joined her. 'What is it?'

She shook her head. Her cheeks were damp.

'Tell me,' I begged, turning her towards me so I could lip-read if needed.

'We're together again,' she said. 'But we're *not*.'

'I don't understand.'

'We're only *half*-sisters,' she said.

'We're not,' I cried. 'I hate that phrase! We had the same mother, and we grew up together, for so long anyway. We're *sisters*. This doesn't change anything.'

'It feels...'

'What?'

'I don't know,' she admitted. 'Like I've found you ... and lost you in the same moment.'

'You haven't.'

Eventually, she nodded. 'Tell me, what happened that day?'

I described as best I could, in ways that might not hurt or be blunt, how my dad had applied for my care and brought me to America. I insisted that he had wanted Heather too, and I'd only gone because I believed it, because I thought she would follow in a few weeks. 'I'd *never* have left you,' I said. 'I wrote you but never heard back. You had probably left the home by then.'

'I never got any letters.' Heather looked broken.

'I'm so sorry.'

'You don't have to be sorry. This wasn't you, Harriet. You were a child. This was adults, making decisions. But it's just so ... *sad*. That we haven't had each other all this time.'

I nodded, struggling now to catch every word.

'How could they keep where you were from me?' Heather looked angry now, and it was understandable.

'Maybe ... maybe they thought it was for the best ... but I agree. We could have written to one another, at least.'

'Wait ... there was something in my records about Grandma Dolly saying that due to circumstances she wasn't interested in seeing you...' Heather looked sadly at me. 'That she thought it better that we now live apart. I've just realised. She would've known you had a different father. What if she encouraged this to happen?'

'I never liked her,' I said.

'She was cold, wasn't she? She never even came to see us. But what if she told the care home that it was better we lived apart? I guess we'll never know for sure. She died when I was thirteen apparently.'

'Good.'

'Harriet!

'Well, she was awful,' I laughed. 'Were your new parents nice?'

'Oh, yes.' Relief flooded me. I needed to know that someone had taken care of her; it eased my guilt at feeling I had left her. 'They were older, never had kids of their own. Kind. Loving. Patient. Everything I suppose a child who's been through trauma needs. They died a few years ago. How about your ... dad?' Her voice faltered on the word. 'Tell me more about him.'

I said he had also passed away and told her the things I thought might put him in the room with us; the little tics he had, the way he spoke, the trips we had taken.

'That's why he did it.' Heather had clearly just realised something.

'Who?' I asked. 'Did what?'

'Our ... *my* father. That's why he was so cold with you that last day. He knew you weren't his. He'd found out. I couldn't understand it, because he loved you so much. That must have hurt him.' She quickly added, 'I'm not excusing him, I'm just saying that it explains his actions. It means that whole day ... Well, it makes sense now.' She paused. 'I can't believe he ... he...'

'I know,' I said. I'd missed some of this but was getting the gist.

'Our mum,' she said.

'I miss her.' I wanted us to be united in our memories, in our love, in the things we both knew, not explore the horrible things yet.

'I hadn't even seen her lovely face since she died, not until I saw that awful newspaper piece the other day.'

'I have a picture she sent to my dad. I'll show you tomorrow. We'll get you a copy. I know how you feel though – I've not got a single picture of you.'

'I have a Polaroid of us that was taken in the children's home.'

'Really.' I wanted to bounce on the spot. 'I can't wait to see it.'

'It's in my cabin. I'll bring it tomorrow.'

'Bring it tomorrow.'

Heather laughed. 'Do you still do that? Repeat things people say? It was so cute! Do you remember?'

I giggled too. 'I do remember. I don't do it now, but it felt like a "repeat it" moment.'

'A "repeat it" moment,' she laughed.

Someone interrupted our 'repeat it' moment. A young couple with matching tattoos of red roses wrapped in ribbon on their bare upper arms. They stopped and she cried, 'Oh, it's the two pianists. The sisters! Gee, we just adored that song. We filmed it. Everyone was. Did you really just meet here?'

'Really,' I said.

'Really,' said Heather.

And we laughed at our own joke; our second 'repeat it' moment. The affection I felt for her was similar to that which I had for Sera, protective and completely consuming. Thinking of my daughter, I said when the couple had gone, 'I named her after you.'

'Who?' asked Heather.

'My daughter. Sera Heather.'

'That's beautiful. You have a *daughter*. Tell me all about her.'

I did, and I knew pride emanated from my words. 'She reminds me of us,' I said. 'Both of us in one person. Do you have kids?'

Heather shook her head and I sensed regret. 'It just ... well, it just never happened. I was married. It ended amicably, and we're friends now, but ... I guess, I'm a solitary kind of woman. I think I learned to be that way.' She looked at me and then looked away, shrugged.

'That's understandable,' I said. 'I'm divorced too, and we're still friends.'

'What do you do, in your general life?' I had to ask her to repeat this.

'I'm a book editor. You?'

'I do this now, it would seem.' She laughed. 'But I teach piano too and play in small bars at home in Hull.'

'You're in Hull still?'

'Yes.'

'I came there ten years ago. I went to our house. Saw Mr Hibbert's. Do you know what happened to him?'

'I looked for him when I left uni and became a teacher,' said Heather. 'He must have left the area ... I suppose I could have tried harder. But think how old he would be now ... he must be ... gone now...'

We gripped hands again.

'You belong on a big stage,' I said. 'Do you have any idea how good you are?'

She blushed, shook her head.

'You always were,' I insisted. 'Didn't you know? It was always *you*. I looked up to you so much. I wanted to *be* you.'

'You didn't. You wanted to be Richard Clayderman in a green dress.'

I laughed until I couldn't speak at the memory. I saw us, at that childhood piano, filling the house with joy.

'You were the vivacious one,' said Heather. 'I was quiet and ordinary.'

'Not when you played the piano. Never then.'

I wanted to tell her about my loss of hearing, feeling able to tell her anything, but this was a joyful moment. It would keep. We had forever now. We talked for another hour about what we remembered from our childhood, about Mr Hibbert and the books we had read and our mum and the music, as the sea gushed by. The words I missed, I worked out. I realised that Heather looked exhausted and was trying to hide her yawns. It was past one and she had been working all day.

'We should go to bed,' I said. 'You must be shattered.'

'I am,' she admitted, 'but I don't want to leave you.'

'I'm not going anywhere. Even if I wanted to, where could I go?'

We both looked down into the water and then at each other.

'Let's get some sleep,' I said, 'and we can talk all day tomorrow, in between your sets.'

Heather relented. 'OK. My first set is at one in the Sky Lounge so I can meet you in the morning. Say ten?'

'Great. If you come to my cabin, I'll give you Mum's letters and her picture.'

'I'm not supposed to come in your room because you're a guest,' she said. 'But bugger the rules. If I get found out, I'll explain why.'

'Can you come ashore in Tortola the day after tomorrow?' I wondered.

'I'll have free time, so I'm sure we can do that together.'

We left the deck and went into the lobby.

'I'm on deck seven,' I said. 'Down one for me. Where do you sleep?'

'Belowdecks,' said Heather. 'I think my cabin is a lot more basic than yours, but to be fair, I sleep so well here at sea...' I missed the last part but didn't want to ask.

'Oh, I have something for you.' I went into my pocket, took out the small charm bracelet. It might not even fit; it had been purchased with a ten-year-old in mind. 'The day I left, my dad took me shopping. I felt bad that you'd given me your necklace. I've kept this ever since.'

I held it out in the palm of my hand. She took it. Held it up to the light, the small moon full. 'I love it,' she said. 'Fasten it for me.'

It was snug about her wrist so took a few attempts.

'I'll never take it off,' she said.

It was obvious neither of us wanted to go. I suddenly had an intense fear that if we separated again something else would stand in the way of us finding one another. I saw that she felt that too. I could read her like my own reflection in a mirror.

'Ten o'clock tomorrow,' I said.

'What's your cabin number?'

'715.'

'I'll be there.'

We both went down one level, and then I watched as she went further down. Thirty-seven years and in some ways, it felt like we had never parted. But in others, it felt like we had an eternity to fill.

52

Back in my cabin I was desperate to tell Sera that I had found my sister, but it was late, and I didn't want to wake her. It was just me and the night. I went onto the balcony and told the sea instead. 'It's like we were never apart,' I whispered, not caring if the dark was hard of hearing too.

In the morning, I had breakfast delivered to my room and was able to eat most of it. I found our mother's letters and photograph, and I sat on the balcony looking through the pages until, just before ten, there was a knock on the door.

Heather was dressed more casually, in a summery yellow outfit. 'I'll have to go back and change before my set,' she said.

'You should play like that. You look lovely. Shall we grab a coffee and sit outside,' I suggested. 'I haven't even been out there during the day yet.'

We got lattes from a speciality coffee bar and went outside, through one of the heavy wooden doors. The warm air surprised me after the air-conditioned corridors, but then this was the Caribbean, after all. Passengers sat in rows on the deckchairs, faces raised to the sun. We found a couple of free seats with unrestricted views of the ocean, of the turquoise water dappled with streaks like the peel in marmalade.

Heather handed me a picture; the Polaroid of us both, faded now. In it she was how I remembered her – tall, gangly, her flowered dress with puff sleeves clearly too big, and her hair pale yellow. I was chunkier with flushed cheeks and my hair in two thick plaits. We had our arms around one another, cheeks touching, smiles shy. I was swept back in time, to the children's home, to cold rooms, to cold meals, to our final night together. But I didn't need to be sad about it now; we were together again.

'Oh my,' I said.

I took out my phone and got a photograph of it. Then I gave Heather the picture of our mother. She studied it for a long time and then did the same with her phone.

'Just think, we're both older now than she was here,' Heather said. 'What a waste of a life. Such a beauty and she never knew it. You look like her, around the eyes.'

'That's weird because I only see you, though it's the hair and jawline.'

'I guess we see what we want to.' Heather seemed thoughtful. 'I hope she knows, wherever she is, that we're together again.'

'I bet she does.'

I gave Heather the batch of her letters. She fingered the looped writing on one of the envelopes.

'I'll read them tonight. Give them back to you tomorrow.'

'There's no rush. We're here for another ten days.'

'Ten days.' She smiled. 'How amazing is that?'

'I know.' I missed the words after 'ten days' because she looked away. My hearing was worse today. Had I forgotten how bad it was while I was confined to my cabin and away from people and noise? Had the adrenaline at seeing Heather carried me, and now the truth of my impediment was a shock? I glanced at the couple a few metres away, watched their mouths, and it was as though I'd put them on mute.

Heather touched my arm and I jumped. 'Are you OK?' I heard it because I was close and looking at her.

'Heather...'

'Yes?'

'I'm losing my hearing.' As soon as the words were out, I began sobbing. I hadn't been able to open up to anyone until then, and it freed the pain.

Heather moved her chair closer and squeezed my arm. 'Tell me about it,' she said.

So, I did. I told my big sister how scared I really was. 'I feel alone,' I said. 'Alone in this newly quiet world. Everything sounds like a TV on the other side of an apartment wall. Music is muffled, and that breaks me the most. I need subtitles when I watch movies. I miss so many conversations. I'm scared. I'm really scared of what the future holds, of how much worse it might get. But mostly I'm scared I'm going to be totally alone when the world goes silent.'

'You'll never be alone,' she said, close to my ear. 'I'm here now.'

I nodded, communicating my gratitude via my hand over hers. She had always made me feel safe when we were small, and now her words worked their magic again. I thought about the burglary but decided that was for another time.

'How long has it been bad?' I knew she was speaking carefully, and I loved her for it.

'Months ... maybe a year ... more...'

'Have you seen anyone?'

I told her about my appointments.

'That sounds hopeful,' she said. 'Hearing aids, I mean. I could come with you, to find out more, if you wanted me to.'

'But you'll be going back to England.' The enormity of the distance still between us hit me. We had lives on opposite sides of a vast sea. I could never live in a place where Sera didn't live, and I couldn't expect Heather to abandon her home for me.

'I have two nights in New York between this and the next cruise,' she said, 'and then two weeks later I have two more before I go home.'

It was something. We could work it out. We could visit one another. And there was FaceTime. We could talk anytime we wanted now.

'Listen,' she said, 'we'll make it wo—'

We were interrupted then by a beautiful young woman with red hair.

'Frederica,' said Heather, still near my ear. She sat up. 'Harriet, this is the onboard writer. Frederica...' She paused. 'This is my sister.'

'I know,' said Frederica. 'I saw you both play last night. Hi, Harriet.'

'Of course you did! I'm just too excited to think straight.'

Frederica laughed and perched on the end of Heather's deck-chair. 'What a moment,' she said. 'I'm so happy for you both. Heather's been telling me about you the whole trip. And did you see?'

'See what?' asked Heather.

'Don't you ever go on your bloody social media?'

'Um ... I haven't today. Why?'

'The people who filmed you last night uploaded the footage. They tagged you in it. Anyway, one of them is a big CEO of some company, lots of followers, and their video had been shared nearly ten thousand times last I looked. The #NothingElse hashtag was trending in the early hours because a few others shared theirs and used it. Have you got your phone?'

Heather took it out and opened her Twitter app. 'Oh my God,' she said. 'There are loads of notifications. Look Harriet.' I glanced at her screen, at the tiny picture of her at the piano, at the numerous videos now on her timeline. The hashtags were #NothingElse and #SistersReunion and #ReunionSong. She clicked on one and played it. I watched us at the piano, reflected in the window behind, rapt in concentration, but the song was barely audible. I was more moved by Heather's reaction, by the emotion on her face, by what my eyes gave me now my ears were the enemy.

'Look how many followers you've got now,' said Frederica.

'Eleven thousand,' said Heather. 'And another ... and another...' She laughed.

'You need to share it, keep the momentum going. You too, Harriet, if you're on there. Who knows what this could mean for you both?'

Heather was still scrolling. 'Harriet, you made people notice me. You got us trending.'

'No, that's you,' I insisted.

'I've never had this kind of attention.'

'It's both of you,' said Frederica. 'That's what the magic was. I've seen Heather play, and she's hypnotic, but last night, the two of you, that was something else. I got my happy ending after all.'

'You did.' Heather looked at me, spoke clearly. 'Frederica never lost faith that I'd find you.'

'Anyway, I'll leave you both to it,' Frederica said. 'You've got years of catching up and my workshop is in ... yikes, five minutes. See you later.'

She disappeared. 'Let's watch the video again,' I said to Heather, excited.

And we did. She plugged her headphones in, and we had one earpiece each. Knowing why she had done it, and why she turned it up to a volume that must have been uncomfortable for her, touched me. I can't deny the pride in seeing myself play for an audience, at witnessing the crowd's reaction, at hearing our childhood song in its full, perfect, intended beauty. And now it seemed many others would enjoy it too. We dipped our heads towards one another and watched it again.

For the rest of the day, I trailed Heather, her little groupie. She left me to get changed into her 'smart performance attire' as she called it, and I browsed the shops on the Queen's Parade, picking out some earrings and a Guess handbag for Sera. Then I watched Heather play in the Sky Lounge, a sunny place that was packed out. She commented on how many people were there, so I guessed it was unusual. She played John Denver and Don McLean and Bob Dylan, and I was happy to relax with a drink and enjoy it.

As she neared the end of the hour, someone in the audience shouted something. At first I wasn't quite sure what. Then, when others joined in, I realised. 'Play the song! Play the song! Play the reunion song!'

Heather stood up and looked at me. Everyone began cheering. I joined her, took my place. And we played it, my instinct and sheer joy compensating for the moments I could barely hear the notes.

We had a late lunch after that set, reminiscing about the happier days of our childhood, talking now as though we'd been close our whole lives, finishing one another's sentences and saying the same word at the same time. Being slightly older than me, she remembered more and told the stories of our past as well as she had once told me the story of Snow White and Rose Red.

I loved the dark décor of the Piano Bar, and the livelier atmosphere, where Heather played hits from the eighties and everyone sang along. Frederica was there; I sat with her and we joined in. No one asked for 'Nothing Else', but it was understandable considering the party vibe. Heather only had an hour or so before her next performance, so we enjoyed a glass of wine on the deck, watching the sun sink into the sea. Heather asked a passenger to take a photograph of us with her Nikon, and we huddled together, faces close, recreating the faded polaroid in bold, modern-day, hi-definition colour.

And then we were back in the Sunset Bar, where we had been reunited just twenty-four hours earlier. It felt like so much longer. How could the thirty-seven years we had been apart melt into nothing, while one day felt like forever? I sat close to the piano, not only to hear better when Heather played my favourite Chopin – 'Nocturne No 2' – but to see her. I took photos on my phone and shared them on Twitter, where I saw that the footage of us playing last night had been shared a further few thousand times, and by a few musicians and artists who had the blue tick.

At the end of the evening, a woman in black sequins called, 'Play that song with your sister again!' A host of others joined in, demanding the same, cheering and whistling. It was my cue. I joined her at the piano. We unfurled in unison, we paused in unison, we inhaled in unison, and then we played in unison. Just as it should be.

HEATHER
(PRIMO)

53

I came back to my cabin belowdecks after a full day with Harriet, my mother's letters and photo underarm, a bounce in my step, another thousand or so notifications on my phone, and the remnants of our song spiralling around my head. It was as though Harriet's arrival had brought other things with it – a warm wind heralding summer. I'd barely had time to take in, assess, think about the moment Harriet arrived at the piano and made her request. It had been a whirlwind of flashes, like the dramatic highlights from a previous episode in a TV series: flash, flash, flash.

Now, I sat on my narrow bed and smiled; I couldn't help it.

How quickly you get used to nice things. Ugly as it was, the shock of learning the truth about the car crash was receding. Even my upset at discovering Harriet had a different father had faded. Initially, it had felt like yet another thing to come between us. A physical pain in my chest. Now it made perfect sense. Who else could have taken her? I was relieved she'd had a good life. That her time away from me had at least been kind time.

But I was sad about Harriet's hearing loss. When she became upset telling me, I'd wanted to protect her from that sorrow, like when we were small and in our bunks, pretending to play music to drown out the commotion downstairs. Now I *could* be there for her in this crisis. It seemed I'd arrived – or at least she had – at the perfect time.

I showered and climbed into bed with my mother's letters. I dimmed the lamp and kept her photograph close by so I could glance at her face while I read; she looked so much happier in this snap than in the newspaper one with my father. I didn't know if the letters were in date order, but I wanted to dip in and out, read my mother's words indiscriminately, hear her like a fragmented conversation.

Dear Bill,

I'm writing this in the garden. The house is empty. The girls are at school and Robert is at work. I can send this before any of them come home. I need this quiet to be with you. I feel like you're sitting next to me. I wish you were.

I do care for Robert and so I feel guilty. But he doesn't make me happy. Love should make us happy, shouldn't it? His father died when he was two, and he has a cold, unloving mother, who I think was physically brutal with him when he was small. He has said things that hint at this, and he is so meek when she is around. Does violence breed violence? I suppose. I feel for him, I do, and yet he hurts me. He can be tender, he really can. Sometimes. When we met, I thought maybe I'd be the one to heal him, to make him happy, because he was often depressed. When I first met his mother, she belittled and berated him in front of me. I wanted to show him kindness. But when it comes too late, it comes too late.

I love you. This is simple. This is everything. Having you, even just once a year, gives me the strength to stay in my marriage. Because I have to. For my girls. For my Heather and Harriet. I can't break up the home they have. On my own, I could not afford to give them what I can here. Even if I found the courage to leave, what help is there? What skills do I have to support my girls? None. And you don't want to hurt your Gabrielle. Why hurt others any more than they already are when we can survive on our brief time together?

Dear Bill,

Today I wished I could talk to you. Maybe we could sometime. I'd have to go to Sheena's to call, because otherwise Robert would see it on our bill, but I'd do that, if there was a way. It was a difficult day. Robert was in a foul mood this evening. That's all I will say. Afterwards, when he's like that, I go into the bathroom and lie in the bath and cry. And when I then go to bed, he is loving. He kisses my bruises. No one else knows this. It used to work. I'd forgive him. Now I feel myself float out of my body when he does it and I'm watching, thinking how weak I am.

I wanted to thank you from the bottom of my heart for sending money to help with the piano lessons. I was so anxious about how I could cover it out of my meagre housekeeping allowance, especially when I can't tell Robert. The girls love playing, and I love hearing them, though of course they only play when he's not here. I fear him getting rid of it. He's always threatening to. I live to hear their music. I wish they could know the joy it brings me. But I'm sad for them. I know they see what their father can be like. Maybe I should find the courage to leave. Maybe this kind of home is worse than a poor one, where at least there would be an end to the violence. But I'm weak, I know. I'm scared. I have what I call my sense of darkness and my sense of light. They are Robert and you. It seems to exist in extremes in my life. But still, I let the dark in.

Dear Bill,
When I first saw you that day at the Women's Institute and you stood up to talk, I swear I'd never felt anything like it. I was jealous that the other women were watching you too – isn't that silly? I wanted you all for myself. I thought I was imagining it when you kept glancing at me and forgetting your words. When we spoke afterwards, I literally wanted to touch your face. And when we met, alone, later, and you kissed me, I'd never known such passion. Isn't life cruel to put us on opposite sides of the world? But I can survive on just my thoughts of you. Because you are in my head. You are right there. And that's more real than just being in my heart.

Dear Bill,
In Harriet, I have you. She moves a certain way and it's you. But Heather, she is me. Harriet delights me, gives me such big hugs, but Heather is my little soul. You can love equally but for different reasons, and that's how I am with my girls. If Heather

is like Robert, she's like the him that could have been if he'd had a more nurturing mother. Does that make sense? I wish he paid her more attention. I see her face when he acts like she doesn't exist. They are so good on the piano now. I don't have anything to compare it to, but I'm sure they are gifted. I think Harriet plays partly to be with Heather. But Heather, she would play even if the house fell down around her. Thank you again from the bottom of my heart for sending money for the new music books. I know you do it because ... well, Harriet. But thank you.

Dear Bill,
I pass the café where we meet and see couples in there and wish it was us. I even get a bit angry at them, just because I'm jealous. Isn't that silly? I smell the pages of your letter in the hope that there's an essence of you in there, but there never is. I sometimes think about our proper moments together while I'm going about my household chores and I blush and have to sit down for a moment. I think of you when I'm with Robert in that way. I feel guilty for doing so but I can't help it. You're inside me, at all times.
If only Robert could let love heal him. He told me once that his mother locked him in a cupboard to punish him for some small thing, and he wet himself with fear. I cried over that. I cry over a man who hurts me so much. It torments me. All of it.

Dear Bill,
Robert knows Harriet isn't his! Oh God, oh God. I can hardly write this, I'm shaking. It was horrible. He called me so many terrible things. He found one of your letters, the one where you said that, despite it all, you were overjoyed that you had given me Harriet and you'd always longed for a little girl. I should never have put it in the kitchen drawer, but he never goes in there, and I wanted one letter with me, so I had you. Just one. He hurt me, a lot, so I lied and said it was a one-off, a mistake, something I've always regretted. I hated lying when it wasn't something I regretted at all! He is quiet tonight, which I hate the most. I'm

sad I've hurt him but I'm afraid too. I have such a sense of dark-
ness. I wish you were here. God, I wish you were here.

Date-wise, that was my mum's last letter. It touched me profoundly. I could feel her panic, her sense of doom, and oh, how right
she had been, my poor, dear, lovely mother. The passages that stood
out most were the ones where I felt she whispered in my ear, and in
those last few lines, she could have been in the cabin with me.

Our music had given her joy. This made me happy. It was all we
had wanted to do when we played. And her description of having a
sense of darkness, a sense of light, gave me shivers; I'd thought this
was just me, but now it linked me even more to my mother. Though
he could not be forgiven for his behaviour, I understood a little more
of my father. I wished I could have known him as an adult, spoken
to him, tried to help him change. But it was never to be.

My mother had loved Bill, and he had loved her, and of this I
was glad. The final remnants of resentment at Harriet having a different father to me dissolved. We were who we were because of our
unique parentage, because of the childhood that shaped us, because
of the lives we had made for ourselves; change any of those things,
and we wouldn't be part of the right story. In those letters, Harriet
had given me the gift of a reunion with our mum, and I would
cherish it forever.

I fell asleep on a tranquil sea of contentment.

54

I was happy to see Frederica at breakfast so we could catch up. She had caught the sun and looked radiant in an orange blouse with puff sleeves, like the summer tops we wore as kids. We would arrive in Road Town, Tortola, at noon, four hours later than scheduled due to the ship going back for the woman who had fallen. Sarah Briggs had told me yesterday that the poor thing was shaken up from her ordeal, but physically fine. I had the full day off – I only had to perform my last set in the Sunset Bar – and had agreed to call for Harriet at her cabin just before twelve.

'This sea life agrees with you,' I told Frederica, drinking my second coffee.

'I love it.' She devoured lightly poached eggs. 'I'm not getting much actual writing done, though, so it might be best for me not to do too many of these gigs. Not that writers are the kind of draw that musicians are. Will you do another cruise?'

I had to think about it. Meeting Harriet had made me rethink so many things. Before her, I had finally decided that I'd definitely do another. Now, I wasn't sure, and I didn't know why. 'Maybe,' I said. 'Sorry I missed your workshop yesterday.'

'Don't be silly, you were with your sister. God, you look alike. It isn't obvious, with her dark hair and different accent, but it's there in the way you carry yourselves and smile. I'm *so* happy for you.' Frederica paused. 'How's the social media doing? I see the reunion video is still being shared loads.'

I hadn't looked yet. Frederica shook her head as I got out my phone. There were lots of new notifications, and I'd been followed by another six and a half thousand people, including the presenter of an American show called *New Day*. I followed her back, along with a few others.

'The comments are amazing,' said Frederica. 'Everyone wants

to know more, like how you came to be apart. You should respond.'

'I will, I promise, I just haven't had time.'

'Are you going ashore with Harriet?'

'Yes.' I suddenly thought Frederica might be lonely. 'You're welcome to join us.'

'Oh, don't worry about me. I'm going with Gemma.'

I smiled. 'You seem to be getting close.'

'Maybe.' She looked coy. 'She might be more than a fling...'

I called for Harriet just before noon. We still couldn't stop grinning inanely at one another. I wondered when it would become everyday to see her, and yet didn't want that to happen.

'Hey,' she said as we headed to deck seven, where we could disembark, 'I got a message on Twitter from Brianna, a presenter on *New Day*, and she wants to speak to me about our reunion.'

'She followed me,' I cried. 'I followed her back.'

'I was their guest once, with a controversial writer whose book I'd edited. It's a huge morning show,' gushed Harriet. 'I often catch it before work. Anyway, I told Brianna that I'll contact her when I'm back home after the cruise.'

'What do you think she wants?'

'Maybe to go on the show? Everybody loves a reunion, don't they? Look how popular *Long Lost Family* is.'

'How exciting. Would you do it?'

'With you?' She squeezed my arm. 'Of course.'

We had arrived at the gangway that led onto a long narrow quay, which, once we were on it, gave panoramic views of a postcard island: a bay curving around the ship like a lucky horseshoe, leafy hills rising out of indigo waters on both sides, little white villas dotted along that incline. We were moved along by the crowd to the end of the jetty, where bright, white, red-roofed buildings formed the Tortola Pier Park, and friendly locals waited to greet us and offer bus day trips, and shops sold treasures, like jewellery made from ground coral and conch-shell lamps. The tropical heat was dry, and I could smell salt from the water, some sort of flower I couldn't name, coconut, and sandalwood.

'This is beautiful,' I said. 'Now I know why people cruise.'

'What do you want to do?' asked Harriet.

'Shall we just wander?'

'Let's.'

Beyond the pier, we found a palm-tree-lined main street where the wooden buildings were painted bright pink and blue and yellow, where huts sold artwork, and a small market sold local crafts. After recommendations from a store owner who sold us some West Indian spices, we caught a taxi to Cane Garden Bay, where a long white beach stretched forever, and surfers and jet skiers enjoyed the waves. We hired two chairs for five dollars each and set up for the afternoon in the shade of a large palm tree.

I wondered, as we both stared quietly out to sea, if the fact that our reunion had taken place in such beautiful surroundings added a holiday-romance feel to it, and that if we'd met in a dull city, it would have felt less special. No. It wouldn't have mattered where we met; I knew this absolutely.

'If someone had told me a week ago that I'd be sitting on a beach like this with you,' said Harriet, 'I'd never have believed it.'

I shook my head. 'I know.'

'The guy at that gazebo is making seafood paella,' she said suddenly. 'Smells divine. Shall we get some? I'm starving.'

While we ate, I thought of things that I wasn't sure whether to talk to Harriet about, like if she remembered our mother falling down the stairs and being in hospital, if she knew our father had pushed her that day? How much of the violence did she recall? I wondered if I should tell her about that last morning, when my father said what he said to me.

I decided these things didn't matter now. They neither changed nor added to us. They were sad moments in our past, and this was a too-happy moment in our now. We had a whole future to share these details.

'When I was in Hull and I went to our house ... it was a different place. Like we never even existed.'

'But we did,' I said softly. 'We *do*.'

'I wonder what happened to our piano,' said Harriet. 'It probably got ruined that day. Do you know where it went?'

I shook my head. 'No. I remember we had some of our own things at the care home, but beyond that ... Maybe someone ... I don't know, got them all. Grandma bloody Dolly?'

Harriet laughed. Then asked more seriously, 'What are we going to do, Heather?'

'What do you mean?'

'When the cruise is over, and you have to go home. We spoke about it before, but...'

'I don't know.' I didn't. I suddenly thought of young Rebecca, my would-be new student back in Hull, and the reaction I'd had to her. If I returned, could I teach her now? Now that I had Harriet? 'Let's not think about that yet. Let's enjoy now.'

We paddled in the warm waters of the Caribbean Sea, drank rum punch at a beach bar, bought a hand-carved wooden shorebird each from a man on the street, and finally came back to the ship, glowing and tired. I had to get lively again, freshen up and change into my suit for the late-night performance in the Sunset Bar.

At the end of the evening, everyone wanted our song. I did not want it to become customary. I feared it would lessen the magic. But, then, weren't songs supposed to be there for us through every life moment, the light and the dark. As Harriet joined me, in her place, it still felt as though this was the first time we had played in thirty-seven years, and yet somehow also as though she had never left my side.

55

The rest of the cruise flew by, as if time was envious of our days together and wound up her clock so the hours went faster. We were typical holidaymakers when we went ashore to St Kitts, St Maarten, and Barbados, my camera about my neck, our flipflops gritty with sand, buying every souvenir and trying every speciality cocktail, cramming in the memories as though to make up for all the trips we had missed.

During our days at sea, I performed my sets, and Harriet joined me when guests asked us to play. I loved that they called it 'the song'. For me, it always had been *the* song. Hearing Harriet's adult interpretation of it, I realised that when I'd attempted to write it down a few years ago some of her notes were wrong. I rewrote those parts in my cabin one evening and I showed her the following morning.

'Oh my,' she said. 'Our song as an actual *score*. "Nothing Else" by Heather and Harriet Johnson.' She paused. 'It's your song really. You came up with the melody – I just followed you.'

'But I would never have created what we did on my own,' I insisted.

'Can I get a copy of this? I'll frame it.'

'Of course.'

We went to one of the ship's art auctions. Harriet admitted she had been burgled before she came away, that the upset, along with her hearing loss, had contributed to her decision to take a break. They had stolen her favourite pieces. She bid on a colourful painting depicting a pianist playing on top of a skyscraper and was told it would be delivered to her apartment in four weeks.

I caught up with Sarah Briggs and apologised to her about the fact that I'd barely got to know the crew on this cruise, feeling bad that I wasn't mixing with them or going to any of the parties. I explained about my reunion with Harriet. 'I never anticipated something like this happening,' I said.

'I don't think I've ever known anything like it on any of my trips,' she said. 'We've had a few engagements between crew members, then the weddings and the babies, but never anyone meeting a long-lost relative. Listen, Heather, please, just enjoy your sister.'

I desperately wanted to message Tamsin and Dan and tell them what had happened, but I resisted. This was too big for the small space on a smartphone.

I still made time for Frederica, attending two more of her workshops, where I wrote a piece about first seeing Harriet again, and jotted down the notes to a new melody in my head, one that got louder each time I was with my sister. Frederica attended most of my sets, often with Gemma, who she told me lived only seventy miles away from her back in the UK.

'We're going to see each other when we're home,' she said. 'Who knows? Maybe we can make it work. It's quite a distance, but hell, you and Heather have to make three thousand miles work.'

I tried not to think about that.

There were three days at sea after we left St Maarten and sailed back to New York. Harriet and I fell into a simple routine. Between my sets we ate out on the deck, sharing more about each other's recent lives, and delving further back into what we could recall about our childhood. When we shared memories together, I could see the past more vividly than when I thought of them alone.

'You said you've got two nights in New York when we get back, yes?' said Harriet on the penultimate day.

I nodded, not knowing how I'd be able to board the ship again without her, or how I'd eventually then come home.

'I booked another appointment with the audiologist earlier,' she said. I knew she had been reluctant to go back and have to face this health issue. 'We get back on Sunday; it's on Monday morning. Will you come with me, like you offered?'

We had agreed that I would stay at Harriet's apartment. 'Of course I'll come,' I said.

She looked troubled still.

'Are you OK?' I asked.

'Oh yes, I'm fine.' The answer came quickly, and I didn't believe her.

The last night of the cruise came around, and with it my final performance. I had only been away from home three weeks, half of the full duration of my trip, but it could not have felt longer ago. I'd boarded the ship back in Southampton afraid of so many things: afraid of leaving the habitual and dull safety of my flat, of not being able to sleep at sea with strange sounds around me, of not being good enough when I performed, of my care records.

The Sunset Bar was packed. Harvey and his staff were so busy he didn't have time to greet me. I remembered how nervous I was first walking in there; now it felt like it was my room, that I owned it.

Harriet had said she would meet me but hadn't arrived yet. Frederica and Gemma sat at a table, so I joined them.

'Are you two going to do New York together?' I asked them.

'We sure are,' said Frederica. She studied me, her eyes glazed with slight inebriation. 'It's been quite the trip, hasn't it? I'm really glad we met. I hope we'll stay friends when this is all done.' She laughed. 'I'm not drunk, honest. I just ... Well, it's been a pretty special trip.'

'It has,' I said, warmly. 'I'm not the biggest socialiser, so I'm grateful that you made time to talk to me, especially when you're young and should have been off with the rest of the crew.'

'Don't be silly,' she said. 'You made me fall in love with classical music, you know. You should see the new playlist on my phone. Gemma thinks I'm a right weirdo.'

'I *don't*,' cried Gemma with mock outrage.

I laughed.

Then I realised it was time. I wondered where Harriet was but felt sure she would arrive at any moment. I headed to my piano. Applause began before I'd even sat down. This had never happened before. I stopped and turned around; the clapping increased, until it was a roar of thanks. I nodded my head, unable to speak.

Then I sat. I stretched and breathed, in, out, in, out, slow, slower, slow. I remembered my first performance in here, when I thought I saw a child Harriet darting between guests. She had been with me, even then.

I began with Beethoven's 'Moonlight Sonata' like I had that first time, and the room dissolved, and I was in my own world again, where each note was all that existed.

At the end, the usual chanting began. 'Play the song, play the song, *play the song*.'

I smiled and waited for Harriet to join me.

She didn't come.

My heart beat fast like a clumsy beginner on a new keyboard.

Still, she didn't come.

'I ... I'm sorry.' I hurried out of the bar.

I went to Harriet's cabin and knocked softly on the door. I realised she might not hear it and rapped harder. She eventually opened it, face pale, eye make-up smudged. 'I wanted to, I *did*,' was all I could get out of her. I went into the room. It was pretty, more spacious than mine, with a door to a balcony and pastel paintings on the wall. She flopped onto the bed, repeating over and over that she had wanted to, and I sat next to her.

'What did you want to do?' I made sure she could see my mouth.

'Come, tonight. I did, I really did. But...'

'But what?' I put a hand over hers.

'I just don't know if ... if I can play it anymore,' she said.

'Our song?' I asked.

She nodded. 'Yes.'

Gently, looking directly at her, I asked, 'Why not?'

'I'm scared.'

'Of what, Harriet?'

Tears streamed down her cheeks. She shook her head. I didn't push. I waited, hand still over hers.

After a while she said, 'Every time we've played, each night, it's been getting ... been getting quieter and quieter. I was scared ... that if I'd come tonight ... I was scared I wouldn't hear it at all.'

I nodded. I understood. But I didn't know what to say. What

comfort could I give? I had no idea what she was going through, and I had no idea if it would get worse. So, I held her tightly as she cried against my chest. I slept in her cabin that night, cradling her through the night like I had in the children's home. In a gesture I knew she would understand, I took off the quaver pendant and fastened the chain back around her neck.

'I'm here,' I said against her ear. 'I'm here.'

56

In Harriet's apartment I initially felt like a teenager on a sleepover at a friend's posh home. But then – despite the clean white walls, the sleek kitchen units and the expensive wooden floors – when Harriet said, 'My home is your home,' and I saw her favourite magazines and much-loved books with creased spines, I realised there was warmth to the place, and I fell in love with it.

We had docked in New York at 8am, and once I was free to disembark, I met Harriet and we shared a taxi – or cab as she called it – back to her building. I found myself doing the small talk with the driver, knowing she'd find it difficult to hear him when he couldn't turn to look at us.

Now I stood on her balcony, looking out at a river – I wasn't sure which one – and at the tall buildings nearby, the smell of her potted lilacs and lupins cloying and heady, the air warm and dry, probably close to forty degrees. I could hear the traffic below, the odd siren, so different to ours, and I felt I was in one of the American police dramas I loved watching back home.

Harriet put a hand on my shoulder. 'You want coffee?' she asked.

'Oh, yes, thanks.' I spoke clearly as had become habit already.

Learning to play softly – or pianissimo – on the piano is a challenge. It's about staying close to the keys and controlling arm weight; it's also about instinct. I had to learn the opposite now when talking to my sister. I had to be loud, clear, but with calm control; it was about instinct too.

'There're two guest bedrooms,' she said, 'so take whichever you want. It's yours.'

'Only until Tuesday,' I said quietly, not intending her to hear, playing pianissimo.

I went inside and took my luggage to the first bedroom that wasn't Harriet's, a sunny space with a similar view to the one from the balcony. I took a few things out of my case, hung things in the wardrobe, and then returned to the living room. I touched the black baby grand piano in the corner. It had been the first thing I'd noticed on entering the apartment. Harriet was still in the kitchen, so I waited until she brought me an oversized mug of coffee before saying, 'This is beautiful.'

'Michael bought me it on our tenth wedding anniversary.'

'I think I got a set of tea towels. No, I'm only joking. Dan bought me some very thoughtful gifts over the years.'

I realised how bare the walls were and spotted empty shelves where I imagined things must have once been, things Harriet had loved.

She followed my gaze. 'And I never heard a thing … I can't stop thinking…'

'What?' I asked gently.

'When we were small, we tried not to hear the violence downstairs. We tried to drown it out. Now … that night when they broke in … I couldn't have heard it if I'd wanted to. And I'd give anything to have heard it.'

I didn't know what to say.

After a beat, Harriet changed tempo and said, 'I'm going to get that old Polaroid of us put onto one of those canvas prints and hang it above the TV.'

'Oh, I'll do that too.' Why had I never thought of it? 'And the one of us on the cruise.'

She seemed distracted still, but I understood. She was likely thinking about tomorrow, the appointment with the audiologist.

'Make yourself comfortable,' she said. 'I'm gonna go unpack and get some laundry on the go. You need anything washing?'

'No, I did it all yesterday on the ship.'

Alone, I sat at the piano and played the opening notes to 'Nothing Else', but stopped abruptly, not wanting Harriet to hear it if she came back into the room. She had said she didn't know if she wanted to play it again – did that mean I shouldn't? Would it upset her? I closed the lid. What had begun in hope, in us playing it to drown out the chaos around us, had become a song that might cause upset; a melody that now reminded her of what she was losing.

I sat in silence. Tried to imagine that quiet being forever.

I couldn't.

I jumped when Harriet came into the room. 'I've got Brianna on speakerphone,' she said, looking panicked. I knew why. It was on full volume. But she likely couldn't make out the words being spoken. I could hear an American lady.

'Who's Brianna?' I asked Harriet.

'She's one of the anchors on the *New Day* morning show – remember she got in touch on the ship when she saw our reunion.'

I nodded, then spoke to her. 'Hi Brianna.' I wasn't sure whether Harriet wanted her to know she was finding it difficult to hear her. 'This is Heather.'

'Hey Heather, how are you? I *love* your story. I was so touched by your song. Your sister said you might consider coming on the show and telling us about how you lost and then found one another. It's a newsy story but intimate too, and we think our audience will love it.'

'Oh, I guess, yes, sure.' I glanced at Harriet, but she looked blank. I would tell her it all when we hung up.

'I know it's short notice,' said Brianna, 'but could you come in on Tuesday?'

'Tuesday?' It was only two days away, the day I had to return to the ship.

'I know it's quite sudden, but we've been keen to get you guys in since we saw the footage. I know Harriet lives here in the city so our studio should be an easy commute. Could you get here for 6.30am to do an 8am slot?'

'I...' My mind raced. I had to return to the ship by eleven. I supposed I could take my luggage and go there from the studio. It was possible. But would Harriet want to go on TV now her hearing was so bad. I needed to ask her. 'Can I call you back in five minutes? I have to chat to Harriet about it. Is that OK?'

She said yes, and I hung up.

'They want us to go on the show on Tuesday morning,' I said.

'That soon?' she cried.

'I had to make sure you wanted to do it first.'

'Do *you*?'

'Only if you're happy to.' I saw that she was realising why I had to make sure *she* was OK with it.

'I can do it,' she said as though trying to convince herself.

'Sure?'

'Yes – with you, of course.'

I rang Brianna back and got the details of where we had to go on Tuesday; she got a bit more of our story from me: how long we had been separated, where we each lived, how the reunion had come about, I presumed to prepare her questions.

'Oh my God,' I said. 'TV. I've never done anything like this before. I'll have to watch it tomorrow morning, get a feel for the show.'

'It's fun,' said Harriet. 'I've been on with an author, but never for a segment about me. This is way scarier. Do you realise they have an audience of millions?'

'Don't tell me that. I'll change my mind.'

'Let me make us some lunch and I'll see if I can find the episode I was on online. What do you want to eat?'

We had mushroom-and-ham omelettes and watched a show where Harriet featured with an author who had written about her #MeToo experience when the movement was at a peak. My sister looked elegant, accomplished, and I buzzed with pride. But, at my side now, she looked sad. I didn't have to ask why.

For the rest of the day, we relaxed in the apartment. Mid-afternoon, Harriet's phone buzzed.

'Oh, it's Sera,' she cried joyfully. 'FaceTime. She knows I prefer it. Stay out of shot and let me tell her about you, and then we'll surprise her.' The energy was back – she was six-year-old Harriet again, bouncing in her seat. 'Hey sweetheart,' she said to her daughter. I heard Sera but stayed away from the screen. I listened to Harriet animatedly tell her first about the cruise and then about me being there too. Sera swore heartily and said she couldn't believe the co-incidence of it. 'No such thing,' said Harriet, just as I would have done. 'And guess what? She's here now. Sera meet my sister ... *Heather*!' It was my introduction. My set. My performance. I sat closer to Harriet. On screen was a girl, hair and eyes like Harriet's, not lessened by the screen, filling the room with her energy.

'Hello, Sera,' I smiled. 'I can't believe how much like your mum you look.'

'You too,' she cried. 'Oh my God, I love your accent. I can see why my mom talks the way she does. How did this just *happen*? It's incredible. Mom talks about you often. I'm so happy for you guys.'

'I'm happy too.' I squeezed Harriet. 'I can't wait to meet you. I have a niece. I'm so chuffed.'

'Mom says "chuffed"', giggled Sera.

'I'll make sure I polish up her Yorkshire accent,' I laughed. 'Teach her some of our newer words. She's lost a lot of it, and that's a crime.'

'Oh, I hear it,' said Sera.

We chatted a while longer, and at the end of the call Sera said she would visit the weekend I was back in New York before I went home.

That evening Harriet and I shared a bottle of wine and watched old movies. I still couldn't get over the fact that I was in her apartment.

'I can't believe I was in the city for two days, alone, and you lived right here,' I said. 'We could have walked past one another. What a waste it seems, eh? Not just then but all those years apart.'

'But we can make up for it, can't we?' Harriet was flushed; perhaps the alcohol had warmed her.

I looked at her. 'How do you feel about seeing the audiologist tomorrow? Remind me what happened, and what tests you've had?'

'The first appointment was about six weeks ago.' She sounded tired, but it could have been the sedating effects of the wine. 'Feels like a lifetime ago. Dr Resnick said I needed some further tests, for diabetes and I think a brain tumour, though he didn't say it like that. They came back clear. He asked about my family, to ascertain if it's hereditary, but of course I couldn't answer that, since our mother died so young and my dad is gone now too. Thinking, though, my dad did used to joke about how his mum missed a lot of conversations and how they tricked her when they were kids, pretending the phone had rung when it hadn't. I should tell Dr Resnick when we go. He mentioned a hearing aid.'

'And?'

She didn't answer.

'It can't hurt to consider,' I said.

'It can't hurt to consider,' she agreed.

A 'repeat it' moment. But neither of us acknowledged it.

57

Dr Resnick's office was the kind you see in glossy American dramas, where wealthy women find out they have some easily curable condition, an illness worrying enough to progress the story arc and inject drama, but fixable by the season finale; the desk was sparsely adorned, and big enough that ten people could have eaten around it. Dr Resnick sat behind it, not a hair out of place.

'Mrs Romano,' he said. His voice was perfect for this job; it was rich, clear and a few decibels louder than average. I wondered if he had been trained to talk that way or if it was natural. 'It's really good to see you again. Please, take a seat.'

We sat in two cream chairs. I had to concentrate on him and not the fantastic view of Times Square through the tall window behind him.

'This is my sister,' said Harriet, and I still got a kick out of these words. 'I just felt I ... well, I needed her with me today.'

'Of course. How have things been?'

I knew by 'things' he meant her hearing.

'Not good.' Her voice broke and I grabbed her hand. 'I know those other tests I went for didn't give any answers but I think ... if I'm honest with you and with myself ... my hearing is disintegrating.'

He nodded, his face showing no emotion, which was a comfort. 'It could just be that with your acknowledgment of it, it *seems* worse. But let's do a few tests again and see where we are, and then we can talk about what we can try. Are you happy for your sister to stay?'

'Oh, yes.'

Dr Resnick got up and came around the table and checked inside Harriet's ears with a tiny device. Then he led us into a small, black-walled, soundproof room, where she had to sit at a table, don some headphones, and, as I understood it, press a button each time she heard a sound. This produced a graph, which Dr Resnick showed us back in his office, pointing to certain lines and explaining that Harriet's range was now well below normal hearing ability. I noted the word 'now' and presumed that perhaps last time it hadn't been *well* below, only *just* below. Harriet must have noted it too, because she looked distraught. I squeezed her arm, but she barely acknowledged me.

'Remember those word tests we did last time?' Dr Resnick said to her.

She nodded.

'We'll do them again, though obviously with different words this time. OK?'

He stood across the room, about ten feet away from Harriet, and told me he was going to say a series of words, in a normal voice, and she would repeat them.

'Dodge,' he said.

'Dog,' she said.

'Mouse,' he said.

'Mouse,' she repeated.

'Time,' he said.

'Mine,' she said.

And on it went. After twenty words, Dr Resnick said she had got fifteen out of twenty correct. I knew it to be true; I'd been adding it up too. To me, this sounded quite reasonable, but Harriet looked upset.

'I got eighteen last time,' she explained, and I understood.

Then Dr Resnick put a sheet of paper in front of his face and said, 'Thirsty.'

'Thursday,' Harriet said, tentative.

'Almost,' said Dr Resnick. For a moment I thought he was praising her for being close and then I realised it was the next word.

'Can you repeat that please?' asked Harriet.

He did.

'I don't know,' she admitted, distressed.

He moved on. 'Before.'

Harriet shook her head.

And on it went like the previous test. This time Harriet scored just four out of twenty, which she tearfully told me was one less than last time.

'This could just be a particularly bad day,' said Dr Resnick. 'We'll still need to do some further tests, such as a bone conduction test, and a test of your acoustic reflexes, which I can arrange. I can book those today for you if you'd like me to?'

Harriet nodded, her face devoid of emotion. She wore the quaver pendant that I'd put around her neck on the last night of the cruise. I wanted her to keep it.

'Would you consider a hearing aid?'

Harriet nodded again.

'I'll book you in to talk to our specialist – she can tell you more about how it might or might not work, and you can then be fitted for one. When are you free?'

With trembling hands, Harriet went into the diary on her phone, and they arranged an appointment for the following week. She hadn't told the doctor about the realisation that her paternal grandmother might have been hard of hearing, so I now prompted her to, which Dr Resnick said might be helpful.

'Whatever we find out,' he said, 'there is always something we can do. You're young and healthy, and there's no reason why a hearing aid won't mean a normal life with good hearing again.'

Harriet was mute when we left the office. She remained mute when we found a table at an outdoor café, and I ordered us both coffees. It was as though I was the one who had lost her hearing, except I could still hear the rest of the world, the soft tinkle of cup against plate, the clickety-clack of a woman in spike heels walking by, the drilling going on further down the street. I felt desperately sad that Harriet was missing these mundane, everyday sounds that we never appreciate or notice. She looked lifeless, drained of all hope.

'I want to come to your next appointment,' I said. 'And whatever else you need to do, I want to be there with you for that too.'

'You can't.' Her first words, spoken quietly. 'You have to go back on your cruise, then go home again.'

'I can. I *want* to.' I realised then that there was no way I could return to the ship the next day. There was no way I could cruise the Caribbean, even if it was my job, while she went to all these appointments alone. I knew she didn't want to burden Sera, and she hadn't told her friends or work colleagues about this health issue. There was only me. I was her sister. I should be there.

'No, I won't hear of it,' Harriet insisted. 'I'm fine. For fuck's sake, you can't give up your job for me.'

'You're *not* fine,' I cried. 'I can see that you're not. Stop being stubborn. I'll call Sarah Briggs and explain. She can't expect me to abandon my family during a crisis. Because you are, and this is.'

'But you *love* playing on the cruise.'

'Yes. I do. But I love you more.'

She smiled, but it was weak. 'Of course, I'm grateful, *happy* to have you for longer, but I don't want to burden you. We've only been together again a few weeks and already I'm worried that I'm asking too much.'

'Stop being so bloody silly. You haven't asked – I've offered. There'll be other cruises, but this is an important moment in your life.' I paused. 'Maybe it's one I was supposed to be here for. Did you ever think of that?'

She appeared to consider it. 'If Sarah Briggs can't let you go, I want you to return to the ship,' she said. 'I don't want you to jeopardise your future.'

'I'll decide that. Now let it go and accept that I want to stay.'

She didn't speak. The silence said it all.

'Are you sure you want to do the TV show tomorrow?' I asked her when we had ordered a second coffee and some cheesecake to share. 'We can cancel it if you're not up to it.'

'Yes, let's do it,' she said.

'You sound unsure, and I don't want you t—'

'I'm sure,' she interrupted, more enthusiastic. 'Heather, it could change your life.'

'What do you mean? Why mine?'

'You might never play in small bars again.' The life flooded back into her face as though she'd been injected with liquid happiness. '*New Day* gets millions of viewers, and if they play the clip of our reunion, I think you'll end up with a *huge* following. Look at what happened when it trended.'

The idea made me nervous. Nervous but, I couldn't deny, excited too. I remembered a night, long ago, playing in a bar; the chat had been louder than my music. No one looked my way. No one applauded at the end. Was it that I had played terribly, without the attention? Or had I just been playing in the wrong place? Did I belong on a stage, with an orchestra, rather than in small bars?

'I'm doing this show for you,' said Harriet. 'Just as you want to stay with me for my appointments. Because this could change your life. I think people are really going to see your talent. You're going to shine.'

I shook my head, tried to say something, but she told me to hush up.

So, I did.

Then we sat in the New York heat, our coffees cooling despite the sun, the world rushing past us, no words needed, content with the sacrifices we would make for one another; the backing track I heard to the city sounds around us was 'Twinkle, Twinkle' the way Harriet first played it for our father, opening with an arpeggiated left-hand accompaniment. She was my left hand, I was her right, and these hands were only complete when together.

58

The glass building that housed the TV studio towered above us into the dawn sky, tapering to a sharp point at the top, reminding me of The Deep museum back in Hull and how it had been designed to resemble a ship's bow. I had abandoned the cruise – with what had felt like Sarah Briggs' reluctant approval in a brief phone call – but now I saw ocean themes everywhere; in the beautiful aqua dress Harriet had chosen for our appearance, in the two workmen carrying a huge painting of an underwater scene along the morning street, and at the pinnacle of this mirrored building.

We got out of the car that the studio had sent, in which I'd felt like a film star being taken to a movie set. We had been up since five, drinking too many coffees, and changing our minds repeatedly about the outfits we'd planned last night. Harriet had been quiet, however, and though she hadn't said it, I knew she was nervous about how she might manage a TV interview with her hearing affliction. Yet she insisted I should do it, that this was a huge opportunity for me.

'Are you sure you're ready?' I asked her as I looked up at the glitzy tower. I couldn't stop my hands from shaking.

Harriet didn't respond. I turned to her, asked again, more clearly.

'I guess,' she said. 'Are you?'

'I am,' I said.

We went inside and a production assistant – Kellie, all white teeth and eyelashes – came down to meet us, got us signed in and gave us lanyards. But before she could take us up in the lift, Harriet shook her head.

'I can't,' she said.

'*What*?' My heart sank.

'You must though.' She grabbed my hands. 'But I can't. I just...'

She touched her left ear, perhaps involuntarily, perhaps saying with her fingers what she couldn't in words. And she was gone, her heels clacking on the floor.

'No, Harriet, wait,' I cried.

Kellie's professional veneer faltered. 'Oh,' she said.

'I should go after her,' I said.

'No, she'll be fine, I'm sure. You heard her – she wants you to go ahead.' Kellie ushered me into the lift before I could argue. I was too surprised to resist, rendered docile by my sister's shock departure. 'I'm sure they'll make it work with just you,' continued Kellie as we ascended, clearly with her mind on the job.

Harriet had left me. I couldn't believe it.

Had she just wanted to get me to the studio, knowing I wouldn't have come without her, or had she simply panicked?

I was deposited in a green room where the red network logo dominated the wall, and there were a variety of teas and coffees on offer, as well as muffins and bagels. But I couldn't eat a thing. Then it was make-up, where a woman called Gloria explained that the heavy-duty, HD cosmetics might make me look overly made-up here, but on camera I'd be perfect.

I just wanted to run, like Harriet had done, but my legs were leaden.

Brianna, the anchor, came to see me.

'Kellie told us your sister was ill and had to leave,' she said briskly, and I nodded, barely able to speak. 'That's *such* a shame, but I guess we'll make it work with just you.' I felt sick. Perhaps seeing my nerves, she added, 'You have *nothing* to worry about. Think of it as an everyday chat, except you're in a studio. We'll bring you in during the commercial break at eight.'

Kellie got me miked up and took me into a studio that was designed to look like a trendy loft apartment, with brick walls and arched 'windows' showcasing filmed city views behind the two anchors, Brianna and a man called John. I had to wait off camera. I wanted to cry. I was angry at Harriet for abandoning me like this, and yet I also felt sad for her, because I understood her fears.

'And that's commercials,' said Kellie, leading me to an area where red chairs were set around a metal table. Brianna and John left the news desk to join me. Three large cameras were moved smoothly around the floor by head-phone-wearing men and women. One came closer. The lights were hot. My palms got damp.

Someone, somewhere, counted down.

And we were on air.

'Welcome back,' said Brianna, all smiles. 'Now, who doesn't love a good reunion? Millions of us tune in to *Long Lost Family* every week, where families are brought together again after many years.'

'It's always emotional,' said John, all smiles too. 'But what would it be like if that reunion hadn't been planned. If it happened out of the blue ... and after *thirty-seven* years.'

'Well, today,' said Brianna, 'we have a guest who not only *can* imagine it, but who is here to share an incredible story with us.'

'You may have seen the now infamous "Reunion Song" video, as it was hashtagged,' continued John. 'It went viral just two weeks ago. This was the moment sisters Harriet and Heather finally found one another, captured by guests on a cruise ship. Let's take a look...'

And they played our song.

I saw our moment on a large monitor for the first time instead of a tiny phone screen. I saw Harriet sit down next to me while I had my head on the piano top. I saw myself finally look up. I saw us hug and then play, in unison, as though it was a carefully practised piece. Our music filled the studio. Tears streamed down my face. Was Harriet watching? Had she gone home to view the show?

'Tell me first, Heather,' said Brianna, 'how did it feel when you looked up and your sister was there after all that time?'

My voice was a dry croak; I took a sip of water from a glass on the table and tried to speak. When I finally could, I treated the interview like one of my sets – I sat up straight and I gave them what I thought they wanted. I told them our history, our journey, our sadness and then joy.

'Now,' said John, 'I want to know about the song, and I imagine many of our viewers do too.'

'We created it together when we were children,' I said. 'I wanted to distract Harriet.'

'From what?' asked Brianna.

'From ... our home life. There was a lot of ... violence.'

Brianna nodded. 'So, it was a means to escape a difficult life.' She paused, perhaps for effect. 'How did you remember how to play it together after all this time?'

'We just ... *knew*,' I said softly.

'Well, we have a little surprise for you.' Brianna smiled. 'The other day we messaged Harriet to ask if there was a written score of the song, and she sent us a picture of it.'

'She did?' I was caught unawares.

'We sent the reunion video and your musical score to the Grammy Award-winning New York Philharmonic Orchestra,' explained John, 'and they *loved* your story and think the music is absolutely beautiful. They want to perform it with you.'

'With *me*?' I gasped.

'They're performing at the Lincoln Center in two weeks, and they'd like you to join them on stage and play "Nothing Else" with them as the finale to the show. Rehearsals will begin next week.'

I didn't know what to say.

I thought of concerts I'd watched in the past, the power of all those musicians playing together. I thought of our childhood and listening to epic orchestral performance albums on the record player with our mother. What would our little old song sound like when presented in such a way?

Before I could respond, Brianna turned to the camera and said, 'Wonderful. We hope to bring you a full report on how it goes for Heather, with some backstage chat on the night, so look out for more on this amazing reunion story in the coming weeks.'

Then the interview was over, and with a flurry of quick thank-yous I was ushered out of the studio by Kellie, de-miked, delivered to the lobby and back out on the busy street so fast it was hard to believe I'd just been on a TV show.

A message from Harriet awaited me, telling me to get a cab to a restaurant where she was waiting.

59

I arrived at a venue that was all white linen tablecloths and fat, creamy candles, with bamboo furniture and lush greenery. Harriet was drinking coffee at a table by a low wall that allowed a full view of the city, its glass buildings winking in the late-August sun.

'You abandoned me,' I said, still annoyed.

'I'm sorry,' she said quietly.

I sat opposite her. 'Did you plan on running off?'

She shook her head. 'No, I really didn't. I thought I could go on the show. I wanted to support you, I did, but I could hardly hear what that assistant was saying when she came for us, and I thought, how the hell will I hear the host? Then I thought, if I make a mess of it, I could ruin *your* big chance.'

Harriet was close to tears, and I melted. How could I be cross at my little sister, at the girl who'd had my heart all these years?

'It's OK,' I said, not looking away for a second so she could read my lips if she needed to. 'I understand why. I ... well, I just felt alone without you. I bet I was as dull as dishwater in the interview.'

'Don't be bloody ridicu—'

A waiter came over then, interrupting Harriet, and we ordered a feast of eggs, bacon, pancakes, and syrup, and more coffee.

'When did you send Brianna the sheet music?' I asked after the waiter had gone. 'How did you hide it from me? We've been inseparable.'

'It was easy to send messages while you were in the shower,' she said.

'I'm speechless.'

'You're not.'

I laughed, and it lightened the mood for a moment.

'So, you'll play with the New York Philharmonic Orchestra then?' she said, like this was just an everyday occurrence.

'I'd be stupid not to,' I said. 'But that song is about *us*, and it's about our reunion now as much as our childhood. It doesn't work when it's just me.'

'It will have to.' Harriet was firm.

'You're so bloody stubborn,' I snapped.

'Look, I'll come to the rehearsals with you,' she said, 'and I'll be there on your big night, but I want you to be the star you deserve to be.'

'This is because you're nervous about playing it, isn't it?'

The food arrived then, and we paused to thank the waiter. We ate quietly, looking out at the view.

'Will you still come to my next appointment with me?' asked Harriet eventually.

'Of course,' I cried. 'Why wouldn't I?'

'Well, *I* let *you* down...'

I didn't respond at first. Then I said, 'No, you didn't. Expecting you to go on that show with this new ... well, new disability, was asking an awful lot. Me coming to a few appointments isn't. I'll be at your side whatever the results are. And I'll be at your side whatever you then decide to do.'

'Thank you. It means everything to know it won't be just me.' She paused. 'Just me,' she repeated softly.

'What is?' I asked.

'No, I saw this woman,' she explained, getting excited and fidgeting in her seat like she had as a child. 'Back when I booked the cruise. It was like ... well, a *vision*. It looked like an English city. Not Hull, I thought. I couldn't see her face, but her hair was as light as the sun. That's what she said. "Just me".' Harriet smiled. 'It was you. I saw you, didn't I? You were looking at some ships.'

I shivered despite the heat. Remembered that moment. In the hotel room.

Just me.

'Yes,' I replied. 'I was there. I said that. How strange. And yet ... *not*.'

'And yet not,' repeated Harriet, and we smiled at our private joke.

'But ... I feel...' I couldn't finish.

'Yes?' Harriet studied me.

'That, once again ... it *is* just me.'

'But it *isn't*.' Harriet was suddenly passionate. 'Just because I couldn't do the show and bec—'

'That isn't it,' I said, not even sure myself why I felt I was losing her again. 'I buried it all those years. How I felt when you'd gone. It was so ... *huge*, the pain.' A solitary cloud passed across the sun and, just for a moment, the world dimmed a little. I realised that I was angry that Harriet's hearing issues were coming between us. I would never say that when she was struggling so much, of course – felt guilty for even thinking it. But it was there, a low note ruining a sweet song. 'And now I'm terrified of going through it again. Of...'

'Of what?' asked Harriet gently

'You've been so sad. So anxious. I want to make you happy, like I always seemed to be able to years ago, and I feel like I'm failing. That I'm losing you all over again...'

'No, *no*,' cried Harriet, shaking her head vigorously. 'You *are* making me happy. I'd be coping far worse with my hearing loss if you weren't here. I couldn't tell anyone about it before you.'

I nodded, choked up. Deep down, I wanted her to play our song with me at the concert, but I didn't want to pressure her. It wasn't fair. But then this situation wasn't fair either. I had my sister again after thirty-seven years and still some darkness invaded the light.

The waiter interrupted and took our empty plates; we ordered more coffee and sat in silence for a while.

'The world is at your feet now,' said Harriet, and I knew she was trying to cheer me up.

'It feels like it up here,' I admitted.

'No, I mean it figuratively. It's at your feet right now. Heather, this day, that TV show, the upcoming concert, it's for you. I'm a book editor and I love my job. But you're a *pianist*. That's who you are. I was your sidekick. I was your secondo. But now it's time for you to play. Our song, I think, will catapult you into the limelight because of the story behind it, and because it's beautiful. But then, it's all about you.' I tried to interrupt and insist we were a team, but she wouldn't let me. 'Yes, we're a team as sisters now, but musically, it was always you. I think your life is about to change, and I could not be happier.'

I didn't argue. I couldn't spoil her sentiment, the moment.

Maybe she was right.

But, for now, we were two sisters, sitting on top of the world, and I hoped we could find a way to stay there.

60

The David Geffen Hall in the Lincoln Center was a curious concert venue. When Harriet and I arrived for my first rehearsal, I'm not sure what she expected, but I had anticipated an old-fashioned theatre with a dark-wood stage, where musicians played for music lovers in rows of velvet seats. Instead, beyond the impressive façade, the stark interior had walls that looked like cheap laminate, rows of ugly seats and a plain stage; it lacked intimacy with the platform so far back from the audience.

One of the cleaners told me the place was plagued with acoustic problems and they'd had complaints that it was dowdy, but that a huge renovation was planned. 'Oh, but it comes alive though,' he said, leaning against his mop, 'when the orchestra plays. They could play in a bathroom and sound like angels with harps.'

Over the week we met a whirlwind of faces, from the music director, who was overseeing the production of 'Nothing Else' and would conduct the orchestra during their performance of it, to violinists and cellists, to clarinet, flute, horn and bassoon players. There were over a hundred members of the New York Philharmonic, but sixty musicians would play the night our song was performed: plus me.

Just me. Not Harriet.

Just me. The words I'd said at the same time as she had, across an ocean; now sad words that separated us again.

The music director was surprised that the reunion song would not be performed as a duet. I could tell he wasn't happy, that he felt he had been misled, but there was no changing Harriet's mind. I'd tried. She had said no. I had to respect that, and so did the orchestra. None of us knew what she was going through. She sat close by when I practised, incorporating new elements to compensate for the piece now being a solo work. She smiled and gushed about how glorious it sounded.

But I was sad. I wanted her with me.

Dan and Tamsin had each messaged me during the week, saying they had seen clips of me on the TV show, that our reunion was being talked about in the UK media too, asking why I hadn't told them I'd found Harriet. I felt bad and explained that it was the kind of thing I'd wanted to tell them in person, when I got back.

On the big night Harriet and I arrived at the venue early.

The sound of the musicians warming up was sublime; I've always loved it, how the instruments seem to be competing to be heard when, really, they're getting in sync; uniting. This is when the players make sure they are all tuned the same way. The oboe might play a specific pitch of the note A. Then the lead violinist will check he's in tune and allow the different parts of the woodwind and brass section to follow suit.

I was to come on stage for the finale. I'd only rehearsed six times. The music director felt it needed to be less perfect, less finely tuned, raw and real. 'Like it must have been when you were small and played at home,' he said. 'That's the true beauty of it.'

But he was wrong; the true beauty of it was when there were two of us.

Brianna and John from *New Day* met us in the foyer for a quick interview, and I introduced them to Harriet. They were staying for the concert, with a film crew recording my performance to be shared on a special edition of the show next week.

'Can't you persuade your sister to join you?' asked Brianna, when Harriet popped to the toilet. 'That would be so special.'

Much as I also wanted her to, I would not allow anyone else to pressure her. 'She has her reasons, and you have to respect that,' I said, annoyed.

Sera came too with a friend from university, and we had a quick drink in the bar with them. Harriet fussed and talked at speed.

'Mom,' laughed Sera. 'Did you take something?'

'I'm just a bit giddy,' she admitted. 'Excited for Heather.'

Despite everything, I loved seeing her like this. Because she hadn't been. Not in the previous week. It had been a tough few days, but she hadn't shared that with her daughter. I had been there for that. I had sat up until 3am some nights, letting Harriet talk as much as she needed.

'This is just surreal,' said Sera. 'You two have only been together again for a month, and already Heather has done the biggest break-fast show, and now she's playing in a concert. What's next? The moon?' She paused. 'Why won't you play too, Mom?'

'I think this moment should be Heather's,' she said quietly.

'I don't get it,' persisted Sera. 'People want to see *both* of you play it.'

I discreetly shook my head, hinting at Sera to stop, and fortu-nately she saw.

'How much longer can you stay in the US?' she asked me.

'Another two months,' I said. 'Then I'll have to go home.' I looked at Harriet; she was watching me closely. 'But I'm hoping to look at working in New York, even if I can't live here yet. It would mean I'm here with your mum for ... well, for anything she needs.'

'You'd leave England then?' asked Sera.

I had thought of nothing else. Would I leave my home? My Hull. The place Harriet and I had grown up, the place my biological and adoptive parents were buried. But what really kept me there? My family – my only family, my niece and sister – were *here*.

'I don't know,' I admitted. 'But I'm not ruling it out.'

When a voice announced that patrons could take their seats, and Sera and her friend went into the auditorium, Harriet and I headed backstage to the dull, could-be-anywhere room. She had said she would be with me right until the moment I went on. We crept to the edge of the stage, hidden still, and watched the audience arrive, anticipation and nerves pulsing hotly through me.

Then the lights dimmed. We returned backstage and sat next to the open door so we could hear the music. There was a silence between the last of the audience chatter and the first note, like a swoop ... and then it began. My heart. My head. My soul. Every part of me heard it. Mozart, 'Serenade No 13', like I'd never heard it before – refined, delicate, living, breathing, and surrounding me completely.

Harriet was crying.

She felt it too.

But she could barely *hear* it; this I realised; this I knew.

'Are you OK?' I asked.

She had been to get fitted for a hearing aid on Tuesday, though she was still awaiting the results of further tests. Next week she would finally try one out. Dr Resnick said he had no idea if it would work for her. The majority of people with mild to moderate hearing loss benefitted from them, apparently, but those with severe nerve deafness or sensorineural hearing loss, not so much, and until the results of further tests she had taken came back, we couldn't know.

Harriet's distress had been intense. 'I think I'd rather go blind,' she had sobbed in a dark moment, before dawn arrived, when neither of us had been to bed yet and two empty wine bottles sat on the coffee table.

'The hearing aid might work,' I insisted. 'Please don't give up hope.'

'But it's getting worse, I'm sure it is.'

'You could just be more aware of it now,' I said. 'Look, I'll learn sign language, if need be. You can teach me, can't you?'

'I don't want to talk that way,' she cried, angry then. 'I want to hear your voice. I want to hear your music.'

What could I say to that?

With Mozart our background theme, I put a hand over Harriet's. 'Are you OK?' I repeated.

'I don't think ... I don't think I can...'

'Can what?'

'Stay. Watch you ... alone... without being able to...'

'Because of your hearing?'

She didn't answer.

'You *know* our song.' I put my hand over my chest. 'You know it in here. In your bones, in your blood, in your soul. You don't need to *hear* it. You'll watch me and that's all that matters.'

'Music from heaven,' she said, suddenly. 'Do you remember?'

'I do. Mr Hibbert told us that's what Beethoven said he heard when he finally...' I couldn't finish.

'I'm not ready to hear that yet,' she said.

'You don't have to. The hearing aid mi—'

'It won't be the same.' She paused. 'Do you mind if I go home?'

My heart sank. I did mind. I wanted her with me. But she came first. 'If you really can't stay, I won't either. I'll just say I'm ill and we'll go home and talk all night again.'

'But ... you ... your concert...'

'It will wait. They can wait.'

Mozart's 'Serenade No 13' ended. We looked at one another in that brief interlude, holding the last note, waiting for the next. It was Chopin. Goosebumps ran up my arm in time with the graceful upward leaps of the opening.

'Mum,' we both said at the same time.

'She would have loved this,' I said. 'I don't know if she ever went to a real concert.'

'Maybe she's watching now,' said Harriet.

'Maybe.'

We let Chopin wash over us. I could feel the beat through the floor, through my seat, and knew Harriet must do too, even if the notes weren't as clear for her. She wore the quaver pendant and kept touching it, perhaps unaware that she was. The orchestra played Bach, Beethoven, Schubert, and Debussy. We didn't speak. Harriet didn't leave.

And then the music stopped.

Thunderous applause. After a while, when it lessened, the music director must have been announcing me, telling the crowd our story, but I could only hear it like a TV through a wall, the way I knew Harriet heard so much.

'I can't let her down,' she said.

'Who?' I asked.

'Mum,' she said. 'She would want me to be here to support you.'

'No, she'd want you to be happy.'

'How can I be happy if I let you down?'

'You're not—' I started.

'I'll stay,' she interrupted.

Applause again, which was my cue.

'You're sure?' I said.

'If I don't stay, you won't play. And you have to. They need to hear you. Go. *Go*, that's your cue. I'm here. Right here.'

I walked out, onto the waiting stage, the clapping gentle now. I looked back at Harriet as I went. How afraid I was on my own. I knew I'd likely fall, trip clumsily up the few steps, without her holding my hand. The piano waited for me at the front of the stage, ebony, polished, so perfect, its seat comfortably long enough for the two of us. How would I fill it? I couldn't. I *couldn't*. I stopped. Put my head in my hands. Just me, and I didn't want it to be. Muttering in the audience.

Then she was there.

At my side.

My sister.

'I'm here,' she said.

'You're sure?'

'I'm sure.' She paused. 'Just us.'

'*Just us*,' I smiled.

We sat, primo and secondo, older sister and younger sister.

We looked at one another.

'Nothing else,' we said, and it wasn't a song title, but an expression of the fact that no one else was here, just our mother, just us, and we were all safely cocooned within the safety of our music.

And then we played.

Something happened when we did; the something that had always happened when we were small. A something that even now, to this day, I can't define; a unity, an understanding, a synchronicity.

I played it the way I had the very first time in our back room, in a way that evoked the way I heard the wind in the trees at night, that evoked the way I heard our mother's musical jewellery box when she was searching for pearls to hide bruises, that evoked the way I heard my father's footsteps, a mix of lyrical and dissonant, light and dark. Harriet mirrored me, her version at the other end of the keyboard, the same but different, complementary and yet its own truth, her own story.

I didn't hear the orchestra, the violins, the harp, the oboe.

I heard my life. I heard the little girl back in Hull, whose house I had run from – Rebecca – asking 'Are you OK, Miss?' And I hoped she had continued to play. I heard Mr Hibbert's metronome keeping our beat. I heard him walking the wooden floor behind us, click, clack, click, clack, in time with our rhythm. I heard him whispering, 'Keep practising, keep forcing those secrets, keep letting those fingers dance.' And I heard Harriet; I had not lost her again, and I never would. Even if this was the last time we played our song, it would not be the last time our fingers danced like fairy-tale endings across a keyboard, because I'd store the memory like I had our musical score, in a black ash frame.

I knew all the secrets of music in that moment; and I'm keeping them.

The roar of the audience at the end was sudden, intense, emotional.

And then, just for a moment, the world went quiet.

ACKNOWLEDGEMENTS

So many people, as always, helped make this book what it is. Thank you, Claire Nolan, for all the information about working aboard a cruise ship. Thank you, Thomas Enger, for answering my many questions about playing the piano. Some of your lovely turns of phrase made it directly into the book. Also, thank you, Carrie Martin, my singer/songwriter sidekick, because you eternally inspire me. Thank you, Janet Harrison, for the beautiful word, *saudade*. Thank you to my beloved sisters, Claire and Grace, for being the inspiration for Heather and Harriet. I hope I did you proud. And, as always, thank you to my beta readers, Madeleine Black, John Marrs, Thomas Enger, Janet Harrison, and my sisters. You're all so essential in letting me know if what I've written works.

Thank you also to Karen Sullivan for trusting me again to write what I have to, what bursts out of me. And for the sharp eye during edits and the helpful advice about Harriet's hearing loss in particular. Thank you West Camel for seeing the things I don't see, and for making this book a better thing. Thank you Mark Swan for the beautiful book cover that captures Heather and Harriet so perfectly.

Thank you to every single blogger and reviewer and reader who has talked about my books in some way, shared their thoughts publicly or simply sent me a lovely message. It means the absolute world to me. Thank you to the fantastic online book groups, like TBC and the Clare Mackintosh Book Club and Book Connectors and the Motherload Book Club, for the support. And thank you Anne Cater for arranging my blog tours – you're a star.

Lastly, thank you Chopin and Beethoven and so many others for the music. What on earth would be the point without it?